SWEET PEASE

A THORNTON VERMONT NOVEL

CAMERON D. GARRIEPY

Kindle Edition - ASIN: B07691Y9JF

Original Cover Photography courtesy of Brigitte Tohm on Unsplash.

Sweet Pease is dedicated
to all my Kates, literal and figurative–there is a little of all of you in Kate Pease–

and to the memory of Dolores Morin.
I'm sorry I didn't finish in time.

ACKNOWLEDGMENTS

It ought to get easier to write books.
It doesn't. Thank goodness for…

…the tribe of readers, writers, and magical internet friends who nudge me when I'm sluggish.

…R.B. Wood and the Word Count Irregulars for pushing me to create in ways I didn't think I could.

…the Words Aptly Spoken crew.
I live too far away from each of you. That is all.

…Roxanne Piskel, with whom I am joyfully reunited on this project. Editors are incredible.

…my great-big, far-flung, marvelous family.
You are waiting for me behind every cozy door in Thornton.

…Angela Amman and Mandy Dawson. You are, without a doubt, the midwives of my work.

SWEET PEASE

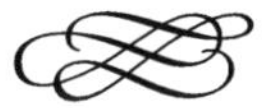

CHAPTER 1

"I'm going to make one hell of a maid of honor."

Kate Pease laughed off the wobble in her voice and blinked back a threatening tear. She smoothed the fuchsia silk shantung over her hips and stomach, twisting to check out her own rear view in the three-way mirror.

Her best friend, Nan Grady, stood on a dressmaker's pedestal while an attendant laced up the wedding gown she was trying on. Nan was radiant; the creamy silk only accentuated her glow.

Kate blinked back tears. It wasn't every day your best friend found the dress she was going to get married in. "That's the one, you know."

Nan blushed happily. "I think so, too."

"There's no thinking about it. It's the one."

The two women regarded each other. Below the second story window, Boston's Newbury Street bustled despite the January cold. Nan's brilliant smile wavered; Kate rushed over and swiped gently at the yet-to-fall wetness in her friend's eyes.

"No crying. We are far too fabulous today for streaky mascara."

Lady Gaga suggested a bad romance from Kate's purse. When Nan snickered, Kate shot her friend a withering look.

She retrieved her phone from the bag and took the call with a grin. "Hello, brother dear."

"Did Nan pick a dress?"

"Yes, she found her dress." Kate winked at Nan, who was posing for the shop attendant's measuring tape.

"Did you leave anything for the other shoppers?"

Her brother Jack might taunt her about her shopping habit, but his own was just as bad... if not worse.

"You're mean."

"Can I make it up to you with an extravagant lunch?"

"You can."

"I have to go; client on the other line."

He gave her a restaurant name and a time, and Kate ended the call.

Nan looked over her shoulder while the attendant created a potential bustle in the skirt. "Lunch?"

"At that sushi place near Jack's office. And he's picking up the tab."

Kate watched as Nan took a moment to drink in her own reflection. The dress was a simple A-line; the corsetry emphasized Nan's lean waist and gentle curves. The skirt clung to her hips just a little before falling like water to her feet.

"Oh, Nan," Kate breathed, "you're gorgeous."

Thornton was in for the wedding of the decade. The Fullers, the Peases—who considered Nan one of their own already—and nearly half the county would gather to celebrate Nan and Joss Fuller's marriage at the Damselfly in June.

That they would all eat cake by Kate Pease, well that didn't hurt either. Especially given her business plans.

Placing the dress order was swift and expensive. Her thrifty friend was pale with sticker shock. Kate squeezed Nan's hand in solidarity.

Kate and Nan gathered coats and scarves and gloves, bundling up against the bluster of a Boston winter. Just as they struck out for the T station at Arlington Street, Nan's phone rang in her pocket.

"Hello, Anna?" Nan motioned for Kate to stop. "He just walked in? Well, we have room. Go ahead and check him in."

While Nan walked her friend and inn-sitter through the registration software, Kate's gaze lingered on a camel hair wool skirt in the window of a nearby boutique, and she slipped inside.

Kate picked up a few additional items on her way to the fitting room. Nan followed her inside. Her half of the conversation was clear across the tiny space.

"I'm as surprised as you are." Nan's smile was wide and gleeful. "I can't imagine why, though. The college must have offered him an apartment."

Kate waved to Nan, motioning at the fitting room door while Nan's eyes widened at whatever Anna was saying.

"He's what?" Nan laughed aloud. "I have to go. Kate and I are meeting Jack for lunch before we drive home. I'll be home in plenty of time for you to tuck Chloe in."

Nan waved to Kate from across the sales floor, pointed at her watchless wrist.

"Bye, Anna. Thanks for calling. Give Chloe a snuggle for me."

Kate whipped through her choices, but nothing was just right. She hung everything on the rack outside the fitting room and sought Nan out among the scarves near the register. She tucked her arm in Nan's and swept them out the door and down the street.

"What did Anna want?"

Nan squinted into the glittering winter sun. "I have a new guest. A surprise. Anna says he, and I quote, 'looks like Mr. Rochester.'"

"Oh, really?" Visions of Timothy Dalton's smoldering gaze danced in her head. She silently thanked her mother for making her watch old BBC dramas when she was home sick in high school. "I always did think Rochester was kind of dreamy."

Nan snorted. "Don't."

Kate grinned, wondering if the newcomer was her kind of dreamy. And if he was single.

~

EWAN LOVATT WOKE TO THE KIND OF RURAL QUIET HE KNEW WOULD BE perfect for his next project.

He stretched and swung his legs over the edge of the bed. He'd long ago perfected the art of sleeping diagonally in a queen-sized bed to accommodate his six-foot-three frame. His feet struck the cold hardwood and he shivered. Pulling on cotton flannel drawstring pants and an NYU T-shirt before he padded over to the window seemed a wise choice.

Ewan was an urban creature, but the stark allure of the Vermont countryside in January wasn't lost on him. The nearby hillsides rolled smooth, painted in slashes of snow, granite, and coniferous greens. The skeletons of cornstalks marched in the neighboring fields. At the far western point of his view the Adirondacks were just beginning their craggy swell over the horizon.

By the time he left Thornton, Vermont he hoped early summer would show a version closer to the one he planned to write.

He grabbed his advance copy of Reed Sharpe's newest novel and headed for the bathroom. He had promised the man—or their shared publicist, anyway—a jacket review, and he couldn't think of a better place to read the damn thing.

After a shower, his appetite called to him more clearly. The small reproduction mantle clock in the room told him he had twenty minutes before the innkeeper closed the kitchen, so he put his feet into his boots, hauled the laces tight, tossed the book and some papers into his laptop case, and started downstairs to meet his hostess.

Watery winter sunlight flooded the kitchen; the scent of toast and coffee filled the air.

"Good morning. Mr. Lovatt, I imagine?" A petite brunette brushed her hands on her apron and offered one to him. "I'm Nan Grady. I'm sorry I missed your arrival, but it's a treat to meet you. I'm a huge fan." The innkeeper paused with a twinkle in her eyes. "Huge enough that it's killing me not to rush at you with all my copies of your books."

"Good morning, Ms. Grady." He enjoyed her praise even as embarrassment spread up the back of his neck like fire. "Thank you."

"Mama? Is Paw Onion stayin' wif Nan?"

Ewan turned to see the blonde who'd checked him in—Anneliese, he recalled —sitting at the enormous farm table which dominated half the room. Next to her was a small version of herself, in pigtails and overalls. Anneliese laughed affectionately and tapped a bowl of what looked to be yogurt.

"Breakfast, Chlo."

"Mr. Lovatt, you'll remember Anneliese Thompson from check-in last night," Nan said. "This is her daughter, Chloe."

"Forgive her, Mr. Lovatt." Anneliese blushed. "We've been reading about Paul Bunyan. Apparently she's grasped the bit about him being very tall."

The two women watched him with gentle mirth in their eyes, and whatever wit he had escaped him. He cleared his throat.

The innkeeper spoke first. "Mr. Lovatt..."

"Ewan. Please."

"Ewan, would you like some coffee? Please have a seat while I put your breakfast together. I've got oatmeal, bread for toast, eggs however you'd like them, scones from Sweet Pease, the bakery in town..."

"Yes, to the coffee. Eggs, scrambled dry, please. And a scone." He moved to a chair opposite Anneliese and Chloe.

Nan brought over a mug on a coffee tray and a carafe. "I have Devon cream or honey-lemon preserves for the scones, if you'd like."

"Cream," he said.

"Of course."

Ewan pulled the novel and his reading glasses out of his bag. He slipped the glasses on his nose and opened to his bookmark with a sigh. Reed Sharpe couldn't string four words together without tripping over his colossal ego, but his grasp of sexual positions and heavy weaponry had catapulted his books to the bestseller list faster than you could say, *"Sell out."*

He folded a corner on page forty-two. There was a touch of literacy there he could reference. He looked up from the coffee tray to see Anneliese staring at the galley with an expression Ewan couldn't quite explain.

She blinked. "Is that a new Reed Sharpe novel? I don't read him, but my h— my ex-husband did. Your books are more my type. I read *The Orchard Gate* when I was in the hospital after Chloe was born, and the nurses recommended a therapist because I was always crying. I finally gave them my copy to convince them I wasn't seriously unwell."

Ewan poured milk into his coffee, his eyes flicking nervously from the billows of dairy to Anneliese's blue eyes as she spoke.

"And I'm babbling. I'm so sorry," she finished with a small laugh.

The little girl—Chloe—clutched a strip of toast and peered into his face from across the table. "Did you bring the blue ox baby?"

He smiled in spite of himself. She was a beautiful child, and funny, especially since she didn't know it yet. "No, Chloe. I'm sorry. Babe stayed in New York for the semester."

Chloe's laugh was sweet, like wind chimes, and he wished he had a notebook to capture the joy in her blue eyes.

Nan set down his plate of scrambled eggs, along with a wedge-shaped scone with double cream pillowed on top and a scoop of minted citrus salad. He tucked into his breakfast, quietly observing the women in the kitchen with him. Their ease and camaraderie was infectious.

"All done Chlo?" Anneliese swiped at Chloe's mouth with a napkin, helped her down from her chair, and cleared their dishes. "Time for your jacket and boots, little lady. We have to meet with CeCe at the florist shop, and then we have a lunch date with Mere!"

"Thanks for staying here while I was in Boston, Anna." Nan came around the island to hug her.

"Sorry we invaded your space again this morning." Anneliese held out a tiny sunflower printed parka for her daughter. "She was willing to sleep one night without Feesh, but she was rather insistent we come get her first thing."

"You are both welcome any time, especially since you took the trouble to keep my business running for me."

Ewan watched them embrace, piecing together details about them between bites of egg.

"It was no trouble, and it's nice to have a night away from my parents' house. Reminds me that someday I might have a place of my own again."

"You will." Nan dropped to her knees beside Chloe. "Thanks for helping your mom take care of the inn, Chlo."

"A-welcome, Nan," Chloe replied seriously, before digging a ragged plush clownfish from her mother's purse and skipping over to Ewan, mushing the toy against his cheek. "Feesh kiss!"

Ewan patted the clownfish, touched by the little girl's affection, and then they were gone, trailing her giggling mother toward the door.

Nan saw her friends out, and turned to him. "You were very good with her. Thank you."

Ewan swallowed his coffee with a fresh wave of shyness. "She seems like a sweet kid."

"She is, but not everyone has the patience for a preschooler."

"Not everyone's taught college freshmen."

Nan laughed and peered at the book in his hands. "Are you a Reed Sharpe fan?" Her delicately raised eyebrow told him all he needed to know—she was not.

"No," he exhaled. "But we share a publicist, and I promised I'd give him a jacket quote."

"I'm glad. You're an entirely different class of author, Mr. Lovatt."

Ewan's cheeks burned.

Nan returned to her work behind the counter, and he finished his breakfast in silence.

Nan brought the coffee carafe back to him just about the same time he realized his mug had gone cool. "I've read *The Orchard Gate* too, but *Moriarty's Daughter* is my favorite."

He waited for it: the casual request for something that more often than not followed praise, but nothing else was forthcoming. "Thank you, Ms. Grady."

"It's Nan," she said. "I hate to abandon you, but I have rooms to turn over by noon, and my assistant won't be in until later. Leave the dishes. I'll come back for them."

Ewan could only nod at Nan's warm charm. He listened to her light steps on the stairs for a moment, before opening the book and pouring a second cup of coffee.

CHAPTER 2

Kate gazed through framed openings for planned picture windows at winter-brown fields spreading down to the long shoreline of Lake Champlain. Dotted with oaks and maples, cross-stitched with stone walls, the view from Cooper Vineyards was breathtaking, and almost hers.

She stretched up to see the acres of dormant grape vines, waiting in their tidy rows for the milder weather to come again. Wineries weren't unheard of in the Champlain Valley, but this one, with its huge success, was something special. That they were willing to take a chance on her, on Sweet Pease, was an amazing opportunity.

As if in greeting, a cold wind blew up off the water and swirled around in the space.

A few feet away, her father and Jack consulted with Joss Fuller on the room's blueprints. "Room" was too small and organized a term. "Space" was more accurate. The unfinished lower floor of the brand-new barn—built into the hillside with one entire face open to the lake—was cavernous, but Kate was already seeing it complete.

She rubbed her gloved hands together, blowing hot breath between them. The men laughed the secret laugh of shared maleness, bringing her out of her reverie. If it weren't for the immense love she felt for them all, she'd have been tempted to throw something at them.

"Are you boys going to let me in on the joke, or will poor, stupid Kate not understand?"

Joss, at least, had the good grace to look ashamed.

Her brother shot her a devilish smile. "'Poor, stupid Kate,' my ass. You planned out the entire expansion. We're only indulging our egos that we have half a clue about any of it."

"Speak for yourself, son." Her father waved her over. "Where were you just now, sweetheart?"

Kate grinned at her brother. "Building the whole thing in my head. So, what's the joke?"

"No joke, Katherine. These two young bucks were giving an old man a hard time."

"Then, gentlemen, if you're done consulting amongst yourselves," Kate asked with a wry smile, "Will it work the way I think it will?"

"I think so, Kate," Joss answered. "I really do."

Kate launched herself at Joss, hugging him hard and kissing him extravagantly on the cheek before pulling her father and brother into her arms.

"Joss thinks he can have it ready by the end of the summer," said Jack.

"Even with the addition at the Damselfly?" Kate asked.

"Even so," Joss replied, looking at Kate's father. "John's going to help me when he can, and we're nearly ready for the subcontractors at the inn, so there's some room in my schedule."

"Daddy?" Kate's smile faltered a little. "Do you have time for this? What about the practice?"

"Oh, the practice only needs me on weekdays, but your mother may smother me in my sleep if I don't find something to do on the weekends."

"Speaking of being smothered while we sleep," Joss added, "Nan's expecting me back at the Damselfly."

Jack made a whip-snapping gesture. Joss replied with a gesture of his own.

"Go home, Joss," Kate giggled. Her brother and his best friend never failed to entertain her. "Maybe we can all hang out before the city mouse goes back to Boston on Monday morning?"

She stuck her tongue out at her brother, but it was Joss who answered.

"Call Nan. If she can get away, we can all go up to the cabin tomorrow night."

"Oh, I love that idea! Jack?"

"It's not like I have a hot date."

"I wonder if the Thompsons would watch Chloe." Kate went into planning mode. "If Nan can get Amanda to stay at the inn, then Anneliese could come, too."

She ignored the shadow that crossed her brother's face.

John Pease chuckled and dug his car keys out of his pocket. "Katherine, you exhaust me."

Kate squeezed him. "I love you, Daddy."

"I love you, too, sweetheart." He leaned in close to her ear. "And I'm so proud of you." He turned to his son. "Jack, I'll see you and that flashy car back at the house for supper?"

"Sure, Dad. I'll be back by seven."

"Good night, John," Joss said, stretching out a hand.

John took it with a wide smile. "I'm looking forward to this, Joss."

The two men walked out, leaving Kate and her brother standing in the empty barn. Kate took a long look around, already building the walls in her imagination, filling the empty space with an open kitchen, booths and tables, a gleaming pastry case. The winery would use the space above for tastings and functions, and she would run Sweet Pease's expansion from here. She would put in a terrace and a garden for the warm months, drawing her customers to the panoramic view of the Adirondacks rising up across the lake.

"I'm going to run up to Burlington before supper," Jack said, sliding his phone into his trouser pocket. "Seth's in town curating a new show. You want to come?"

Kate considered. Not so long ago, Seth Weston had made her a very attractive offer with his eyes. The art dealer was just the sort of man she usually loved to spend time with. There was something about him, though. Something vulnerable. Something lost and seeking that she sensed she'd never satisfy.

"I'm going home to go over my numbers again."

"Who knew it'd be ambition that would settle my little sister down?"

"Stuff it, Jacky Boy."

She started for the sawhorse, where her bag lay on the plywood floor.

"Katie?"

"Yeah?"

"Hang on a sec." He pulled an envelope from his coat pocket. "For you."

Kate took the envelope and flipped it open. Inside was a generous check.

"Jack." She breathed her brother's name.

"Your budget should cover things, but this will cushion you and provide a little cash reserve if you need it."

"I can't take this from you."

"Of course you can. Especially since I'll be running up a tab in exchange for my investment."

Kate bent to retrieve her bag. "I still haven't paid you back for the first loan you gave me."

"Katie, they're not loans. I'm investing in you. Because I believe in you. You're terrifying and you own too many pairs of shoes, but you're a brilliant baker and a hell of a businesswoman."

"Oh, *I* own too many pairs of shoes?"

"Mine all fill a very specific need. You're just a magpie."

"As in, 'oooh! Shiny'?"

"Exactly."

Kate snatched the keys to Jack's coupe and danced away from him, taunting him with the jingling keys as she bolted for the car. "Oooh, shiny!"

"Kate!" He yelled and gave chase.

She had the lead, but Jack had longer legs. Even in dress shoes, he was faster. He caught her and wrestled back his keys by pinching her armpit, just like he had when they were kids.

"Jerk!" She was laughing.

Jack offered her his keys back. "Fine, take them. Give me yours."

"Really?" Kate looked longingly at Jack's car. "You'd take my van?"

Jack wrapped an arm around her shoulder and squeezed. "Just this once. I know you don't get a ton of thrills up here."

Kate blew a raspberry at his back, but Jack was already climbing into the fuchsia van.

She settled into the supple leather of the driver's seat with a little shiver of delight. When the engine roared to life, she had to admit her brother had a point, at least as far as driving went.

EWAN'S TEMPORARY OFFICE ON THE FOURTH FLOOR OF KELLER HALL was quiet and devoid of personal effects. He'd brought little with him on this first visit, just a small, framed lithograph of the Chrysler building and a photograph of his parents standing on the stoop of the Brooklyn Heights apartment building where he had grown up, both of which fit in his laptop bag.

Reed Sharpe's galley taunted him from his desk like a malevolent paperweight. He turned instead to the view over County Road, just in time to watch a sleek sports car roar over the ridge and downshift with a throaty purr as it whipped down the hill that bisected the campus.

He smiled at the blur of the car hugging the curve below the science building. Maybe things didn't move so slowly in the country after all.

Thornton College, nestled in two hundred years of tradition and rustic Vermont hillside, was breathtaking, but it was neither the ivy-draped white granite buildings around the quad nor the charming village straddling the river that thrilled him about this position.

It was a chance to research a tenuous connection between his family and Thornton's best-kept ghost story. There was a novel in it; he just had to find the lost threads of the tale.

A knock at the door pulled Ewan from his thoughts. The intrusion didn't bother him so much as surprise him. He pushed aside the Sharpe novel and took off his reading glasses.

"Come in."

"Excuse me, Professor Lovatt?" A young man in Elvis Costello frames and a Navy surplus pea coat shuffled into the room.

"Mmhm?"

"I'm Ryan Chandler. I write for *The Rose and Talon*. I'd love to do a piece on you for our next issue."

"The *Rose and Talon*?"

"Online daily broadsheet. Thornton, the rose. Falcon, the talon. We started it as a side project for our freshman Shakespeare seminar."

"Clever. All right, Ryan. Have a seat." He gestured to the empty academic chair across the room. The boy pulled the chair up to the opposite side of Ewan's desk and pulled out his smartphone. He unwound a preposterously long, striped scarf from his neck and draped it over the chair, revealing a hipster band T-shirt whose logo Ewan actually recognized.

"Do you mind if I record this?" Ryan gestured to the phone.

"Nope."

Pulling a composition notebook and a gel pen from the front pocket of his bag, the boy touched the screen of his phone and spoke.

"Interview with Professor Ewan Lovatt. Office 402, Keller Hall, Thornton College, January twenty-eight." He looked up at Ewan. "Well, Professor, how are you finding Thornton?"

"I've only just arrived. I checked into the Damselfly Inn yesterday."

"And how are you enjoying it?"

"Charming."

"Charming?" The boy echoed. "Your characters, especially Dearest in *Moriarty's Daughter*, often use one word replies to deflect attention from their private agendas. Would you say this is something you do as well?"

His interviewer had at least read the right reviews of his work. "I suppose all authors draw on themselves a little."

"That's a very diplomatic answer."

Ewan chuckled. "My room is very comfortable. Ms. Grady is a generous hostess. My breakfast scone was a little dry. Probably the last one of the morning."

He watched the young journalist notice the Reed Sharpe novel and switch tacks. "The critics loved your last two novels, but I've read that *Moriarty's Daughter* was passed over by a major Hollywood studio while Reed Sharpe's Hawk Johnson books are being optioned for a multi-film series. Authors like him are more of a hit with bestseller lists and Hollywood executives. Does that ever factor into your writing style?"

"Not particularly." He didn't want to talk about Reed Sharpe.

Ryan was quick to take that in. "You self-published your first few books, the Alasdair Sledge novellas, which you've continued to put out between your traditionally backed literary fiction. There are a lot of people who wonder why a man, whose historical female leads are so treasured, also writes a steampunk mystery series with no women at all."

Ewan went for levity. "Alasdair just hasn't found the right woman yet."

"Is that autobiographical?"

Ryan Chandler wasn't half bad at interviewing. Ewan reached for his glasses, though he didn't need them. "Just a coincidence."

"You're offering an intro to speculative fiction, a junior seminar in novella structure, and an independent project opportunity in literary fiction. Those are some very interesting course options. Are these courses you've taught before?"

"They are. I'm also co-instructing a course in publishing industry legal issues with Will Dancy."

Ryan consulted his notebook. "You've taught at NYU, Emory, and UVA over the last few years. That's an impressive spread. What drew you to Thornton?"

The Damselfly Inn. Ewan pushed aside the true answer and gave his interviewer the quote he needed for the piece. "I'd heard the students here were some of the best minds I could learn from."

Ryan laughed out loud. "Well-played, Professor. I won't take any more of your time. I appreciate you talking with me."

"Not a problem," Ewan said. "I'll keep an eye out for that broadsheet of yours."

"The profile will be online around midnight. I'll be sure to send you a link."

"You do that."

"Good day, Professor."

Ryan stood, madc a production of buttoning the six buttons on his coat and winding his scarf just-so, shouldered his expensive messenger bag, and hunched his way out into the corridor. Ewan leaned back in his chair and kicked his boots onto his desk. The Reed Sharpe novel hit the floor with a solid thump. At nearly five hundred pages, the damn thing would make an excellent weapon. He let it lie where it had fallen and watched students trickling out of the granite and ivy buildings which ringed the quad. Winter term was finishing up; the campus was preparing for a short break and a new semester.

His student interviewer had come closer to the heart of the matter than he could have known. Thornton held the key to the next stage of his career.

CHAPTER 3

Kate heard the front door to the bakery open just before seven the next morning. A moment later, Andy Greenberg came into the kitchen to hang up his coat and swap his customary fisherman's sweater for an apron. Kate wiped a stray curl from her cheek with a finger dusted in confectioner's sugar. She took a sip of her coffee and smiled at him.

"Morning, Kate." Andy blushed furiously. The blushing was an improvement over the stammering and fidgeting he had exhibited when she first hired him.

"Morning, Andy. Who's on the breakfast shift with you today?"

"Moira."

"Great. Breakfast is trayed up on the rack. I've got a wedding cake for tomorrow that's going to take all of my time today. Think you two can handle the morning?"

"No worries, Kate. We've got it."

"Great."

Andy went back out front. The familiar sounds of his morning routine faded into the background while she rolled gum paste out on the stainless steel counter. She studied the pinboard on the backsplash, where a photograph of the bride's bouquet design and a piece of lace from her veil were centered.

When the gum paste was suitably thin, she took up her tools and began to fashion lily petals, setting them aside in groups to be assembled into flowers. The bride had called the night before, wondering about adding a few white lilies to the cake, and Kate was never one to turn down a client's last minute add-ons—at an upcharge, of course. These would take up most of her day if they were going to be dry for the event the next night.

The bell over the front door jingled; she heard Andy greet Moira.

A moment later, Moira hastily ducked in to grab an apron, gave Kate a worried glance, and slipped away again.

Kate frowned, but continued to trace lily petals with a fine blade. As the newest hire at Sweet Pease, Moira got all the jobs the others didn't want, but she was easy-going and the customers loved her for her friendly, chatty nature. Kate enjoyed the benefits of Moira's vital position in the town's gossip chain, which was based largely on Moira's elementary PTA involvement.

This shifty silence was unsettling.

The bell jingled as the first of her regulars began to appear. The sounds of conversation, orders taken and filled, the hiss of the espresso machine, all of it gave her a thrill—this place of hers, just as she liked it, succeeding, poised on the verge of expansion. Two hours later, with the lilies fashioned and propped against foil and egg carton molds to dry, Kate popped out front to check in with her employees.

A silver-haired woman in faded Levi's and a Patagonia fleece waved to her. "Morning, Katie."

"Good morning, Mrs. Mayhew," Kate replied. "Can I get you and Mrs. Marlow another cup of coffee? On the house?" Her now-retired kindergarten teacher came in every morning with her next-door neighbor. They stayed an hour in their favorite booth, walked Main Street, then drove together to the twin Cape houses they lived in on Snake Mountain Road, rarely pausing to draw breath. Kate liked to think that Mr. Mayhew and Mr. Marlow each drank concurrent, silent cups of coffee on their adjacent decks without needing to speak a word.

"No, thank you, Katie," Mrs. Mayhew replied.

It was then that Kate noticed Moira and Andy with their heads together over Andy's phone, whispering.

"What's the big secret?" Kate asked, coming around behind the counter.

"No secret," Andy said quickly, stowing his phone in his pocket. Moira busied herself with a milk pitcher which needed cleaning.

"Seriously you two. What gives?"

"She's going to see it sooner or later." Moira mumbled. "News in this town travels quicker than lightning,"

"It's just an article in one of the student newspapers. Nothing big," Andy said as Kate held her palm out expectantly. He dug the phone out and placed it in her hand.

She swiped the screen, bringing up the article. It was a profile on a professor who had recently joined the Thornton faculty. *Ewan Lovatt. Why was that name familiar?* Books. Novels. Nan read his books. Kate skimmed until the offending paragraph jumped out at her:

> On the topic of life in Thornton, Professor Ewan Lovatt was reticent, save for an apparent dislike for the scones served at the Damselfly Inn. "The room is very comfortable. Ms. Grady is a generous hostess. My scone was a little dry," said Lovatt. An informal investigation revealed the scones in question to be provided by Sweet Pease, a favorite local bakery and pastry shop.

Kate felt the blood rush up to her face. Andy and Moira looked on, waiting.

"Kate, it's really nothing," Andy reassured.

"The hell it's nothing. My scones are perfect." She bit the word off.

Andy backpedaled. "The seniors who publish this thing, Kate, they like to stir up trouble."

"I have lilies and royal icing lace to finish." Kate slapped his phone into his hand and stormed from the room.

Back at her work table, she rolled out a ball of ivory fondant. Unpinning the lace from the corkboard, she laid it over the fondant and pressed it gently with a small plastic smoother to indent the lace pattern into the fondant. The work forced wounded pride from her mind. There was no room for temper or defensiveness in a wedding cake. Kate believed in that, and after a few hours of painstaking fondant work, with five nearly-finished cake tiers to show for it, she'd almost forgotten Ewan Lovatt's commentary.

Kate covered the cakes, took them to the walk-in, checked the lilies, and set about tidying her workspace. Her Lady Gaga ringtone punched into the relative quiet of the empty bakery. Nan's number and a goofy picture of the two of them together lit up the screen.

"Hey Sugar Plum, what's the plan?"

"Amanda is watching the inn; Joss and I are on our way up to open the cabin. Pack some treats," Nan said. Kate heard Joss's voice in the background. "And can you swing by and pick Anna up?"

"Is my darling brother not going to pick her up?"

"He said something about there being no room in his car. I guess your mom is sending a bunch of his stuff back to Boston with him."

Kate snorted. "She's been threatening to clean out the attic for years. Figures."

"Joss wants to know if there are any day-old *financiers* for him?"

"He'll find out when I get there. Which, factoring in a swing up to River Ridge to get Anneliese, should be an hour and a half from now."

"Perfect. We'll light the wood stove and get dinner started."

"See you in a bit."

Kate ended the call, pulled up her to do list and typed in a few items. Satisfied that her workspace was ready for a busy wedding prep morning, she opened the walk-in to raid for treats.

Ewan wasn't normally given to gestures of the supernatural kind, but he couldn't help but stroke the white granite mantelpiece in the Damselfly Inn's parlor, hoping some gift from its original owner might simply appear in his imagination. The mantel was warm from the fire which crackled merrily below it, magnificently carved with vining botanicals, but devoid of messages from beyond the grave.

If the secrets of Faye Bartram's love and death were ever locked in this stone, they would remain for now.

With only the century-old diary of a teenage girl and third-hand family stories to push his curiosity, he would have to unearth Faye's secrets on his own—or build them from the world he now inhabited. He hadn't meant to book himself into the Damselfly; he'd only meant to drop in and meet the current owner before collecting the keys to the apartment Thornton College had offered him along with the teaching fellowship.

Instead, he'd felt the thrill of a character in his chest; the request for a room had come from the place in his heart where his characters lived. How could he have refused?

The extravagance of staying at the Damselfly Inn—in Faye's own home—would have to be reckoned with.

Novel writing alone—even the critically acclaimed and modestly successful variety—didn't allow for nest-egg building, but Thornton had been calling to him for years. The siren song of a story—a complicated, heartbroken story—lured him. If his agent's promises of backlist sales boosts and his share of the new project panned out, the expense of the inn would be a drop in an almost Reed Sharpe-sized bucket

He wandered out of the parlor and down the front hallway to the back door, stepping out into the brittle sunshine. He shoved his bare hands into his pockets and curved his shoulders in, hunching away the chill. The morning sun cast the back patio into shade, and Ewan regretted coming out here without going back upstairs for his jacket.

A dairy herd grazed in the pasture to the north, their shaggy hides soaking up the weak warmth. Patches of grimy snow still dotted the fields. Though there hadn't been any new snow recently, it was cold enough for some to have survived the bovine hooves churning the winter ground.

He momentarily envied the cows their slim foraging; his stomach was beginning to complain.

When he'd first researched Faye Bartram's story, he'd wondered what on earth would have drawn a sophisticated bluestocking, bred to Manhattan's bustle, rocked to sleep to the heartbeat of railway expansion, to build her country home among Vermont dairy farms. Great Granny Lovatt's girlhood diary echoed these sentiments. She'd been an upstairs maid in the Bartram household, one of the entourage who'd traveled to Vermont for the first few glorious summers, and the only one to see the final, tragic one.

Now, with mountains blurring one horizon and creating the other, he began to understand why Faye might have wanted to be part of this place. Its beauty seeped into the soul, even in these darkest, most frigid months of the year.

A gust of early February wind swirled around the corner of the house, and Ewan left the cows lowing in the north pasture, hoping to find something tastier than half-frozen pasture to graze on.

Nan Grady was in the kitchen, an ergonomically curved laundry basket on her hip, shifting folded tea towels onto the center island. She greeted him with an easy smile.

Ewan held out his hands. "Can I take that for you?"

"I've got it, but thank you." She nudged the stack of towels away from the edge of the counter and set the basket down on the floor. "Is there anything I can get you?"

He wanted to plumb her for any knowledge of the house's history, but manners and instinct held him back. One excellent breakfast and a few moments in the company of her friend didn't mean he was entitled to her life story. He settled for satisfying his rumbling belly. "I heard a rumor from the couple in the room next to mine about leftovers."

She lifted a glass pie dome resting on the counter. "English muffins, and sausage and rosemary focaccia. Help yourself."

He reached for a thick slab of focaccia, the soft bread redolent of a savory breakfast, its dark-golden crust studded with rosemary. "This smells amazing."

Nan bent to retrieve her laundry. "If the pie dome is out, it means there are treats for grabs. Please feel free to take them. I get deliveries from the bakery daily, except for Mondays."

She grinned when the first bite of the breakfast bread left him happily speechless. "Enjoy, Mr. Lov—Ewan. Have a great day."

~

KATE TOOK THE LAST CURVE BEFORE THE THORNTON RIVER FAST AND hard.

Anneliese grabbed the "oh-shit" handle and hung on. "I love that you drive your minivan like it's an Aston Martin and you're 007."

"You can take the fast car away from the Pease…"

"I know." Anneliese cut her off, looking out the window as Kate crossed the bridge over the river and took the next switchback a little slower. "The river's mostly frozen."

Her friend's voice was far away. Kate regretted the quip about Peases and fast cars. There was definitely some tension between her brother and Anna.

"This winter's been cold, even by my father's strict standards," Kate said.

The road up to the gap twisted and wound its way up toward the bony backbone of Vermont that was the Green Mountains. As the river dropped away into its ravine, and the mountains rose up around the van, Kate turned to some shop talk with her driving companion. Anything to dispel the sudden mood shift in the car.

"Thanks for the O'Hara graduation referral. That's going to be a fun cake."

The wistful fog cleared from Anneliese's expression.

"You're welcome. Are you all set for the Lynch wedding tomorrow?"

"I have to do the royal icing on the lace overlay and position the flowers. I'll assemble on-site. How are things from your end?"

"We had a small hiccup with the seating chart, but I checked in with the maid of honor and the best man about an hour ago, and the rehearsal dinner is underway at Vittorio's as we speak."

"Have you eaten there?" Kate asked.

"I've had their function sampler. The catering menu is excellent, and the price point is really attractive. It's funny to me, a hot-shot Food Network chef opening a restaurant in a sleepy Vermont town."

"Vergennes is the smallest city in the country," Kate reminded her with a sideways smile. "And Mike Labonte, the executive chef? I totally made out with him in culinary school."

Anneliese's lips curved. "Who haven't you made out with?"

"Pretty much just Joss," Kate shrugged. Both women giggled as Kate pulled off the main road and onto the dirt driveway that led up to Joss's cabin in Catmint Gap. He'd kept it after he moved back down to the valley to live with Nan at the inn, just for nights like this. As they wound through the fir and white birches, coming to a stop with the forest thick around them and the night sky endless above them, Kate understood why.

"What do you want me to grab?" Anneliese asked.

"I've got it. It's just this one bag of snacks and dessert." Kate shouldered a reusable shopping bag and slammed shut the door to the van.

Nan opened the front door as they approached. "Come on in."

The cabin glowed warm against the night, and Kate and Anneliese hurried for the door. As the door was closing, Kate heard the purr of Jack's car coming up the drive.

She shut the door behind her. "And my brother makes five."

"Thank god," Joss joked from his spot in the recliner by the stove. "It's a bit of a hen party right now."

"And that's so hard for you." Nan replied with an expressive eye-roll even while she settled on the arm of his seat.

Outside, Jack killed the engine. They heard his boots on the packed-dirt driveway. He didn't knock, but opened the door and let himself in. "Joss, you wanna come give me a hand out here?"

"What the hell did you bring?" Joss asked, setting down his beer and pushing himself up.

"I've got my stuff—since I'm crashing here tonight—and a half dozen bottles of my Dad's home brew."

Joss vanished out the door with Jack. Kate wasted no time.

"Nan," she said, "is the Thornton professor staying with you? The novelist? Lovell, Lobel?"

"Ewan Lovatt," Nan answered slowly. She could hear the unrest in Kate's voice.

"He's kind of ruggedly handsome," Anneliese remarked. "Like..."

"Rochester," Kate snapped. "I remember. He's got about as much tact as fucking Rochester, apparently."

"Kate?" Nan began, but was cut off by the men returning with the beer and Jack's bag.

"Rochester? Are we angry with upstate New York?" Jack interrupted.

"We're talking," Kate snapped, "about the jackass professor who trashed my scones on the internet today."

Nan sat up. "What?"

Kate was already pulling her laptop out of her leather bag. "Joss, do you have internet up here?"

"I'm not a total savage." Joss set the beer on the counter and peered over Kate's shoulder. Jack left his things by the front door.

"Password?" Kate demanded.

"579 capital-F falcon one," he replied.

"Katie, what's going on?" Jack asked.

Kate pounded on the keys, bringing up the *Rose and Talon*. "Here," she offered, tilting the screen back for her friends. "This is what's up."

Ewan's headshot filled the top left corner of the screen. His dark eyes, shaggy dark hair, and serious expression dominated the photo.

Jack peered at the screen. "I'd buy him as Rochester. Who's playing the crazy wife in the attic?"

"Read the damn article," Kate said through clenched teeth.

Joss had pulled the article up on his phone. "Wait. The guy staying in the Chittendon room is *the* Ewan Lovatt? My mom loves him. She's going to want to meet him."

Nan found the offending paragraph first. "Oh, honey," she said, squeezing Kate's arm, "it's just a soundbite. And no one but students read this thing anyway."

"Give it a day or two and it'll come up in a Google search for Sweet Pease, and then I'm the baker with the dry scones."

"Kate," Jack said seriously, wrapping an arm around his little sister, "do not feed the troll."

"I'm not going to feed the troll," Kate hissed. "I'm going to kick the troll in the shins and tell him to go back to New York where he belongs."

Joss and Anneliese both giggled, but Nan and Jack exchanged a knowing glance over Kate's flushed cheeks and glittering eyes.

"Seriously, Kate, the guy's quiet, kind of shy," Nan said. "I doubt he was trying to offend."

"He struck me as sort of awkward," Anneliese added. "Chloe was the one who got him to open up."

Jack popped open his cooler. "Who wants some of Dad's winter spice brew?"

"No one thinks this is a big deal?" Kate asked, looking around at her friends.

"I think it's only a big deal if you let it be," Nan said. "You have incredibly loyal customers, and a comment from an outsider, on a student website, isn't going to undermine that."

"The last thing I need with the expansion is negative press."

"This isn't negative press, Katie," Jack soothed. "This is what Nan says it is. A flatlander with no taste giving a college kid a soundbite." He handed her a pint glass.

Joss laughed. "Ouch."

"Let's not let this spoil the evening," Anneliese said, taking the glass Jack offered her without touching his hand.

Kate closed the laptop with a deep sigh. "Okay, if you think it's no big deal." Apparently, her friends had no further thoughts on Ewan Lovatt and his opinions. She could play along.

Nan went to the stove to check on dinner. Joss returned to his recliner by the stove, and Jack took his backpack up the spiral staircase to the sleeping loft.

Anneliese sat down on the sofa with her beer, tucking her feet up under her legs. "Do we have an agenda for tonight?"

Nan replied from the kitchen. "Rummy or the new Russell Crowe movie? Since you and Kate have a wedding tomorrow, we figured we should keep it low-key."

"I vote Rummy," Jack said, coming back downstairs. He'd pulled on his old Harvard Law sweatshirt and switched his snow-hikers for leather moccasins. He sat on the sofa with Anneliese, frowning a little at her barely perceptible shift away from him as he did.

"What's for dinner, Nan?" Kate asked, joining her friend at the stove.

"Macaroni and cheese," Nan said. "And a pickled beet salad, courtesy of Molly."

"Yum. I love when Joss's mother insists on supplementing my diet." Kate sniffed at the casserole in the pot. "I brought two French boules and a box of petit fours for dessert."

Jack raised a glass. "We shall feast like kings."

"Actually, we're just about ready to feast," Nan said. "Jack, Joss, why don't you boys set the table."

The two men raided the cabinets and drawers for plates and silverware. Nan brought the food to the table with Kate and Anneliese.

With her friends around the table, Kate very nearly let Ewan Lovatt and his snarky quote slip her mind.

CHAPTER 4

Ewan sped out County Road to the Damselfly under a pale morning sky, taking the turns wide and fast, feeling the swoop and fall of the rolling countryside under his painstakingly restored 1974 International Scout. It was an unlikely truck for a guy who never drove off-road, but he'd fallen in love with it on a lot in Poughkeepsie, and that was that.

The weather was exceptional: blue skies, a touch of thaw. He'd spent the morning with a colleague, in a meeting that had turned into a lunch and a tour of the campus art museum. Will Dancy was an amateur historian and his wife was an assistant curator for the college's art collection. The talk had turned briefly to Faye Bertram's local legend, and Will had offered to connect him with a historian in Lake Placid who had written on the railroad expansion that had made the Bartram's fortune.

"Do I get a mention in the new book if this works out?" Will asked. They were about the same age, but Will Dancy's entire bearing spoke of academia, from his pale, owlish face to his polished loafers. Will exuded earnestness.

"Yeah," Ewan said, uncomfortable with the half-truth; he had no idea how that worked in the endless scrolling credits after a film. *Would they let him thank anyone?*

Would the folks at the studio be as fascinated with this story has he was?

He slipped into autopilot, contemplating Faye and her father, Faye and this valley, Faye and her late-blooming, doomed love affair, and he had to swerve suddenly to avoid a runner. The woman—the kind of woman who gave birth to the word statuesque—stumbled mid-stride and tumbled into the scrub and dirt by the side of the road.

Ewan pulled the car over, but she had already pushed herself up and was dusting gravel off her knees. The high-tech fabric shed the road shrapnel like wax and water.

"What the hell?" Her irate voice was dark and polished. It rang of old money and prep school.

"I'm sorry." Ewan approached her guardedly. "Are you okay?"

"No thanks to you," she snapped. "Keep your eyes on the road next time or you'll kill someone."

"I can give you a lift somewhere if you need." She pursed her lips, and he realized how such an offer might sound. "I'm a guest at the inn down the road."

She eyeballed the Scout. He watched her take his measure.

"I'm fine."

He got back in the truck, not at all comfortable with leaving her there, even though she looked no worse for her fall. She stood, resolute by the side of the road.

"Suit yourself." He fired up the old engine and popped the emergency brake.

By the time Ewan sat down at his computer, he'd almost put the blonde out of his mind. That is, until he looked out the window to see her jog into the parking lot and lean fetchingly against the picket fence to stretch her toned calves and quads.

He watched her finish stretching, take a small water bottle from her fuel belt and chug the contents, then stop mid-swallow as she caught sight of the Scout in the parking lot. She looked up at the window—he'd swear at his exact window—with a scowl and started for the front porch.

Ewan saved his progress as he listened to her running shoes pound the stairs up to the second floor. Her knock was forceful.

"It's open." He hoped he'd masked the resignation in his voice. The characters' voices were fading and he knew he was losing momentum on an afternoon's writing session.

"It's not every day I get run off the road by a critically acclaimed author." She stuck out a flawlessly manicured hand. "Elisha McNair."

"Ewan Lovatt." Ewan took her hand and shook, standing as he did so. "But it seems you already know that."

"I can see I'm interrupting," she said, taking note of the still steaming coffee mug and his open laptop. "I won't keep you."

"Thanks," Ewan replied, feeling genuine gratitude toward this cosmic event of a female. She at least respected the process.

"I'll see you around. You and I are soon-to-be colleagues."

She flashed him a brilliant smile and vanished behind his door as it closed. The snick of the knob flipped a switch in his thoughts, and he was back in the story. *Could there have been another woman? Perhaps a polished Boston socialite who stole Faye's summer love when he returned to his life away from Lake Champlain; a cool, fashionable woman who would never permit herself to be thrown over for a spinster like Faye...*

He dropped into the desk chair and began to type.

Later that evening, very nearly done with a full outline and first scene, Ewan padded downstairs in his flannel pants and holey T-shirt in search of coffee. The carafe he was quickly coming to feel a serious affection for was sitting out, and it sloshed cheerfully when he picked it up. He rinsed the mug he'd had in his room and refilled it.

He nearly dropped the coffee when Elisha McNair's voice slipped out of the shadows in the front hall.

"It's nice to see I'm not the only one keeping long hours. You'd think after the drive up here from New York and a fourteen-mile training run, I'd be passed out cold. I swear there's something in the air up here that lets you go longer and harder."

Her expertly colored blond waves tumbled around her face, and her ruthlessly sculpted body filled out her pricey yoga clothes. She was a knock-out, and Ewan knew an invitation when he heard one.

"Yeah," he said with a shrug. "I don't know what's possessing me to cram in a late-night, over-caffeinated writing session when I've got early meetings with potential independent study students in the morning."

"Speaking of your students—sort of—are you going to the new faculty reception? I was here last semester, but I still get to go since this is my first semester teaching a full course load."

Ewan pushed his hands through his hair. "Yeah. I guess I am. Will Dancy tells me I have to, and Dr. Sporinger expects me."

Elisha laughed like carillon bells. "Will you introduce me to Dr. Sporinger? He's a living legend."

"I will." He wondered suddenly why Elisha was still in residence at the Damselfly. "Are you planning on staying here indefinitely?"

"I'm actually moving out over the weekend. I've got a condo lined up. What about you?"

"My rooms are in Lawrence House. I checked in here on a whim, but I'll be moving out on Monday."

"Lawrence House isn't that far from downtown. You'll be able to walk everywhere." Elisha stretched. "Speaking of, have coffee with me tomorrow. At Sweet Pease. I don't indulge often, but the croissants there are divine."

"I've got meetings..."

She snagged a stray brochure and a pen from the sideboard, carefully inking her phone number and sliding it toward him. "Here's my number. Text me when you know you'll be free."

"Maybe after eleven? I don't want to keep you."

"I've carved out my morning to work on a book proposal. I can work there as easily as anywhere."

"Okay, sure." He caught his reflection in the window glass. "I should shower before I go to bed. I look like a crazy hermit."

"I'm sure your students expect that kind of thing. It fits the image of the tortured writer they're expecting from your work."

"Thank you?" He half-questioned the sideways compliment.

"Oh, you're welcome. As a former college co-ed, I can say, without a doubt, that there's nothing sexier and more anticipated than a course taught by a tortured writer." She looked him over. He wondered if the heat in his cheeks betrayed him. "You'll do just fine."

With that, she was gone again. He had half a mind to follow her upstairs and see if her invitation still stood, but there was already a jealous woman waiting for him in his room.

CHAPTER 5

Just before noon, Kate took a quick sweep of the pastry trays. She was out of beignets and Danish, as well as the oatmeal brown sugar muffins. She made a mental note to keep those in rotation for another few days.

The room was nearly empty, just Jim, who worked Andy's off days, and a single customer.

She recognized Elisha McNair immediately. The blonde professor wasn't one to frequent the bakery. Kate attributed that both to Elisha's known devotion to her figure, and to the fact that Kate had mistakenly insulted her in a dress shop not six months before. Nan was fond of the woman, though, so Kate swallowed her embarrassment, and tried for warmth.

Elisha was camped out in the booth in the corner, a favorite with most everyone in town who came in to get work done. She had a slim laptop open and a mug quietly steaming by her elbow.

"Hey there." Kate approached with caution. "Can I get you anything?"

"No. I'm waiting for someone before I get anything more than tea." Elisha glanced at the time on her screen. "Though if he's any later, my croissant will end up being my lunch."

Kate heard the complaint loud and clear. "Student missed an appointment?"

"Colleague, actually." Elisha sighed. "There's a novelist I admire staying at the Damselfly and teaching at Thornton this semester. I thought we had a date, but I haven't heard from him all morning."

There was only one novelist at the Damselfly. Novelist, casual scone maligner, and, apparently, jerk who stood women up.

"I wish I knew what all the fuss was with him. You'd think Shakespeare had taken up residence in town."

Elisha laughed. "His books are amazing, and I don't know about you, but I like that gruff good-looking type. And he's really tall."

"I love tall," Kate agreed with a grin, "but I have zero patience for no-shows."

"We'll see." Elisha picked up her mug. "I like this tea. Where do you get it?"

Kate took the topic change in stride. "What are you drinking?"

"It's an herbal blend. Minty. I took a chance."

"I'll tell you, since you're a friend of Nan's, that I get it online. Just search 'Steeped Zen.' You can buy it in bulk as loose leaf, or bagged."

"That was easy," Elisha said. "You don't strike me as the type to give away her secrets."

"I don't figure I'm losing too much business by telling you where to buy my tea. You're not exactly a regular here."

"I'd have to buy a new wardrobe if I was. You've got a gift with baked goods."

"I'm glad you think so, anyway."

Any reply Elisha might have made was interrupted by the jingle of the bell over the door. Both of them looked up, hoping for Ewan Lovatt, but by Elisha's expression, the man who came in with his family certainly wasn't Nan's new guest.

Elisha set her mug down with an exasperated thump, and Kate took her cue to leave, wondering as she did what special kind of jackass this Ewan Lovatt was.

~

Ewan's office phone rang four times before he was able to look away from the screen. He'd been writing for hours, taking advantage of the quiet academic building.

"Ewan Lovatt."

"Ewan, it's Mallory. I called your cell, but I assume they don't have signals in Vermont."

"There's a signal. I just turned it off so I could write."

"Perfect answer," she said. "So, how's the great northern wilderness?"

His agent was a city creature herself, though he recalled that she had a brother somewhere in New England. Near the water, he was pretty sure.

"Cold."

"Cold and productive, I hope. I want pages."

Ewan looked at his laptop screen. "And you'll get them. Soon."

"Good. Now, tell me all about the revered halls of Thornton College."

Ewan turned in his chair so he could see the quad outside the building. "It's gorgeous. I don't know much more yet. The kids are on break until Monday." A young man bundled against the cold made his way across the frozen grass below. "I did meet one the other day. A reporter from a campus paper."

Mallory laughed. "I love press, and so does Alex. Send us the link."

The mention of his publicist reminded him that he needed to finish Reed Sharpe's book. "I'll send it when I send the jacket quote for the Hawk Johnson nightmare."

"Right." Mallory was all business again. "You need to do that. Cross-pollinating your name with Sharpe's readers is good for you."

Ewan sighed. "If you say so."

"I do." Mallory's bracelets jingled in the background. "Now go write. Lots."

She was gone before he could come up with a quick response.

CHAPTER 6

Kate woke a little after eight. She could tell by the bright glow behind her blinds that the day was her favorite kind, glittery and cold, a pure winter diamond of a day.

A day for slaying dragons. Or rude professors.

The Thornton College website had revealed Professor Lovatt's office location, and Kate figured that was a good place to start. This man had some explaining to do.

But first, the gym.

She pulled on yoga pants and a hoodie, slipped her feet into her scarred Uggs and pulled her down-filled jacket from the closet. Finishing her outfit with a slouchy cable-knit hat and thick mittens, she packed her gym bag and struck out on foot for the Thornton College Athletic Complex. She paid for the privilege, but the facilities were top notch, and Kate valued her workouts. A baker needed to sample her wares, but a woman didn't want to jeopardize her relationship with her favorite jeans.

The quarter-mile walk down South Avenue gave her time to contemplate the Ewan Lovatt situation. Time on the treadmill sharpened her resolve. Her friends didn't understand how much the small criticism stung. She couldn't describe it, but she felt compelled to demand some kind of apology from the man.

Sweat and vintage Madonna pushed her through a steady run, before she slowed to a brisk walk for a few minutes. Finishing up on the treadmill, she set herself up in a corner of the studio and stretched through a half dozen sun salutations. Smiling to herself at the admiring glances from the college boys, she made her way to the locker room and indulged in a long, hot shower.

When she stepped out into the cold, her long dark hair pinned back into a messy, wet bun under her knit cap, she felt unstoppable. Her courage carried her through campus toward Keller Hall. She might not have studied at the prestigious little college, but she knew the campus like the back of her hand. Just how well she knew some of its nooks and crannies was something she sincerely hoped her father —or her brother—never found out.

She pulled open the side door and started up the four flights of stairs, swiping a fine sheen of sweat from her forehead and congratulating herself on not being winded. Room 402's door was open, sunlight spilled into the hallway. She knocked briskly on the door jamb as she stepped into the room.

Her first thought was that Ewan Lovatt appeared more rumpled in person than he did in his head shot. Her second thought was that the man looked positively haunted. His body hunched almost protectively over his desk. The dark eyes behind his tortoise-shell glasses were far away.

"Yes?" His voice, like the planes and angles of his face, was craggy and gruff. Kate's confidence flagged briefly, but she squared her shoulders and walked across the stark office. She stuck out a hand.

"Katherine Pease, Mr. Lovatt," she said, hoping her last name might form a connection for him. He reached across his desk to shake her offered hand.

"What can I do for you, Ms. Pease?" he asked. "If you're interested in the Independent Essay, you need to see the department assistant to verify your pre-requisites before I can officially meet with you. I assume you are a senior?"

"No, Mr. Lovatt." Kate spoke slowly to mask her disbelief. "I'm not a student. I'm the owner of Sweet Pease."

He looked at her expectantly.

"The bakery downtown?" She winced as her voice went shrill. She breathed in through her nose, fighting for composure. "Sweet Pease?"

"I'm sorry," he said. "I don't understand." He closed the notebook he was making notes in and pulled off his glasses.

"Do dry scones ring a bell?" She spat the words at him.

"Dry scones?" he asked, blinking slowly, then tilting his face at her as he put the pieces together. "Ms. Pease, I—"

"Save it," Kate snapped. "I'm sure you think you're clever, belittling the country girl's baked goods. Big city writer walking among the common people or whatever, but you're trifling with my livelihood."

"I—" he began.

"I'm sure it's very entertaining to give the students witty quotes, to set yourself up as aloof and superior, but I call bullshit, Professor." Kate drew a breath. "Come into Sweet Pease sometime. I promise you, my scones are perfect, and I dare you to find anything to complain about in my establishment."

She turned on her heel and sailed out of his office as gracefully as a woman can sail in Uggs. She flew down the stairs and out into the cold on a current of righteous anger. Her fury and pride carried her back down the hill from the college to her apartment over the bakery. She dropped onto her couch still in her boots and coat.

There she let her hands shake.

EWAN COULD ONLY STARE AT THE EMPTY DOORWAY, BETWEEN SHAME and admiration, listening to Katherine Pease's steps fade on the stairs. He was torn. He didn't know her, hadn't meant to cause her pain, but her anger was magnificent. Before the sensation faded, he jotted down his thoughts and a quick sketch of her face, something to help him remember her high color and glittering eyes, the fury rolling off her in waves: an avenging angel in denim and down.

He had a sudden flash of his steampunk hero, Alasdair Sledge. He'd been thinking about the direction of his independently published series, but the Victorian explorer had stalled in his imagination. *What would Alasdair, a confirmed bachelor scientist, do when confronted with a fierce, clever, and beautiful woman? A woman like Katherine Pease.*

He found himself itching to get back to the inn to start fleshing out this new character in more detail. The reason for her visit faded the deeper he tumbled into his work.

Katherine Pease's face stayed with him long after she'd left his office, long after an afternoon of meetings and his solitary dinner at the bar at Temple. He headed straight upstairs to his room at the Damselfly, and wrote her into Alasdair's life until the small hours of the morning.

If Faye Bartram's ghost objected to his temporary loss of focus, she didn't feel the need to speak to him about it.

Ewan woke early the next morning. The clear light and rural quiet pulled him from sleep, despite a long night at his computer. He slipped out of bed and fished in his luggage for the hiking boots he'd bought at a sporting goods store he'd passed on his way north. His laptop called to him from the small writing desk by the window. This new character wanted his attention, but he needed exercise. A hike might satisfy them both.

A fire crackled in the parlor hearth. Ewan thumbed through a display of pamphlets about the area on the sideboard until he found a State Parks map which showed several nearby trails.

He stopped in the kitchen on his way out to the car. He was midway through filling his travel mug with Nan's excellent coffee when the innkeeper herself entered the room from the breezeway. He could hear the sounds of construction from beyond. He wondered what work was being done in her private space.

"Good morning."

"Good morning." Her tone was pleasant, but he thought he detected something cool in the delivery. For a moment, he wracked his brain for some offense he might have committed. He'd already offended the baker…

The baker. The scones. The two women were at the very least colleagues, probably friends knowing his luck. The extent of the damage his idle remarks had done settled in his belly. Best to make amends. This woman held the key to his next book in her unknowing hands.

"Ms. Grady—"

"Nan," she corrected.

"Nan," he echoed. "I'm sorry about that article in the *Rose and Talon*. I wasn't thinking."

Nan's expression gentled. "I'm not the one you should consider apologizing to."

He had the sinking sensation of having disappointed her, which didn't sit comfortably.

"I'll bear that in mind." He showed the map he was carrying. "Would you recommend Arcadia Falls or Tiger's Eye Rock?"

"Arcadia Falls," Nan said decisively, slipping easily back into her professional charm. "We've had a series of partial thaws and cold snaps. The water makes gorgeous ice sculptures when that happens. I'd guess it looks amazing up there right now."

Nan was right about Arcadia Falls. The water spilled over three falls, horse-tailing and tumbling a hundred feet from top to bottom. The stream flowed musically under sculptures of ice created from its own spray. The combination of road walking and easy trail hiking pushed his blood a little faster and his imagination raced with it.

He wondered if Faye had ever come here. She'd been a naturalist at heart: a hiker in woolen skirts, a hot-springs bather, a sketchbook tourist on the lake. He was sure this place would have enchanted her. He knew Faye's basic biography, but the years in which she was an iconoclastic spinster, a railroad heiress who never married, the years in which she built her summer house and fell in love with an enigmatic older man, those were missing.

He'd seen old black and white photographs of the woman herself, but as he walked, the eyes that sparkled in his imagination, cheeks rosy with exertion and cold, belonged to Katherine Pease. Thoughts of Alasdair Sledge's new research partner stole into his already crowded head. The bakery owner's fiercely beautiful face pushed Faye aside for a second time, and an invented backstory for this new heroine—Cordelia, a naturalist, a scientist like Sledge—wove around him as he walked.

It was useless to try to tame his imagination. He gave Cordelia her way, and spent an hour clambering over rocks, exploring the vantage points of the two pools formed by the natural tumble of water. He imagined that in the wet heat of July, these pools would invite swimmers, but now they were ice-skimmed and bubbling with cold.

Cordelia, in all her clever, adventurous beauty, rebuked him on Katherine's behalf. She would have upbraided Sledge for his casual sarcasm, and she would have had the right of it.

His feet began to protest the chill, so he picked his way back to the trail and hiked down to the parking area. If the walk up had given him the solitude of forest and birdsong in which to be a god, forming lives and worlds and destinies in his mind, the walk back humbled him with a panoramic view of Lake Dunmore and the topography of the valley rolling down to the steely sliver of Lake Champlain just visible under the Adirondacks.

By the time he reached the parking lot, the god was a man again, and a blend of curiosity, remorse, and hunger were already driving him back into town and toward Sweet Pease. He found the bakery easily enough. Downtown Thornton was essentially an intersection of two streets, complicated a little over the years by a state road and a new bridge. The common squatted amidst that intersection, pushing the two main thoroughfares out to form a kind of roundabout. The bakery sat several blocks west of the common, where County Road finished its descent from the campus.

He parallel parked his truck a block past the bakery and fished in his glove compartment for change for the meters. At fifty cents an hour, parking for lunch was a bargain. He thought twice about the necessity of locking the truck, but his urban caution won out. The color of Sweet Pease's awning made him think of Prince's raspberry beret, but he was afraid of the welcome, or lack thereof, that waited inside.

The bell over the door tinkled cheerfully, and Ewan fought the urge to duck his head. There was a shortness to the doorways and ceilings in the older buildings in New England that frustrated him. He normally managed to forget his unusual height, but the shops and eateries in Thornton gave him the uneasy sensation of holding up the structures with the top of his head. He was no Atlas, shrugging or otherwise.

It was early for lunch. A quick glance around the room told him he would have his choice of tables. He walked purposefully toward the display case, noting the baskets of brown paper wrapped breads and plates of samples set atop the counter.

He read through the sandwich offerings on the chalkboard over the counter, deciding on roast beef and hot house tomatoes.

"Can I help you?" asked a young man in a navy apron with a tag which named him *Andy*.

"Sure." Ewan noted a light cough from the young woman switching out a nearly empty tray of tiny French cookies and the boy's widening eyes. "A roast beef sandwich with tomato and country Dijon."

"What kind of bread would you like, sir?" The young man wouldn't meet his eyes.

Ewan paused, unsure. He found a list of the daily options and chose the first one. "Seven grain."

"You get pickles and a side with that."

Ewan stared helplessly at the board.

"We've got an arugula salad or mustard roasted sweet potato oven fries today."

That was easy. "The fries."

"You can have a seat," the boy said. "Moira will bring your lunch over."

Ewan fought the urge to leave without his lunch when he caught a weighted glance between the two. Gathering the composure that had bolstered him through two book tours, he chose a seat by the window and crowded his long legs under the table. He was aware, in the corner of his field of vision, of both Katherine's employees venturing into the kitchen, though he'd seen that the food prep was done behind the counter.

To distract himself, he turned to watch Main Street, and was immediately rewarded when an elderly man in formalwear passed by the bakery, his bearing military-straight even though his feet shuffled a little on the sidewalk. A carnation in the man's lapel lent him a wistful, debonair charm.

Ewan forgot his discomfort and pulled a small wire-bound pad and ballpoint pen from his jacket pocket. He was adding the flower to his sketch when the velvet rasp of Katherine Pease's voice interrupted him.

"His name is George Cartwright." She was looking at his drawing.

She set a plate down in front of him and took the seat opposite. His sandwich and fries were heartily piled on the plate. The young woman, Moira, followed with two to-go coffee cups. He frowned slightly and Katherine spoke up. "The coffee's on me."

Ewan hated that his brows knit in confusion. *Who was this woman?*

"Mr. Cartwright's memory started to slip about five years ago," Kate said. "He was my parents' English teacher back in the day. Jack had him, too, but I didn't take AP English."

Ewan raised a questioning brow, but he didn't speak. He didn't want to spoil her story.

"Jack is my older brother. Anyway, Mr. Cartwright sort of went back along his own timeline to when he was young. Mrs. Cartwright decided it was kinder to play along, so every evening they would stroll Main Street together, all dolled up in clothes no one had seen for half a century."

She gazed fondly at the old man as he passed out of sight down the sidewalk.

"What happened to her?" Ewan asked gently.

Katherine laced her fingers around her coffee cup. "She died last year. Cancer. He's more or less lost in the early fifties now, and his daughter, who looks after him, won't let him out after dark, so he goes for his walk around midday now."

Ewan watched, enchanted, as she blinked back tears.

"Your sandwich will get soggy," she said.

"He must miss her," Ewan wondered aloud.

"He'll tell you, if you stop to say hello, that he fell in love with her the moment he saw her, but she fell in love with him on the bridge." Katherine's voice had gone hoarse. "His face lights up like a boy's."

She sipped from her cup. "He breaks my heart."

Ewan fought the urge to draw the slight tremble of her lips on his napkin. Instead, he spoke. "Katherine—"

"It's Kate."

"I'm sorry about the quote," he said. "I was inconsiderate."

"Yes, you were. Apology accepted, Mr. Lovatt."

She was even more beautiful when she was haughty.

She stood and drained her coffee cup. "Enjoy your lunch. Next time? Try the honey-oat bread and the aioli with the roast beef and tomato combo."

She was gone before he could gather the words to reply; her employees did their best to look occupied when he picked his sandwich up. He could feel their eyes on him as he chewed, but he was too busy wondering what other stories from Thornton's past she might have up her hot pink sleeves.

PACING THE KITCHEN LIKE A LION, KATE CREDITED THE LATE MORNING coffee for her sudden burst of nervous energy. She refused to give Ewan Lovatt that much power over her. She'd indulged in a moment of pure, self-indulgent gloating when Andy and Moira had each snuck back to the kitchen to tell her that Professor Lovatt was in the bakery. He had taken up the gauntlet, he had dared, and she would show him that she was made of the same stuff as all the pretentious *boulangers* and *pâtissiers* in the big cities.

She'd trained in Paris under a revered pastry chef. Mathieu had loved to bring his friends around then. She'd always managed to get him a special something on the house.

In the end, Mathieu hadn't stuck, but that training had, and she'd be damned if some stranger was going to use her for a clever soundbite.

She'd taken Ewan Lovatt's lunch order to his table herself, planning on delivering an ass-kicking on the side.

Seeing him alone at the table by the window, the ass-kicking hadn't seemed so necessary. Better to show him exactly how gracious the local hospitality really was. After all, he was staying at the Damselfly Inn. Nan's reputation as a hostess set a high bar. Sweet Pease wouldn't be the business that brought the town down in his eyes.

When she caught Ewan watching George Cartwright with a tender expression, she'd been helpless to resist the wistful romance of the Cartwrights' story.

The way he'd watched her. Like being a curious child absorbing a bedtime story. He'd breathed in her words, pen to notebook through her telling.

And then he'd apologized.

With the wind gone from her sails, she'd fallen back on the only defense which remained: scorn.

Kate slipped her discarded chef's coat back on and tucked her ponytail around itself before stuffing it inside her baker's cap. She loaded a rack with the afternoon's offerings, focusing more on snacks and treats, less on the *viennoiserie*—after the noon hour fewer people were looking for muffins, croissants, Danish, or scones.

Scones. She'd learned scones from a fellow intern in Paris. The Glaswegian boy with the brilliant ginger hair and unintelligible accent. He'd given her his Gran's recipe in exchange for her friendship and her devotion to getting them just right.

Her scones were perfect.

Her thoughts churned; she fought for focus. There was production work to finish. The next morning's pastries weren't going to bake themselves, and her student-intern wouldn't thank her if the kitchen was left in shambles.

Kate opened the dry storage cabinet, in search of inspiration for the next morning's muffin special. She grabbed macadamias, dried hibiscus, and candied pineapple. Tropical to balance the winter chill.

She pulled a two gallon bucket of thawed plain muffin batter out of the walk-in refrigerator and poured it into her industrial stand mixer. She eyeballed scoops of her custom ingredients and made a last-minute decision to add a glug of rum to the batter. While the mixer turned, Kate ran down her checklist: assemble a tasting for a wedding couple, finish the next morning's production set up, and place her order for sandwich and lunch options with the co-op.

"Excuse me? Kate?"

Andy loitered in the doorway, holding his apron. Kate flipped the mixer off.

"Yeah?"

"If it's a bad time?"

"It's not a bad time."

"It's just about two o'clock. Moira has another hour, but I've got to go. I have a meeting with my chemistry TA before cross country practice."

"Don't worry about it." She turned back to her list and reached for the mixer. "Take off. Moira can handle things out there until three, and then I'll cover until closing at five."

"You sure?"

Kate looked back at him over her shoulder and sighed. "What is it, Andy?"

"I—" He fidgeted, then straightened his shoulders and spoke. "I know you were upset when he came in. I don't want to leave you alone here if you're upset."

Kate blew out a breath and stifled a smile.

"I'm okay, Andy." Kate hoped she sounded convincing. "Thank you. You're very kind."

Andy blushed. "I'll head out then."

"Good night."

"G' night, Kate."

She gave up on the list and set paper liners in neat rows on a pair of half sheet pans and fished in a drawer for her batter scoop. When the liners were filled, she covered the tray and moved it to the walk-in.

She cleaned up and stripped off her jacket. She was untucking her ponytail from her cap when Moira came in to get her coat and bag.

"I'm off to get my kids. See you on Thursday?"

"Yep. Have a great afternoon, Moira."

"You're all right here?"

"I am." Kate suppressed a laugh, but her heart was full. Her employees cared for her, and she could do far worse than that in a team.

Out front, the tables were empty save for a pair of students sharing a slice of pie and drinking tea over some reading. She poured a to-go cup of coffee and grabbed a chocolate cherry cookie from the display. Settling behind the counter, she pulled up the co-op's catering menu on the computer and logged in to place her order for the coming week.

The bell jingled cheerfully when the students left, and the bakery settled into a kind of silence. It was never truly quiet, with the hum of the refrigerators and the noise of Main Street outside, but it was peaceful. Kate looked at the front window. In the days before Mrs. Cartwright's passing, this would have been the time they walked; thinking of them conjured the memory of Ewan, sitting by that same window.

A browser window was already up, so she let her fingers do the walking. His name and those serious features filled the screen. His author site came up first. That she bypassed; she could read his press kit any time. Lists of interviews and reviews and retail sites to buy his books followed.

The faculty rating site she found was at least entertaining. The reviews were largely glowing, citing a no-nonsense teaching style, a tough but fair grading system, and he had a little flame next to his photo which Kate understood to mean he'd been voted *smokin'*. Kate made a mental note to check the site for a few of her former instructors. One or two of them definitely qualified as such.

After that, her search yielded little more than links to his speaking engagements, signings, and teaching gigs. He seemed to be everywhere and nowhere all at once, though she knew from Nan that Ewan based himself in Manhattan.

Ten past five. Past time to close up shop. Ewan Lovatt's somewhat nomadic lifestyle was none of her business.

She shut down the computer, then made the rounds, flipping switches and checking the instructions she'd left for Margot. Her intern started her shift at four a.m., baking the morning pastries according to Kate's notes.

She locked the front door and was walking around the corner when her phone buzzed from her pocket. The number didn't look familiar, but she was curious. "Hello?"

"Kate? Hi; it's Seth Weston."

She stopped short, a bemused smile playing around her mouth. "Hi Seth."

"I'm glad you picked up—"

Here was just the kind of distraction she needed. "Lucky me."

"Jack gave me your number. I hope that's okay."

She leaned against the brick wall of her building. Above her the night sky raced westward and a cold waning moon hung low. "Yes, of course it's okay. How have you been?"

Half a year, more or less, since his gallery opening in Burlington.

"I'm on my way south tonight," Seth said. "I'm about twenty minutes north of Thornton and I'm hungry. Let me take you to dinner at the Riverbend Hotel."

Kate was impressed with his confidence. "I think I will."

"What's your address? Or should I just put your bakery in my GPS?"

"486 Main. My apartment door is around the corner on Gristmill Way."

"Got it. ETA is seventeen minutes."

"See you then," she said, ending the call.

She fished her apartment key from her pocket, unlocked the door and jogged upstairs, kicking her clogs off at the top. She had a lot of work to do in the next sixteen and a half minutes.

~

Only fifteen minutes later, Kate's cheap battery-operated doorbell chimed.

Her studio apartment over Sweet Pease was roomy for one, but she could still make it from the boudoir screen by her dresser to the stairs that led down to her door in about twenty steps.

She flipped her head forward, spritzed the back of her neck with Chanel No. 5, and flipped back over. She took a last glance in the mirror and congratulated herself on a job well done. The aubergine Diane von Furstenberg knock-off wrap dress was sophisticated without being fussy, and it suited her long, lean frame.

She carried her faux alligator sling-backs looped over one finger as she went down to let her date in.

Seth Weston looked like a lawyer. Or a stock broker. But not an artist. Which was perhaps why he was such a successful dealer. Kate gave him an appreciative once-over. He wore his denim well, snug without being obnoxiously tight, and Kate recognized his half-zip sweater from a recent Brooks Brothers' catalog.

Seth beat her to the compliments. "You look beautiful."

Kate leaned in and kissed his cheek, pleased by his dazzled expression. "Thank you."

He checked his watch. Kate indulged in a private sigh at the tasteful Rolex. "The computerized siren who gives me directions was exactly right." He tugged his cuff down over his bared wrist as a cold wind barreled down the alley. "I called on the way to reserve a table."

"Let me put on my shoes."

He waited while she slipped her feet into shoes and collected her clutch from the shoulder bag hanging from the coat tree. He held her coat and the passenger door of his BMW for her.

Kate stopped him when he started to put the restaurant's address into the GPS. "I'll be the navigator."

"Works for me. You've got a better voice than my phone."

"Flatterer."

Seth smiled and turned down the satellite radio. "Jack says you're getting ready to expand."

"I am," she said, shifting toward him in her seat. "I've got the go-ahead from the bank and an amazing location. Plus, the John Pease Seals of Approval, Junior and Senior."

Seth chuckled. "Jack said there was quite the powwow at the winery."

"Oh, that's right. You two had beers at the University Tavern last week."

"How could you forget?" Seth asked. "You stole his car and left him to drive a hot-pink minivan into downtown Burlington."

Kate laughed out loud. "I tried to. And failed. He ended up giving them to me anyway, whatever he told you."

"He loves you like crazy."

"He's my big brother; of course he does."

The inn was no more than five miles away; they made good time in Seth's car. Kate approved of the way he handled the coupe.

The Riverbend Hotel's great claim to fame, other than its position on the historical register, was being the inspiration for the setting of a gruesome, bestselling horror novel. When they were seated at a cozy corner table near the fireplace, with drinks ordered, Seth looked around the room.

"Did you read the book?" he asked. "I have to admit, I've wanted to eat here ever since I did."

"I did," she said. "Saw the movie, too. Honestly? They should have filmed it up here. No one with half a brain would believe that the Green Mountains look anything like the Sierra Nevadas."

Seth laughed. "I've never seen the Sierras in person. But you're right, it didn't look at all the way it was written."

"My friend Nan, the innkeeper? She says the people who own this place get hundreds of calls from people who want to sleep in the room where all the murders happened in the book."

"I thought it wasn't a functioning hotel, though?"

"Just a fantastic restaurant in a former public house." Kate rolled her eyes. "I guess people get pretty irate."

"How is Nan?" Seth asked. "Is the… Damselfly? Is it doing well?"

"It is," Kate nodded. "I think she'd be thrilled if people wanted to check into her place for its ghost story."

"Does it have a ghost story?"

"Depends on who you ask. Joss was close with the Swifts, who owned the place before Nan. He says it's a little bit haunted. I don't know the whole story. Something to do with a Victorian socialite."

The server arrived with their drinks. "Gibson for the gentleman and a Manhattan for the lady. Would you like a few more moments with the menu?"

"Please," Seth said to the server, confirming with Kate in a glance. The server slipped away.

Seth looked over the menu quickly and shut it with a decisive snap. "So, when are Nan and Joss getting married?"

"June." Kate looked up from her menu. She and Nan had talked about Seth's Big Hurt. They'd both seen it in his eyes before, and here it was back again.

He'd lost someone special; Kate would bet on it. She had more experience there than anyone—even Nan—knew of.

She quickly banished those thoughts with a sip of her drink and some spontaneity. "I don't suppose you're going to be in town in three weeks?"

"Actually..." Seth considered the rim of his glass for a moment. "I'm curating a show in my gallery for three UVM Studio Art majors. Trying to draw in more local talent, and more local commerce."

"Come with me to Nan and Joss's engagement party," Kate said. "I don't have a date, and you'll already know a few people. It'll be fun."

For a moment, the shadows behind Seth's eyes faded. "I'd like that."

The waiter reappeared. "Are you ready to order?"

Kate nodded. "I'll start with the sunchoke *frites,* then the *canard à la grenade.*"

Their server nodded, taking the order without notes. "And for you, sir?"

Seth closed his menu. "The seared kale and the veal, please."

"Excellent. Any wine this evening?" The waiter looked expectantly at Seth.

"Kate?" He said, "I defer to you."

Kate turned the page, reading the wine list thoughtfully before choosing a bottle she knew would knock his socks off.

The dining room at the Riverbend Hotel was fussy and old fashioned. The brass and wood, heavy fabrics, and patterned floral wallpaper should have dated the room beyond redemption, but it had a special kind of charm, like an elegant woman in her old age.

A memory of Paris blindsided her. She'd been walking with Mathieu when they stopped to admire a window display. A woman who was eighty if she was a day, wearing a menswear-style structured three-piece suit and a small fortune in emeralds dangling from her ears had stopped them to ask for directions to a particular café.

When she'd continued on her way, Kate had marveled at her style, but Mathieu had been unfazed. "You see it all the time here. Age doesn't mean a woman can't dress as she likes."

There has been a coolness in his eyes when he spoke to her, a superiority that she'd taken for worldliness. She should have seen it a thousand times; she was a novelty for him. He never meant for them to stay together.

Nan might tease her about the boy in Paris, but her killer scones and passable French weren't the only things she'd brought home from her year abroad. Hamish had shared his granny's recipes; Mathieu had shared her bed and stolen her heart.

But not before leaving her shattered and miserable when he'd told her she was nothing but an amusement, an American distraction, and that she wouldn't find him waiting for her if she came back to Paris.

"So, what did you decide on?"

Seth was looking at her expectantly.

"It's a surprise." She closed the wine list and grasped at a new topic of conversation. "So, tell me about the craziest thing you've sold lately?"

"I still show the very first photographer I ever discovered. Peregrine. Peri. She's nuts, but we've done well together. She just did a thirteen-image series, macro images of moths, left to decay where they died. I sold the whole collection to a Senator with a flat on the Upper East Side."

Kate liked the protective way he talked about his artist.

"I love New York, but I never get there."

"You should. I'd love to show you around." Seth's eyes issued a deeper invitation.

"Maybe once the dust settles at the new location." She licked pomegranate sauce from her fork with a grim laugh. "Which might be in a year or two."

"I could always bring some New York to you?" Seth's tone was flirty, but Kate only thought of Ewan.

"I have enough of that already," she muttered.

"Hmm?"

Seth hadn't heard, for which Kate was grateful. Ewan had no business creeping into her thoughts like that.

They finished the meal with a shared gingered pear tart, a cappuccino for Seth, and an after-dinner drink for her. Seth paid the check and they walked back to his car.

Kate was savoring the warmth of spiced fruit and good cognac when Seth took her hand.

"Kate." His voice was husky and intimate under the frosty, starry sky. "Do you think Jack would be very angry if I kissed his sister?"

He brushed his hand up her arm, drawing her close. She knew he was teasing, but wasn't it her he should be asking? Still, he was an attractive and attentive man.

His lips were cool and questing. It was a practiced kiss, intended to tease and seduce. She should know; she'd given enough of them.

Seth pulled away and they tripped over their words.

"I'm sorry."

"Don't apologize—"

"Kate, it's okay."

He opened the passenger door, so she sat, smoothing her skirt and tucking her chilled feet into the car.

"It's not—" she began, once he'd joined her in the car.

Seth cranked up the heat. "It's okay. Really."

They drove in silence, the dark roads confined to the blue-white spread of his headlights. When he pulled up outside her building and put the car in neutral, Kate turned to him. She unbuckled her seatbelt and leaned across the center console. The kiss she gave him was brief but warm.

"Drive safe, and I'll call you with the party details."

He frowned slightly when she pulled away, but his expression was gentle. "Good night, Kate."

He was still idling outside when she turned on the light and waved down from her window. The car sped out past the athletic center headed for the route south-west along the Northway, down through the Hudson River Valley, and on to Manhattan.

In the quiet of her studio apartment, she peeled off her dress, scrubbed her face, and wrapped up in her favorite robe. She picked up her phone, intending to finally just text her brother and ask what the deal was with Seth's past, but it felt like an invasion of his privacy. She knew she wouldn't want her own pathetic failed romance paraded in front of her friends.

Her text notification chimed, as though conjured. Her brother's face popped up on the screen.

Just got off a call with Seth. Seems you two had dinner?

Curling up in the corner of her sofa, she typed a quick reply. *Yep.*

Having your revenge on all New Yorkers through poor Seth?

He was a beast. *Shut up, Jack*

Make me.

Was she having some sort of revenge, though? She opened a new search, chasing Ewan Lovatt from guest appearance to talk to research trip via the blog on his author website. He was nothing to worry about. Her friends were right. He would be gone before the summer, his poor taste in scones—and those fascinated eyes —with him.

CHAPTER 7

Kate loved having an intern. Margot was nearly finished at New England Culinary Institute—Kate's own alma mater—and a perfect fit for Sweet Pease. Kate had her working an academic internship on the production shift, but was planning to ask her back next year to manage, if things worked out. She said a quick prayer to Saint Honoré that she had a bakery and sufficient funds for a few paid interns this time next year, then laughed at herself. She was pretty far from being any kind of Catholic, but a year in a Parisian kitchen left her with a few lingering superstitions.

Margot was on her break, and everything was spotless. The ovens convected, blowing hot over the croissants for lunch service; the counters were clean and bare. Kate peeked into the proof box and smiled at the neat trays of breakfast pastries lined up for the next morning.

She checked her schedule, pleased to note that she'd have a wedding cake tasting to occupy her after closing. Her evening with Seth still sat awkwardly on her shoulder, but right now she had a meeting with Joss at the winery. From the cluttered corner desk she referred to as her office, she grabbed the two-inch binder which held all the files related to the expansion and stuffed it in her bag.

She found Margot reading on the back stoop of the building.

"Everything looks great. If anyone's looking for me, I'm meeting with my contractor up at Cooper Vineyards."

Margot looked up from her book with a guilty smile. "Thanks, Kate. I'll let Andy and Moira know you left."

Kate recognized the cover of Margot's book. She'd seen it the night before on Ewan's website. She'd also seen it—now that she knew what she'd seen—in the window display at the book store down the block. On a whim, she detoured in that direction. She wasn't a reader like Nan, but she'd been known to pick up a paperback now and then.

Vellichor smelled like lavender, clove, and paper.

A voice floated up from the back of the store. "Can I help you?"

Kate knew the bookstore's owner through her mother, but she rarely dropped into the shop. "Marian? It's Kate Pease. I'm just here to browse."

"Lemme know if there's anything I can help you find, hon."

"'Kay; thanks."

Kate found the fiction shelves easily enough. She traced the spines until she came to Lovatt, E. She pulled out a copy of *Moriarty's Daughter* and opened the book jacket.

> *In brilliantly re-imagined Victorian London, Sherlock Holmes and James Moriarty's intellectual battles have left scars on the city. On the sidelines of their private war is Gertrude Bosworth, the criminally brilliant professor's illegitimate daughter. Brought up among the glitter of the demimonde, Gertrude—called "Dearest" by her actress mother—struggles against social constraints and the awful rumors of her paternity. As she grows, it becomes clear that she has both the best and worst of her parents in her, terrible beauty and diabolical cleverness. When circumstances surrounding the death of her mysterious father bring her into the path of recently widowed Dr. John Watson, Dearest takes up her father's legacy. Watson's seduction is only the beginning of a far deeper masterwork.*

She carried the book to the counter. Marian met her there with a knowing expression.

"I can't keep his books on the shelves now that people know he's in town."

"I've never read one, but I met him yesterday," Kate said, feigning nonchalance. "I thought I'd see what all the fuss was about."

"You'll love it," Marian said, ringing up the book. "I can't get into Sir Arthur Conan Doyle's Sherlock Holmes, but Lovatt's version?"

She hummed appreciatively and bagged the book.

"He writes amazing women. This one? Dearest? She's incredible."

"Really?" Kate wondered.

"Really," Marian confirmed with a wink. "Even my old man reads them, though he really loves the Alasdair Sledge novellas. Can't wait for the next one. The only thing I don't love is that they're missing a really kick ass female lead so far."

Kate looked back at the stacks. "Should I get that instead?"

"Nah," Marian took the book and scanned it into the register. "This is the one to start with. Enjoy."

"Thanks, Marian. Take care."

"Have a good day, Kate."

Kate drifted back out into the gray day, headed for the small lot at the bottom of Gristmill Way where she parked her van.

Kate could see Joss's truck parked at the barn when she made the turn at Cooper Vineyards. Since their meeting the previous week, the siding crew had nearly finished the exterior of the building. A hopeful flutter blossomed in her belly as she pulled her van up next to the truck. *What wonders awaited inside?*

Joss was leaning against the cab, hands in his pockets.

Kate waved. "I hope you're envisioning the gorgeous bakery we're going to create."

Joss pushed off the truck and joined Kate on the walkway that led to the lower level entrance. "You know the lower level of a barn always makes me think of Charlotte and Wilbur."

Kate's breath released somewhere between a laugh and a sigh. "I could use a clever spider to announce to the world that I'm *terrific* and *radiant*."

"Everyone knows you are both, Kate."

"You're just saying that because you're marrying my best friend."

"And because I keep hoping you'll pay me in my favorite cookies."

Kate shot him a sidelong glance. "I would totally pay you in baked goods."

Joss reconsidered on the spot. "Maybe not."

Kate laughed as she unlocked the double doors and pushed them open with a flourish.

Joss started in immediately. "First thing we're going to be doing is running plumbing and electrical, and we're going to want to consider some add-ons like hard-wiring for internet and speakers. I'll schedule a time with Al so he can walk you through your options there." He gestured to the northeast corner of the room. "Do you still want to partition this area off for an office?"

"I do," Kate said, walking over to a spot about twelve feet from the corner. She paced out a rectangle. "A large enough space for a desk and office storage, as well as a small conversation area and efficiency kitchen so I can do tastings in this location."

Joss looked at her strangely.

"What?" she asked. "Can I not have that?"

"No. I mean, yes," he said. "You absolutely can. It's just that sometimes I still think of you as Jack's kid sister"

"Sister, always," Kate laughed. "Kid, not so much."

"Listening to the way you talk about this project reminds me that none of us are in high school anymore."

The preliminary drawings for Joss's wedding cake were hanging on her board at work. They'd both been away and back again; the world had broken their hearts in different ways. They surely weren't teenagers any longer.

She smiled through the pinch of nostalgia and chose levity. "We were idiots in high school."

"Fair enough," Joss said. "Now, we have the plumbing specs from the architect, and we have your additions to the plans. I'm going to try to get Ray, my plumber, up here the same day you meet with Al. That way they can put their heads together."

"As long as I can have everything I want, and we don't use up all of my money, I'm happy."

"We're going to do our best, Kate. My fiancée will flay me if I don't get this right for you."

"Your fiancée!" Kate squealed. "I love when you say that. You get these two bright spots on your cheeks. It so cute."

"Cute?" Joss grimaced, scrubbing his jaw with his hands. "Let's walk through the built-ins, and then you can go. I've got to measure for your appliances and cabinets before I head out."

"Okay," she said, pulling out her binder. She thumbed through the pages under the green tab, then held the book open to a rough drawing and two magazine cut-outs. "This is the booth style I was hoping for, and I'd like to do one under each of the north-facing windows to maximize the space underneath. I want an airier, table-and-chairs feel over on the south-facing side where the windows are larger and the view is spectacular."

Joss took the page she popped out of the binder. "I can do this. D' you mind if I take this home and work up some actual drawings for you?"

"Take it." Kate flipped ahead a few sections. "Do you need the pages for the cabinets in the office space? And the book shelves?"

"Sure." Joss took the extra pages from her.

Kate slung an arm around Joss. "You are too good to me."

Joss gave her a squeeze. "It's going to be great."

"Hey, do you think Nan would mind if I drop by today? Is she busy for lunch?"

"Are you asking me about Nan's schedule?"

"I guess I am," Kate laughed. "I must really think she loves you."

"She said she was going to update the reservation software and catch up on some bookkeeping."

"She so needs a lunch distraction."

Joss dropped his arm. "Get out of here, Kate. I'll drop your pictures off at the bakery tomorrow."

"Thanks, Joss."

~

The Damselfly Inn huddled amongst the pine stands and dairy pastures in the middle of the valley. Kate hopped out of the van and shuddered as a harsh wind yanked her jacket open. There was a warm light on in the office, and as long as she didn't run into her friend's literary guest, a good girl-talk was waiting for her inside. She grabbed a shopping bag from the passenger seat and ran up the front steps, through the front door, and into Nan's office.

"Lunch time!"

Nan looked up from her computer screen. "I love when you say lunch time." What's in the bag?"

"A triple crème brie, rosemary-and-currant crackers—a prototype I'm working on—a pomegranate, and a Toblerone."

Nan laughed. "You stopped at the little specialty shop in Vergennes, didn't you?"

"Maybe…"

"Is the really good looking guy with the mysterious Eastern European accent still working there?"

"I didn't notice. He wasn't at the cash register."

"You didn't notice?" Nan spoke slowly, peering at Kate wide-eyed. "Do you have a fever?"

"Oh, shut up. Let's eat." Kate flounced out of the room.

She was spreading out the food on Nan's serving pieces when Nan came into the kitchen.

"Make yourself at home," Nan said wryly, grabbing two sparkling waters from the fridge.

"'Course," Kate said, slicing an edge off the brie. "Oh, I love when the rind doesn't overpower."

Nan reached for a cracker, crunching warily at first. "Okay, I was a little skeptical about rosemary and currant. I take it all back. Give me that cheese."

Kate slid the brie across the island. "Ewan Lovatt came into the bakery yesterday."

Nan picked up the cheese knife. "Really?"

Kate made a show of breaking open the pomegranate, but she heard the false disbelief in Nan's voice. "You already know."

"I might have suggested it."

Kate frowned as she inverted the pomegranate peel and pushed the seeds into a bowl. "And here I was thinking I dared him to come in."

Nan swallowed. "Dared him?"

"I might have gone by his office on Monday."

"Kate," Nan said, setting down the knife. "Seriously?"

"It seemed like a good idea at the time," Kate began. "And I was brilliant, all angry and, for me, eloquent."

"Meaning you didn't turn the color of an eggplant and swear like a sailor?"

"I sometimes hate that you know me so well."

"You love it." Nan grabbed a handful of pomegranate seeds. "So he stopped in. I kind of like the guy, Kate. I'm not going to lie."

Kate pouted. "Of course you do."

"Don't be mad. He was sweet with Chloe."

"He was interested in George Cartwright."

"Oh." Nan clucked her tongue. "He can't be all bad."

"I know," Kate grumbled. "He apologized for the *Rose and Talon* thing."

"Of course he did." Nan shook her head knowingly. "And I'm sure you were gracious about it."

Kate broke a section of seeds apart and popped a handful into her mouth.

"I bought his book," Kate admitted when she finished chewing.

"You did?" Nan asked. "Which one?"

"*Moriarty's Daughter.*"

Nan lit up. "It's so good. Three pages in, and you won't care who wrote it, you'll just want to read it until you finish." She smeared another cracker with the brie and stuck a few pomegranate seeds on top. "Can we have this at the engagement party?"

"Oh, shit!"

"What?"

"The engagement party." Kate giggled. "That's why I came over. Well, sort of."

"Sort of?"

"Seth Weston called me last night."

"Seth Weston—Jack's friend?"

"Yeah." Kate sipped from her water bottle. "He took me to dinner at the Riverbend Hotel."

"And it took you until now to mention this?"

"I got distracted by lunch."

"You are a bottomless pit, and I hate you for it, but right now you need to tell me about dinner with Seth 'I own two galleries' Weston."

Kate set down her water.

"Did he confess The Big Hurt?" Nan asked with a giggle.

"It was only a date," Kate snapped. "Not everyone marries the first nice-looking man to cross their threshold."

"Hey now."

"Sorry." Kate backpedaled. She hadn't meant to let Nan get so close to her own Big Hurt. "You know I love you and Joss. The Seth thing? It should have been perfect."

"How was it not?"

"I don't know; it was a gorgeous night. He calls, asks me out. Shows up exactly when he says he will in a sexy, steel-gray BMW, lets me choose the wine, asks me about my business, about you and the inn..."

"And?" Nan asked, tilting her head.

"And he kissed me under the stars and it was... meh."

"Meh," Nan repeated.

"Yes, 'meh.' And I felt awful about it, so I kissed him when we got back to my place—"

"It was 'meh,' and you still went back to your place?"

"No, I just mean when he pulled up at my apartment. Anyway," Kate rambled on, "I'd already asked him to be my date for your engagement party, so I told him I'd call him with the details."

"You invited him to the engagement party before he'd been properly vetted?"

"You mean before he passed the make-out exam?"

"Of course that's what I mean," Nan countered. "You've had a firm system in place the entire time I've known you."

"I don't know, Nan," Kate sighed. "The whole evening just felt... off somehow."

They lapsed into silence for a moment.

"I blame Ewan Lovatt. He threw me off my game." The confession surprised her, but it was true. He had thrown her. She did blame him.

Nan's knowing *huh* bordered on smug. To dispel the feeling she'd cornered herself, Kate smeared brie on another cracker and dotted it with pomegranate seeds. "We can totally do these for your party."

THORNTON'S LIBRARIAN CONFIRMED WHAT EWAN ALREADY KNEW; HE needed to ask Nan about the house. He had assumed that once he'd checked in to stay, he'd have ample opportunity to press the innkeeper for stories.

He hadn't expected to be caught up in their lives, to feel so welcomed. Suddenly, his curiosity felt invasive, as if he were using them for their home.

In fairness, that had been his plan when he arrived.

Mrs. Williams, as her desk plaque named her, was a straight-backed woman in her sixties. She maintained a flawless platinum blonde bob, and dressed like the saucy secretary in a black and white movie. Her knowledge was more based in Thornton's history and its relationship—or lack thereof—with Faye Bartram. She had known Margaret Swift, the previous owner as well.

"Meg thought there was a kind of benevolent spirit around the place, but nothing you'd call a haunting. A couple of families in town sent servants out to the summer house, according to the records we have, but I couldn't tell you if anyone today has any connections there.

"The Fullers, who own the dairy next door, they've been out there longer than anyone. I'd bet Walt Fuller heard a story or two over the years."

She vanished into the stacks for five minutes, returning with several microfiche cards.

"The newspaper from the year she took up residence here. Maybe you can find something interesting there. You'll think we're awfully backward, but I haven't managed to get the funding to convert all the old stuff to digital. There's a reader in the room to the left of the fireplace."

The microfiche reader was a behemoth. A relic. A familiar beauty. Ewan thanked his stars for the hours he'd spent researching at the Brooklyn Heights library as a kid. He settled down and devoted himself to Thornton in the year the railroad heiress came to town.

CHAPTER 8

Kate got to Temple early on Sunday. She ordered one of Deirdre's locally famous pint-glass mimosas and caught up with her bartender friend.

"So?" she asked, nodding slightly at the five o'clock-shadowed guy in a Pats sweatshirt nursing a Bloody Mary near the small flat screen TV.

"Oh, Robbie?" Deirdre said with a small smile. "It's good. He's lovely."

"I love when I'm right."

Deirdre cleared a few glasses from the spot next to Kate. "So who're you meeting for brunch this morning?"

"Joss and Nan, Anneliese and Chloe."

"D'you want the table that looks out over the waterfall? The little ones usually like that view."

"You're too good to me, Dee."

"Anything for the woman who once raided a boy's locker room to save my poor immigrant pride."

Kate snorted. "As if you weren't three steps behind me. Josh Burke never lets me forget that when he brings his kids into the bakery."

"He's adorable. Now." Dee grinned. She looked up at the door as a gust of wind blew in. "And speaking of adorable."

"Kate-kate!" Chloe Thompson ran toward her, pigtails flying. Kate hopped off her stool and scooped the little girl up.

"Hi, Chlo!"

"I'll grab a booster seat. You three go sit," Dee said.

Anneliese followed as Kate walked Chloe to the picture window at the back of the restaurant. The falls tumbled down underneath Main Street, sending up a rainbow of mist. Chloe pressed her face to the glass. "Look, Mama!"

"I see, sweetie," Anneliese said.

Deirdre buckled a booster seat to the chair nearest the window. "Now into your seat. I brought your crayons."

"Eggs!" Chloe crowed.

Kate laughed.

"Yes," Anna said. "And we'll get you some eggs." She turned to Kate. "Are Nan and Joss still coming?"

"Yep," Kate said. "Got a text from Nan about a half hour ago. She's got three rooms checking out this morning, then they'll be over."

"Who'll be over?" Nan asked from behind them, handing her coat to Joss. "Hey, Kate. Hey, Anna."

Joss picked up the other women's coats, noting that Chloe had hidden herself behind her coloring book. "Where's my prettiest cousin?"

The little girl giggled.

"Anna?" Joss scolded, "Did you forget someone at home today?"

"No?" Anna answered with exaggerated wide eyes. "Who would I have forgotten?"

Chloe laughed, her book shaking.

"I thought you had a little girl," Joss went on. "Maybe that's my other cousin?"

"Must be," Kate commented. "You are related to half the town."

Chloe peeked over the edge of her book, eyes shining with glee. "I am here!"

"Chloe!" Joss exclaimed. "There's my prettiest cousin!" He leaned over and gently tugged a curl. "I'll be right back."

Kate caught a glance between Nan and Joss before he left to hang up their coats. Images of little tow-headed Grady-Fuller children around a brunch table came unbidden, followed by a pang that felt suspiciously like longing.

When Ewan Lovatt walked into the restaurant, ducking his tall body under the door frame, Kate did a double take.

Their eyes met and held. Ewan's expression softened a touch, then turned serious as he scanned the bar for a spot. Kate turned away and sat down. Nan had pulled up a chair; she and Anna were already discussing the furniture rental for the wedding.

"I can't let you two alone for a moment," she joked. "It's like the Wedding Channel around here."

"I'm still wearing a tux and saying 'I do' to the beautiful woman, right?" Joss asked, dropping into the chair next to Nan, skimming a casual hand over her shoulder. Kate took the remaining seat with a sigh. Ewan dominated her view of the room.

"Is everyone here then?" Deirdre asked, setting out menus. "Flag me down when you're ready to order."

"Thanks, Dee," Kate said.

"Isn't that Mr. Lovatt, Nan?" Anna asked. "I'm still embarrassed about the way I prattled in front of him the other day."

"I'm sure he gets worse on a regular basis," Nan said. "Joss, if you get the eggs Benedict and I get the French toast, can we share?"

"I'm having the Irish breakfast," Kate said, without opening her menu. She stole a glance at Ewan, who was reading from the same thick paperback he'd had in his office on Monday.

"Eggs!" cheered Chloe.

The adults all laughed, and Dee returned with her order pad to distract Kate from Ewan. Wedding talk and Dee's excellent Irish breakfast kept her thoughts at the table.

The conversation turned to the expansion before long. Anneliese asked Joss how his end of things was going.

"Well enough," he said, grinning at Kate over a Bloody Mary. "There are worse ways to take your friend's money."

"Speaking of," Kate said, "My sweet, sweet brother made a generous donation to the cause, so I might be able to afford some upgrades."

Joss toasted Kate with his drink. "I can get behind that."

Kate noticed a slight frown on Anneliese's face at the mention of Jack, but it vanished when Chloe tugged on her mother's shirt. "Mama? I gotta go pee."

Anna was already standing and unbuckling her daughter as she answered. "Okay, baby. Let's go."

Kate wondered if that reflexive movement was natural or learned.

Kate watched Chloe sitting on her mother's hip on the way back from the restroom, and then noticed Ewan sitting by the bar.

"Mama!" she announced to the whole room, "it's Paw Onion 'gain!"

Nan and Joss looked up, along with half the brunch crowd. Kate couldn't help laughing at Ewan's obvious distress at being the focus of the room.

"Miss Chloe," Ewan said with a nod. The gesture seemed to Kate like something from an old Western. "Anneliese? If I remember correctly?"

"Hi, Mr. Lovatt." Anna pushed her thick gold hair away from her face. "Sorry about that."

"I don't mind at all," he said. Kate thought he was trying to mean it. "And please, call me Ewan. Or Paw."

His behavior with Chloe and his tender reaction to George Cartwright seemed at odds with his prickly professor attitude. His warm tone with Anneliese set Kate's teeth on edge.

"We've got an empty seat at our table." Anneliese shot her friends a look. "Won't you join us?"

Kate stayed stone-faced.

Nan decided it. "Please, Ewan, join us."

Ewan motioned to Deirdre, who set his check down. Ewan left his empty plate and some cash, and brought his coffee cup to their table.

"Ewan Lovatt," Nan said, introducing him to Joss, "this is my fiancé, Joss Fuller."

The men shook hands.

"Nice to meet you," Joss replied. "How do you like the college so far?"

"I think it's going to be a great semester," Ewan said. "The kids are really dedicated."

"That's how it was when I went there, too."

"You're an alum?"

"And a native."

"What did you study?"

"Visual art."

Nan scooted her chair over closer to Kate and Anneliese. "I think he needed another boy to talk to."

Kate gave Ewan a sidelong look before turning to her friends. "Now you can tell Anna about your dress."

Nan blushed. "Okay."

Anneliese leaned down to retrieve a dropped crayon, bouncing Chloe on her knee. "Of course I want to hear about the dress, but we do need to talk about musicians. Bookings go out pretty far."

"We were thinking strings for the ceremony, and actually," Nan paused and Anneliese raised a brow, "don't be mad. Just renting some good sound equipment—"

"It's entirely possible these women are incapable of talking about anything but the wedding," Joss said to Ewan. "Tell me you can talk sports or big game hunting or the weather."

Ewan smiled into his coffee. Kate gave herself a mental shake. She was trying to follow both conversations and failing. Badly.

"I know there are two pro baseball teams in New York City." He shrugged self-deprecatingly. "That's about it."

Nan was describing her ideal playlist. "Instrumental jazz for the cocktail hour, and then just fun songs for dancing."

"Mama? I wanna go home," Chloe said. Kate heard the hint of whine and figured it was time to wrap up brunch.

Joss was laughing with Ewan; the two men seemed to have found some common ground. "You should consider staying up at the cabin for a few days if you need a break, some quiet. You know over a weekend or something."

"I'm moving over to my own space in a couple of days, but I may take you up on that sometime, thanks."

"We should get the check." Kate said, catching Anneliese's eye while Chloe squirmed.

Joss tossed some cash on the table. "That'll cover Nan and me."

Anneliese fumbled for her purse, but Ewan beat her to it.

"Let me," Ewan said, pulling a card from his wallet.

Kate lurched to grab her bag. "No. We've got it."

"Please," Ewan said, addressing Chloe. "A gentleman should always pick up the lady's tab."

Chloe gave him as sharp a salute as her small hands could manage, which made Nan and Joss laugh.

Ewan picked up his coffee cup with a quick glance her way. "Kate."

"Ewan." She was sure the others were staring.

"You're very kind," Anneliese said to Ewan as she took Chloe by the hand. "See you all soon?"

"Of course." Kate hugged Anneliese and kissed Nan and Joss both as though on autopilot.

Ewan stood at the corner of the table, a monolith of a man.

"You didn't need to do that." Kate disliked the petulance in her voice; the man brought out the worst in her.

"I know. You're welcome." Ewan took his empty mug and left her standing there.

Shaking off the sudden hollow feeling in her chest, she gathered up her coat and purse.

KATE TURNED IN EARLY THAT NIGHT, WITH EWAN'S BOOK FOR COMPANY. Brunch or no brunch, *Moriarty's Daughter* had been burning a hole in her proverbial pocket for days. She tried not to feel silly and spinsterish, curled up in her bed with thick socks on her feet and the sound of the falls in the background. She opened the book tentatively.

Get a grip, Kate.

She turned to the first chapter and began to read.

Destiny is peculiar.

I heard the stagehands whisper his name—Moriarty—when I drifted past them, but I never knew just how dangerous a man he was until he died.

Rumours swirled like velvet travelers in the theatre where I was raised about my mother's long-ago affair, but she was silent on the subject until the box appeared.

Terrible events come in threes, and the first was the arrival of Moriarty's solicitor. He had a letter for my mother and a box for me. Letters from dead men are nothing to seventeen-year-old girls, but I was told I couldn't open the box until my mother had read the letter.

Adelaide Bosworth was not to be disturbed during her siesta, and the stage manager made the solicitor wait. "Dearest," he'd said, using the pet name my mother did—a pet name the whole theatre insisted on parroting to please my diva mother, "make Mr. Jones comfortable."

Mr. Jones had a hangdog, nervous look about him, but he was a man nonetheless. The evidence was in the hungry glances he cast my way. I was poised, at seventeen, to be a tremendous beauty, perhaps even more beautiful than my infamous mother. I heard the lead chorus girl once say that my father must have been more an interesting than a handsome man, owing to the cleverness in my face. Cleverness and a carefully cultivated touch of danger animated my flawless features. That I knew even at seventeen.

"Please, Mr. Jones." I was careful to be a bit breathy, just innocent enough. "If the box is for me, what is the harm in my seeing its contents?"

"I'm sorry, Miss," he stammered. "But I am obligated to see out my client's last will and testament as instructed."

I leaned in close, let him smell the rosewater in my hair, let him see the swell of my breasts against the fabric of my dress. I could smell the lust coming off his skin.

In the end I bought the box from his trembling hands with the smooth skin of my thighs and the wet whisper of my tongue.

Whether my mother read the letter before it murdered her, I never knew. She was dead on her settee when the stage manager found her.

I met Dr. Watson thirteen days later.

What luck.

Kate plumped the pillow behind her as she turned the page. She had a feeling she wasn't going to be sleeping for a good long time.

CHAPTER 9

Monday morning was surprisingly bittersweet. Ewan had finished Reed Sharpe's pile of pages in the small hours of the night, firing off a clever and ambiguously positive jacket review—but not the link to Ryan Chandler's interview—to their publicist. He had a long day of moving and meetings, but before he checked out of the Damselfly Inn, he was hoping for one last excellent breakfast with his hostess.

Nan was at the kitchen island with a magazine and a steaming mug at her elbow. Ewan pulled a small sketchbook from his bag and outlined her face before she looked up from her reading.

"Good morning, Ewan."

When his hostess smiled and pushed her pixie hair out of her eyes, he thought, not for the first time, that the contractor was a lucky son of a bitch.

"You caught me with my guilty pleasure." She closed the slim celebrity glossy. "Breakfast?"

Ewan sat down at the long farm table by the windows with his drawing, fleshing out Nan's contemplative expression from memory. He wanted to remember the way she looked in this house, content and in love. Faye Bartram had been, too, for a while.

"Is that me?" Nan had brought a coffee cup and the carafe over and was peering at her own face, roughed out.

"I'm no artist, but yes." Embarrassment stung; he didn't want to offend her, either. "You reminded me of someone just then. The drawings help. Is it okay? That I did it?"

She set the cup down, blushing a bit. "I'm flattered. And yes." She touched his shoulder. "You are an artist. Remember, I've read all your books."

"I hope my students feel the same way."

Nan laughed. "They're taking a class with Ewan Lovatt. Pardon me for sounding star struck, but that's not a small thing."

"I'm hardly Michael Chabon."

"Don't sell yourself short," she said. "Now, omelet or oatmeal?"

"Oatmeal?" He hadn't had homemade oatmeal since he was a kid. "The real thing? With maple syrup?"

"And an assortment of options," Nan added. "Coffee?"

"Yes, please," Ewan said. "To both."

Nan turned to the kitchen and Ewan returned to his sketching. His limited ability meant the drawing was as finished as it would ever be by the time Nan brought him his breakfast.

She'd been generous with syrup and brown sugar. "I'm going to miss these breakfasts as much as your company."

"You'd be welcome as a visitor. Anytime."

He blinked. She meant it. Even after his blunder with her friend.

"Thank you."

Spending time in this house—getting to know its moods, learning more about its history—had been the goal, hadn't it? Here was his chance, among these kind people, but he found that it was the prospect of running into Kate that appealed more than researching the screenplay.

He lingered over his coffee, taking out his laptop and delaying his check out and departure as long as he could.

The kitchen looked out toward a stand of fir trees which separated the inn's grounds from the neighboring dairy farm. He could just make out the long red dairy barn built into the easy slope of the hillside. The day was mild for Vermont in early February, and the herd was in the pasture enjoying the weak sunlight.

He let his mind wander, typing as he daydreamed, imagining a century past and bringing it to life in his book file.

When the kitchen door opened, he noted with some surprise that an hour had passed.

"Good morning, Ewan." Anneliese came in and hung her purse on the coat tree. "I'm sorry to interrupt."

"Don't apologize. Where's Chloe this morning?"

"She's with my mother. They're baking brownies and visiting my grandmother at the nursing home." She shrugged. "A thrill a minute."

"My niece and nephew are a little older than Chloe. I think they'd like each other."

"Do you see a lot of them?"

"Not enough." He took off his glasses. "My folks still live in the same brownstone in Brooklyn that they brought me home to thirty-six years ago. My sister lived all over, but she ended up pretty far from Brooklyn."

"Really? I thought New Yorkers never left?"

"My sister lives on Bainbridge Island."

"Puget Sound?" Anneliese's disbelief was comical.

"The same." Ewan said.

"Wow. That sounds wonderfully romantic."

"That's what Ailie thought when she moved there."

Anneliese's phone pinged. "If you'll excuse me, I've got to find Nan. I need to measure the parlor and the terrace for fairy lights and heat lamps."

"Heat lamps?"

"For the tent."

"Tent?" Ewan forgot in his curiosity that she needed to leave.

"For the engagement party." She helped herself to some coffee. "It's in two weeks."

"Here at the inn?"

"Yes," said Anneliese. "Three weeks from Saturday. They're closing the inn for the party."

"And you're planning it? I didn't know you did that."

"Weddings and events." Pride glowed on her face. "I'm pretty good at it."

He could see that. "I'd hire you."

"We could do a book event…" She regarded him over the rim of her cup; he saw her come to a quick decision. "Ewan? Come with me to the party. Not to sound too pathetic, but I'm a divorced mother of a small child living in a small town. Opportunities to have a conversation with a man who's not related to me or marrying a close friend are few and far between."

He allowed himself a moment of male pride. His second offer from a pretty blonde, and all in a single morning. This offer he could take.

"I'd love to be your guest at the party, provided the happy couple won't object."

"Nan's far too generous to say no."

"That's exactly my fear."

"Really, Ewan," Anneliese reassured. "You'll be welcomed." Her phone pinged again. She swiped and handed it to him. "I do have to get moving, but leave your number in my phone, so I can give you the details."

He tapped his phone number into her contact list. "I'm looking forward to it."

When she was gone, he took out his phone and texted a quick hello to his sister. His conversation with Anneliese left him missing Ailie and the twins.

EWAN SPENT THE REST OF HIS MORNING AND A GOOD PORTION OF THE afternoon meeting with Will Dancy and the TA the department had hired for his novella course, and had a phone conversation with the features editor of the Rutland paper about doing a series of columns while he was living in the area.

The idea appealed to him, but in the end he turned down the offer.

He'd already made the mistake of underestimating a college journalist, had ended up on the defensive and said foolish things.

Before the call was over, the editor asked, "While I have you on the phone, I have to ask: what's next?"

"That's a very good question, but I don't have a clear answer for you yet."

It was true, despite the knowing chuckle from the editor. He'd sent some pages to his agent, but what happened next was beyond his control.

As the late sun slanted into his office, the desire to pack up and drive—anywhere—distracted him. There was something about a college campus on break—even in the frozen glory of January—that sang to him of road trips and spontaneity. Before he had time to second guess himself, he tossed his computer and files into his bag and sent an impromptu text.

His car was in a lot about three blocks uphill from Sweet Pease. Ewan's stomach reminded him that he hadn't eaten since the excellent bowl of oatmeal at the Damselfly, and Kate had suggested he try the roast beef with a different bread. And the aioli. It seemed too perfect an opportunity to pass up.

By the time he'd dropped his things in his car and walked to the bakery, he was wholly committed to the sandwich plan.

The cheery bell announced his entry. A striking Asian man closer to his own age was behind the counter.

"Good afternoon. What can I get you?"

Ewan pulled a sparkling water from a low cooler near the counter. "Roast beef and tomato on... honey oat. With the aioli."

"One Kate," he said to a pigtailed young woman wiping down the prep surface. He turned back to Ewan. "To go or for here?"

"What?"

"The sandwich? To go or for here?"

"To go. The sandwich is called Kate?"

"It's the owner's favorite. Just shorthand. It's not official or anything."

"Ah." Ewan fidgeted with his wallet while the man rang him up, then settled into an empty chair to wait for the young woman to assemble his lunch. A hint of a tattoo peeked out from under her sleeve; the same shirt proclaimed her attendance at a local Greek festival the year before. He briefly considered starting a list in his notebook of all the people he met in cafes and shops along Main Street, starting with Sweet Pease's four employees, but banished the idea when he realized he didn't know their names.

Strains of Ella Fitzgerald floated out from the kitchen, but the road was calling.

There was a clatter and bang, followed by a wet *thwack*.

"DAMN it!" Kate hollered from behind the closed door. "Jim!"

The owner was on the premises. All thoughts of leaving vanished.

"Hold the fort, Kim," the man said, hurrying to the kitchen door and slipping through without affording Ewan a glance inside.

"Here's your sandwich, sir." Kim—now he knew both their names —held his lunch out across the counter. He took it without moving. He could hear Kate's voice, urgent and angry, and Jim's answering tone, serene, almost placating.

The kitchen door banged open, and a floury Valkyrie stormed out.

"Kim?"

The ponytailed girl turned at Kate's call, flicking a pointed gaze at Ewan.

Kate swung around, stopping when her eyes met his. "What are you doing here?"

"Is everything okay?" he asked, trying hard not to look past her into the kitchen.

"If you call fifteen pounds of bread dough and a flat of locally sourced eggs on my floor fine, then why yes," she snapped. "Everything's fine."

"Kate?" Jim called from inside. "The oven,"

"Shit." Kate looked between Ewan and the kitchen quickly. "Are you any good with a mop?"

"I—"

"There's one in the supply closet, just inside to the left." Kate was instructing before he'd even thought to put his sandwich down and follow her. "Scrape up the dough ball from the floor. You'll want to try to collect the broken eggs before you mop or you'll smear them."

Jim was already wrestling the stand mixer bowl into the dish sink. Kate continued to marshal her small army.

"Jim, get that bowl into the sanitizer, and then give Ewan a hand while I get these out of the oven." She slipped her hands into a pair of high tech oven mitts. "Jim, Ewan. Ewan, Jim. Who says I'm not the goddamn Emily Post of pastry chefs?"

Ewan got as far as the mop water and a roll of paper towels while Jim was pulling the lever on the dish sanitizer, gathering up a pair of enormous flat spatulas, and kicking the trash barrel—cleverly set on a swivel-wheeled dolly—over from another corner of the room. Ewan watched with fascination as Jim scraped and formed the bread dough from floor to barrel with a few well-placed flicks of his spatulas. He did the same with the viscous remains of the eggs.

Kate meanwhile was pulling several trays of something wonderful-smelling from the ovens. Ewan caught notes of rosemary and caramel and wondered what she was up to.

"Your show now, friend," Jim said, kicking the trash away and heading for the sink to deposit the dirty utensils and wash his hands.

Ewan pulled the mop out of the hot water, wrung it twice and took care of the mess on the floor. When he finished, meaning to take it to the sink, Kate appeared at his elbow and stopped him.

"Jim?" she called through the door. "Can you take care of the mop? We've already asked enough of Mr. Lovatt, and Kim's going to have to make him another sandwich."

"It was to-go anyway," Ewan said uncomfortably. "I don't need another."

"Here," Kate said, handing him a brown paper lunch sack. The bag was warm to the touch. "Take these with your lunch. It's the least I can give you after drafting you to clean my floor."

Ewan took a moment to look around at Kate's workspace. She had a long stainless steel work bench down the center of the room, with clean up on one side, and what Ewan thought of as finish work on the opposite side. He could see an assortment of photos and fabric samples pinned to a cork-board above the finishing station. The mutinous stand-mixer dominated one end of the room; a cramped desk, the back entry, and a small bathroom occupied the other. The space was tight, but efficient and tidy. Ewan liked it immediately.

"Thank you," he said, weighing the bag in his palm. Now he smelled toast and... raisins? "What is this?"

"Crackers for Nan's party. Something I tasted in a shop and thought, 'Hey, I can do that.'" She sniffed. "They smell right. Rosemary and currant."

Ewan reached into the bag and pulled one out. It was good, and Kate seemed to like his wordless appreciation.

"Now imagine it with a nice, creamy brie. And Nan wants them topped with pomegranate seeds."

"Very good."

Kate glowed.

Ewan rolled up the bag. "These will make the drive north that much more pleasant."

"North?" Kate wondered aloud. "Burlington?"

"Farther. I'm going to Montreal for the weekend. Spur of the moment trip to visit my friend Chel before I start teaching on Monday."

Kate's glow cooled. "We should get Kim to remake that sandwich."

"No, really. It's okay. I'm sure it's perfect."

Kate turned abruptly back to her stainless steel kingdom. "I'll let you get on your way. Thanks for lending a hand with the mop."

"No problem." He tried to warm the sudden chill. "I'm a man of many talents."

Kate pushed through the door to the front of the bakery and began sorting through the loaves of bread which remained in the baskets on the counter. Ewan followed, painfully aware—and baffled—that she was finished with the conversation. He picked up his abandoned sandwich and water and left, quashing the sudden desire to knock the cheery bell down off the door frame.

CHAPTER 10

Kate would not have described herself as an eavesdropper, but she paused in Nan's foyer when she heard her name. Nan and Anneliese were in the parlor at the Damselfly. Kate had been running late, and ran into Joss at the door, who held it for her on his way out. Clearly the girls hadn't heard her coming.

"Did Kate tell you?" Nan said to Anneliese. A tangled string of fairy lights lay between them on the parlor rug.

Kate held herself still. She could just see them sitting together on the rug. Nan had laid a fire, and there was tea on a tray on the coffee table.

"Tell me what?" Anneliese pushed the pronged end back through a knot. "Why exactly can't we buy new ones?"

"Because I need every cent in our budget," Nan replied, working a snarl on her end. "Kate's bringing one of Jack's friends to the party."

"I saw she had a plus one." Anneliese dug her hand into the tangle to loosen it. "Anyone I know?"

"Jack's old roommate from New York."

"The art dealer? The one who sold those pieces of Joss's a few years ago?" Anneliese threaded a plug back through a snarl in the strand. "You should hear my mom go on about how Joss was a famous artist."

"The famous part, not so much, but there's history there." Nan took the plug from Anneliese and started winding it. "But, yes. Seth. I met him last fall. He called Kate the other night. Took her out to the Riverbend Hotel while he was in town."

"She didn't say a word at brunch!"

Kate was all set to announce herself when Nan set down the coiled section of lights and started working on another. "Speaking of brunch, have you noticed Ewan makes her uncomfortable?"

"Well, he did malign her baked goods," Anneliese said diplomatically.

More than malign, Kate thought. *He went on the record.*

"It's not like Kate to be squirrelly about a guy," Nan said.

"No," Anneliese admitted. "It's not."

Kate frowned. *Was she being squirrelly?*

They continued to untangle the fairy lights in silence. Anneliese broke the silence. "I asked him to your engagement party."

Nan looked up, "Who?"

"Ewan."

"No."

"Yep," Anneliese said, "and you're worried about him making Kate uncomfortable. I should have asked her. She's the hostess."

Kate knew it was ungenerous, but she couldn't manage to disagree. Never mind that she already had a date.

"I'm the bride, and I chose the guests. I gave you a plus one. Who you ask is your business, Anna." Nan put the light-string down. "You asked Ewan Lovatt to my engagement party." She paused dramatically. "When were you planning on telling me?"

"It only happened yesterday. I saw him when I stopped by to measure the square footage of the terrace for the heat lamps. We were talking about Chloe and his niece and I kind of put my foot in my mouth about the party—"

"I doubt it."

"Oh, I did," she said. "And then I just thought, 'Well, he's here. I'm here. I'd like a reason to wash my hair. Why not?'"

"You need a reason to wash your hair? Really?" Nan laughed.

"I know it's been nearly a year since I moved home, but my marriage was over long before that. I haven't dressed up for the sake of feeling attractive in a long time."

"Oh, Anna, I'm sorry," Nan said, scooting across the floor and hugging Anneliese. "I didn't mean—"

Anneliese hugged her back. "It's okay."

Enough. Kate jingled her keys and moved into their view.

"What's okay?" She walked in and dropped down on her heels next to her friends. She wrapped an arm around each of them. "Anna, are you okay?"

"Fine, just... well..."

"Did your asshole ex-husband do something?"

"No, Chad's safely in Palo Alto." She looked at Nan, who nodded. "I found a plus-one for the party."

"Well, a date's totally hug-worthy," Kate said. "Who's the guy? And why wasn't I consulted?"

Anneliese flushed, and Kate swallowed the bitterness on her tongue. The lie tasted as bad as the envy she would have preferred not to name.

"Hey," Kate said. "I'm teasing. What's up?"

"I asked Ewan."

While Kate struggled to act surprised, Anneliese filled the silence.

"He's nice, Kate. And he's safe."

"Safe?" Kate was astonished. "What's the point of safe? And how exactly is Mr. Tall and Craggy safe?"

"He's nice, and I don't want to drag him into bed."

"I love you, girlfriend, but Chad really messed you up if you don't want to drag that man into bed."

Nan intervened. "So do you want to drag the man into bed?"

"No," Kate snapped. "No. I just mean he's a man, and she's asked him on date, and...Shit. You know what I mean." She sat down heavily.

"What is it about him? I can't even properly congratulate my friend on her date without him screwing it up."

"What's he done now?" Nan asked.

"He came into the bakery yesterday…"

"I can see how that's a challenge for you." Nan's reply was tart.

"And I didn't know it, because I was out back having a tantrum over tipping a thirty-quart mixer bowl full of bread dough on the floor, along with a flat of eggs. Next thing I know he's helping Jim mop the goddamn floor while his sandwich is getting soggy on a table out front."

Anneliese and Nan replied in chorus. "He mopped the floor?"

"He mopped well," Kate admitted. "And I almost burned the crackers, but I rescued them, and I gave him a bag to take with him, and we were having a somewhat normal conversation."

"No, not that. Anything but that," Nan teased.

"Anyway," Kate continued, "he makes some comment about driving and I find out he's spending the weekend in Montreal with some woman called *Shell*—"

Nan looked sideways at Kate. "Do I detect a note of jealousy?"

"Great," Anneliese huffed. "The first guy I manage to ask out after my divorce, and my friend's got a thing for him."

"There is no thing." Kate watched her friends' bland reactions. "There is absolutely no thing."

Nan and Anneliese looked at her skeptically.

Kate knew she was cornered. "I Googled him. We all know he's Mr. Manhattan author, but it seems like he's always somewhere else. He's lectured and taught all over, and very likely has some bilingual booty call over the border."

Anneliese giggled. "That sounds okay to me."

"Sure," Kate snapped. "It's great when you're him, and single ladies are begging you to take them to parties."

She regretted the nasty words the moment she spoke them. Anneliese's smile vanished, and Kate could feel her chest tightening.

"Hey now," Nan's voice was measured. "You have a date. And you probably had your share of *bilingual booty calls* in Paris."

That was the bill of goods she'd sold her friends because it fit the image of *Kate In Paris*. No names, no heartbreak, no misplaced love for a man who was never going to stay with her.

"Paris isn't the point." Kate could hear defensiveness in her own words, and hated herself for it. "He's not staying here, so what would be the point of a thing?"

"You heard Kate," Anneliese said, her voice as close to acid as it ever got. "There is no thing."

"I'm sorry Anna, that was icky of me," Kate said.

"Apology accepted," Anneliese went back to untangling lights. "I don't want to fight over a guy. Especially one neither of us is dating."

"Right." Kate sucked in a breath. Despite the thread of tension between Anna and herself, she was uncomfortably relieved at Anna's words: *neither of us is dating*. The man hadn't so much as flirted in her direction, and she was as tangled up as the fairy lights. Kate reached into her bag for her notebook—and a distraction. "Now, can we talk about the menu? This party is two weeks from tonight."

CHAPTER 11

"If there are no more questions, we'll see you all in discussion group." Ewan closed his notes and leaned back in his chair.

The fifteen students around the scarred wood table closed laptops and slipped smartphones away. Ewan noted one who still traveled with pen and ink and allowed himself a private moment of admiration for the young man.

"That went well, don't you think?" Will Dancy leaned against the corner of the table.

"I think I learned a few things, and I've been considered a pro for a few years now."

"And this is only day one." Will gathered up his notes and a few books. "Want to grab some lunch? To celebrate the start of the semester."

Ewan stowed his notes. "I've got about two hours before my seminar meets. What do you have in mind?"

"I love the manchego and quince paste on Moroccan flatbread at Sweet Pease—when it's available. Have you been yet?"

Ewan laughed. "I have, a couple times. No reason not to go back."

Under the noon sun, in the moment just before the door closed behind him, Ewan was deceived. The light was warm, the sky clear. Without a snow cover over the green quad and the ivy-wrapped granite buildings, it could have been June. Then the stinging wind kicked up and the cold sucked the air out of his lungs.

He and Will didn't speak much on the walk down the hill.

Inside Sweet Pease, they draped coats over two chairs at the bar which ran along one wall. The bakery was full, the line a few customers deep. Ewan was glad for the distraction. He read the lunch board thoroughly, fighting the urge to watch the kitchen door for Kate's dark hair and shocking pink chef's coat.

"Hey Professor Dancy." The boy from his first visit, Andy, spoke warmly. "How are you?"

"Fine, thanks, Andrew," Will replied. "How's your thesis coming?"

"Well enough. How's Mrs. D? And MJ and Owen?"

"They're well, Andrew. Thanks for asking. Do you know Professor Lovatt?"

"We met briefly." Andy nodded at Ewan, but there was none of the same warmth. "What can I get for you today?"

They ordered sandwiches; Will insisted on picking up the tab. When they were seated again, Ewan asked Will about his connection to Andy.

"I started here three years ago. Andy's freshman year. Before that I'd been practicing with a small firm in Montpelier. I came on as an adjunct instructor, and my wife as a residential counselor."

Ewan nodded.

"That meant housing on campus," Will continued. "An apartment in the dorm. We were advisors, mentors, to the kids in our building. Andrew lived on the same floor that our apartment was on. He joined my wife's staff sophomore year as a resident aide. This year he's got a floor of freshmen in addition to his course work and his job here."

"Impressive," Ewan said.

"So," Will popped the lid from his tea bottle, "Am I allowed to ask yet why you're so interested in turn-of-the-century railroad expansion?"

"You're allowed to ask." Ewan wondered how much to divulge,

especially as Will had just made it clear that rumors carried. "Something a little different, I hope. A new avenue, but I need to keep it close to the vest for a while."

Andy brought their sandwiches.

"There are so many things here that amaze me," Ewan said. "I'm not sure I could live this way all the time, bound up in the lives of the students and the locals."

As if he'd conjured her, Kate pushed through the swinging door. She wore jeans designed to light a man's eyes on fire, slightly ridiculous fuzzy boots, and a turtleneck sweater and down vest combination that shouldn't have made him lose his train of thought.

"It's special," Will said, "but it's not for everyone."

"Hmm?"

Will caught Ewan's distracted gaze and hummed appreciatively.

"She's beautiful," Will said. "My wife hates her."

"Why?"

"She doesn't really. Kate's nice and successful and everybody loves her; I don't know if it's envy or admiration or both." He laughed. "Meg says it's a female thing."

Kate had yet to see them there. Ewan was torn between wanting her to notice and hoping she'd pass him by. She unnerved him.

"Andy, Moira, you guys have the place until Jim and Kim show up at one," she was saying. "I'm going to run an errand or two before I head to Charlotte to check on the progress at the winery."

Will turned to Ewan. "Did you hear she's opening a second location? I don't think it's strictly public knowledge yet, but I heard through the grapevine that she's contracted out a space at Cooper Vineyards. Some kind of partnership."

"Does Kate know she's got a leak?"

Will snorted. "This is a small town, Ewan. Word spreads." He polished off his sandwich. "Do you have any skeletons in your closet? Rest assured they'll be old news by spring."

The way Kate's gaze turned towards him, he would have sworn she was a bit fey. She crossed the room.

"Will, Ewan."

"Hi, Kate," Will said easily.

"How were your sandwiches?"

"Fantastic," Will said. "And I've got a half dozen spiced donuts here to bring home to Meg and the boys."

"That's great, Will." She turned her blue eyes to Ewan. "Ewan, do you mind a word?"

"No. Sure." He wondered what he could have possibly done wrong. "Will?"

"I'm good, and I'll clear the table." Will glanced between the two of them. "I'll see you at next week's lecture."

Kate was already disappearing back into the inner sanctum. Ewan followed.

Inside, she was already sitting on a stool at her worktable.

"You need to level with me."

"I need to what?"

"Look, I know you're going to my best friend's engagement party with another very dear friend of mine."

"And?"

"And Anneliese is just putting a very sad divorce from a truly terrible human being behind her."

"I'm sorry to hear that. She's a sweet woman."

"Exactly my point," Kate fidgeted with some notes on her pin board. "Which is why you can't toy with her. Getting her hopes up is unfair, since you're not staying here beyond the spring."

"No, I'm not." This was not the conversation he'd expected. "She asked me to the party, you know. Maybe my hopes are the ones that will get dashed."

Kate's jaw dropped. "Do you have hopes?"

"You certainly seem to think so, and if I'm understanding you correctly, you seem to think they include breaking your friend's heart." He sighed and raked his hands through his hair. "You have an awfully low opinion of me, Kate."

"It's not that." She spun in her seat. She was upset, that much was obvious, but there was something else. He was almost sure of it.

"Then what is it?"

Kate slapped her hands down on her desk, blowing a stack of notes to the floor. "Shit."

He started to bend down to help her retrieve them, but she beat him to it.

"I've got it." She crammed the papers back on the desk. "You should go."

"Jesus, woman," Ewan said. "You've assumed the worst of me from the moment I set foot in this town."

"You—"

"I said something stupid. For which I apologized. I accepted an invitation to a party. I won't apologize for that."

Kate seemed to deflate in front of him. "I'm sorry."

"Thank you." Ewan pushed off the wall. "I have to prep for a class. Do I have your permission to take Anneliese to the party?"

Kate's already flushed face flamed.

"I'll take that as a yes." He turned to go. "See you at the party."

Ewan pushed through the swinging door. *See you at the party?* Were they twelve?

CHAPTER 12

The second Saturday of February dawned steel gray and foul-tempered.

Gloomy weather suited Kate's mood. She couldn't shake the mental replay of her conversation with Ewan. Her own words shrilled back to her on a shameful loop while she readied herself for the day.

She was aware that she occasionally flew off the handle. She also knew she regretted it. Every time. Not that she was entirely in the wrong on this one, but if only she hadn't completely abandoned her cool in front of Ewan Lovatt of all people.

He had a knack for knocking her off balance. That it was accidental would have been endearing if she weren't so embarrassed about it.

She jogged down Gristmill to the lot where her van waited, and drove the half-mile, one-way loop that brought her back to Sweet Pease's front door. Piling her things into the back, she set out to collect Anneliese.

Were she and Anneliese not hosting this party, Ewan would be the one to pick up his date. She knew Seth would have done the same.

Seth was his own complication. He would be a fine companion for the evening, but Kate didn't love the idea of leading him on. As she drove, she played through their dinner looking for friend zone loopholes, but her mind wandered.

There was no denying Ewan's height and stormy, intelligent eyes appealed to her. Or that she was a little jealous of Anneliese.

The clouds parted over River Ridge just about the time she pulled in front of the Thompsons' house.

Maybe the weather, at least, would be pleasant for the party.

Kate rang the doorbell of Anneliese's parents' house and stifled a yawn. Chloe's feet pounded down the hall from the kitchen in back.

"Kate-kate!" Her small voice cheered from the other side of the door.

"Miss Pease." Kate heard Anneliese's mother gently correct Chloe on the other side of the door.

There would be no time for strained feelings. She hadn't seen Anneliese since the unraveling—of herself and the damned fairy lights.

The Thompsons' house on River Ridge was part of an Eighties subdivision of cookie-cutter split levels—two-car garage, three-season room, half-acre lots—built north of town. Growing up, Kate had always envied the kids in the neighborhood, who enjoyed TV sitcom sidewalks and a bike-riding friendly cul-de-sac. Her own parents' four-square Mansard house had seemed so old fashioned. Now she was grateful for the historic downtown location of her parents' place.

Mrs. Thompson opened the door. "Good morning, Kate. Come in."

"Morning, Mrs. Thompson. Thanks," she said, stepping into the foyer. "Hey, Chlo."

"Miss Pease, I'm going to the 'quare-a-num today." Her voice was endearingly serious, as was the eager look she gave her grandmother.

"The aquarium?" Kate asked, looking at Mrs. Thompson for confirmation just as Anneliese came down the stairs with Chloe's clownfish and a frayed knit blanket.

"Who's gonna go see the fishies?" sang Anneliese.

"Me!" the little girl exclaimed, tugging her loveys away.

"Thank you for going upstairs to get Feesh, Mama," Anneliese sing-songed after her three-year-old daughter's backside as she danced away with her blanket dragging. She shrugged at Kate and ignored the exasperated look she received from her mother. "Her manners are a work in progress. Give me a sec to grab my stuff, Kate, and we're off."

"Thanks for keeping Chloe this weekend, Mrs. Thompson," Kate said.

"Robert and I are taking her to ECHO this morning, and we'll take the scenic route down to Waterbury in the afternoon. Ice cream at the Ben & Jerry's factory and then we're staying with Anneliese's brother tonight, so Chloe can play with her cousins."

"That sounds really nice."

Anneliese came back, scooping Chloe up for a hug and kiss. "Be good for Mere and Pep, okay, sweetie?"

"I will," Chloe said solemnly.

With Anneliese's party clothes and overnight bag safely stowed in the Sweet Pease van, Kate fired it up and gestured to the center console. "Coffee. And there's crumb coffee cake muffins in the bag."

"You're a very useful woman to know, Kate Pease."

"Does that mean I'm forgiven for being a jerk the other day?"

Anneliese reached for the bag. "You are."

"In that case," Kate grinned, "I know it."

"Thanks for the ride. Hell of a weekend for my car to die," she said, tucking into a muffin. "And thanks for letting me crash with you tonight."

"No worries."

"My parents sat me down for a nice long chat about how I can't go on like this: dead car, freeloading, divorced..."

"Your mom and mine are old friends, Anna, but that doesn't mean I can't say I think that's shitty." Kate swung the van south through the industrial section of town, gritting her teeth.

"I've been a disappointment to them since Chris Greene took me to prom. Being broke and divorced is just what happens when you disappoint your parents."

"Bullshit," Kate said. "That's unfair of them. You're a great mom, you've got a business that's growing..."

"And no husband, a fatherless daughter, and not even a nice boyfriend from their congregation who might redeem me." Anna gave Kate a wry look. "Speaking of boyfriends, if things go well with you and Seth, I can always stay with Molly and Walt. I'd just need to let them know by about nine."

"Anna," Kate said sternly. "You are staying with me. Seth will be staying at the new hotel down on Route Seven. I told you."

"I have to say, I don't get it," Anneliese said. "Word is he's attractive, he's successful, he's nice, and your brother already knows him, so he won't get all crazy about you dating the guy."

"He is all of those things," Kate agreed, "but I can't get into him."

"Can I ask why you invited him?"

"I was trying to force it, I think," Kate said. "I mean, I like him. I just don't feel that fluttery, sinking, champagne-lust thing with him. You know?"

Anneliese was silent as the road crested a small hill and the town of Thornton spread out beneath them. When she spoke, her tone was wistful.

"I haven't felt that way in a very long time. I remember it though." Wistful became dispassionate. "Then there was Chad, and I followed him west. We got married; he got mean. I tried to save the marriage and got pregnant. He stopped loving me. I left, and here I am." She crumpled her paper muffin liner. "I have my daughter, though. It wasn't a total wash."

Kate reached over and squeezed Anneliese's arm. "And now you have a date with a sort-of famous author."

Anneliese caught the slightly sour tone. "Are you sure that's okay, Kate? If it's a problem, I can cancel."

"No," Kate said. "If you can stand more than five minutes in his company, more power to you. And you deserve a nice night out."

The gunmetal sky was beginning to give way to blue by the time they arrived at the inn. Kate handed Anneliese a load of food and linens and led the charge to commandeer her friend's home and business.

"Morning, Sugar Plum. Morning, Handsome," Kate said to Nan and Joss. Joss was loading the dishwasher while Nan polished the table. "Are you ready to turn your place of business over to Anna and me, so we can throw the second best damn party this valley's ever seen?"

Nan stopped polishing. "Second best?"

Kate didn't even pause. "Your wedding is yet to come, my loves."

"Have you always been this exhausting, Katie?" Joss asked, closing the dishwasher and giving her a quick hug. "Is there more in the van?"

She giggled. "You know I have, and yes there is. Go fetch."

"Joss will help Anneliese with the terrace. The kitchen is yours," Nan gestured to her spotless kitchen. "I'm going to get the rooms ready for Joss's family, and then I'll be back to help you with clean up."

Anneliese flipped open her fearsome planner.

"The serving staff should be here by six, but I expect everyone to break by five, so there's time to get pretty."

"Am I not pretty as it is?" Joss asked, coming back in with a box from Kate's van.

"You're perfect, Handsome." Kate patted his cheek. "But you need a shave."

"That he does," Nan agreed.

"When should we expect your deadbeat brother?" Joss asked. Anneliese snickered.

"Yeah, where is Jack?" Nan added.

"My darling *frère* is driving up with my date," Kate answered. "Seth's dropping him off at home before he checks in. Jack's going to borrow my mom's car for the night."

"He's such a weasel," Joss laughed. "He gets to swagger in here and schmooze without lifting a finger."

"Don't worry," Kate smirked, "I'll leave the kitchen for him to sort out when he slinks back in the morning, looking for breakfast."

~

Ewan checked his face in the Scout's rearview mirror after parking along County Road just past the sign for the Damselfly Inn. Anneliese had asked him to come find her when he arrived at the engagement party, but she hadn't offered any advice beyond that. He hoped he would pass muster.

His shirt buttons were done properly, anyhow.

He was met in the front entryway by a coat check attendant who took his parka and scarf and directed him down the hall to the rear door. Where there had been a frozen vista of dairy cows when he'd been a guest at the Damselfly, now there was a huge heated event tent. A small swarm of wait and catering staff came and went through an egress off to one side.

He scanned for Anneliese, wondering if Kate was somewhere there, or in the adjacent tent, conducting a symphony of sweets. The fanciful thought made him smile.

"Something here you like?"

That deep, polished voice again. He turned to see Elisha McNair at his elbow. She was smiling, but there was something in her eyes that set off alarms.

"It's good to see you," he began. And then it came to him. He'd planned to meet her, weeks before, but had written right through the afternoon. He'd opened his laptop and tumbled into an imagined outing on a long ago lakeshore, forgetting Elisha entirely.

"There it is," she said. The cool glitter in her eyes vanished, replaced by the same affectionate pity his mother had mastered in his dreamy, absentminded youth.

"I'm so sorry; I had a story idea after my last meeting. I should never have opened my draft file."

Elisha laughed. "Once my poor, bruised ego recovered, I realized it had to be something like that."

"I can't see how I could bruise your ego."

She arched a brow. "Really?"

"No. That's not what I meant. Jesus." His hands went to his hair, but Elisha reached up to stop his nervous gesture.

"I know. Truly. Apology accepted. I'm just playing with you now."

Elisha sipped from a plastic champagne coupe. Her drink matched her nails, a pale blackberry color; Ewan wondered if she'd planned that. "Who are you here with?"

"Anneliese Thompson. She—"

"The wedding planner. We've met."

Kate emerged from the same door he'd imagined her beyond. Following the trajectory of her path, he found Anneliese amongst a knot of guests in the far corner of the tent.

"Kate Pease is wasted on this town," Elisha said. "She's a force."

Ewan felt distinctly as though he'd been caught with his hand in a cookie jar. He also sensed that Elisha wasn't completely won over by Kate's charms.

"I see my date coming back from the restroom. If you'll excuse me?"

"Of course. Elisha, I'm—"

"No hard feelings, Ewan. I promise." She placed a hand on his shoulder and stretched up to speak closely to him, gaze lingering on Kate. "But I wouldn't stand that one up if I were you."

Elisha had the right of it. Kate's display of temper at Sweet Pease aroused his curiosity. Her protectiveness of her friend was admirable, but he didn't quite buy it.

He stepped into the thick of the party to join Anneliese.

She saw him coming and waved. He noticed the frank appraisal on every face that turned to greet him.

"Everyone," Anneliese said, "this is Ewan. Be nice. He's new in town. Ewan, this is…everyone."

There was cocktail party laughter around the circle, and then the questions began. He attempted to turn the conversation back to Anneliese, but she had a knack for falling into the shadows. He wasn't entirely sure if it was a professional trick or a survival skill.

Kate leaned against the back railing and surveyed the party. The heated tent around her kept the cold at bay, and the fairy lights and rented potted trees brought a festive, summery landscape inside. Food and drinks circulated freely. The music was a soundtrack of Nan and Joss's favorite songs, just loud enough for dancing, not too loud for conversation.

Anneliese certainly planned a hell of an event.

A server walked by with a tray of pilsner glasses and Kir Royales. Seth materialized out of the crowd, plucking one of each from the tray and handing her the coupe.

"You've outdone yourself."

"This is all Anneliese. I just planned the snacks. And made the cake."

"Don't sell yourself short," he said, taking in her full six-foot-one inches, thanks to some truly spectacular heels, "as you're anything but."

Jack joined them from inside the inn. "Hello, beautiful sister." He kissed Kate on the cheek. "Hello, friend escorting my beautiful sister."

Seth turned, deftly snagged another beer from a passing tray and handed it to Jack. "Long time no see."

"Yeah, the last two hours have been challenging without your conversation." Jack turned to Kate again. "Is he behaving himself?"

Kate gave Jack an arch look. "Would I tell you if he wasn't?"

"Fair enough." Jack took a healthy swallow from his glass.

"I was just praising Kate on a fantastic party," Seth told him.

"And I," said Kate, "was deflecting his praise to Anneliese, where it belongs."

"Where is Anneliese?" Jack asked, looking over the crowd.

"The blonde in the pink dress, right?" Seth said. "She's over there with the guy who looks like that guy from Gladiator."

"Russell Crowe?" Kate laughed. "No."

"No," Seth said. "The one with the scar. Only her date doesn't have a scar, and he's crazy tall."

Kate laughed. "So, basically not at all like that guy."

"Who is he?" Jack asked, quietly casual.

"He's Anneliese's plus-one," Kate replied matter-of-factly, giving her brother the side-eye.

"Where have I seen him before?" Seth asked.

"Ewan Lovatt," Kate answered. "He's an author, teaching this semester at the college, and apparently going to parties with lovely women."

"So they're not dating?" Jack asked.

"What's it to you?" Kate challenged her brother. *And they called me squirrelly.*

Jack changed the subject. "Have you seen the happy couple around?"

"They're somewhere in that hoard of Fullers over there, the one that's about to swallow Anna whole."

"And Ewan, too, it seems," Jack noted.

"He said yes," Kate remarked. "I hope he knew what he was doing, being seen out with a cousin to the Fullers. They'll be booking the First Congregational so fast his head will spin."

"She's a second cousin." Jack reminded her. "And I thought you said they weren't dating."

"Touchy." Kate smirked over the rim of her glass.

Seth laughed out loud. "You two are awful. Kate? You want to dance?"

Kate passed her glass to her brother and took Seth's hand. "I always want to dance." As she followed him onto the makeshift dance floor, she turned briefly to her brother. "Don't scowl, Jack. You'll wrinkle."

EWAN WAS THREE CIRCLES DEEP IN ANNELIESE AND JOSS'S FAMILY WHEN he noticed Kate take to the dance floor with the guy he assumed was her date.

He had to admit, the guy was smooth. Watching Kate twirl in his arms to the soulful ache of the music, he wondered what might be going on there. He got the sense her date was far more invested than Kate was, and he didn't get the sense that she would toy with a guy just for the sake of it.

Kate was an accomplished flirt, but she didn't seem cruel.

With half an ear on the conversation around him, Ewan tuned in to Nan and Joss, who'd excused themselves and started toward the dance floor to greet a lean, striking man making his way to them. He shared Kate's eyes and wicked smile. *The brother she'd mentioned?*

"Jack!" Nan reached out to the man, and Ewan filed his name away.

Jack hugged the bride-to-be. "Congratulations." He turned to Nan's fiancé. "You're a lucky bastard, you know that?"

Joss laced his fingers with Nan's. "I am well aware."

Ewan watched Jack seek out Anneliese in the crowd, though he was still speaking to Nan and Joss. "This terrace is always beautiful, but tonight is something special."

Nan followed Jack's gaze. Ewan had to agree. White lights twinkled in potted trees and delicate tulle and light garlands ringed the dance floor. Heat lamps under a huge canopy negated the February chill. Bar-top tables dotted the perimeter of the tent, decorated with purple, gold, and rust-colored arrangements of mums and winter cabbage.

"You should tell her that," Nan was saying to Jack. "In typical Anneliese fashion, she's fretting the details and not relaxing enough to enjoy her date."

The tips of his ears started to burn. He was Anneliese's date, it was long past time he asked her to dance. He got the feeling he was something of a safety net for her, and it made him feel strangely protective. As he made his way out of the group who'd waylaid him, he ended up closer to Nan, Joss, and Jack.

"Yeah, what's with that?" Jack's tone fell somewhere between disbelief and derision. Ewan didn't like it.

A party guest interrupted the couple, leaving Jack free to approach Anneliese. Ewan knew he wouldn't get there first, and he had a sinking suspicion he was watching a natural disaster unfold.

"Anna." Jack intersected Anneliese just as she noticed Ewan's approach. "This party is amazing. Well done."

Anneliese blushed. "Thank you."

"You look lovely."

She sipped. "Thank you again. Who are you here with?"

"Myself," Jack said wryly. Ewan reached the pair, and Jack acknowledged him coolly. "I haven't met your date."

"Jack, this is Ewan Lovatt. Ewan, Jack Pease. Kate's brother."

The handshake Jack offered was brisk.

Both men spoke simultaneously. "Nice to meet you."

Jack gave Ewan a feral smile. "You don't mind if I ask her to dance?"

Anneliese stared helplessly between the two of them. "I can't, Jack. I—I have to keep an eye on the party. You know, I take one eye off the servers, and they miss a plating, or worse, the music skips and I miss it—"

"Message received," Jack said. He set his empty glass on the table nearest him and smoothly vanished into the crowd.

The unshed tears in Anneliese's eyes tugged at Ewan's heart. It was obvious there was something strong between them. Something strong and sour.

"You should be dancing, though." He sounded lame in his own ears. "Am I too late to ask?"

Anneliese pasted on her party planner smile. "I think I just need the ladies' room for a moment."

She faded into the crowd again.

Without Anneliese, Ewan was once again adrift in a sea of Fullers, Thompsons, and a dozen other families related to the groom. He'd attended his fair share of parties, and often as a stranger or someone's date, but he'd never grown fully comfortable with it.

He was scanning the room for Anneliese's return when Kate fell into his field of vision.

She was all bare legs and high heels and some kind of soft, shining midnight fabric clinging to her as she strode across the terrace. Toward him.

He met her at the bottom of the stairs.

"Ewan," she said matter-of-factly. "Are you enjoying yourself?"

"Sure," he replied. He was wary of her response after the way they'd behaved the last time they'd exchanged words.

"You're going to need to keep a close eye on your date," she warned.

"Why exactly?" Ewan stopped her. "I'm hardly her keeper."

"I saw you met my brother. I'm sorry. He's in a mood."

Kate seemed to catch herself on the verge of saying something. Ewan decided to push it.

"Is there something there I should know about?"

Kate tossed her hands up. "If there is, it's none of my business."

"Then what's the problem?" *What possessed him to fight with this woman?*

Kate bristled. "You're here with her. Act like it."

"She went to the ladies' room."

Kate looked as though she was about to say something, but her date appeared at her elbow.

"Ewan Lovatt, Seth Weston." She kept the introductions professional.

Ewan let the other man take his measure, noting the way Weston kept himself angled toward Kate. He also noted the way Kate still glared at him; he was unable to look away.

Seth broke the silence. "I just saw Anneliese over at the cheese board. She told me to dance with you again so other people will follow."

"What?" Kate blinked, breaking the contact between them.

"Dance?" Weston asked again, holding out a hand.

"Oh," Kate flashed a smile Ewan was certain was practiced. "Of course."

Practiced or not, she slid into Weston's arms easily enough. Ewan found it difficult not to imagine the feel of burned out velvet over her body, even as he sought out his own date.

He found Anneliese easily, chatting with a couple in hippie fancy-dress, and went to her.

"Anneliese." He spoke lightly. "I thought I'd lost you."

"Ewan." Anneliese gestured to the couple. "This is Berk and Lily Anderson. They run the co-op in town, as well as a locavore advocacy non-profit."

"A pleasure." Ewan offered a hand to Berk Anderson.

"Lily, Berk," Anneliese continued, clearly at home in her role of social director, "this is Ewan Lovatt. Ewan's a novelist, guest teaching at the college this semester."

Ewan was reaching to shake Lily Anderson's hand when the woman clasped his arm.

"I've read both your books!" she gushed. "I had no idea you were teaching here!" She turned to her husband. "Berkeley, this man is amazing."

Ewan extracted his hand. "Thank you, Lily, but I—"

"Hush," she said. "Dearest Bosworth is a wonderful heroine, and your anti-patriarchal stand on Victorian mores was—"

"Lil," Berk put a hand on his wife's arm, "let the man enjoy the party."

"Oh," she giggled. "Right. Sorry. I get carried away. But really, Ewan. I love your work."

"Thank you," Ewan replied, not sure how to continue. He caught Anneliese watching the dance floor. Another man might have thought she looked wistful, but he was quite sure he could see her counting the couples. "If you'll excuse me, Berk, Lily, I'd like to dance with Anneliese."

"Of course," Lily said, touching Anneliese's arm fondly.

Anneliese looked up at him. He towered over her by a full foot, but she took his arm and fell in step with him. He risked a glance at her tiny feet in festive silvery flats and hoped he wouldn't trample her.

"You should know, I'm not a fantastic dancer."

"I haven't danced in years," she said. "I should apologize to you."

Ewan placed a tentative hand on her waist. Kate and Seth twirled and swayed nearby, Kate's laughter bubbling up over the noise of the room. He focused on his steps, feeling ungainly next to Anneliese, who craned her neck to meet his eyes.

"I can almost see you counting the beat," she said. "Don't worry about it."

She was so gentle with everyone. He chuckled. "I almost always do."

It would be hard to screw up a simple turn, though, so he spun Anneliese under his arm; her answering smile was radiant.

When the song ended, she stretched up to kiss his cheek. "Thank you."

"You're very welcome," he said. "You make me look far more elegant than I am."

They walked off the dance floor in time with Seth and Kate. Kate slid him an approving glance. Against his better judgment, he was glad to have pleased her.

Anneliese excused herself to check in with the servers, leaving him alone with Kate and her date. Seth moved closer to Kate; Ewan wished for something to occupy his hands.

"You gentlemen look like you could use a drink." Jack approached with three beers in hand and a stunning redhead by his side. Kate's expression turned dark.

Ewan regretted his wish immediately, but took one of the proffered glasses. Seth took the other, casting around for a server. Ewan guessed he was looking for something—anything—for Kate.

KATE NARROWED HER EYES. JACK'S ARM CANDY WAS THE PHOTOGRAPHER —the two cameras around her neck and her all black ensemble gave it away. "Madison, this is my sister Kate, my very good friend Seth, and Ewan Lovatt, professor and eligible bachelor."

The redhead tilted her head in Ewan's direction with a come-hither smile. "Madison Walsh."

"Madison's a photographer. I talked her into a quick drink on her break."

Kate caught the slight slur in Jack's voice; he was working on getting drunk. "I'm sure you did."

"She did all the promotional photography for the inn. Joss is talking with her about a portfolio of his work, and she's going to do their wedding photography."

"That's lovely, Jack," Kate said frostily. "Seth? Would you mind getting me a fresh drink, since my brother couldn't be bothered?"

"Sure." Seth sounded relieved as he left them.

"I should see if Anneliese needs anything," said Ewan.

"Yeah." Jack practically growled, "Maybe you should."

"Jack," Kate snapped.

Ewan had turned to go, but Jack's words stopped him.

Madison's eyes widened; she put a hand on Jack's arm. "I should find my assistant."

Kate looked around the room, grasping for a way to diffuse the situation. "Ewan, can I borrow you to get the cake ready for the wait staff?"

"Of course." Kate heard relief in his voice as well.

"The cake's in the catering tent out back," Kate said, taking him by the arm. She shot a look at her brother and the redhead. "If you'll excuse us."

The ten feet between the party tent on the terrace and the catering tent proved cold, and Kate was chafing her bare arms by the time they got there.

Ewan shrugged off his sport coat. Kate couldn't help but appreciate his tall frame in indigo denim and black cashmere.

"Here." He draped the jacket over her shoulders. "You're cold."

She was cold. That he noticed mattered; that he did something thoughtful and gallant about it mattered more.

"Thanks."

STANDING AMIDST THE BLACK TROUSERED, WHITE JACKETED WAIT STAFF and the prep areas, coolly assessing the plating and arranging of the food, Kate looked like a general.

"So where's the cake?" He wondered aloud, not seeing anything resembling dessert in the controlled chaos.

"Oh, the staff's got it all taken care of." Her confidence here was palpable. "I just needed to get you the hell away from my brother. He's spoiling for a fight for some reason, and he seems to like his chances with you."

Ewan chuckled. "I can't imagine why."

Kate pursed her lips. "I think I'm missing something here."

"Your brother is interested in Anneliese. That's fairly simple," Ewan said. "She's either not interested or afraid?"

Kate's entire body tensed for an offensive. "Based on exactly what?"

"I'm a pretty decent judge of character."

"Says you."

"Says me. Your brother has had a little more to drink than he ought to, and he's flaunting the redhead to make himself feel better."

Kate shrugged; he saw agreement in her face.

"I guess what I want to know is," Ewan went on, "if your brother is interested, why didn't he ask her to this party?"

"I suppose you have a theory on that as well?" Kate countered.

He did, and was feeling just irritated enough to be smug about it, though he knew he'd regret pissing Kate off. "She hasn't dated since she came back to town. He isn't here often, but he knows that and just assumed she'd be free and he could monopolize her time."

"You're awfully sure of yourself."

"I'm a writer. I see people," Ewan said. "It's part of the job. And you and your brother? You're used to getting attention, I think. Jack's just mad that Anneliese picked someone else tonight."

"You're amazing, you know that?" Kate snarled, eyes flashing. She turned on her stiletto and stormed out of the tent.

He'd more than pissed her off, but he was past caution. He couldn't let her walk away now, and he was unhindered by precarious shoes. He caught her in three steps, and she spun around to face him.

"Who the hell are you to say things like that to me?"

"I'm a man without my coat," he said and kissed her.

He half-expected her to slap him. Instead, she grabbed a fistful of his sweater, pushed him away long enough to look into his eyes—in her shoes she was nearly his height—then dragged him close again.

It was a greedy, white-hot collision of a kiss. There was nothing sugary about her; she was silk and dark chocolate, heat and furious passion. He held her tight and let instinct say the things he didn't have words for yet.

~

Every coherent thought in Kate's head spun out like hot sugar. Ewan kissed her the way he'd spoken to her—intense, fierce, and without caution. Never one to hesitate when roused, Kate threw herself into the kiss. Even as she opened to him, softened against him, he held her back, exploring and captivating, driving out all ideas save *more*.

She wound her arms around him, pressing her palms against his back. His mouth tasted of hops and toast.

A faraway round of applause brought her back to the moment. Someone was making speeches.

Thought returned on a hastily drawn breath as Kate pulled away from him.

She searched his face for triumph, for mockery, and only found a naked desire that tempted her to throw her hostess responsibilities to the wind and drag him back to her apartment. He still held her close, the heat between them starting to cool in the frosty night air.

"I—" she began. "You've got to be freezing."

"I'm warm enough for the moment." A low laugh rumbled in his chest. "Your friends are going to notice you're missing."

"Oh my god, you're right." She could hear laughter, could just make out Joss speaking, but she couldn't tear herself away from him.

He released her. "Go."

She could feel his gaze on her as she walked away, and fought the urge to put a little extra wiggle in her walk.

"Kate," he said.

She turned back to him just before the plastic strips that kept in the heat closed around her.

"This isn't finished."

CHAPTER 13

The party wound down by midnight. Nan and Joss excused themselves when the last guests left, going upstairs to the apartment over the garage. Jack was nowhere to be found. Kate called the lone taxi service in town to see Seth back to his hotel. When she walked him out to his cab, she saw in his eyes that he understood.

"Thanks, Kate," he said. "This was a great evening. I'm glad you asked me."

"I'm glad you came." She meant it, in her own way.

"Maybe we can grab a beer the next time I'm up in Burlington?"

"I'd like that."

"Goodnight, Kate." He kissed her cheek and climbed into the backseat of the car.

Anneliese had thrown an apron on over her dress and was loading a few dishes which belonged to the inn into the dishwasher when Kate came back inside.

"Having the wait staff set up outside, and renting all the barware and serving pieces? Genius. There's a reason you're getting to be the most sought-after wedding planner in the valley."

"I'm certainly glad of it now." Her tone was more bitter than tired. "I think we can be sure Jack won't turn up tomorrow."

Kate stacked some clean serving pieces. "Do you want to tell me what's going on there?"

"Even if I did," Anneliese said softly, "you're his sister."

"Fair enough." Kate felt guilty for prying. She tucked the stack away and returned to the sink. "Shove over."

She pulled her chef's coat over the cocktail dress and slipped out of her heels. "I'll do the counters while you start the machine."

"Ewan headed out a few minutes ago." Anneliese spoke his name tentatively. "He said to tell you it was a great party."

Kate steadied her voice; her lips still felt his kiss. "I'm glad he had a good time."

Anneliese echoed Kate's words. "Do you want to tell me what's going on there?"

"There's nothing to tell."

Heat bloomed over her skin, and Ewan's parting words lingered. *This isn't finished.*

Anneliese was kind enough to drop it.

She drove the two of them back to her apartment on autopilot, grateful they were too weary for more talk. Sleep came quickly, but so did morning.

One of the mixed blessings of owning a bakery, Kate supposed, was that her body was conditioned to wake early. As a result she got to see more than her fair share of sunrises.

She nursed a cup of tea alone on the fire escape outside her bedroom and watched the first gold light of morning peek out over the rooftops of downtown Thornton. Anneliese slept soundly on the pull-out couch, and Kate saw no need to disturb her friend. Bundled in silk thermals, flannel pajamas, her duffel coat, and a hat and mittens, she was sure she looked ridiculous, but the quiet cold soothed her.

Kate watched a man in high-tech winter running gear jog over the footbridge that ran across the river. A sleek, black Labrador ran alongside him. Quarter after seven, she thought. Ed Marcotte was the pastor at the Congregational Church, and ran the six miles from his family's orchard into town every Sunday before services. The Lab's name was Eve, "Man's best friend," Ed would say with a charming smile.

Ed had baptized her. He had married her parents. He welcomed her whenever her parents dragged her to church, which had been less and less after she got back from Paris.

She had mistaken Mathieu's thorough seduction for passion. Barely twenty-two, a hometown sweetheart who had gotten her head-strong way when it came to boys, she was dazzled by everything from his accented English to his disdain for tourists and knowledge of the best clubs on any given night.

Since Paris, she'd kissed more frogs than she could remember, playing the field to bury the memory of that hollow prince, and by the time her best friend arrived in Thornton, she had reclaimed her independence.

Independence she planned to keep.

Ewan's kiss still burned her lips. No practiced sensuality there; for those brief moments, he possessed her. She hadn't played at her response; she'd reveled in it.

Ed turned right at the end of the bridge and disappeared from view. When her parents celebrated their twenty-fifth wedding anniversary, Ed had given a toast, praising them on a strong marriage and a beautiful friendship. She could still recall the way her dad looked at her mom, still madly in love.

If she was ever to give up what she worked so hard for, it wouldn't be for less than that.

Light tapping on the glass at her back startled her. Anneliese waved. Kate pushed the window open and clambered back inside.

"Morning," Anneliese yawned. "You're up early."

"Occupational hazard." Kate shrugged. "Tea?"

"Please."

Kate put the kettle on and rustled around in a wicker basket on the counter for teabags. Anneliese pulled down a mug and leaned on the narrow peninsula that separated kitchen from living room.

The kettle whistled; Anneliese poured and dunked her teabag into the hot water. "Are you sure you don't mind taking me home after we finish cleaning up? I can ask my Dad to come down and pick me up."

"Anna, it's no trouble."

"I feel like such a burden to everyone lately." Anneliese fidgeted with the tea bag string. "Pity party, table for one."

"Driving you a couple of miles is hardly a burden. If this is about your parents and Chloe..."

Anneliese sighed. "Ignore me."

"Make me." Kate wondered how much of Anna's mood had to do with her brother. She opened the fridge and pulled out a box of left-over macarons. "Cookies for breakfast?"

"Kate?" Anneliese was staring at the newel post at the top of the stairs. "I wasn't paying very close attention last night, but isn't that my date's jacket?"

Kate popped the box open. "Cookies?"

"Kate."

"I got cold. He lent me his jacket."

Anneliese took a pale green macaron from the box. "*That's* your story?"

"There's no story. You said yourself he was nice. Letting a cold person borrow your jacket is nice."

"You are a terrible liar." Anneliese swept a crumb from her lip. "What did Seth think about his date being *a cold person* and wandering around in another guy's jacket?"

"I might have carefully stashed it once I was back under the party tent." Kate closed the box and tucked it in her huge purse. "Let's go tackle the inn's kitchen, maybe bang some pots together to remind the smug lovebirds how lucky they are."

She made a point of grabbing Ewan's suit jacket on her way down the stairs.

~

EWAN WOKE TO MIDMORNING SUN STREAMING INTO HIS WINDOW. THE last shadows of his dreams still played behind his eyelids, so he let himself drift. He'd dreamt of thunder rolling across the valley, Kate's voice at its center; that he understood. The part about suit shopping in Burlington and winning a Prius in a raffle he was less clear on.

He wrote down what he recalled of the dream-storm in his notebook, words coming fast and messy when it transitioned into an idea for an encounter between Sledge and his new character. He channeled his desire into his imagination and filled pages with ideas.

When he finally pushed himself out of bed, it was nearly ten. He felt like his fifteen-year-old self lusting after Jenny Kramer. His imagination had gone into overdrive for Jenny, too. The writer in him struggled to analyze the shift from irritation toward desire; one way or another, Kate had been under his skin since the morning she'd stormed into his office.

The need to see her pushed him through a shower and fresh clothes. He fired up the truck and drove out to the Damselfly, hoping to catch her. Anneliese had mentioned they'd be there to clean up so Nan could reopen the inn in the afternoon.

He could smell coffee even before he knocked on the kitchen door.

Anneliese opened the door with a warm smile. She had a ladle and a dishcloth in hand. "Ewan."

The serving spoon in Kate's hand splashed into the soapy sink.

"Morning, Anna." He looked at Kate. "Kate."

Kate dug around in the soapy water for her lost spoon. "Morning."

"You have great timing," Anneliese said. "We were just talking about the Stone Garden."

"The Stone Garden?" he repeated. Kate continued to wash the serving pieces.

"It's this clearing out in the woods off Mountain Road up in Morgantown," Anneliese began. "But first, where are my manners? Coffee?"

"Sounds like heaven. I'll figure it out for myself." Ewan grabbed a mug from the rack. "Tell me more."

"All around the middle of this clearing, in all these fantastic groupings, are these boulders. Some are on the ground, some are stacked. I'd say the smallest is maybe as tall as Chloe, and the larger ones are enormous."

"It's like a small Stonehenge, only it doesn't look man-made," Kate added, drawn into the conversation by Anneliese's enthusiasm and Ewan's curiosity. "There's a deer trail from the road and an old cart path down to one of the Morgantown farmsteads, but the woods resist further attempts to make a trail."

"It's a local legend," Anneliese finished.

"And apparently, last night, a bunch of local teens got lost out there and had to phone their parents and EMS for rescue," Kate laughed. "Honestly, I hate to sound like a cranky old lady, but when we were teenagers, no one ever got lost out there."

"I'm not sure I can imagine you hiking." He could though, and it fit perfectly with the character he was writing.

"You didn't know her then," Anneliese laughed. "I grew up with her older brother. Kate was like a wild creature. She knows these woods like the back of her hand."

"Really?"

Kate put down her dishes and dried her hand on a rag hung from her pocket. "I had an old bike of Jack's and nothing stopping me. I could track Jack and Joss." She smirked at Anneliese. "And their friends, for hours. I bet I still know about more places than they do."

"Like what?" Anneliese asked.

"Do you know about the stone fireplace and the waterwheel out in the woods behind Strickland's Farm?"

"No," Anneliese replied, wide-eyed.

"But there it is," Kate said. "Used to be if you followed the north pasture wall, then stayed straight west into the woods about a quarter mile, you'd find it. A proper colonial stone hearth and chimney—house long gone, and a nearly collapsed waterwheel near the creek bed."

"I'd love to see that. And the Stone Garden," Ewan said. While Kate was speaking, he was already wondering if Faye would have known about the Stone Garden. Or the water wheel. He felt a pang of guilt at neglecting the story idea that had brought him to the Damselfly.

"Today would be such a great day to go," Anneliese said, peering out at the clear sky. "It may get into the fifties later, and there's not a cloud in the sky."

The prospect of researching, exploring with Kate was intoxicating. With Anneliese to chaperone, he might have a chance of staying focused. "You ladies free?"

"I have to get home," Anneliese said. "My parents will be back with Chloe."

"Speaking of which," Kate said, "I need to get you home or I'll be late, and we need all hands on deck at Sweet Pease for the post-church crowd."

Anneliese looked at the pile of linens destined for the laundry room downstairs. "I hate to leave the kitchen a mess for Nan and Joss."

Ewan saw an immediate solution, though sadly it didn't involve traipsing through the forest with Kate. "Why don't I help, Anneliese? I'll give you a hand with the laundry, then drive you home. That way Kate won't be late, and Nan and Joss still get a clean kitchen."

"Kate?" Anneliese asked, taking a small earthenware dish from Kate's still hands. "What do you think?"

"Sure." Kate glared at him, then at Anna, with narrowed eyes before tossing both hands up in the air. "Perfect."

She dried her hands and tossed the cloth into the pile of linens.

Before either of them could say anything more, Kate was shrugging into her coat. She paused at the corner of the island, waving in the direction of the long farmer's table, where his jacket was slung over the back of a chair. "Don't forget your jacket."

Anneliese looked like she'd been slapped, but Ewan felt a guilty shiver of satisfaction. Kate was a little jealous.

When she breezed out the door, letting the storm door slap against the jamb, the satisfaction soured.

KATE HIT THE GAS PEDAL HARD, REVVING THE ENGINE AND SPRAYING pea-stone out behind her tires as she pulled away. For a moment, the thought of waking her friends pinched her conscience, but she buried the guilt under an irrationally adorable image of Ewan and Anneliese cozied up together in Nan's kitchen, washing and drying dishes.

The farther she drove, the closer they got, getting playful with suds and towels, and—damn him—she knew what it would be like to kiss him.

By the time she got to the parking lot off Gristmill, she was in a nasty mood, with a full-blown headache to boot. She slammed in the back door, stripped her coat off, scraped her hair back into a tail, and checked the coat rack for her chef's jacket and cap.

Which weren't there.

"Where the hell?" She could hear the happy, blurry sound of the crowd out front mingling with the sound of the bell over the door, and it only worsened her irritability.

"Where the hell is my jacket?" She asked the empty room. When the kitchen didn't magically produce her missing jacket, she pushed through the door to the front room, nearly colliding with Margot.

"Have you seen my jacket?"

Margot blinked. "Your jacket?'

"My pink jacket?" Kate snapped.

"Oh!" Margot smiled wide. "No, but the linen service came yesterday. The clean things are bagged next to your desk."

Margot continued past Kate in search of a tray from the supply rack. Kate retreated back to the kitchen to find the bag from the linen service. True to her intern's word, there were six clean pink jackets in with the rest of the staff's aprons and caps. Chagrined, she slipped one on, tucked her ponytail into a cap and went out to help her crew.

She joined Margot, taking orders from the line. Touching Margot's arm, she said, "I'm sorry I snapped at you. I'm forever telling you all to leave your baggage at the door, and here I am letting my mood get the better of me."

"No worries, Kate," Margot said easily before scribbling down the order for the next family in line.

Kate pressed her temples. What was the matter with her? He'd thrown in on chores when he was under no obligation to, and he'd offered up a solution that benefitted everyone. She was coming unhinged over one—admittedly scalding—kiss.

EWAN EASED HIS TRUCK INTO ANNELIESE'S PARENTS' DRIVEWAY AND SET the brake. Anneliese had withdrawn on the ride home, and he wondered what was bothering her.

"Is there something the matter?"

She drew in a breath, as if to steady herself. "It's nothing."

Ewan understood not to press the issue, but he couldn't help but be curious. There was a story to her and Jack Pease, a story everyone was avoiding telling. The heavy expression on Anneliese's face when she looked at her parents' home spoke of frustration. There was a story there, too.

The front door opened, and Chloe barreled out wearing a purple sweater and matching leggings, huge clomping snow boots and a baseball cap.

"Mama!"

"Hi, baby." Anneliese caught the little girl up in a hug.

Chloe looked up from her mother's shoulder and saw him. "Mister Love It!"

Anneliese turned, hoisting Chloe onto her hip.

"No more Paul Bunyan?" He'd warmed to the nickname.

"Oh," Anneliese said, "yeah. My mom asked who 'Paw Onion' was. When I explained, she gave me her *you're-raising-this-child-no-better-than-a-wolf* look. When I got back from a client meeting later, Chloe could say your name." She kissed her daughter's cheek. "Sort of."

Anneliese's mother met them at the door.

"Anneliese." Her reaction to Ewan was nearly cold. "You didn't mention you were bringing company."

"Mom, this is my friend, Ewan Lovatt."

Her mother's eyes widened slightly at his name. Recognition almost always looked the same.

"Ewan, this is my mother, Jane Thompson."

"Come in!" Jane brightened, opening the door wide.

Ewan noticed Anneliese's pinched expression and stepped back. "No, thank you, Mrs. Thompson. I've got to—"

"Ewan is working on a draft, Mom," Anneliese improvised. "He was nice enough to take time out of his day to drive me home, but we can't intrude anymore."

"Well, then." Jane Thompson cooled again. "Anneliese, you should bring that baby in before she freezes."

"It was lovely to meet you, Mrs. Thompson. Thanks again, Anna, for inviting me to the party." Ewan turned to Chloe. "See you around, Miss Chloe."

"Bye, Mister Love It!"

Chloe waved goodbye to him through the big window adjacent to the door while he climbed into the Scout and navigated out of the Thompsons' driveway.

Ewan drove back south into town, but instead of turning west toward the college campus and his apartment, he parked the car on Main Street and walked three blocks to Sweet Pease. The bakery windows were blurry with steam. The bell jingled and the people standing nearest the door skootched in to make room for him.

It wasn't just Kate's height and fuchsia jacket that set her apart from the crowd. She was the captain of her crew. She was taking orders from the line, bagging and plating and queueing pastries and sandwiches in an elaborate choreography with her employees.

Ewan recognized Jim and Kim from the incident with the eggs and dough. The young woman with violet-streaked hair wasn't familiar, but the way she shadowed Kate spoke of something akin to hero-worship.

They were so attuned to her that she moved among them unimpeded and without disturbing their work. The longer Ewan watched, the more like a symphony the service of Danishes, bagels, and coffee became.

When Kim asked him for his order, he was embarrassingly unprepared. And tongue-tied.

"Hazelnut muffin," he muttered, asking for the first item he noticed, "and a black coffee."

"Right away, Mr. Lovatt," Kim said.

Ewan reached for his wallet as he approached Jim at the register. *Mr. Lovatt?* He was hardly a regular. Will Dancy's words came back to him: *Do you have any skeletons in your closet? Rest assured they'll be old news by spring.* Maybe he didn't have skeletons, per se, but word certainly got around.

He perched at the bar that lined one wall and listened to the conversations swirling around him, filing snippets and snapshots away for later writing sessions.

The rush died down around him; he watched Kate snag a Danish from a tray being switched out by the purple-haired girl. She poured herself a coffee, sweetened and lightened it, and approached him, color high and eyes tired. He thought that underneath the fatigue, she might be glad to see him.

"Hi." She sat down next to him and pulled her cap off. Shoving it into her pocket, she tucked into the Danish like a starving woman. "I'm going to lead with an apology for being a brat earlier."

"Hi. Apology accepted. Everyone was tired."

Kate wiped a crumb from the corner of her mouth. "You're being nice. Thank you."

"Is it always like this?"

"On Sundays, yes." She sipped from the coffee, blowing lightly on the surface. "The Congregational Church service ends at 11:00, the Catholic Mass at 11:30, and the second Methodist service gets done just before noon. So, from eleven to one this place is a zoo."

"Do you usually put in a full day?"

"I usually spend the early morning doing production work—that's big batch baking, stuff that gets frozen and baked off at a later date. Then afternoons are for office work. Mondays are my day off."

"Sounds brutal."

Kate nodded. "And it's only going to get tougher when the new location opens."

"New location?" He tried to sound like he'd never heard of it.

She narrowed her eyes. "I'm sure you've heard. You can't buy stamps in this town without your mother knowing about it by supper."

He laughed at that. She might complain, but it was clear she loved her home.

"I'm opening a second bakery up at a winery closer to Burlington. I'll have a bigger kitchen up there, and I'll be expanding the menu to include some bistro food."

"That sounds great."

"Great and exhausting. I'm going to have to hire a whole staff for the second location, and a sous chef to run this place, and it's possible I won't sleep again after it opens. Thank goodness Nan and Joss are getting married in June. That's my soft open, and I'll have July to work out the kinks."

He suspected he was getting a rare glimpse of honesty about the scope of her new venture. "I can't imagine how busy you'll be."

"Keep your fingers crossed that I will be that busy." She looked at the clock. "I should get back to work. The payroll doesn't update itself, and Margot's been on since five a.m. She's got to go home."

"I don't want to keep you." Ewan collected her napkin and empty cup along with his own. "But Kate? If the weather's nice tomorrow, would you want to show me the Stone Garden in the afternoon?"

She stopped. "I would love that." A slow, sweet smile spread across her face. "Are you teaching in the morning?"

"Until noon."

"I'll come by your office a little after noon. And I'll bring lunch."

CHAPTER 14

Kate hauled their lunch up the four flights of stairs to Ewan's office. This time she noticed the new security measures in place since the days when she and her girlfriends had walked into campus buildings without invitation or identification. Of course, they hadn't been walking into the academic buildings, she thought. The signs now clearly posted public hours and warned that ID would be required to use the building after hours.

She knocked on the jamb of Ewan's open office door. "Good afternoon, Professor."

He looked up from his laptop and pulled his reading glasses off. "Hi."

Kate's fingers itched to put them right back on his face. They were incredibly appealing.

"Lunch here?" She asked, brandishing a hamper. "Or al fresco?"

Ewan blinked. "Really? It's not too cold out there?"

"Flatlanders." Kate clucked and shook her head. She was rewarded with a look of bewilderment from Ewan. "I'm teasing. Clear some space. I brought a feast."

She set a picnic basket on his desk and pulled out a pair of soda bottles. “A guy I went to high school with brews his own line of sodas. I sell them at Sweet Pease. I hope you like cream soda?”

Ewan inspected the bottle. “What’s not to like?”

“Dee’s fresh chips from Temple and my second-favorite sandwich,” she continued, setting out a basket of still-warm, thick-cut fries and two wax-wrapped sandwiches.

“I’m intrigued,” Ewan said, picking up a sandwich and snagging a fry.

“Cashew butter and raspberry-cocoa preserves on my own seven-grain bread,” she said with a pleased smile.

She studied him while he bit into his sandwich. Watching someone taste something new was a private pleasure of hers. She loved the mixture of anticipation and uncertainty in someone’s eyes when they took that first bite. Her childlike delight in capturing that first, unguarded reaction to a new flavor spurred all of her creations.

She wasn’t disappointed; the look she always hoped for lit up Ewan’s features.

He smiled, eyes wide, and licked a stray smear of cashew butter from his thumb. “That’s wonderful.”

“Isn’t it?” She unwrapped her own sandwich. “You couldn’t have picked better weather for a hike.”

Ewan looked out the window. “Unless it were June?”

Kate chuckled. “Fair point. But it’s sunny, dry, and at least ten degrees above freezing.” She dug into the fries. “Snow coming in by evening, but if we have time, I’ll take you to the waterwheel.”

“How is it that one small town has so many secret places?”

“Well,” she chewed a moment, “the waterwheel isn’t technically in Thornton.”

He laughed. “One small county, then.”

“There aren’t a million secret places you love where you live?”

“Maybe half a million.”

She liked the teasing gleam in his eyes. “Tell me about one.”

He picked up a French fry, but his eyes glazed over in thought. When his eyes lit up, Kate saw a whole different man in his expression.

"There's this bookstore in my neighborhood in New York... It's too small, half-underground, and you can barely breathe for all the books everywhere, but the couple who owns it knows everyone, and they have this... ability to match you with the book you never knew you needed to read."

She wanted to go there with him, just for the look on his face.

"And," he continued, "you don't need perfect weather to go there."

"Touché" Kate wrapped up the uneaten half of her sandwich. "It would take a year of perfect weather to exhaust my list of secret, amazing things to show you."

He blinked, and a blush heated her cheeks. Neither of them spoke, but ate their fries between cautious glances. She hadn't meant to suggest anything, but he neither did he seem spooked.

Ewan broke the small silence. "I read about the Robert Frost trails near the mountain campus. Can we add that to your perfect weather list?"

She bit her lip. "Don't hate me. I've never actually hiked them."

"Not a Frost fan?"

"I like the wild places better."

The look he gave her was professorial. "So did Frost."

"If you drive over the pass, there's a state park about halfway down the mountain with a triple waterfall." She dropped a little extra sass into her voice. "Way better than walking paths for the tourists."

"Maybe we can save that for spring." Ewan popped the last corner of his sandwich into his mouth.

"Maybe." Spring was still an uncertainty as far as she was concerned. Blistering winter kisses were one thing; sharing her secret haunts in a new season was another. "You about ready to head out?"

"Where're you parked?" Ewan asked as they walked down the stairs together.

"In the faculty lot," Kate said with a grin. "They never ticket me. Maybe they think I'll stop delivering to department meetings."

Evan glanced at the sky. An ominous bank of cloud was forming on the far western horizon, despite the pale blue skies above them.

"You want to take my truck?" They crossed the road and a small quad toward the parking lot in question.

"You mean it?" Her car-loving heart flipped over.

Ewan gestured to the tomato-red truck. "There she is."

Kate ran toward it, leaving Ewan behind. She trailed a reverent hand over the body. "It's gorgeous." She turned to him as he caught up to her. "Will you ever let me drive it? You don't have to say yes, I just need to know not to get my hopes up."

He tossed her the keys; she snatched them from the air with a quick flick of her hand. "Really?"

"You know where we're going."

"Oh my god." Kate hoisted herself up into the driver's seat and smoothed her palms over the steering wheel. "It's so beautiful."

Ewan climbed in next to her. "You surprise me."

Kate gave him a sidelong glance. "Hang on." She turned the key and the engine roared. She dropped it into reverse and backed out.

The drive north up Mountain Road took them through pastures and marsh land, along roadside creeks and past homesteads running the gamut from tin-roofed shacks to gluttonous modern colonials. Kate regaled him with the stories of people who had lived in the older houses over the years.

At a hairpin bend in the road, about twelve miles out of town, she hauled the Scout off the road and yanked up the e-brake.

"Let's go." Kate pulled a wool hat down over her head and slipped her hands into mittens she produced from the pocket of her ski jacket.

THEIR BOOTS CRUNCHED ON THE FROZEN FOREST FLOOR AS KATE navigated the deer trail. Ewan followed her closely; until she'd set off between two leaning birch trees, he hadn't seen a trail at all.

The forest seemed aware of their presence. He was a child of concrete and city parks; the breathing of trees was unfamiliar to him, but Kate was a child of these woods. He understood it as soon as the road disappeared behind them. She stepped softly, ducking and side-stepping the trees, hopping over roots and rocks.

"I can't tell you how many times people have tried to make this path easier to travel," Kate told him as she navigated a series of stepping stones across a small brook. Ewan traced her steps exactly. "The forest takes it back. This place is fantastic. I promise."

"These woods are alive," he said. "They have stories."

So many stories. Faye Bartram's story had to have a moment here. Maybe a stolen tryst with her lover, or grief-stricken wanderings in the forest. He started to ask her if she knew of any. The way she told George Cartwright's history, he could only imagine how she might tell Faye's haunted past.

Kate stopped to watch him crossing after her. The way she was looking at him reached in and squeezed the frozen air in his lungs. Pink-cheeked and windblown, she was alive and full of stories.

"They do." She turned and scrambled up a short ledge. "Just a little farther now."

Ewan took the ledge in one large step. He was right behind her when she pushed past an overgrown mountain laurel and the sky rushed down to meet them.

All thoughts of Faye fled his mind.

The openness of the clearing disoriented him. The sky, cool blue when they'd left the Scout, was solid grey, steely and bright. Snow scented the air. The fir and birch forest gave way to a nearly square clearing, softened by short, rocky deposits at the corners. The henge—if that's what it was—looked as though a giant's child had left her jacks and marbles scattered over the grass. Where the little markers at the corners wore their lichen like a patina, the stones within the clearing were clean and rain-smoothed.

Ewan hesitated, but the huge stones called to him.

"Go." Kate kept her voice low. "They don't bite."

He wove his way around the stones, running his palms over them, pacing the distances and the angles, feeling Kate's eyes on him all the while. He was so engrossed in his exploration that he didn't notice the snow begin to fall.

He turned to find her only a few feet away, face upturned to the falling snow, arms spread as if to gather it close.

"Kate?" He held her gaze as the snowflakes tumbled and twisted between them. He wondered what snow tasted like on Kate's lips.

"We should head out." Kate still kept her voice down. "I don't want to get caught up here in a storm."

"Will you bring me back?"

"Of course."

Ewan followed Kate through the forest with no real sense of time or direction, unsure of how she knew her way. Snow fell harder, quieting the woods as it surrounded them. When they reached the truck, both it and the road were coated in a little more than an inch of snow, and it was falling fast and thick.

"How's the four-wheel on this thing?" Kate banged affectionately on the door as she unlocked it.

"Never tried it out in snow," Ewan confessed, "but for what I paid the mechanic in Jersey City to restore it, it'd better be blizzard-proof."

"It's not *that* bad yet," Kate said. "Let's take it for a spin."

When they had to stop a mile down the road because of a spruce tree blocking the way, she was less optimistic.

"We'll have to head north and pick up Route Seven. I hope you don't have anywhere to be for a while."

"I'm all yours."

Kate raised a brow, then hopped out to lock the wheels. Ewan followed suit, and they got the car ready for the increasingly bad roads. She threw the car into four-wheel drive and they headed north.

"How did you find that place?" Privately, Ewan was grateful Kate had a handle on the truck. The snow was coming down hard, and he wasn't sure he could tell where the road was if not for the woods.

"My dad brought Jack and me up there as soon as we were old enough to make the walk—I was maybe five." Kate was focused on the road, but the strain in her eyes softened with remembering. "In high school I'd go up there sometimes with friends. We'd sit under the stones and talk about boys."

He couldn't help but tease her. "And then bring the boys back later?"

Kate was quiet for a moment. The headlights cut through the snow, and Ewan guessed that twilight was falling behind the storm clouds.

"You're the first boy I ever brought up there," she said. "Take that how you will."

He weighed his words while the snow streaked past the windows. "Thank you."

"You're welcome." She fell silent while she concentrated.

Snow turned the world white around them, blinding him to everything beyond the Scout. After a while the woods gave way to homes, then to pastures, and then to the street lamps, placed like stitches in the landscape on the near-distant state road.

Kate broke the silence. "The roads are pretty slippery. Do you mind if we stop for a while?"

"Here?" He looked out into the empty semi-darkness.

"No." She laughed, but there was strain in her grip on the wheel. "The winery where I'm opening the second bakery is just down Seven from here. I have the keys to the building. I'm hoping Joss left the space heater. And that the snow lets up enough to drive back to Thornton tonight if he didn't."

"Okay."

Kate tapped on the brakes to slow the Scout as they approached an intersection. The few cars on the road drove slowly, leaving tire trenches in the fresh white. The plows hadn't even been out yet to sully it.

THE BARN LOOMED AS KATE BROUGHT THE TRUCK TO A STOP. The daylight was gone; the snow nearly horizontal. Kate fiddled with her keys to find the one for the downstairs space.

"Ready?" She waved the little silver key up between them. "Do you have a flashlight in here?"

"Yeah." Ewan dug a Maglite out of the glove box and handed it to Kate, then pulled the hood of his parka up. "Ready."

They raced for the door by the beam of the flashlight. Inside, Kate used the Maglite to find the infrared space heater Joss used on the job. She fired it up, thankful for the power being on during construction. She searched around for the work lamps and turned on the two nearest.

Ewan dragged a huge coil of wires and a packing blanket over into the warmth and light. Kate eyed them questioningly.

He glanced at the bare floor. "Warmer—and more comfortable—than sitting on the concrete slab."

"Clever."

They sat together on the makeshift seating, backs to the roughed-in service bar.

"Tell me what it's going to look like."

"You really want to know?"

"I do." He sounded sincere.

She pointed to the northern wall. "I want to put in booths there, under the small windows, to fill the space."

Unless she was talking to Jack, Joss, and her dad, Kate tried not to wax poetic about the project. She knew it was her particular passion, and that not everyone cared about table layout and kitchen design. But here Ewan was, asking, and she found herself wanting very much to share. She brought the raw bones of the room to life, coloring them in with her imagination for him.

Her voice went hoarse fleshing her dream out for him in the otherworldly stillness of a snowstorm.

"Kate." He reached out to take her hand. She stopped in the middle of describing the summer terrace and the view of the Frontenac and Marquette grapes on the hillside.

"Kate." He leaned over, closing the slight distance between them. With his gloved hands he turned her face to his.

This kiss was different, Kate thought, just before she gave in to the simple joy of it. She held his shoulders with her mittened hands and pulled him close. His skin smelled of snow and the Scout's upholstery, his lips were cool and questing over hers. He nipped at her lower lip when she moved to pull away. She smiled and slipped off the mittens, letting them fall away behind him as she buried her hands in his hair and kissed him hungrily.

Ewan wrapped his arms around her and tugged her across his legs. Kate savored his strength, reveled in the purr of pleasure in her own throat when he left her mouth to forge a path along her jaw. He pulled his hands free of his gloves and unwound her scarf without stopping his trail of kisses.

Kate was breathless and foolishly happy when they came up for air. "It's apparently a day for firsts."

Ewan kissed her temple, then her forehead. "Why's that?"

"I'd never brought a boy to see the Stone Garden, and I've never kissed anyone in an empty winery, or while sitting on—" She checked under the blanket for the label on the wire. "Metal clad cable."

Ewan kissed her again, hushing her.

"I like that," he said, punctuating his words with his lips at the corners of her mouth.

"But..."

"But what?" He ran his hands under the hem of her parka. She shivered from his chilly fingertips.

"Even with the heater, it's freezing in here," she said. "And I can't tell if the snow's let up."

"Let it be for a moment."

He pulled her close again and loosened her ponytail, letting her dark hair fall around them. His fingers cruised along her skin, leaving warm imprints where they traveled.

She let it be for a minute.

"Ewan." She laid her cheek on his shoulder briefly before getting up to check the weather.

Stopping at the French doors, Kate watched the snow travel past the windows. Her eyes slowly adjusted to the darkness beyond. Fat heavy flakes still fell steadily, but she could see out to the vines now.

"We should head back. There's a lull in the storm."

Ewan stood and joined her at the doors without touching her, but close enough that their mingled breath fogged the glass.

"Okay," he said lightly. "You're driving."

The plows had been through on the state highway, and Kate got them safely back to the door to her apartment.

She left the Scout running, and hopped out of the truck, meeting him by the rear bumper. Stray snowflakes whirled around in the lingering wind. "Think you can make it back to your place on your own?"

"I'll manage."

Kate stretched up on her tiptoes to kiss him. "Another night, I'm going to ask you to come up."

Ewan touched his hand to her face. "Another night, I'm going to say yes."

CHAPTER 15

Ewan taught his early lecture in a fog, then let his students take the lead in the discussion group that met afterward. He didn't realized until they began packing up their laptops and tablets that the hour was up.

The Stone Garden in the snow haunted him, as did the mystery of Kate's woods. Never in his broad imagination would he have placed himself in a construction site in the same day, kissing a woman like Kate by the light of a naked bulb in a safety cage.

The heat between him and Kate was more intense than he'd been prepared for. It didn't feel like a flirtation or a casual fling. That was something to think about.

He returned to his office, determined to turn the buzzing in his brain into creative output, but found an email from his agent waiting for him. *Call me.*

Mallory's assistant put him straight through. "Ewan?"

"Mallory. What's up?"

"They liked the outline you sent me. They came to me over the winter, right? Mitch and Yvonne asked me what you were working on, if you'd be interested in a script. You know I had to tell them what you'd pitched to me about your great-grandmother or whatever. I had to show them your pages. It's not my fault they loved them. I'm going to send you out to L.A. to meet with them once you've got more to show me. Which means, you need to have more to show me."

She had a big voice, which sped up the more excited she got about a project. He wasn't sure how she breathed sometimes.

"You sent that? It was just a rough sketch."

"It was enough for them to want a meeting."

"I can't now, Mal. I've got classes…" *And whatever this is with Kate Pease.*

"I know. I told them you were hidden away, teaching and writing their next Cannes winner, and that I'd send you west once you were done."

"You're at Cannes already?"

She laughed. "I think big. And I want you to be a breakout screenwriter, my critically acclaimed friend. I want one of the big houses to commit to turning Alasdair into a franchise. Films, graphic novels, someone dishy to play him, comic cons. The whole circus."

He had to admit, Mallory's vision exceeded his own, which was a good quality in an agent. She was relentless and ambitious enough for both of them most of the time.

"I'll get back to writing. We'll talk about travel later."

"L.A. is literally calling us."

"Bye, Mal."

She was already gone, but that was okay. He had pages to write. Pages that, as deeply intriguing as he found them personally, suddenly felt a little like selling out.

JUST BEFORE LUNCH, KATE LEFT THE BAKERY IN ANDY'S CAPABLE HANDS and drove out to the Damselfly Inn.

Joss's truck was long gone, but there were a few cars in the driveway—a rainbow of out of state tags that made Kate smile. Nan's hospitality was going to be the stuff of living legend in the valley. While she felt a pang of regret that the red Scout was conspicuously missing, she was glad he'd decamped. Having Ewan in the building wouldn't have been conducive to a gab session with her best friend.

She found the innkeeper herself in the basement laundry room wrestling with a load of sheets.

"Hey, Sugar Plum."

"You've come to fold sheets for me." Nan handed her one end of a fitted sheet. "My wish came true!"

"Of course I did." Kate laughed. "Put me to work."

"I swear," Nan said, "as soon as I can clear the funds, I'm getting a linen service."

Kate nodded. "I love mine. Tell them I sent you. They'll give you a deal. The regional manager is related to my mom somehow."

Nan pouted. "I think I missed out, not growing up in this town."

"Meh," said Kate with a shrug. "In a few months, you'll be a Fuller by marriage, and a de facto relative of two-thirds of mid-state Vermont."

"I can't wait." Nan replied without a touch of sarcasm. "So, aside from my wish for help with the laundry, what brings you out here on a Wednesday morning?"

"Ewan."

"Kate," Nan said sternly, "you've got to let that go."

"What I've got to do," Kate said sheepishly, "is catch you up on what's happened since the party."

"Oh?" Nan knew her well enough to sense a shift in her demeanor.

"First, I think I should apologize for my brother, who was behaving like a beast on Saturday."

"I heard." Nan's brow wrinkled disapprovingly.

"He's a jackass when his nose is out of joint. Seems I missed a few signs. Anna's got him more bent out of shape than I realized."

"That's an understatement." Nan traded the freshly folded sheet for a basket of tea towels. "Now what about Ewan?"

"We had this big fight last week." Kate told Nan about the scene in the Sweet Pease kitchen while they snapped out and folded the towels. "I was out of line."

A smug smile played around Nan's lips. "He's really gotten under your skin."

"Yeah." Kate inhaled the fresh scent of the linens. "You could say that. Anyway, we had a couple of tense moments at the party, but near the end, Jack was behaving badly and I felt bad for Ewan. I brought him to the catering tent with me to rescue him from my brother. One minute we're arguing, and the next minute I'm wearing his coat and we're making out in the yard."

Nan stopped mid-snap. "Making out in the yard?"

"He's a spectacular kisser," Kate said, biting her lip to keep from smiling too wide.

"You are amazing." Nan shook her head in wonder. "So what's happened since then? I know you're not done."

Kate took a stack of towels and dropped them into a laundry basket. She hoisted the basket up and set it on the long work table. "You definitely need a service. He turned up at the inn—come to think of it, I don't know why."

"Don't you?"

"Shut it," Kate said. "So, he dropped in while Anna and I were doing dishes Sunday morning. She and I were talking about the Stone Garden, and he seemed interested."

Nan added a tablecloth to the basket. "Oh?"

"He offered to drive Anna home, and I was a beast to them both."

"Oh?"

"Yes. Jealous and weird and horrible. Then he came by the bakery, and we ended up making plans to go up there yesterday."

"You've never taken me to the Stone Garden." Nan raised an eyebrow. "And we slept together for years."

"Smart ass. Pulling the ex-roommate card." Kate tossed a stray washcloth at her. "I'll take you up there this spring."

"The thrill is gone, now that I know you're taking my former guests on guided tours."

"Well, then I guess you'll have to get that hunky man of yours to take you up there sometime," Kate countered with a sly grin. "Now, can we get back to my story?"

"Of course," Nan said, handing Kate an armful of pillow cases.

"The storm came in while we were up there, but I got us down to the road by the time things got bad," she said. "Oh, and I should add, he let me drive that gorgeous Scout of his."

"He did not!"

"He did. And the visibility was awful, and there was a tree down across Mountain Road, so I had to go north up to Route Seven. I ended up stopping at the winery with him to wait out the white-out."

"You were stranded with him at the winery?" Nan moved on to a huge pile of fluffy towels. "Honestly, Kate. If I didn't know you better, I'd swear you planned these things."

"Yes," Kate countered. "I have an in with the weather gods. And I so enjoy being stranded in a freezing building with a man. Seriously, if I were going to engineer being stranded with a man, I'd strand myself in a ski condo at Stowe with a Jacuzzi."

"Fair enough," Nan said. "So what happened at the vineyard?"

Kate took a towel from Nan. "He proved himself resourceful."

"Mmhmm. So, now what?"

Kate sighed dramatically over a fresh pillow case. "I want to see him again. I can't figure it out, but there it is."

"You like him," Nan said. "You really like him."

"Don't gloat," Kate said darkly.

Nan tossed her one last pillowcase. "Fold that, then we can take this stuff upstairs and I'll pour us some coffee. I want to hear more about this change of heart."

Kate folded the pillow case and grabbed a basket of laundry before following her friend up the stairs. "Let's just call it a change of attitude."

CHAPTER 16

Thursday morning the temperatures soared to nearly fifty, the air off Lake Champlain was mild, and the effect was balmy, especially after the stretch of deeply cold, dry days preceding it. Ewan walked into downtown after his morning class. He had a mind to check out the local bookshop.

Despite the distraction Kate posed, he still needed to research Faye Bartram, the Industrial Revolution, and the railway expansion into Vermont and upstate New York. He figured that the bookshop might have some locally flavored references.

He made a mental note to ask Nan about the Ticonderoga and Crown Point historic parks on the New York side of the lake.

He turned from College Street onto Main and saw, to his delight, George Cartwright out for his daily walk. The elderly man was impeccably turned out, down to a sturdy pair of boots for navigating the sidewalks, which, due to the warming temperatures, were puddled with slush and rivulets of melting snow. Ewan recalled that he had a daughter who cared for him.

Thornton's history could wait. He had a wonderful opportunity walking just ahead of him in the present.

He jogged across the street and quick-stepped to catch up with the older man.

"Excuse me, Mr. Cartwright?" Ewan fell into step with him.

"Yes?" George Cartwright replied brightly.

"My name's Ewan Lovatt," he began. "I'm new in town. May I walk with you a bit?"

"Of course. And please, call me George. No need to be so formal on a Thursday morning."

"I will," Ewan replied with an easy chuckle. "If you'll call me Ewan."

"What brings you to Thornton, Ewan?"

Ewan began to wonder if Kate was exaggerating the old man's memory loss. "I'm a writer, and I'm teaching at the college for the semester."

"My daughter Rosemary studied literature at the college," George remarked with pride. "Takes after her mother. My wife had sparkle."

"I'll bet she did," Ewan said. "You studied there yourself, or so I hear?"

"When I got back from Korea. Same time I met Ginny."

They walked half a block in companionable conversation. Ewan paused at the corner of Main Street and the road that curved around the common to Route Seven, seeing the four-story, early twentieth-century mercantile building with fresh eyes. That this man's family had founded the business after the Civil War, expanded it to a local empire, and that George had preferred a life of teaching, fascinated him. He wondered what George might know about the Bertram house and the Swift family who owned it then.

He realized he'd let his mind wander when George turned to him with a young man's eager expression.

"Will I see you at the American Legion dance on Friday? I'll be there with Ginny. You could bring your girl."

"I'd love to meet Ginny." Ewan was surprised by George's easy slide back in time, and sorry he'd never met the man's wife.

George Cartwright beamed. "She'd like you." He looked at Ewan with a twinkle in his cloudy eyes. "She's got the prettiest smile in the county. I'm a lucky man, Ewan."

Ewan smiled through his melancholy. "Sounds that way."

"Pardon my asking, do you have a steady girl?"

"Not at present." Ewan glanced back at Kate's bakery, wondering what she would think of being someone's steady girl.

"Find yourself a girl who keeps you on your toes. Of course, it doesn't hurt if she can cook." George winked conspiratorially.

Ewan's thoughts flew to a girl who certainly kept him on his toes, and could she ever cook. "Does that mean you're going to ask Ginny to marry you?"

"We're getting married in the spring."

They passed the two-screen movie theatre. Ewan half expected to see posters for *Roman Holiday* or *Gentlemen Prefer Blondes* instead of teasers for the newest blockbusters.

"I think your Ginny's a lucky girl."

"We're just about the luckiest pair in town, I expect, but it wasn't easy. Love isn't always, you know."

Ewan noticed a middle-aged woman in a barn coat and felt fedora watching him from the steps of the sporting goods store opposite the Congregational Church.

She waved and called in their direction. "Dad!"

Ewan watched George Cartwright's face as his mind made the journey from past to present. He swore he saw the glint of tears before the old man smiled broadly at his daughter.

She made her way to meet them. She extended a sturdy, mittened hand to Ewan.

"Rosie Keller."

"My daughter," George added. "Rosemary, this is Ewan. He's a professor at the college."

"Nice to meet you, Ewan." Rosie had a firm, friendly grip. "Dad, we've got to be heading home now."

"Of course, Rosie. Do we need to pick anything up for your mother?"

Rosie's face clouded for a moment. "No, Dad. She doesn't need anything."

"It was nice speaking with you, Ewan. Take care, now." George touched his arm, then took his daughter's hand.

"Good day to you, George."

KATE WATCHED THROUGH THE FRONT WINDOW OF SWEET PEASE AS Ewan passed by the bakery with Mr. Cartwright. Her pulse kicked over at the sight of him: tall, not exactly handsome, but compelling. He kept pace with Mr. Cartwright, hands in his pockets like an earnest little boy, leaning in to listen.

She could only speculate as to what they might be discussing.

When his gaze turned briefly to Sweet Pease, she hoped it was her.

There was a change in Ewan since January. His prickly awkwardness was melting with the snow, replaced by this tender, curious, passionate man.

He treated Mr. Cartwright with the same respect—bordering on reverence—he'd had for the Stone Garden.

The passion, it would seem, he saved for her.

When Rosie Keller collected her father at the end of Main Street, Ewan shook Rosie's hand, but it was the gentle pat Mr. Cartwright gave him, and Ewan's answering smile, that sent a warm thrill up her back. As if he'd felt her reaction, he turned toward the window and saw her standing there looking at him.

That smile widened, just for her.

She met him just inside. "Hi."

Her body wanted to curve itself to his, but she wasn't ready just yet for her employees and customers to see what was brewing between them. Mrs. Mayhew and Mrs. Marlow could alert the entire town to fresh news within a half-hour with two well-chosen phone calls.

"Kate." His tone was neutral, but Kate could see the fire in his eyes.

"Are you here for lunch?" The blaze between them undid her; she struggled to pull herself together. His proximity and her own thoughts had the blood hammering in her veins. "Why don't you order, and we'll go into the kitchen. Moira can bring your lunch back when it's ready."

"I'll do that," he said.

He followed Kate through the swinging door a few moments later. Before it could fully close, she hauled him away from the doorway and up against her. She caught his face in her hands and pulled him down to kiss him.

"I've been thinking about that since Monday."

Ewan laced his fingers together behind her back. "I'm glad I'm not the only one."

The door swung open, and Moira coughed lightly. "Kate? I've got Mr. Lovatt's lunch."

Ewan dropped his arms just in time for the young woman to come in with a tray.

Kate stepped quickly away from Ewan and took the tray from Moira. "Thanks. Will you and Andy be okay for a while?"

"This place practically runs itself on Thursday afternoons." Moira flashed a knowing grin at the two of them.

Kate set the tray down on her work table.

"Kate." Ewan said, "I understand if you don't want people to know what's going on here. Just tell me what the rules are."

"No, Ewan. I—" She pulled at the ends of her ponytail. "It's not that. At all."

He waited while she put the words together.

"It's more that news travels faster than sound in this town, and I don't want people speculating while we're just figuring out what this is."

"So, does that mean I can ask you to dinner?"

His tentative words in contrast with his huge presence in her kitchen kicked open a door in her heart Kate hadn't known was closed.

"You absolutely can ask me to dinner. Chances are very good I'm going to say yes."

He laced his fingers together again, holding her lightly. "What destination would be most likely to get that yes?"

The hell with it. As Nan had said, she really liked him. "Temple. You should ask me to Temple."

Ewan raised his eyebrows. "Kate, would you like to have dinner with me at Temple tomorrow night?"

"Yes, Ewan." She kept her tone playful, but there was joy coursing through her, threatening to spill over. "Yes, I would."

"Good then," he said, his voice going low. "Now that's out of the way."

He pulled her close and kissed her hard. Kate purred her approval and melted into him.

"I have work I should be doing," she said when they came up for air.

"I have a discussion group in half an hour." Ewan kissed her softly, tucking a stray strand of her hair behind her ear. "I'll be thinking about dinner for the next thirty hours or so."

Kate tipped her face up. "I know you will."

He was just about to let the door swing closed behind him when Kate remembered his uneaten lunch. "Ewan!"

He paused in the doorway and Kate's heart inexplicably turned over.

"Your lunch. Let me bag it for you." She batted her lashes. "Since I distracted you."

Ewan stepped back into the kitchen, while Kate wrapped up his sandwich, closed his soup container, and put it all in a small handled shopping bag.

"I'll pick you up tomorrow at seven." Ewan took the bag and left the kitchen.

Kate sat on the edge of her desk, for the second time in a week watching the door swing shut behind Ewan, feeling like the world was poised to shift, whether she was ready for it or not.

Andy pushed through the door with the day's mail. "Hey, Kate? Moira said to mention that we're low on chocolate chip cookies and she couldn't find any in the freezer."

Ewan was still occupying space in her thoughts. "Hmm?"

Andy handed her the stack of catalogs and envelopes. "We're low on chocolate chip cookies out there and Moira can't find extras to bake off."

"Oh, shoot," Kate said. "Let me check. I think Moira's right, though."

She got up and headed into the walk-in, already pushing Ewan from her thoughts. With her mind back on work, she fished around in the freezer. She needed sheet cakes to build tasting cakes for a client meeting later that evening, and Moira was right. Time to add cookie dough to Margot's production list for the morning.

CHAPTER 17

Ewan was in his office when the chair of the English department knocked.

Murray Sporinger was a spry walking-stick of a man with an incongruously deep, robust voice. At eighty-two, he still taught three full courses and advised a thesis student every semester.

Sporinger sat down opposite him. "How are things going?"

"They're good, Murray." Ewan set down the essay he was reading. "I wasn't sure exactly how I'd feel about small college—small town—life."

"But?" Sporinger templed his fingers and grinned.

"No 'but,'" Ewan countered. "I like it here. I love my students. Will's a pleasure to work with."

"You were staying at the new inn out on County Road," Sporinger observed, knowing the answer. "How's Lawrence House compare?"

"I am cozily housed. Not as well-fed, but the village is close enough. A lazy New Yorker could do worse."

Sporinger laughed. "You said it, not I." He reached out and straightened a stack of papers with his thumb. "Ewan, I have a proposal."

"Oh?" Ewan took off his glasses.

"Caroline Waterford is leaving after this year," Sporinger began. "And while I can't formally offer you her position on the faculty, I can strongly suggest you apply for it. You've impressed the powers that be."

"I can't imagine how."

"Let's be realists a moment," the older man said. "You are a published and well-received author without the less desirable attributes of commercialism attached to your work. That kind of person is attractive to establishments such as this."

"You want me because I'm not a fame-whore?" Ewan asked with a wry smile.

"Something like that," Sporinger replied. "Your classes are full, and we're hearing good chatter from the students about you."

Ewan began to speak, but Sporinger hushed him.

"You've been a bit of a vagabond, but you always go back to New York."

"You've done your homework," Ewan said.

"I'd be remiss if I hadn't," Sporinger replied. "I'd like to keep you here, at least during the academic year. Writers-in-residence are good for our image."

"I'll think about it," Ewan said. "But I can't make promises."

Sporinger pushed himself up from the chair and offered Ewan a hand. Ewan returned the grip, struck by the constellation of age spots on the man's hands. He'd read Murray Sporinger's book on literary style in his own college courses. To shake the man's hand was an honor, never mind to receive what amounted to a job offer from him.

"I will think about it," he repeated.

Sporinger smiled as he turned to go. "I know you will."

For the second time in a week, Kate pulled into the Damselfly Inn in search of Nan. A flurry of texts had confirmed Nan's availability between check-in and afternoon tea. Kate arrived ready, with a flexible plastic basket full of her favorite date clothes.

She found her friend upstairs, curled up on her bed with a trade magazine.

Kate dropped the bag and ran a hand down the satiny, twisted wood of the bed frame. "I still can't believe Joss made this."

Nan sighed happily. "He's pretty amazing."

"How quickly we become smugly coupled." Kate plunked down on the bed with Nan. "Speaking of which, we have a lot of bachelorette planning to do. I assume you want a pizza delivery guy strip-o-gram, and..."

Nan snorted and whacked her in the chest with a throw pillow. "Ew."

"Or one of those dudes who wears a G-string and we eat sushi off his immaculate pecs?"

"Kate!" Nan collapsed into giggles.

Once the laughter bubbled up, Kate couldn't stop. She gasped for air. "Or maybe a sex toy party with Molly—and Jane Thompson?"

"I can see Joss's mom getting a kick out of it, but Anneliese's mother at a sex toy party?" Nan wiped away tears of mirth. "Are you really asking?"

"What kind of adult-themed hat you're going to have to wear? I'm not sure yet..." Kate dodged another pillow.

"Mani-pedis. That belly dancing class we saw advertised in Burlington last month. Something fun for dinner." Nan sat cross-legged. "You, me, Anna, Penny, Molly, maybe see if Janelle and Priya can come up?"

"Perfect. I'll make it happen." Kate hopped down from the bed, dumping the contents of the plastic carry-all on the bedspread. "Now, what should I wear to dazzle Ewan tonight?"

"The irony of you modeling for me is astounding," Nan remarked as Kate stripped off her dark gray tee and slipped into a shimmery red strappy top. "Since you dress me for all my important moments."

Kate struck a pose. "Without this," she added, plucking at the lacy straps of her bra. "And, Sugar Plum, we need each other. I make you take advantage of that adorable figure of yours, and you keep me from going completely over the top."

Nan giggled. "True." She considered the red top. "What are we thinking on the bottom?"

"Skinny jeans and boots." Kate shimmied out of the distressed blues she was wearing and grabbed the first of two pairs of dark indigo denim.

"I didn't even ask. Where's he taking you?"

Kate buttoned the jeans. "I told him to ask me to Temple."

"I don't picture him liking being told where to take you."

"Turns out, he can flirt a little. He asked where he should ask."

"That's practically your second home." Nan let the implications sink in. "You really do like him."

"Don't get all starry-eyed on me, Sugar Plum," Kate warned, sliding her legs into a dangerously high-heeled pair of tall black boots. "He's a visiting professor, something I'm not planning on losing sight of. Yes, I like him, but it's not a long term thing."

"Who are you trying to convince?" Nan was teasing, but there was a hint of seriousness in her eyes.

Kate ignored the question. "What do you think?"

"My early opinion is those jeans are trying too hard, but I'll have to see the other options. Keep the red thing. Is that even a shirt?"

"Yes, it's a shirt, and you should borrow it sometime." Kate regarded herself in Nan's mirror. "You might be right." She rustled around in the carry-all, producing a slightly less snug pair of jeans. "I'll wear my black wool car coat and that silver fake pashmina."

Kate swapped the boots and jeans, then twirled for Nan.

"Better," Nan said.

Kate gathered her hair up in a messy bun. "Up?"

"Up," Nan agreed. "When are you expecting him?"

"Seven," Kate said, "so I have to get a move on."

Nan got up from her perch on the bed. "Joss and I were thinking about getting everyone together for brunch again this weekend. I have a serious jones for the home fries at Rick's."

"You really are becoming a townie if you're jonesing for Rick's Diner."

"Isn't it great?" Nan grinned.

Kate shoved clothes back into the basket. "I can do Sunday before eleven—which is really more breakfast than brunch, or Saturday morning. Have you talked to Anna?"

"No, but unless she's got a day wedding on Saturday, she's probably free, especially if we're going to Rick's."

"She can bring Chloe, if that's what you mean."

"Only sort of speaking of Anna," Nan said tentatively. "Have you heard from Jack?"

Kate shook her head. "He's gone dark. I expect he'll talk to Joss first. Re-establish his male pride or whatever."

"Right," said Nan. "I'll leave them to it. I have tea to serve to a full house tonight."

"Gotcha," Kate said. "I'm off to get pretty."

"Heaven help poor Ewan. Who's probably pacing his room in Lawrence House as we speak."

Kate rolled her eyes, but the idea of Ewan in need of divine intervention at the sight of her did have some appeal. "I'm sure he's not."

EWAN WAS NOT, IN FACT, PACING HIS ROOM.

He was hunched over his laptop, importing research sites into his writing software. Faye was drawing him into the forests of Vermont. He'd done his best to shelve Alasdair's Kate-like ladylove in favor of Faye, but Faye wanted to explore the Stone Garden. Which led him back to Kate, so he focused on reading about the forest anomaly, saving local blog entries, hiking trail reviews, history buff articles, and haunting lore.

His thoughts wandered from the research and before he knew it, he'd sketched a woman wearing a combination of bustled silk taffeta and scientific instruments, her hair in a Gibson girl pompadour, in three-quarter profile. She had Kate's dark hair and strong features. Faye simply wasn't compelling enough to drive Kate from his thoughts.

It was only the insistent electronic beeping of the alarm on his phone that dragged him into the twenty-first century. He gave himself twenty minutes to shower and change before he left to pick up Kate. Moments like this, he was glad of a wardrobe largely chosen by an assistant back in New York. He might have been initially embarrassed to hire the fashionable young woman to sort out his wardrobe, but as a result, everything he owned was classic, correctly tailored, and easily coordinated.

He figured ten more minutes for the drive, and five to walk up Gristmill from the parking lot to Kate's door.

In the bathroom, he ran his hand over a day's beard, trying to decide if it was dangerous-looking or just scruffy. He concluded he wasn't as much of a Clive Owen-type as he might wish, and opted to shave.

CHAPTER 18

Kate stole the breath from his lungs the moment she opened her front door. The golden light from her apartment backlit her upswept hair like a corona. She was winding a pale gray scarf around her throat while he gaped.

"Hi." She stretched up on her toes to kiss him lightly before buttoning up her black coat and locking up. He caught a flash of scarlet shimmer and snug denim before she fastened the coat.

"Hi." He took her hand and walked with her around the corner and down Main Street, understanding, under the flicker of the street lamps, why George Cartwright still walked this stretch every day. There was enchantment in crossing over the waterfall with a beautiful woman. He wondered briefly if someday his own ravaged memory might revisit the spray from the falls catching the amber glow of the street lights and Kate's voice carrying over the rush of the river below.

Dismissing the maudlin thoughts, he pulled open the door to Temple.

Ewan had taken to coming into Temple once a week for dinner and occasionally Sunday for the Irish breakfast, but on a Friday night, the local watering hole came alive in a way he realized he'd been missing.

Holding the door open for Kate Pease in all her splendor was, admittedly, part of the glamour.

He'd accused her of wanting attention, but the simple truth was that she had it, whether she wanted it or not. She was beautiful, but Ewan knew it was more than that. She drew people to her. She was a flame—a glowing, living, dangerous creature. She approached the bar, still holding his hand and flagged the bartender down. The curly-haired blonde Ewan knew to be the owner took them in with a practiced eye.

"Table for two, then, Katie?" Deirdre asked. Ewan was acutely aware of the eyes on them as the proprietress led them to a table at the far end of the dining room. He noted, too, that while they were in a quiet part of the dining room, they were in full view of the bar. "What can I get you to drink?"

"Manhattan for me, Dee," Kate said.

"I've heard good things about the local porter," Ewan said.

"A fine choice," Deirdre remarked, then left them with their menus.

He dropped his coat over the back of his chair. Kate slipped her scarf and coat from her shoulders. The subtle red shimmer he'd caught back in her apartment revealed itself to be a nearly backless, silky halter top. She twisted to lay her coat over her scarf, and Ewan had to fight the urge to touch the smooth skin of her back.

A little green finger of jealousy flicked his heart when several nearby men also visibly appreciated Kate's dramatically bare flesh.

"How long have you and Deirdre known each other?" Ewan asked, diffusing his own reaction. He sat down himself, fascinated by the way she tucked a stray curl behind her ear.

"Me and Dee? Since the first day of sixth grade. Her father moved the family here from Cork just before the start of school. She and her brother Dermot started school their third day in the States."

Ewan recalled the way she'd spoken of the Cartwrights that day in the bakery, wondering if she knew how incredible her gift was, the ability to draw people in, to feed them, to slip into the fabric of their world.

Or maybe that was just what she did to him.

He studied her face as she spoke, near desperate to capture her animation, her fire.

"We had gym class second period, and everyone knew the drill. Showers, gym clothes and shoes. Even Deirdre. She'd come prepared," Kate recalled. "And Josh Burke, resident humorist of the sixth grade, thought it would be hilarious to take her gym things and hide them in the boys' locker room."

"Why is it I think I know what happens next?"

"Because you have a well-honed sense of justice? Anyway, there's Deirdre, beet-red and frizzy in her anger, tears of new-girl-in-school humiliation in her eyes, and I got mad. I stormed the boys' locker room, pantsed Josh Burke, and retrieved the stolen clothes. And in my moment of triumph, Dee stormed right in on my heels and laughed out loud at Josh in his tightie-whities with his Levi's around his skinny ankles. We've been close ever since."

Ewan laughed. "Remind me not to take your gym clothes."

Kate peered at him from beneath darkened, sooty lashes. "I can promise you, you'll enjoy it when I take off your pants."

Her eyes sparkled with unmistakable invitation and a punch of lust hit him in the gut. Before he was required to be clever in reply, Deirdre turned up with their drinks.

"Ready to order?"

Kate looked sheepishly at the untouched menus between them on the table.

"Another few minutes, then?" Deirdre tucked her notepad in her apron pocket with a laugh.

"Thanks, Dee." Kate gestured to the menus. "Maybe we should take a look."

"You don't know it by heart?"

"Fine," she admitted. "I do. I'm having a rare cheeseburger with sweet potato fries. And the amber lager on tap."

Ewan picked up his menu and made a show of reading it, peering over the edge to catch her eyes as he did.

"While you decide what you're going to eat," Kate led off, "I'm going to ask you all sorts of obnoxious first date-ish questions."

"You are, are you?"

"Mmhmm." She plucked the cherry from her Manhattan. "Did you know I sell Dee all the candied cherries for her cocktails?"

"No." Ewan flipped a page. "I didn't."

"I do. So, were you ever a little boy?"

Ewan looked up from the menu. "I was. Believe it or not."

"And where were you a little boy?"

"Brooklyn Heights. My parents own the building now, and rent the apartments I grew up in to consultants and boutique bankers."

"But you're not bitter about it?"

"Rack of lamb." Ewan closed the menu. "And no, not bitter exactly."

"Then what?" Kate sipped her drink.

"My grandparents owned the building when I was a kid, and it was like this magic thing that Gamma and Pup lived downstairs. When I was small, we lived on the third floor and my mom grew vegetables on the roof. My uncle and aunt and three cousins lived downstairs. With my sister, that was five kids. I was never wholly alone my whole life until I got my own place when I was twenty-eight."

He tasted the porter, and continued. "I used to hide out in the library in college, just to have quiet. Anyway, my uncle moved to Ohio for a job when I was ten, and my family moved downstairs. It was this big thing, moving down. My mother was thrilled. But I hated it. The new tenants upstairs got the garden, and my cousins only came back for Easter.

"Then my grandfather got sick when I was in college. They sold the building to my dad and moved to an assisted living village in Florida. Mom and Dad moved to the first floor, and my oldest cousin moved back to New York with his new girlfriend, and they rented the middle apartment for a while, before it all went to more transient tenants."

"Can I say, without a touch of irony," Kate said, "that I love that you still refer to your grandparents as 'Gamma' and 'Pup?'"

Ewan went pink at the ears, but Kate didn't notice.

She was caught up in the idea of his childhood. "I can't imagine. It sounds so romantic, growing up with Manhattan right there."

"It's just where we lived." Ewan shrugged. "It wasn't until I left that I realized people actually aspired to live there." He took another sip from his pint glass. "What's romantic is growing up here. It's like a movie with you and your friends running wild in pastures and forests..."

"There was a lot of Barbies and playing in the sandbox and bugging the crap out of Jack, too. It was all pretty normal."

"Not normal for a kid who chased his cousins through Prospect Park."

A young man with a shaved and tattooed head and an incongruously gentle voice came to take their order.

Kate rattled off her order, then raised her brows at him.

"The lamb rack, thanks."

Kate took his menu from him and handed both to the server, who wound his way to the next table.

"So, you grew up in Brooklyn." Kate started ticking items off on her fingers. "You have a sister and you love your grandparents a lot. So, where was this college where you would hide in libraries for quiet?"

"Bard College, it's in—"

"Red Hook. Hudson River Valley," Kate finished. "My parents made me look at it when I made them drive down to visit the Culinary Institute of America. Vassar, too." She ran a finger around the rim of her glass. "They were skeptical of my culinary ambitions and convinced I was smarter than I am."

"You don't strike me as a stupid woman, Kate."

"You're a smart man." Kate grinned. "Truthfully, I got into the CIA, but the money wasn't there, and NECI was the strongest choice after that. I never wanted a four year academic thing. I wanted to cook; I wanted to work in Paris."

"And did you?"

"I did. For a year I—" She broke off mid-sentence.

Ewan waited for her to continue. Wherever her thoughts were, the way her lips tightened told him it wasn't all good, but she came back to the conversation with a smile that appeared only half-forced.

"I lived in a tiny apartment with a Scottish kid who worked in a bar when he wasn't pulling shifts at the pâtisserie." She gave him a pointed look. "He taught me to make scones."

"How will I ever make that up to you?"

"I'm thinking of ways right now."

He had no words.

The inked server returned with their dinners in time to rescue him a second time. Ewan caught Kate sneaking a glance behind the bar. Deirdre was trying very hard not to watch them. Ewan made a mental note to buy the proprietor a round some time.

"This place is fantastic," Ewan said over a forkful of roast lamb.

"It really is." Kate picked up the fresh pint glass that had arrived with her dinner. "Dee hired a great cook and handed him her mother's recipe book. So you get pub-grub and classic Irish comfort food, as well as the whims of a creative young chef all in a local watering hole. That there's a really decent small brewery in town doesn't hurt things either."

"No, it does not," Ewan said, tipping his glass at hers.

Eating with Kate was an experience. She wanted to share her fries, and spoke lovingly about the grilled roll her burger came on. She stole two bites of his lamb, and had a story about a vendor or a colleague for every ingredient on their plates.

"You know," Ewan said, once the waiter had cleared their plates, "I once considered making a main character a chef. I would not have done him justice."

"*Him*?" Kate finished her drink.

"My first mistake."

He felt Kate's smile to his toes.

"I started your book a couple of weeks ago," she said. "I have to confess, I'd never read anything of yours before I met you."

"Before you barged into my office and called down a hail of righteous fury?"

"You're exaggerating."

To his delight, Kate hid a blush behind her glass.

"I never exaggerate." Ewan set his silverware down, wincing as the knife clattered. "I hate to ask, but now I have to know. Did you like it?"

"My righteous fury? I guess I enjoyed it."

Ewan shook his head.

"The book is…" she paused, searching for words. "I'm not a huge reader."

Ewan's jaw tensed slightly. Kate saw him brace for criticism; tenderness bloomed in her heart.

"I didn't want to put it down." She reached across the table and laid her slim fingered hand over his larger one. "I fell for Dearest completely, in all her wicked, broken glory."

Ewan looked up and held her gaze. "That's exactly how I think of her."

"I have to find out how it ends."

He wondered if they were still talking about his book. "I can't wait."

Kate curled her fingers around his. "Let's get the check."

KATE COULDN'T HAVE SAID HOW THEY GOT BACK TO HER APARTMENT, but she found herself backed up against the inside of her apartment door, Ewan's hands in the waistband of her jeans, her fingers working the buttons of his shirt, jackets tangled at their feet.

His mouth was clever and insistent on hers. The air around them was electric. Ewan's hands slipped up her back, his fingers cool on her flushed skin.

"Your skin feels as good as it looks," he murmured against her lips.

Physical pleasure and feminine pride reacted in her blood. She pulled away breathlessly.

"I have a perfectly good bed," she panted. "Or a couch if you want to go the making-out-like-teenagers route."

Ewan scooped her up, eliciting a squeak from Kate. "Which way to the bed, woman?"

"Straight back from the top of the stairs." She slithered down and wrapped her legs around his waist.

Ewan took the stairs with barely a hitch, navigating her living room while Kate whispered in his ear.

"Do you remember what Dearest does to Watson in chapter fifteen?"

Ewan groaned. "I wrote it, didn't I?"

She slipped back the fabric of his shirt and traced the line of his collarbone with her tonguc. "Let's give it a try."

Kate dropped to her knees onto her bed and pulled him down along with her. Ewan threaded his fingers into her hair. With his free hand, he gently unwound her artfully messy bun, curling locks falling between his fingers as he did. Kate hummed and stretched against him.

With her dark hair freed, he turned her, and with tender fingertips and warm, damp kisses found his way from hairline to the delicate strap of her top. As it fell away, he smoothed his palms over her shoulders. She melted back against him as one hand grazed a bare breast and other teased her taut belly.

She sighed. "I don't remember this from chapter fifteen."

"Shh. We'll get there." He unfastened her jeans and slipped them over her hips.

Kate reached for his hands, laid them both down and shimmied out of what clothing remained.

"Enough of these." She quickly unbuttoned his shirt. Ewan took his cue and shed his clothes.

Kate ran her hands down his chest, raking teasing nails over the line of muscle at his hip and stomach, and smiled knowingly at his reaction.

"I know how you feel," she said, guiding his hands.

When their bodies came together, this time there was no more room for words, only the hitch of breath. They explored one another hungrily, with hands and mouths, drawing out their desire until it was strung tight.

When their control snapped, they held one another and let the tide take them.

In the full and glowing silence which followed, Kate allowed her heart to slow. She shifted her body to cradle him against her.

"I see where Watson gets his skills."

"Dearest has nothing on you." He shifted in her arms.

Kate snuggled up against him and tugged the duvet up over her shoulders to ward off the chill she hadn't noticed, but she swung her legs over his, leaving her bare feet uncovered.

"Mmm. You're so warm."

"You paint your toenails," Ewan mused.

"Technically, Cheryl at Lacquer paints them, but yes," Kate said. "You seem surprised."

The sky outside her window was inky and starless; she hoped that the cloud layer would burn off in time for brunch at Rick's. She found that in addition to a pleasant soreness, she had a yen to walk in the morning sunshine with a man who made her blood sing.

"Your fingernails aren't done," he said, taking her hand and running his thumb down her fingers.

"It's not sanitary—" she started. He followed his thumb with his lips. Rational thought skipped like a record. "Don't start what you can't finish."

He rolled over her, capturing her mouth, still holding her hand. "I rarely do."

Kate woke tangled up with Ewan in her double bed. He threw heat like a furnace, but the covers had fallen away and she shivered, reaching to pull her duvet up under her chin.

The room was dark, but the cool blue glow around her blinds told her dawn wasn't far off. The cozy scent of smoke drifted on the air, and Kate at once applauded and cursed the drafty windows. Ewan stirred when she tugged a little extra blanket around her arms.

"Hi." His breath warmed the cool skin of her shoulder.

"Hi," she answered, rolling over to face him. "Do you think Jane Eyre woke up feeling this good?"

"Jane…Eyre?"

Kate giggled. "When you first turned up at the Damselfly, Anna told Nan you looked like Rochester."

"A cranky bigamist?"

Kate laughed out loud. "You're such a man. She meant a movie Rochester. All BBC, tall, dark, and brooding."

He attempted a moody scowl. "How's this?"

"Divine." Kate traced the line of his collarbone. "Very Timothy Dalton."

Ewan skimmed his palm over her hip, fitting their bodies together. Kate closed the remaining distance, pressing her lips to his, offering him her mouth.

"Mmm…hold that thought."

Ewan rolled off the bed, affording her a fantastic view of his ass as he padded naked to the bathroom.

Kate dozed while Ewan was in the bathroom, but when he didn't come back, she began to wonder. "Did you fall in?"

"Got sidetracked." He showed her his phone. "I shouldn't have picked it up."

"Anything good?" Kate leaned up on one elbow and pushed her hair out of her face.

When Ewan didn't answer right away, her curiosity was piqued, but she played it down. "Super-secret academic spy stuff?"

"Sort of…" Ewan set his phone down on the back of her sofa and started collecting clothes.

She sat all the way up, holding the blankets up around her bare chest. "I didn't mean to pry; I was just playing."

He stepped into his boxer briefs and pulled his T-shirt over his head, then scooped up his phone. He joined her on the bed, but she could tell he was halfway to somewhere else. It irked her.

"Don't let me keep you."

"It's not like that. I just got some news." He leaned over and kissed her. "I shouldn't have let it distract me."

His kiss was sweet, and her body responded, but she couldn't shake the feeling that there was something he wasn't telling her.

She swung her legs off the bed and pulled her robe from the screen that divided her bed from the rest of the studio. "I'll make coffee."

"It's still early, Kate. Come back to bed."

It was a tempting invitation. She banished thoughts of fizzy, champagne lust. God, she'd wanted him, and they'd had their fill of one another. That sparkling desire had been exactly what she'd told Anneliese was missing the night she'd gone out with Seth.

And now she could feel the effervescence slipping away into a void between them.

"Coffee."

The studio apartment gave her nowhere to hide, so she busied herself with the coffee grinder and pot. She was out of practice—another occupational hazard—but her fumbling gave her some cover.

The machine burbled to life and the fragrance of coffee filled the room. She let herself look back at Ewan, who'd returned to whatever he'd been reading on his phone. The screen threw blue light over his features in the dimness.

Frustration and worry played across his features; Kate fought the urge to smooth them away, despite her irritation.

She picked up her own discarded clothes and tossed them into a half-full laundry basket at the foot of her bed. The remainder of Ewan's things she laid gently over the back of the sofa.

He looked up. "You don't have to do that."

"I know." She made a show of setting his socks and shoes together.

"Hey." He left the phone, and crawled off her bed to take her hand. "What is it?"

"Just tidying up."

"I got an email from my agent. There's a project she's trying to line up; it would mean a lot more west coast travel than I'm used to, and the truth is, I'm not sure I'm up to it. I'm going to have to go to L.A. whether I'm ready or not."

So he was leaving. Already. Sitting in her bed in his underwear and planning his next adventure.

"I'm sure you'll be great." She pulled away from him and went to get mugs from the kitchen. "I don't have anything but skim milk and sugar. How do you take your coffee?"

"Milk is fine." He followed her around the peninsula that delineated the kitchen. "Kate? What's going on?"

"Coffee."

"You've said that three times."

"So?"

"I like coffee."

"If this is about L.A., it's just meetings for now, and probably not until after the semester is over. It doesn't mean I'm not here with you right now. I'm sorry I let it distract me." He wrapped an arm around her waist and nuzzled her shoulder. "I promise, I'm right here."

Kate broke free. "Let me get your milk."

"I don't want coffee."

She opened the refrigerator door too hard and something rattled inside. "It's pretty clear you want to go."

"I'd rather take you back to bed."

"I want you to go."

She reached for a glass liter bottle from Fuller Dairy, the smiling cow mocking her mood.

Ewan hadn't done anything wrong. Insensitive, maybe. He couldn't know that his casual mention of the end of the semester echoed another man's effortless dismissal.

"It's nothing, Katherine," Mathieu had said. His accented pronunciation—so romantic just a heartbeat before—felt pretentious. "Just some travel arrangements. My brother and I are going to New Zealand for a few months. After you go."

After you go. Not to work, not out dancing with Hamish and the crew from pâtisserie, not off for a weekend to Normandy.

"I don't know why, but you want to be angry with me," Ewan said. "I don't want whatever is in your head to come between us. Not now."

She pushed the milk bottle at him. "So, it's all in my head?"

He caught the milk, but it sloshed out, puddling on the counter. "That's not what I meant."

His eyes weren't the eyes of a man who wanted to leave. There was frustration there, yes, but also a plea. And the steady heat that burned there just for her.

The milk puddle began to spread, heading for the counter's edge. Kate tossed him a kitchen towel. "I know."

He mopped up the milk before it tipped over the edge, then carried the towel around to the sink to rinse it. He wrung it out and laid it carefully over the faucet. "I put my foot in my mouth."

There it was: the earnestness she found so sweet. "Again."

"It's a character flaw."

She could send him on his way, punish him for another man's sins, or she could give him the benefit of the doubt. A date, a handful of delicious kisses, mutual attraction, even their outrageous physical chemistry, these did not give them exclusive rights to each other's futures.

It wasn't Ewan's fault that she could imagine a hazy future with someone like him.

"I don't like coming in second to your phone," she said. Evasive, but not untrue.

He relaxed visibly. "You couldn't. You're amazing."

He reached for her, and Kate leaned on sass to close the gulf she'd opened between them.

"My father says I'm exhausting."

Ewan pressed a kiss against her temple. "Speaking of exhaustion, is there anything I can do to help you get ready for your day?"

"I think I'm good. Jim, Kim, and Margot will all be downstairs in less than an hour, and I'm ducking out later to meet..." She stopped, remembering that she'd wanted to walk with him in the sun. "Would you like to have brunch with us? I'm meeting Nan, Joss, Anneliese and

Chloe at eleven, over at Rick's Diner, and I'd like you to come, if you're not completely sick of me."

"They won't mind me being there?"

She shrugged. "They've been fans of you longer than I have."

"Fair point." He kissed her again. "Yes. I'd like that a lot."

Kate framed his face with her hands. "Whatever will you do with the next three hours?"

"I may take a nap." He yawned. "I don't usually do dawn."

She socked him playfully in the arm. "Don't you dare."

"You could always play hooky. Keep me from sleeping."

It was tempting, but the sun was up and there was work to be done. She gave over to the pleasure of kissing him, drawing out their parting until they were breathless, then leaning back to catch the dazed, hungry look in his eyes.

"I'll see you later."

THE MORNING NAP HE'D TEASED KATE ABOUT ELUDED HIM. INSTEAD, HE ate cereal at his desk and lost himself in Alasdair's first failed romantic encounter with Cordelia.

It was easy to imagine. Cordelia, like Kate, would be fiercely independent. Smart, self-sufficient. Not without temper. She would naturally clash with a bachelor who'd barely looked up from his work in a decade.

A brisk knock on his apartment door disturbed Ewan from his laptop.

"Come in," he said warily.

"Ewan?" He was fairly sure it was Nan. "I'm sorry to disturb you."

"Not at all." He got up to answer the door.

Nan was bundled up and waiting for him. "Are you ready?"

He was at a loss. "Huh?"

"Brunch?" Nan said. "Kate says you're joining us. And that we should pick you up on the way into town."

She'd made sure he didn't sleep through brunch.

"She's so bossy." He grabbed a coat from the arm of the nearby sofa. "I'd love a ride, if it's no trouble. Let me get my shoes on."

"I'll let you get yourself together," Nan said, "since I obviously disturbed you. Joss is waiting with the car."

She clomped downstairs in sensible hiking boots, and he reached into his pants pocket for his phone, which showed a missed message from Kate: *Asked N&J if you could ride with them. Okay? K*

He'd have to get used to being managed if he was going to get involved with this woman.

If. There was no "if" left. He was involved with her. It only remained to be seen where it would take them. He saved and closed the book file.

Nan and Joss were waiting for him in the driveway. Joss was shifting some boxes out of the back seat of the Jetta Wagon he'd seen around the Damselfly Inn.

He took a box from Joss and moved it to the trunk. "I thought you said it was no trouble."

Nan climbed into the back seat. "Oh, that's just a few things I picked up when we drove up to Williston to do the shopping yesterday. His truck was full of stuff for a job site, so we took the wagon, and... You're not interested in my big box shopping adventures."

"Actually, I kind of am. I can't imagine how you keep the place running. I guess a big box store is a necessity." Ewan got into the passenger seat. He looked back to Nan. "Are you sure you don't want the front?"

"Yeah." Nan laughed. "You're what? Six-foot-five? Sit up front."

"Six-three, but thanks."

Joss backed the car out and started out for town. "How are your classes going?"

"I can't complain," Ewan replied. "My students are really psyched about the material, and the work ethic is admirable."

"Trust me," Joss chuckled. "So is the play ethic."

"If the gray faces of my Monday morning students are any indicator, yeah," Ewan said. "But they show up."

“I have to ask,” Nan said, “are you working on a new novel? I kept seeing you with your computer.”

Ewan took a moment to consider how to answer.

“Oh,” Nan said apologetically. “I’m being nosy. Sorry.”

“No,” Ewan reassured her. “I have an idea for a book. I’ve been meaning to ask you about Ticonderoga and Crowne Pointe.”

“Revolutionary War stuff,” Nan said, eyes twinkling. “I’m intrigued.”

“I meant what I said about the cabin, too,” Joss added. “If you need a break from the noise, it’s really quiet up there.”

Ewan laughed. “This is pretty quiet for me. I live in SoHo.”

“Right,” Joss agreed.

“But if the offer stands, I might just take you up on it sometime.”

The easy downhill into town only took a few minutes. Ewan wondered for the first time how much his hosts knew about where he’d spent the night. They parked the car outside the diner and it stopped mattering. Kate was waiting on the bench outside, playing some complicated-looking rhythm game with Chloe Thompson. Anneliese came outside to join them as they all climbed out of Nan’s car.

“Look, Chlo,” Kate said. “Who’s that?”

“Mister Love It!” Ewan walked over to the sidewalk and Chloe sprang at him. He caught her and picked her up, hoisting her over his head like his niece and nephew loved.

“You’re so tall.” He tilted his face up and squinted against the sun to see her.

“I’m the tallest!” Chloe crowed.

He heard Joss lean over and stage-whisper. “I think I’m losing my favorite guy spot.”

Nan leaned against Joss, smiling in Ewan’s direction. “She’ll come back to you. Probably.”

Ewan held Chloe like an airplane and flew her to Anneliese while the little girl made extravagant motor noises. When she was safely in her mother’s arms, he turned to Kate and kissed her.

Kate tried to glare at him, but her lips wouldn’t curve down.

"I was going to tell you all that they've got a table for us as soon as we're all here," Anneliese said, "but I was just rather gallantly upstaged."

"Kiss for me?" Chloe asked, puckering up for Ewan. Ewan flushed, but to Chloe's delight, he kissed her cheek. Kate's smile was worth indulging Anneliese's sweet daughter.

Nan sidled up to Kate as they started for the entrance. Ewan caught her words, though they were low, intended for Kate. "Looks like you had a good date."

"Stuff it," Kate said cheerily. "Or I won't tell you a single juicy detail later when the boys aren't around."

Ewan looked helplessly at Joss, who only shrugged.

Anneliese opened the front door of the tiny diner. "We can talk about it over food. The table's ready, and my daughter needs breakfast. The four Cheerios and glass of milk she had this morning aren't going to cut it."

CHAPTER 19

The following Monday, Kate's phone rang at 7:30 a.m. She fumbled with the phone, catching it by its charging cable before tapping the screen to answer the call.

She sounded as bleary as she felt. "Hello?"

"Good morning, sleepyhead," Ewan laughed.

"Ewan." Kate cringed a little at the schoolgirl lilt her voice took on. "Hi. Good morning."

"What's on your agenda for your day off?"

"A whole lot of nothing." She stretched a toe out from under the blankets to test the air, then nipped her foot back under the covers. "Staying in bed is starting to sound more and more attractive." She dropped her voice low. "Wanna join me?"

"I have elaborate fantasies about just that," he answered easily. "But I have a plan, and I would love it if you came along."

Kate sat up, fishing around in the heap of discarded clothes at the foot of the bed until she found a camisole and a pair of fleecy sweats. "Oh, yeah? What's that?"

"I want to drive out to Crown Point to look around, take some pictures."

"It's awfully cold." Kate could hear the excitement in his voice, but it was well below freezing, and would be colder on the lake. She might be a native Vermonter, but she wasn't crazy.

"I've seen the wide range of outerwear in your apartment, Kate. It's like an L.L. Bean showroom."

"Fine." She grumbled, but her heart swelled. "Have you had breakfast?"

"I was going to grab some coffee at the wonderful little bakery downtown."

"Hold that thought. We need proper sustenance for touristy stuff." She switched to texting for a moment, firing off a quick succession of messages to Nan. "I'll pick you up in twenty minutes. We're going to the Damselfly. I'll commandeer Nan's kitchen and make French toast."

"What about her guests?"

"If the guests want my French toast, I'll make it for them too."

"You're something else entirely."

"Yup," Kate agreed. "Now, I need to put myself together. I never guest-chef with bed head. See you in a few."

True to her word, Kate pulled up to Lawrence House twenty minutes later. A happy thrill raced up her arms at the sight of Ewan waiting for her by the front door.

At the inn, they found Nan serving coffee in the kitchen. Two couples sat at the farm table.

"Morning, Kate," Nan said. "I pulled a loaf of cinnamon bread out of the freezer for you."

"You're my hero." Kate stretched up and kissed Ewan just where his hairline met his temple before looking at the other four people gathered around the table. "Good morning everyone; I'm Kate Pease, and this is Ewan Lovatt."

A short, balding man in a cotton-knit sweater and khakis stood and offered her his hand. "Curtis Croft. This is my wife, Elaine."

Kate shook his hand. "Pleasure to meet you all. I hope everyone's hungry."

The young couple opposite the Crofts moved over to make room for Ewan, who poured two mugs of coffee, handing one to Kate before he sat.

Nan set out a tray of muffins and a basket of fruit. "Kate owns the bakery in town. I promise, you're in for a treat."

~

EWAN MADE SMALL TALK WITH THE CROFTS AND THE YOUNGER COUPLE, a pair of shy newlyweds from South Carolina who were honeymooning on a tight budget. He loved that none of them knew—or cared— who he was. It was pure pleasure to watch Kate at the stove. She moved like a dancer— her body certain of the fundamentals, mind focused.

When she set down a platter of thick slices of French toast, rich and eggy with a vein of cinnamon swirling through each piece, even the young couple broke their reserve. Kate convinced Nan to sit; the scent of breakfast drew the remaining guests down from their rooms.

It was nearly eleven when they climbed into Ewan's truck to drive out to the Lake Champlain Bridge. Kate pointed out some of the local history as they crossed the lake.

"They say the cannon on the resort's lawn is from a ship Benedict Arnold scuttled in the bay."

Ewan soaked in the history and Kate's enthusiasm. "This is why I brought you along."

"And here I thought it was my good looks."

He reached over, skimming a hand up her thigh. "Those haven't gone unnoticed."

Kate plucked his hand from her jeans and dropped it back on the shift knob. "History time, Professor. You can explore my leg later."

He steered the Scout into the Crown Point historical site's parking lot.

Ewan let her take a photo of him against the view of the lake as they crossed the road.

"You don't look nearly so serious this way," she said.

The cornflower sky was feathered with clouds, but the wind off the water stung his cheeks.

"I'm sure my eyes are watering and my nose is red."

She laughed. "Are we researching a new novel?"

Ewan kept his reply casual to avoid the whole truth. "Yeah."

"Can you tell me about it?"

"It's mostly ideas at this point," he began. "There are two stories, really. One I was planning before I got to Thornton, which is why we came out here today. The other has been brewing since a certain brunette stormed into my office. My series hero needs a little magic in his life."

"Magic?

He caught a hitch in her voice, but her eyes were hidden behind her sunglasses.

"I think you do that well." The hitch was gone. "Dearest isn't magical, like a witch or anything, but the way she uses her surroundings and what she's learned growing up; it's a kind of magic."

"You see right through me." She did, and it unnerved him in the best way possible. "Dearest isn't supernatural, but I think she's magic. Twisted, cruel, and tragic, but magic."

Kate snickered. "If you like twisted and cruel magic, you'll love being here in a couple of weeks when mud season hits."

They prowled the site of the British fort, soaking up what heat the sun offered, then walked under the bridge and along the path to the Champlain Memorial Lighthouse. They read the placards together, wordlessly joining hands at some point as they explored. He couldn't have said who reached for whom, but he didn't want to let go.

"Speaking of cruel and tragic…and my project," he said. "What do you know about the Damselfly Inn. The history, I mean?"

Kate tilted her head sideways, keeping one eye on the path. "The whole railroad heiress thing? Or the ghost story?"

"All of it."

She shook her head. "Not much besides the basics. Some people think there's a benevolent ghost that haunts the place. I don't know. Joss knew the Swifts pretty well. They owned the house before Nan bought it; it was in Meg Swift's family for a couple of generations."

"I'll have to ask him."

"Why? Is the Damselfly in your book?"

There was a suspicious note in her voice.

"In a way. Is that okay?"

She paused, looking up at the lighthouse memorial. The sun was glorious. It picked up a thousand different hues shining in her dark hair. He was glad of his cold-weather gear while he waited for her answer; the wind off the lake that tangled those locks was frigid.

"I'm not sure." She flashed him a mischievous look. "I guess you'll have to let me read it." She turned away from the monument, starting down the road that led back to the parking lot.

Could he let her read what he had so far? Would she appreciate just how much she and her world had influenced him in such a short time?

When he didn't follow, she waved him along. "It's still early. We can drive down to Ticonderoga and be back for a late supper."

CHAPTER 20

Kettlebells were the devil's own handiwork; Kate was sure of it. After a grueling fifty-five minute class and a long stretch with a yogi classmate, Kate was certain she would never squat again.

She showered and dressed in the gym locker room, then set out on foot for Keller Hall and Ewan's office. The day was steel gray and still, the ground hard with frozen, dirty snow. Mud season would follow the first deep thaw, and gray would give way to brown for a few weeks. A lifetime of mud seasons still hadn't endeared them to her.

A stream of students filed out of Keller, swarming along the paths leading to the chapel, dorms, and dining hall. Most days, Kate would say she felt like a twenty-year-old. Until she was actually around twenty-year-olds.

She found Ewan at his desk. He'd started out reading from a stack of papers on his desk, that much was obvious, but his mind was somewhere far away.

"Professor?"

"Kate." The way he looked at her, blinking back to the present behind his reading glasses, curled her toes. "To what do I owe this welcome distraction?"

"My impatience, mostly." She stepped into his office and perched on the corner of his desk. "And maybe a little bit of hot for teacher."

He snaked an arm around her waist and pulled her into his lap. "You're incorrigible."

"I am." She kissed him, threading her hands in his hair. He laughed when her nose bumped his glasses, and she pulled back with a smile. "I'm also on my own this evening. Want to join me for dinner?"

"Very much. What time?"

Kate considered her day. "Seven?"

"I'll be there, but I should probably finish reading these essays before then."

She kissed him once more before leaving him to his work. On the walk back into town, she wondered what Ewan had been thinking about when she'd first arrived. Ever since he'd mentioned being inspired by her first visit to his office, she'd been curious about his new work. The idea that maybe he'd been thinking about her, or some version of her, was thrilling.

Margot was waiting for her in the Sweet Pease kitchen, clipboard in hand.

"I drove up to the new location with your checklist, and took notes like you asked. Kate, I know it's early to ask, but I'll have my certifications by the end of summer. Would you consider hiring me on full time?"

Kate took the clipboard, looking over Margot's assessments. The young woman was observant and detail-oriented, in addition to having the temperament and talent she needed. She'd been considering a place for Margot anyway, to have her take the initiative was gratifying.

"I would love to bring you on. It's obvious you enjoyed your visit to Cooper, but how would you feel about managing the kitchen here?"

"Managing?" Margot's face lit up. "Do you mean it?"

"I'll want to be on site there for at least a year, hopefully setting up a sous chef to manage that kitchen, so it would be a huge relief to have someone here who's familiar with how I like things run."

Margot bounced on the balls of her feet. "Would it be weird if I hugged you?"

"Not at all," Kate said with a smile.

Margot threw her arms around Kate and squeezed. Kate hugged her back.

~

EWAN TOOK A DRIVE OUT TO THE DAMSELFLY AFTER HIS LAST CLASS. HE was feeling brave. And curious.

Nan was at her desk when Ewan knocked.

"Ewan." She looked up distractedly. "What can I do for you?"

He stepped into her office and perched lightly in the chair opposite her desk. "Am I interrupting?"

She put aside the paperwork in front of her. "A little, but nothing that won't keep. What's up?"

"I meant to ask you when I was staying here, but it seemed…intrusive somehow."

Nan leaned back a little, rolling her shoulders. "I doubt that. What is it?"

"Do you know anything about this house's history?"

He could see that this was not the question she'd expected.

"Only a little. Joss is the resident expert. He did a lot of work here for the previous owners, and grew up next door. He told me about Faye Bartram, and the drawing."

"The drawing?" His heart rate sped up.

"Meg Swift, who owned the house before me, her family owned the house for generations. They bought it when Faye died, I think, and renovated it after the fire. Joss tells it better, but they found a drawing by their bedside shortly after they moved in. Legend says it was signed by Faye."

Chills crept up his arms. "Is it here?"

Nan laughed. "No. Joss never even saw it. It was just a family story, or so he says. Like I said, he tells it better."

"I'd love to have seen it."

"If it ever surfaces, we'll be sure to let you know, but why are you asking?"

"Well, I…" But he saw that she'd put it together by the sparkle in her eye.

"You're writing about her. Faye."

He felt silly, having been uncertain about asking her. "Yeah. My family is descended from one of Faye's maids. There's a diary. I always wanted to know more. When an opportunity my agent loved collided with the offer to teach here, I couldn't resist. Faye's proving to be a challenge, though, so I'm digging deeper."

She clucked her tongue. "You should have asked sooner. I'd have told you all of it. Or had Joss do it."

"Can you get me in touch with Mrs.…Swift, was it? I'd love to have her permission to use that part of the story in my novel."

"Molly Fuller, Joss's mother, will know how to find the Swifts. Can I put her in touch with you?"

"Would she mind if I stopped by the dairy? I hear it's quite the operation."

"She would love it."

"Thank you." He stood; it was time to let her get back to her work, but he was ridiculously eager to get his dinner date with Kate right. "Can I ask you one more thing?"

"Of course."

"It's kind of a personal question."

Nan sat back. "Oh?"

"I'm having dinner at Kate's tonight," he began.

"I know," Nan replied.

"Of course you do," he said quickly. "Anyway, I was going to bring wine, but I'm at a loss."

Nan's answering smile was brilliant. "I'm going to tell you a secret: Kate is a brilliant baker, but largely uninterested in cooking dinner food. I'm not saying she can't…"

"But she's more concerned with wedding cakes?" Ewan finished.

"Exactly," Nan said. "You can't go wrong with a red, but not something meaty like a cabernet." Nan pondered a moment. "Maybe a pinot noir?"

"I can do that."

"Or," Nan offered, "you can really wow her."

"I'm listening."

"Take a ride up to Vergennes this afternoon," Nan directed. "There's a specialty food shop that carries a Prosecco she loves. Ask the wine guy. He knows her."

Ewan felt his brow wrinkle with sudden envy. When Nan tamped down a giggle, he knew she'd caught him feeling jealous of the wine guy.

He made a lame attempt to save face. "I will. Thanks. I've been meaning to check out Vergennes."

"Of course." Nan slid back toward the desk with a knowing smile. "Enjoy your evening."

~

KATE SNATCHED THE HANDLED BROWN-PAPER BAG FROM EWAN AS SOON as she saw it. She was riffling through the contents and walking upstairs while he slipped out of his shoes and hung his coat on a free peg. He trotted up the stairs after her, snagging her back against him and speaking low behind her ear.

"You only invited me over for the treats."

"Right you are," she replied, sinking back against him. She held up the bottle of Prosecco he'd bought. "And how did you ever know to get this?"

"I'm resourceful," he muttered, turning her for a kiss. Her mouth tasted of mustard and thyme, the apartment redolent with the scent of roasting poultry. He recalled George Cartwright's advice: *Find yourself a girl who can cook.* Cartwright was a smart man.

"I need to check the sprouts," Kate said, pulling back. Still holding the Prosecco in one hand, she went to the oven and opened the door. She bent over and poked into the oven with a wooden spatula. Ewan appreciated the view.

She straightened, turning with a sly smile. "Were you checking out my ass?"

"Right you are." He echoed her earlier response.

She gave her rear a little wiggle before reaching to open the fridge and deposit the sparkling wine inside. Closing the door, she said, "I have a bunch of stuff in my Netflix queue. How about a movie with dinner?"

"The true test of my worth as a date."

"That remains to be seen." Kate sat on the arm of her sofa and swiped a finger over the trackpad of her laptop and an infinite scroll of choices waited for him. A romantic comedy and a recent Shakespeare adaptation vied for top billing.

"May I?" Ewan asked. Kate scooted over as he sat in front of her computer, typing into the search box. "They've got it," he said, turning the laptop to face her. He'd pulled up a cable-network drama that had been popular that fall.

Kate's answering smile was surprised. "I totally wanted to see that, but I don't have fancy cable."

"I missed it when it originally aired. I was teaching in Georgia and promoting *Moriarty's Daughter*. Too busy for TV."

Kate reached across him to click the title. "A series means you'll come back to watch the rest with me."

He slipped an arm around her waist, pulling her against him. He kissed her, gently working his hands under the untucked tail of her shirt. Breaking the kiss, he pointed out another advantage. "Hour-long episodes mean more time for this."

He certainly had his priorities straight. She pressed him backwards onto the couch. "We've got about twenty minutes 'til the chicken comes out. Want to make out?"

Her mother's chicken recipe perfumed the apartment, which might have been the only thing that kept Kate from abandoning dinner altogether. Ewan kissed her breathless. His touch promised without demanding, leaving her aching for his bare skin hot under her hands. Leaving her wanting all of him. Until the oven timer, and her growly tummy, tore her away from him.

They watched the pilot episode while they ate. Kate watched him watch the show; she analyzed him while he ate. He got extra points for going back for seconds. Experiencing her family's favorite meal was a crucial test she hadn't realized she was administering.

Ewan cleared the dinner dishes while Kate broke down the chicken carcass. She put the bones in the freezer and the meat into a glass container for the fridge.

"Shove over." She nudged him away from the sink with her hip and brandished her greasy fingers. "I have chicken hands."

"Is it weird that I find that completely sexy?"

"It is, but I'm okay with your brand of weird." She plunged her hands under the hot running water. He offered her a kitchen towel when she was done soaping and rinsing. "If you load the plates and stuff, I'll refill the wine glasses and we can watch the next episode. See if it..." She trailed off as she walked over to the coffee table where their empty glasses flanked the bottle, "...can hold our attention."

"I doubt it," Ewan said, dropping the silverware into the dishwasher caddy. "Chicken hands."

CHAPTER 21

Mallory's attachment to her phone was going to be his undoing. She called three times while he was teaching. Though his phone was set to vibrate, it was still painfully obvious that the professor's phone was ringing.

His students, of whom he was growing increasingly fond, couldn't help but give him a little attitude about it.

He returned his agent's call once he left the lecture hall. While he waited for her to pick up, he paused in a patch of sun and drank in the view. The Green Mountains were almost cozy from his vantage point, rolling along from north to south, still crested with white at the highest peaks, but softening as though they would see spring coming from the west. In the brilliant daylight, they begged to be traversed, but Ewan knew his limits.

"Hey." Mallory's voice yanked him right down out of the hills. "Everything okay up there?"

Not the question he'd anticipated.

"I think so," he said. "Why?"

"Faye's lost some of her sparkle." Mallory sighed. "The pages you sent me. They're…bland."

"They're not—"

Mallory cut him off. "They're bland. You can do better, so tell me. What gives?"

She wouldn't stop hounding him, and if he were honest, she was right.

"Fine," he said. "My heart wasn't in that bit. I've been toying with a love interest for Alasdair. She's magnificent. You'll love her."

"I'll love her more once we've negotiated a major contract for the series, which is infinitely more likely if you're a household name for penning an Oscar winner."

"Mal," he stopped her. "You're getting a little ahead of yourself."

"That's my job."

"Look, your books are beloved by NPR and critics no one reads, and you have this fan base who love your work. I can sell your literary fiction, but if you want to take the Alasdair Sledge stuff up a notch, we need something splashy."

"And a costume drama is splashy?" Ewan adjusted his bag on his shoulder and started to walk again. If he finished his grading, Kate had invited him to keep her company in the Sweet Pease kitchen.

"Mitch and Yvonne are a power couple; they've got connections everywhere. You'll see when you're there. This is going to be a game changer. You could end up being a regular collaborator."

Something about being labeled a collaborator struck him as wrong.

"I've got to go, Mal. Papers to grade, and apparently more pages with more…sparkle."

"Yes. You do. Email what you've got at the end of the week."

Ewan pocketed his phone and took a left toward Lawrence House. There was still time to finish the grading and maybe get something down to send to Mallory.

JACK'S ASSISTANT ANSWERED KATE'S CALL ON THE SECOND RING. "JACK Pease's office."

"Hi, Angela. It's Kate. Is my brother available?"

"Just a moment. Let me put you through."

"Thank you."

While bland hold music did what it could to entertain her, Kate wandered around her apartment, tidying up her bed, tossing dirty laundry in her hamper. Jack's smooth, clipped voice picked up after a moment. "Jack Pease."

"Hello, brother dear."

"Hey, Katie," Jack said slowly. "What can I do for you?"

"So formal," she teased. "It's almost like you know you've been bad."

She heard his sharp inhale. He would be drumming on his desk blotter while planes took off and landed across Boston Harbor from his thirty-eighth floor office.

"I'm sorry."

"Sorry for what?" Kate knew she was badgering him, but they hadn't spoken in weeks. Not since the engagement party.

"Sorry for not checking in with you in ages. Sorry for behaving badly and skipping town the weekend of the party. Sorry for—"

She cut him off. "You're forgiven, you know."

"I was an ass. No one here knows that, so it's easier to stay here."

"You were an ass." Kate laughed. "But Nan and Joss still love you."

"How about my sister?"

Kate heard wariness in his voice. Jack wasn't one to brood. His usual confidence made her feel like a wallflower. This tentative brother was a new animal.

"I will always love you. What choice do I have? It's not like you're going to stop being an ass any time soon."

"Mom says you're dating that professor."

Jack was apparently trying to dodge the insult. But was she dating Ewan?

"Maybe I am. We can talk about that in person."

"So, how is everyone?"

"I'm sure you've talked to Joss." Kate let an unspoken accusation hang for a beat. "So you know how they are, and how work is progressing on my new space."

"Fair enough." Jack sighed heavily into the phone. "How's..."

He stopped short, but Kate knew exactly who he meant. She debated just telling him how Anneliese was, but in the end whatever was going on there was none of her business.

"So," Jack began again, "do you think Nan will let me have Joss for a guy's weekend?"

"If you ask nicely. Which you'll have to call her to do." Kate grabbed a pad of paper from her kitchen counter. "And we should coordinate, since I'm doing the bachelorette."

"I can't do it until closer to the wedding, but Joss knows that." Jack sounded beleaguered. Kate figured her work was nearly finished.

"I'm not trying to be a nag, you know. I miss you. We all miss you."

"Got it," Jack said. "So, tell me how the expansion is going. Not the construction stuff, your stuff."

"Really well." Kate tucked her phone under her chin and reached for her binder. "Want to hear the changes?"

"You bet I do."

CHAPTER 22

"Who was it," Ewan asked, "and how crazy were they, to imagine heating sugar past the point of reason and then playing with it?"

Kate was poised in front of her cooktop, spooning amber strands of sugar syrup over a greased sharpening steel. As the filaments of caramel cooled, they hardened in fanciful curls and loops. She set the finished pieces onto a silicone mat inside a shallow-edged sheet pan.

"I would give you a culinary history lesson," Kate answered without turning, "but it would slow me down." She risked a quick peek over her shoulder at him. "And I don't think that's what you want anyway."

"No, you're right." Ewan had his small notebook open and was drawing the framework of Kate's body, a schematic of her bones and muscles as they translated to shape and shadow. His gaze flicked between the woman and the forming image. "I was thinking about going up to Montreal the second weekend of spring break."

"Oh?" Kate's tone was frost-dipped. He was aware enough of her moods to sense the shift.

"My friend—the one I mentioned a few weeks ago?" He didn't look up, but she didn't respond so it didn't matter. "Anyway, Chel invited me to spend a few days."

The cool silence continued.

Finally, Kate's steel clattered into the sink. Ewan looked up from the drawing to see her furiously scraping at a dollop of hardened sugar stuck to the counter. She turned to him with a smile, but it didn't reach her eyes.

"That sounds nice. I'm sure you'll have fun." Her words were sharp.

Ewan put his pen down with a sigh. "Is there a problem?"

"Of course not." She shrugged and returned to the sink, running hot water over her tools. She stared into the steam for a moment before snapping the faucet into the off position. "I know we haven't talked about whatever..." She gestured between the two of them, "this is, but I assumed it meant that for the time being we weren't involved with other people."

She reached into the sink, attacking the pot with steel wool. She put the rinsed pot on the rack in front of the sanitizer.

"I know that was stupid of me to assume." Her sigh wobbled. "But I thought—"

"You thought what?"

"Your friend Shell might be more than a friend," she finished in a half-whisper, swiping at her eyes. She didn't hear him step up behind her.

"Kate, what are you talking about?" He realized the mistake even as the words were coming out of his mouth. He spun her around and took a wet ladle from her hand. "Michel Gaultier: Canadian celebrity journalist, blogger, childhood friend. *Man.*"

"Oh god. Michel. With a horrible, un-French nickname." Kate pressed her forehead against his chest. "I'm an ass."

"Yes to all of that." Ewan agreed with a chuckle. "But it looks good on you."

He kissed her forehead, then tipped her face up. "I was going to ask if you'd like to come with me."

Kate's mouth dropped into an O of surprise.

"If it's too soon," Ewan backpedaled, "just pretend I never asked."

"All I've got coming up that isn't work is Nan's bachelorette, but I'm free that weekend."

Ewan took his phone out, typed in a text message, and pocketed it again. "Michel's relationship with his iPhone borders on obscene. He should—"

Ewan's pocket chirped.

Kate eyed Ewan's phone admiringly. "He is quick."

"He says next weekend will be fine, but we'll have to go with him to some sponsored party he's agreed to be at."

Kate clapped. "Does that translate to dancing at a ridiculous club and maybe free drinks?"

"Very likely." Ewan shuddered. "And photographers, annoying press, and impossibly dressed Canadian party kids."

"It's like Michel knows me already. Maybe I should date him?"

Ewan looked her over. "You're really not his type, but he might just make an exception."

"I see." Kate stretched up to kiss him. "I think dating you is enough for now."

"Are we, then?" Ewan's smile crinkled the corners of his eyes. "Dating?"

"I think we are," Kate admitted.

Ewan thought of Murray Sporinger's words earlier in the week. If he was being honest with himself, Kate was part of his decision to consider the offer.

"Kate," he said. "I—"

"What?" She bit her lip.

He started to speak again, but stopped. She was only just able to admit out loud they were involved with one another. Asking her to think about his future in town, or the possibility of a future together beyond the semester, seemed like pushing. Kate tilted her head in concern; he'd been silent too long. "I like 'dating.'"

"Speaking of dating." Kate pulled away, as if she remembered they weren't completely alone. "There's a string quartet playing at the college a week from Tuesday. I've got a wedding cake tasting at six p.m., but I'd like to see the performance. Want to come with me, maybe get a late dinner after?"

Ewan knew several members of the faculty would be at the performance, including Will and his wife.

"I would love to."

Kate looked over her work. "I'll call for the tickets when I finish up here."

"Let me do that." Ewan stopped her. "I've got clout."

Kate laughed. "Of course you do. I have to get started on tomorrow's production list. Go teach or something. I'll call you later."

"I'll look forward to that."

CHAPTER 23

Kate tied a jingling scarf around her hips and gave a little shimmy, loving the sparkly sound.

"That's it." Their belly dancing instructor nodded encouragingly. "When everyone is ready to begin, I'll take you through some beginning movements."

The dance studio was draped in gauze and softly lit. She, Nan, Anneliese, Molly, and their friends Penny, Priya, and Janelle watched the teacher demonstrate a series of fluid undulations. Kate was grateful for the yoga classes she'd taken, until she saw Priya mirror the instructor as though she'd been doing it all her life. Her friend had moves.

The music picked up, and everyone began to relax into the lesson, even Joss's mom.

A sweaty hour later, Kate felt more or less like a sex goddess, and Nan was flushed with happiness. They cleaned up and made their way the few blocks to a spa Kate had booked for makeup, nails, and blowouts.

Janelle gave a little staccato hip lift while they waited for a crosswalk. "Why have I never tried that before?"

"I haven't been out dancing since before I got married, but we should tonight." Penny twirled sinuously. "Not bad for a woman who spends all day with her hands in the dirt."

Molly laughed. "Penny, I've never 'been out dancing.' When I was young, we had bonfires with guitars and questionably acquired beer. Then I married a farmer."

"That seals it," Kate said. "After dinner, we go dancing."

In the end, it was Molly and Penny who stayed on the dance floor the longest. Kate hugged Nan while they watched her future mother-in-law shake and shimmy hip-to-hip with university students.

Anneliese leaned in. "Who knew my aunt Molly could do *that?*"

In the limo on the way home, Priya fell asleep on Penny's shoulder, and Janelle snuggled up to Kate. "You need to tell me about this man everyone is going on about."

"There's not much to tell." Kate knew she was hedging.

So did Janelle. "Your pants are smoking, Katie, and it's got nothing to do with your fine ass. Spill."

Kate let her head drop onto Janelle's shoulder. "He's a visiting professor. It's just a fling."

It wasn't, though, and she knew it.

"Bullshit."

Anneliese snickered. "What's she calling you on, Kate?"

"Nothing." Kate grumbled.

Janelle guffawed. "Her new man."

"He's nice," offered Anneliese.

"Nice?" Janelle lifted a flawlessly groomed brow. "Katie's never been into nice."

Nan giggled. "What Anna means is, he's kind. He's also a little awkward, kind of broody, and looks like Rochester."

"And which one of you is dating him?" Molly asked.

Kate laughed at that. "Me. Fine. I am dating him."

"I thought so." Janelle always raised smugness to an art form.

From her spot pinned under Priya, Penny was the one to point out the obvious. "He's not *only* a professor, Janelle. Kate's not telling you that he's also a critically acclaimed novelist."

Janelle turned on her. "Katie, you are in so much trouble."

The laughter woke Priya, who rubbed her eyes. "What did I miss?"

~

THE LIMO DROPPED PENNY AT HER HOUSE, THEN STOPPED AT FULLER Dairy for Molly. Nan had put Priya and Janelle in the Damselfly's bridal suite for the weekend, and sent Joss off to his cabin in Catmint Gap. Kate collapsed into Nan's bed, plumping a pillow under her cheek and turning to Nan.

"I haven't danced like that in years. I feel like I could sleep for a week. Did you have a good time?"

Nan mirrored her, eyes shining. "Yeah. Thanks, Kate. You're the best."

"I really am."

Nan snorted, which sent them both into a fit of giggles. When the laughter died down, Nan yawned.

"What's really going on with Ewan?"

Kate flopped on her back. "Why is everyone so obsessed with me and Ewan?"

Nan propped herself up on her elbow. "I'm not everyone, and I'm not obsessed. I just can't see why you haven't sorted him into the proper dating category and proceeded accordingly."

"Do I do that?"

Nan only blinked at her.

"Fine. I do. I just didn't think you noticed." She rolled back over to face her friend. "Aren't I allowed to play by different rules every once in a while?"

"He seems pretty smitten."

"He's having a campus fling. I'm enjoying it."

"Liar. And you know it." Nan let the accusation hang between them for a moment. "I've watched you dance through plenty of flings, casual relationships, hookups. I've watched half the men who've ever met you wonder if they had a chance, but I've never known you to be secretive or unsettled."

You weren't in Paris. That wound ached like the old injury it was.

"I'm not being secretive." She rolled away to avoid being less than truthful to Nan's loyal—and very perceptive—face. "We just haven't talked in a while, Ms. Engaged-to-be-Married Lady."

"I'm sorry. I don't mean to grill you. You're not avoiding me because of Joss, are you?"

"No." Kate yawned. "Sorry. I'm not yawning at you. I'm not avoiding you at all. Life gets in the way."

"*Life?*" Nan pushed her hair out of her eyes. "You're so full of it."

"Sometimes, yes." Kate burrowed into the blankets. "Things are just…complicated right now."

"Complicated? Is that what we're calling it?"

Nan's sarcasm wasn't enough to keep Kate's eyes from drifting shut.

CHAPTER 24

Ewan left the phone on his dresser with Michel on speaker. "Please tell me what you're planning."

"*Non, mon ami,*" Michel said, leaning hard on his slight Québécois accent. "Then you would talk me out of it or try to make other plans."

Ewan sighed. Michel was right. "You sound more like your mother with every passing year."

"My mother is a Frenchwoman," Michel said. "I could do worse."

"Your mother would never expect me to turn up in a foreign city without knowing what I should pack."

"*Bien sûr,*" Michel said. "Dress to impress."

Ewan looked at the carefully selected wardrobe he'd brought to Vermont. Blacks, grays, dark jeans, outerwear he still didn't fully understand. "I guess I'll just figure it out, then."

"I guess you will." Michel was still laughing when he ended the call.

Ewan folded a sweater and a pair of jeans to pack. At least he didn't have to worry about matching. Did Kate fret about clothes, or did she have that effortless knack for fashion that some women did?

The painted screen in the corner of her apartment was often decorated with discarded clothes, her hamper was frequently overflowing, and she always made his mouth water.

That had little to do with her clothing.

The vision of her boudoir screen draped in fabric gave him an idea. He pulled out his notebook and sketched it twice, then opened his laptop to search images of outdoorsy clothing for the turn of the twentieth century heiress.

He loved the idea of Faye in the golfing outfits, the white blouses and ties, so he drew them over the screen on the right, laid mindfully where a maid—someone like his great grandmother—would retrieve them for cleaning. The one on the left was Cordelia's. Here it was a hat, a belt, the trappings of steam-powered scientific pursuits, and a fanciful scarf.

His phone trilled; he half expected to see Michel's name on the screen, but it was Mallory.

"How's our movie coming?"

Ewan abandoned the drawing. "Good to talk to you, too."

"Guess where I am?"

The giddiness in Mallory's voice tipped him off. "Los Angeles?"

"I had lunch with Yvonne. I'm here for a conference, but I couldn't resist. Her place is adorable. She says the one next door is a vacation rental type thing. I think you'd love it, especially after a New England winter."

"It's spring here, or so they tell me." Outside, the gunmetal sky was threatening a cold rain, and the grounds were shaded in browns, patched with dull green.

"You're going to fall in love with this place. I know it."

Ewan looked down at the second screen he'd drawn, the tools of Cordelia's trade, the frivolous scarf. Inspired by a woman who lived and breathed less than a mile away.

"We'll see."

It never ceased to amaze Kate that just over the border was a city wholly European in attitude. The peppering of French, the cosmopolitan feel of the shops and restaurants, all of it made Kate miss Paris with a pleasant kind of homesickness. She'd been any number of times with Nan and her brother, but to walk the streets with Ewan and Michel was a treat. The two men had history, or rather Michel had stories and Ewan's friend reveled in embarrassing him.

"I have never seen a man so uncomfortable in a strip club, and that includes myself." Michel chortled. He was telling Kate about Ewan's first trip to visit after Michel's family moved from Brooklyn back to Québec. They'd been college students, and Ewan, despite his appearance as the worldly New Yorker, had his eyes opened amongst Michel's university friends.

"I'm still not comfortable in them," Ewan grumbled.

Kate slipped her gloved hand in his to dispel any grumpiness.

"Shall we hit Rue Sainte-Catherine after the thing?" Michel winked broadly at Ewan's scowl. "A lot of the old places are gone, but I'm sure we can find some trouble?"

"I think I'm too jaded." Kate rolled her eyes. "Tempting though it is."

Michel leaned around her to stage whisper at Ewan. "She does like you."

"I know. It's a shock." Ewan's reply was dry.

"So, what is this thing we're going to?" Kate asked. "Between dressing, dinner, and the tales of Young Men In Strip Clubs, you've neglected to mention it."

"He wasn't neglecting." Ewan smirked. "He was avoiding, because he knows I hate these things."

"*Vraiment*," Michel replied with an exaggerated shoulder shrug. "I do know he hates these things. But for *la jolie Katherine*?"

"I like him. A lot." Kate whispered and squeezed Ewan's hand. Even with two layers of leather and lining, she still got a thrill from holding his hand as they traveled the sidewalks.

"It's the premier party for the club itself," Michel continued. "Word has it the major investors are an Eastern European pop-star, a minor British aristocrat and the front man of that band from Vancouver that everyone in the US is going crazy for."

"Seriously?"

"That's what I heard," Michel dished. "I'll find out more. They want me here so I can 'leak' information when I blog about the party."

"Ooh!" Kate purred. "Can I be in your fancy celebrity blog?"

Michel adopted an aloof expression and began quoting his future-self. "American novelist Ewan Lovatt lent me his beautiful date for a few moments—"

Ewan growled affectionately. "Like hell."

"Ewan," Michel chided. "I promise not to steal her away."

Ewan grinned. "That's not what I'm worried about."

"Ah," Michel said. "You're afraid I will tell her the truth about you."

"And what's that?" Kate asked.

"That he is incurably grumpy," Michel said, waxing poetic, "and while the words from his brain are like twenty-year Scotch on your tongue, the words from his mouth are like stones in your shoe."

Ewan shot Michel a friendly warning look.

"I am sorry, but it's true." Michel's tone was anything but apologetic.

"I'll tell you a secret," Kate said, leaning toward Michel. "I know he's grumpy. But if he didn't occasionally put his foot in his mouth, I'd never have met him."

Michel's eyebrows pushed up, wrinkling his forehead. He touched the tip of Kate's nose with his gloved finger. "That is a story for later."

Kate batted Michel's finger away. "Oh, it certainly is."

Michel linked arms with her. "He never tells me the stories that make him look bad."

"No," Ewan interrupted. "Because you make enough of them up on your own."

Michel feigned offense.

Kate pulled them both in close as they walked. "This weekend was a wonderful idea!"

~

It was well after two a.m. when they made it back to Michel's apartment.

"Adieu." Michel winked saucily before vanishing into his bedroom, weaving slighting and texting, Ewan supposed, with the film critic who'd caught his eye at the club.

Ewan held the guest bedroom door for Kate, whose steps weren't completely steady either.

She put a hand on his chest at the doorway. "Chivalry is alive and well, I see."

Ewan covered her hand with his own. "The better to get you into bed, my dear." He dangled her shoes, which she'd abandoned in the lobby of Michel's building, from his fingers. "You're tired, remember?"

Kate gestured expansively at the guest bed, which resembled a luxury catalog photo shoot. "Not that tired."

She let her teeth scrape over her bottom lip, smoothing her hand up over his shoulder.

Ewan shivered.

Kate hooked a finger through her shoe straps, and with a little tug, freed them from Ewan's hand. She dropped them with a clatter and a giggle. Ewan hushed her half-heartedly, but the heat in her gaze was more than he was willing to douse.

He pulled her close, aligning their bodies from toes to lips, drinking in her warmth when she melted against him. He cradled her head in his hands, threading his fingers through the deceptively messy chignon of her hair, and growling when they struck the pins.

She would be his undoing with the hair pins alone.

Kate let her head fall back and her eyes drifted closed, but it was Ewan who surrendered.

While he worked the pins from her hair, he explored the smooth expanse of her throat with his lips, relishing her small sounds of pleasure. Each pin tumbled to the floor, the resultant pings an unsteady counterpoint to Kate's hitching breath.

She wound her arms around his shoulders and clung; he tugged the last locks of her hair free and drew the thin straps of her emerald sheath dress down over her shoulders.

When he paused to look at her, to marvel at her, she opened her eyes. He knew she saw his unspoken emotions there. He felt the pleasure and understanding ripple through her. Her lips curved against his, and again he was the one who surrendered.

She took a half-step back and reached for her zipper. With a glance calculated to bring him to his knees, she unzipped the dress and let it puddle at her feet. He had wondered how she'd managed anything at all under the slinky dress. Now he knew.

She hadn't.

From her painted toes to her tumbled curls, she stole his breath.

He started toward her, but she danced away toward the bed, giddily tossing Michel's artful throw pillows to the floor and peeling back the thick comforter. She climbed onto the bed and faced him, on her knees and in her skin, with all that wild hair gloried around her shoulders.

"Ditch the suit, Ewan. I want you."

His pulse jumped and he reached for his shirt buttons, his body betraying him. Kate leaned forward, arranging herself into a boudoir model pose that broke his control. He shrugged out of the dove-gray dress shirt Kate had chosen, yanked off his shoes and belt, and cursed his suddenly clumsy fingers.

All the while she regarded him like a cat's saucer of cream. She was his Siren, changeable and tempting, and she knew that in that moment he would have crossed hot coals to get to her.

Clothes dispatched, he was barely at the bedside when Kate pulled him down—onto his knees and into the endless softness of down and cotton, the endless softness of her skin, the endless heat between them.

He held himself above her, torn between lust and delight. "Do you always get what you want?"

"Mmhmm."

He snaked an arm around her waist and hugged her against his chest.

She showered him with playful kisses, ran her palms over the contours of his flesh, made him weak with her clever touch. She took his hands and put them on her body, falling back into the mattress and wrapping her legs around him to pull them together.

For a moment, Ewan held them both there, body to body, with the percussion of their pounding hearts marking time. He smoothed away a stray twist of hair caught in the corner of her mouth, then leaned in to kiss the spot. She sighed against his lips and rocked her hips to take him even deeper inside. When he felt her body close around him, felt the shudder roll through her like a tide, he surrendered to her for the third time.

CHAPTER 25

Kate woke when a bright bar of sunlight passed her eyes. She rolled over and blinked at the clock. Nearly nine in the morning. Ewan was gone, his pillow cool. The morning light sliced between the thick shades and the window casings, striping her bare legs where the sheets had fallen away.

She took a deep breath, caught the scent of coffee, stretched. She hoped the boys had left some for her.

She tugged on jeans and a soft, impractical sweater and made her way toward Michel's kitchen. Once in the hallway, her nose picked up a waft of warm dough, sugar and cardamom to accompany the coffee. She smiled to herself, imagining her feet lifting off the floor like a cartoon character, drawn to the food by the diaphanous whorls of flavor in the air.

"What will you do?" Michel's voice rose over the hiss of tap water.

"Do I have to know yet?" Ewan's reply was grumbled; just the sound of his gruff tones loosed a flutter of happiness in her belly. She paused at the end of the hall, curious about their conversation.

The water stopped abruptly, followed by the clank of stainless steel on china. "Yes, *mon ami*, you do. At least some idea. Katherine is beautiful and chic and very funny. She would sparkle anywhere, but she is a tree, Ewan. A birch, perhaps, wild, elegant, and able to compromise, but rooted nonetheless."

Kate smiled at the description. She wouldn't have summed herself up so, but much of it felt right.

"Two nights and a day, and you know that?"

Kate heard skepticism, but also a touch of sadness in Ewan's question. She knew this was the point where she should cough or shuffle her feet, but she found she needed to hear where the conversation was going.

Michel's response was serious in tone. "I do, just as you do, or you would not have brought her here. You have feelings for her."

She had to resist the urge to peer around the corner as the silence stretched out between the two old friends.

"Let me ask you something, then. What happens when the semester is over and it's time for me to go?"

"If I were choosing?" Michel said, "I would choose your Katherine."

Eavesdropping was a bad business; Kate had heard enough. "Choose me for what?"

She had to give Ewan's friend credit. He thought quickly.

"To attend every club premier with me."

"You are adorable." Kate hugged Michel before going to Ewan.

She relaxed into him, letting him take her weight, trying not to purr when he wrapped an arm around her, stroking her hip through the denim. This would have to be enough.

Michel toasted them with his coffee cup. "No, you are adorable. I'll need a week to recover."

Michel took them to lunch. Kate mentally added two extra workouts to the coming week. *Poutine* was a particular weakness of hers, and when in Quebec… They walked off the indulgent lunch, and Kate popped into a small shop for a sea green cashmere scarf she felt Ewan needed to have.

Something to remember her by, at the very least.

Long lines at the US border delayed the drive home, making it hard for Kate to avoid replaying the conversation she'd overheard. She snuck a glance at Ewan; he was still wearing the green scarf, though they'd ditched their coats in favor of the Scout's aggressive heat.

What will you do?

She reached for the radio dial, seeking a distraction, but was interrupted by her phone chiming from her bag.

She fished around for the phone. The text was from Joss. "Ooh."

"What's up?" Ewan's eyes stayed on the road, but she felt the almost physical sensation of his attention.

"Joss says the commercial appliance delivery is done. Sweet Pease North has a kitchen!" She grinned. "Ish."

"You want to stop in when we get there?"

Kate could see his smile in profile. "Do you really need to ask?"

"I don't." He glanced at her. "I can't wait to see it."

Kate couldn't either. She'd been busy with her bridesmaid duties, with the day-to-day running of the bakery, with phone calls and paperwork for the opening, but the reality of what she was about to do had seemed very far off. Suddenly that reality was about to be tangible: gleaming stainless steel, just waiting for her.

The hour passed in giddy anxiety. Kate knew she was talking Ewan's ear off with her plans and ideas, but he didn't seem to mind. His hand crept from the gearshift to her leg while she talked, and the easy warmth steadied her singing nerves. Joss hadn't elaborated, so she assumed everything had been delivered as planned, but she was desperate to touch the surfaces herself, to feel the oven door handles and the weight of the walk-in doors.

"How much more has changed since we were there?" Ewan asked.

A welcome heat spread along her arms at the memory of that stormy afternoon. "I'm pretty sure we won't have to sit on the wiring anymore."

Ewan slowed the truck and flipped the signal indicator. "I guess we're about to find out."

The "Opening August" banner fluttered in a breeze. Joss's truck was backed in near what would be the main entrance. Deep tracks in the cold earth spoke of a large truck's recent traffic. Kate picked her way across the mingled ice and mud in the yet-to-be-paved lower parking area. The boots she'd packed for Montreal were adorable, but hardly suited for off-roading.

Ewan took her hand to steady her, as he'd worn more versatile footwear. She thought she could get used to his chivalry.

She pushed the door open. "Joss?"

"Back here, Katie."

Ewan squeezed her hand and whispered, "Can I call you Katie?"

"Not if you ever plan to see me naked again," she whispered back.

"Duly noted."

"What's noted?" Joss came out of the kitchen area. His shoulders and ball cap were dusty, and a smudge of grime crossed the bridge of his nose and one cheek.

"Nothing. You've got a little something…" Kate reached out to poke his cheek.

"I'm sure." Joss ducked the poke and reached out to shake Ewan's hand. "Good to see you. How was Montreal?"

"Good. Except for the mistake of introducing Kate to my oldest friend."

"Yeah," Joss said. "Probably a huge mistake."

Joss turned to Kate, who could feel the pull of her kitchen from behind the newly framed walls.

"You ready, Chef?"

She could only nod. Joss stood aside for her.

They'd left the appliances in a rough configuration of the kitchen. Kate assumed that was for the benefit of the plumbers and electricians. She could see it, though. Could feel how it would work, flowing from oven to walk-in to cleaning stations. The long stretch of workspace was marked with plywood, but she could already sense it in her muscles, the dance of the kitchen.

"You look like you were born for it," Ewan said. He was leaning against the framed door opening. She wondered how long he'd been standing there watching her.

"I'm pretty sure I was, and this opportunity coming along when it did, exactly when I was ready for it? I'm not superstitious, but it felt like a sign."

"I wish I could be here to see it."

He meant what he was saying. She knew that, but the truth of it was like ice down her spine.

What happens when the semester is over and it's time for me to go?

"Maybe you can visit after the opening." She kept her tone bright. "Labor Day is gorgeous here."

A wariness she didn't like, but chose to ignore, crept into the slight wrinkles around his eyes.

"Maybe," he said.

Joss joined Ewan in the doorway, drying his hands on his jeans. The smudge was gone from his cheek. "How does everything look?"

"Amazing." Kate took Ewan's hand and buried her doubts. "Now, show us the rest."

CHAPTER 26

Monday's classes were slow. Spring break was still clinging to his students. His weekend in Montreal was clinging to him, but it wasn't like any hangover he'd ever had.

He was infatuated. Spring was emerging from the ground and he was tumbling helplessly into Kate Pease's web. Even his writing had shifted. Faye still waited in the wings of his imagination, but it was Cordelia who took center stage. He'd nearly drafted another Alasdair Sledge novel, and his poor hero was as confounded by her as he was by Kate.

He thought of Ryan Chandler's interview. So many of his own feelings poured into the story; it felt autobiographical—if he were a reclusive Victorian engineer and explorer in an alternative steam-driven computer age, whose heart had been stolen by a brilliant, head-strong micro-zoologist.

When Ewan's phone rang, he half hoped it was Kate, calling to distract him with baked goods or an adventure. She hadn't called in a few days, only texted replies to him. Tiny alarm bells were starting to ring, but he wasn't sure how to bring them up without starting an argument that would eat into the increasingly precious time they had left in the semester.

The number wasn't Kate's, or any number he knew, but he was glad to have answered nonetheless.

It was Thornton's resident bookseller.

Marian Muse's voice was both warm and brisk. She took no time getting to her purpose. "It would be a shame if I never got to host a National Book Award nominee in my shop while he was in town."

"I'm more proud of being shortlisted for the PEN/Faulkner, but the National Book Award does better for commercial recognition."

Marian's earthy laugh rang through the earpiece. "Read from *The Orchard Gate*, then. I loved it."

"I'd love to. I'm flattered."

It was settled quickly. He would meet her at her bookshop the following day to discuss the particulars.

Downtown Thornton was waking from its wintry slumber, and mud season was drying out. The bravest shopkeepers had optimistic window boxes and container arrangements out under a bluebird sky. He kept his eyes on the bookshop's bright yellow awning and black and gold wooden sign as he made his way down Kate's block.

Marian, like her voice, was both gracious and lacking in pretense. She was slim and soft, all silver and maple curls, batik scarf, and hemp bracelets.

"I just love your stories, you should know that. I'm shameless." She guided him past end-cap displays of local photography books and a table of regional poets to a cozy reading nook at the back of the store. Her view of the river, winding away below the falls, was spectacular.

"I'm glad. I like your selection. I read Larry Golden's poetry in college." He picked up a volume from a side table where it had been left, tracing the sticker proclaiming it autographed. "Is he as cranky as his interviews make him out to be?"

"Worse!" Marian stage whispered, glancing around as though she expected the octogenarian Northeast Kingdom poet to materialize from behind the stacks. "But he reads here once a year—at the college,

I mean—and always stops in to sign some copies for me, so I love him."

"I hope you'll love me, too." Ewan was smitten with the bookseller already. "After you see what an atrocious public reader I am."

"As long as you leave me with a pile of signed books to sell, you have my undying devotion."

He knew the moment he left Marian's shop that he was not going to be able to resist the call of Kate's foggy windows and fuchsia door.

The bakery's proprietress was, however, not in. Her staff muttered apologies that sounded like excuses. There was no sound from the kitchen, though, so he bought a muffin and a hot tea for the walk back to his apartment.

He hadn't made it two blocks when he ran into the woman herself. Kate was with Deirdre Temple, and the two looked as though they'd been to the gym.

"Good afternoon, Ewan." Deirdre waved. "Our Kate was just telling me about your trip up north."

"I hope only the good parts." He spoke to Kate's friend, but it was Kate he watched. Her silence woke those little warning bells again.

"And what fun would that be?" Deirdre said. "Kate, I'll leave you here. Robbie's minding the bar until I get back, then we're both off tonight."

"Robbie's pouring drinks?" Kate looked honestly shocked. "It *is* getting serious."

"Night, loves," Deirdre said with a wink, and sauntered away, gym bag knocking against her hip as she went.

"A class?" Ewan took in Kate's sleek form in her yoga clothes. Unlike her friend, she wasn't carrying anything but her phone and a keyring with a gym tag on it.

"Yeah. Bollywood dance. Dee was dying to try it, so I went with her. Earned my shower tonight."

"Let me walk you home." He fell into step with her. "I volunteer to wash your hair."

She turned sharply, so much so that he expected a rebuke. Instead, there was an astonished grin on her face that defined "saucy."

"I think I just might take you up on that offer."

THE MAN KNEW HOW TO WASH HAIR. HE'D MANAGED TO SOAP THE REST of them both, before and after they'd made love in her narrow shower stall.

Tangled up with him on her bed, her wet hair like a rope over her shoulder, Kate was sorry she'd avoided him for those few days. Their time together was dwindling. Having him in her bed like this was a precious luxury.

"Where've you been?" He stroked her arm from shoulder to wrist.

Goosebumps followed the trail of his fingertips. The sun still set early, and her apartment cooled quickly.

"Busy, but that's no excuse." She wriggled a bit, snugging herself into the curve of his body. He was warm and solid beside her, and the feel of his skin against her soothed an ache she'd been ignoring since they returned from Montreal. "Where did you learn to wash hair?"

His laughter rumbled between them. "I've never done that before."

She craned her neck to look at him. "You're not lying."

"Nope. I just take quickly to pleasurable tasks."

"Mmm. You do." She peeked at the clock on the wall in the kitchen. "I have a cake to start tonight. Come over and keep me company."

HE WENT HOME TO GET HIS LAPTOP, THINKING HE WOULD USE THE TIME at Sweet Pease to catch up on grading papers.

Andy waved him through to the back just before closing; Kate was already busy at her massive stand mixer. For a moment, he simply stood by the swinging door, fascinated by the wet smack of the paddle in whatever wonder she was whipping up.

She didn't notice him until she turned off the machine. She dipped a clean offset spatula into the bowl. "Buttercream?"

"I've never been a frosting man," he said. That wasn't going to stop him from trying.

"I'll convert you." She watched him lick the spatula.

This was not grocery store frosting. It was silky, both delicate and rich. He let the buttery sweetness melt on his tongue. She was a witch. There could be no other explanation.

"Italian meringue. This is just a blank canvas. The groom is adamant: only vanilla cake. The bride wants a bunch of flavors, so I'm doing different fillings and flavored buttercreams on the four tiers."

"I volunteer as taster," he said, leaning around the bowl to kiss her hello.

"Looks like you brought work." She shot a glance at his laptop case, and waved at her corner. "You can use my desk."

He set himself up while she raided her pantry, but he overestimated his ability to focus on anything but Kate. He raised an eyebrow when she emerged with a large bottle of dark rum.

She laughed. "Rum buttercream to cover the tier and caramel pastry cream between the layers."

"You'll need a quality control check, right?"

"I thought you weren't a frosting man." She set down her ingredients, and headed for the walk-in fridge. She returned with several citrus fruits and two containers. "I'm going to be mixing up sample batches. You're not missing anything yet."

He took the hint and unpacked his computer, but he couldn't resist the draw of watching her work. She hummed tunelessly while she stirred and scraped, often stopping to inhale the contents of her mixing bowl.

She looked up from testing a lime and caught him staring.

"Key lime buttercream for a mojito themed tier. You want some?" She fished around for a clean spoon.

He drank in the sight of her, ratty yoga pants and sturdy clogs, long, lean limbs and wicked expression. If you'd asked him two months before what was sexy about a woman in a chef's coat, he'd have found himself at a loss, but Kate, in her hot pink coat and baker's cap, with those few loosely curling tendrils lying against her neck, offering him a spoonful of creamy, sweet perfection...

"Ewan?" She was watching him, brow furrowed.

"Sorry," he said. "Got distracted by those sexy Danish shoes of yours."

"Ha." She waved the spoon and its contents over the bowl, then handed it to him, and went back to her mixing.

It was divine. The tang from the lime rind balanced that buttery sweetness, and a hint of something he hadn't seen her add gave it extra depth. "That is amazing. I may never leave."

He realized his error before the words were out of his mouth, but Kate said nothing. He thought maybe the corners of her lips tightened, but she was too intent on her frosting to be sure.

He set the dirty spoon down with the others by the dishwashing station and returned to his work with a heightened awareness of Kate's mood. They worked in silence for a while, but Ewan couldn't help but replay his gaffe. He needed a distraction, or he'd say something even more stupid. "Am I allowed to make coffee, or are there rules about that?"

"Hmm?" Kate looked up from a bright pink cream she was stirring raspberries into.

"Is it okay for me to make us some coffee?"

"Oh, yeah. Can you use a French press? Andy gets grumpy with me when I mess with his espresso machine."

Ewan located the kettle and French press on a shelf above the stove. "I doubt Andy ever gets *grumpy* with you."

Kate caught his meaning with a lazy smile. "Jealous?"

Perhaps he'd overthought his earlier slip.

"No. You know," he said, coming up behind her to kiss the bare back of her neck, "I'm not jealous at all."

CHAPTER 27

"I've never seen this many people in here." Nan whispered.

Kate absentmindedly nibbled a biscotti. Vellichor was packed. "Marian should have ordered the pastries from me."

The turnout at Marian's book shop confirmed that the women—and a few of the men—of Thornton were curious about Ewan Lovatt.

"Reader, reader, gossip..." Kate whispered to Nan over the rim of her plastic champagne flute, running down the line for autographs. "Definitely gossip. Little of both. She'll Instagram that faster than you can hashtag *selfie*."

"Won't we all?" Nan was carrying a bag full of hardcovers, but she'd avoided the official signing crowd. They stood aside watching the queue as it wound around the vegan cooking section and spilled over into textiles and fiber craft.

Kate gave the bag a significant look. "I'm getting those signed for you, I assume?"

Nan lifted the paper bag like an offering. "Would you like them now?"

"I'll take them home with me. Right now I need to look cool and mysterious. Otherwise, what will Mrs. Thompson and her bingo crew have to talk about while they wait?"

Nan was giving her a look. “Easy now. Jane Thompson is practically family to both of us.”

Kate rolled her eyes. “I know, but I just get the feeling that they’re not thrilled about Anna’s current situation.”

“Joss says they were pretty strict with her growing up.”

“I didn’t pay that much attention, honestly. I just feel like Anneliese is being treated like a teenager. She’s been married. She has a child, for chrissake.”

“Which for strict, traditional people, probably stings. And they let her stay there until she gets her feet under her.”

“I just don’t remember her being so… deferential to everyone all the time when we were kids.”

“I don’t know.” Nan nudged Kate’s arm. “The woman who asked your boyfriend to my engagement party wasn’t very deferential.”

Heat bloomed on Kate’s cheeks. “He wasn’t my boyfriend then.”

“So, he is now, Ms. Cool and Mysterious?”

Kate let a touch of the foolish grin she was feeling show in the curve of her lips.

Nan didn't hide her smugness. “That's what I thought.”

Ewan looked up from inscribing the front matter of three copies of *Moriarty’s Daughter* for Reverend Marcotte’s wife. The unrepentant heat in the glance they exchanged would be news by morning, but Kate found she didn’t care.

Nan tapped her shoulder. “It looks like Marian is trying to flag you down.”

The bookshop owner was, in fact, waving and weaving her way toward them through the crowd. Kate snuck a peek at the refreshment tables and wondered if Marian was going to ask her for emergency backups. Whoever she’d ordered from had clearly underestimated the draw of a tall, dark, and brooding writer with a penchant for strong, memorable heroines.

“Let me go see what she needs.” Kate set down her plastic flute and touched Nan’s elbow. “Will you be okay for a few?”

Nan laughed out loud. “I’m not the new girl in town anymore. And

I'm going to be a Fuller by the end of the summer. I can handle your absence for five minutes."

Kate met Marian halfway to the front of the store.

"Kate, Ewan says you know where his office is." Marian was flustered, which was rare. "I'm sold out, but he says he has a box of books in Keller Hall." The bookseller brandished Ewan's faculty lanyard. "Would you mind terribly?"

Kate glanced back to the signing table. Ewan was making small talk with a buyer. Only a touch of tension around his eyes betrayed how little he enjoyed this part of his career.

"Sure, Marian. I'll grab my van and be back as soon as I can." She took Ewan's lanyard from the bookseller, and slipped out the front door.

EWAN LOOKED UP JUST IN TIME TO SEE KATE LEAVE THE BOOKSTORE.

He blinked, realizing the town librarian was waiting for him to finish signing her copy. He focused on her again. "I'm sorry, I got distracted for a moment. Who should I inscribe this to?"

"Kitty Williams, thank you."

He scrawled his name below the inscription and pushed the book across the table, cursing the thirty people still in line.

KELLER HALL WAS DARK, BUT EWAN'S KEY CARD GOT HER INSIDE. SHE took the stairs as quickly as she could, not wanting to leave Marian in a lurch.

The key to his office hung from the ring along with the key card. Inside, she flicked on the lights. The box of books was wedged into the corner of the room, but it was his desk that caught her attention.

He'd left pages on the blotter. She peered over the desk, ignoring the guilty butterflies in her belly. Not pages, but a printout of a travel itinerary.

Highlighted meeting times. A hotel reservation. Los Angeles. June.

A handwritten note from a woman named Mallory.

If we're lucky, we'll have to find you a little bungalow so you can FINISH!

The desk seemed to swim away from her. It was one thing to know with her head that Ewan would move on, and sooner than she was ready to face. Seeing his plans in writing knocked her sideways.

Her phone chimed. A text from Nan popped up: *Do you need a hand?*

Instead of replying, Kate hoisted the box, and deposited it in the hallway so she could lock Ewan's office. She hauled the box down the four flights of stairs and into her waiting van.

Patrons were spilling out of Vellichor. Kate could hear the laughter and chatter from half a block away with her windows down. She wanted to be one of them, giggling with Nan about the crowd again, exchanging hot glances with the author, but the evening's glamour fell flat.

Marian was waiting for her to take the books to Ewan. She handed them off. Nan was chatting with some women Kate recognized from the local craft guild. Ewan was still signing books. She could see that he was tired by the set of his jaw.

She placed Ewan's lanyard around Marian's neck. "Do you need anything else?"

"Nah, hon. I think we've got it."

"Tell Ewan I'm sorry, but I don't feel well, please, Marian?"

Marian's eyes creased in concern. "You okay?"

"I just need some quiet." Kate mustered a smile, then let herself out the door on the heels of a couple still bent over their freshly autographed books.

EWAN LOOKED UP FROM THE LAST COPY OF *MORIARTY'S DAUGHTER* hoping to find Kate's face across the room.

Nan was still there, laughing with a group of women. Marian was ringing up a few stragglers. Kate was nowhere to be found.

Marian saw him searching the room, and handed the register off to an employee.

"I didn't want to interrupt before. Kate asked me to tell you she wasn't feeling well. She went home to get some rest."

Nan had seen them talking; now she made her way over. "What's up? Where's Kate?"

"She must've had a headache or something. She looked kinda pale. Left and said she needed quiet."

Nan was looking at him with questions in her eyes, but he had nothing to answer them.

"Marian said she went to get more books from your office," Nan said. "I texted her while she was there, but she didn't answer. When I saw Marian with your books, I assumed she was back."

"I'll stop by her place before I head back to the apartment," Ewan said to Nan. "I'll ask her to text you."

He thanked Marian for the signing, but she was already shooing him out the door with a knowing expression. "Go find your woman. We can settle up another time."

The bakery was dark. The light over Kate's apartment door was dark, as were her windows. He tried her number, and got no answer. His gut told him there was no headache, but that didn't make him feel any better. He'd have bet the advance he didn't have yet that she wasn't up there.

Halfway back to his apartment, he stopped for a moment to catch his breath. In the distance, the falls rushed and roared through town. He found the sound comforting.

Comfort. Where would Kate go for comfort...besides Nan's inn?

In his haste, he hadn't bothered to look down Gristmill to see if her van was in its spot. He texted her a quick where-are-you, and turned back for downtown.

Her van wasn't in the lot, so he fished his keys from his coat pocket and unlocked the Scout, grateful he'd left it there instead of back at his apartment. He had a pretty good idea of where to start looking for her.

His hunch paid off, and twenty minutes later he parked the Scout behind her van in the dirt parking lot outside Sweet Pease's unfinished expansion.

He found the chef sitting on the unfinished landing outside the door by the light of the security floods. Her hands were pulled up inside the sleeves of a fleece pullover to ward off the wintry chill that lingered over late March.

"Kate. What happened?" Ewan closed the truck's door. The sound of his feet on the cold dirt was too loud in the country silence.

"When were you going to tell me?" In the glow of the security lights, she was pale as a china doll.

"Tell you what?"

"About L.A.?"

"I told you about that weeks ago." He crouched down in front her. "What's going on?"

"I saw the note. In your office. About a bungalow and the hotel, and it seemed so real. You leaving. I wish you'd said something."

"Jesus." Ewan raked his hair back. "Half of that will get canceled and rescheduled six times before it happens. If it happens. Mallory is my agent. She's got her teeth in this Faye Bartram thing of mine. The truth is, Kate, I don't know when I'm leaving. I have the apartment until a week after commencement, but nothing's certain beyond that."

"Shit." She cradled her face in her hands.

"That's not the reaction I was expecting." His knees were killing him. "Do you want to finish this conversation inside?"

"We can't." Kate looked up at him. "I grabbed the van's keys, but my key to this place is on my other ring with the ones for the bakery."

"I don't mean to laugh…" But he was. "It's cold. Can we at least do this in one of the cars?"

"Do what?" Wariness crept over her features.

"The part where I explain about L.A."

He held a hand out to her.

She took it, but didn't move toward the van or his truck. "What does L.A. have to do with a book about a New York railroad heiress and a small Vermont town?"

He wanted to tell her. He started to explain, but it didn't make sense anymore. A chance conversation, a question from a director to a literary agent, and suddenly he was forced to choose between Kate's smile in a crowded room and his career?

"I sent my agent some pages. She has contacts in Los Angeles who want to be involved. She thinks this thing could mean the difference between critical success and big franchise, Reed Sharpe type fame. She wants my indie titles to get picked up by a publisher."

"What do you want?" Kate asked.

Every unspoken question he could imagine, every conversation they weren't having about the direction they were heading, played out in the silence. Ewan heard them all, but he didn't know which one he should grab on to.

"I'm not sure," was all he could say.

She dropped his hand, trading it for her keys. "I owe you and Marian an apology, then."

"You don't owe me anything, Kate. But talk to me. I just hadn't had the chance to bring it up."

"I'm still sorry. I spoiled your big night."

Levity, then.

"I hate those things. At least after the first five people."

"I know we were going to get a drink after, but I'm worn out, and I have an early morning tomorrow."

He swallowed his disappointment. He didn't want to let her slip away while there were bruised feelings and confusion still between them.

"It's okay. I should get back to Vellichor and collect my things. Marian doesn't need all that taking up her space. Will you be okay driving home?"

Kate's smile fell far short of sassy. "I'm a big girl. Are we still on for the chamber concert?"

"Yeah. Of course."

He watched her get in her van and drive away, wondering what exactly they were doing.

The bookshop's windows were lit gold across the river when he approached the village. Marian had a check for him, and was tidying up the shop. He apologized, letting her draft him into helping her with the cleaning.

Marian, he learned, rented out two apartments over the shop, and lived in a log cabin in an apple orchard two towns south. Her partner played cello in the Vermont Symphony Orchestra and taught private lessons through Thornton College's performing arts department. When she said good night, she was off to feed her chickens, since her kids were at art class.

He drove his truck back to his apartment, wishing all the while that it was Kate's tiny apartment he was heading to. He pulled into a parking spot with a faculty sign and dragged himself up to his own cramped space. The adequate furnishings and bland decor taunted him. He'd done his best, but he was a spartan traveler. Most of his favorite things were in his apartment in New York.

He thought of his apartment in New York, of his parents' brownstone, of some anonymous bungalow in West Hollywood or wherever such things were. None of his spaces called to him like the fuchsia awnings at Sweet Pease or Kate's apartment above.

Marian's tales of chickens, apples, and wild, artistic children had filled him with longing. Not for precisely that life, but her comfortable satisfaction. Partner, kids, poultry, trees… What would his satisfaction look like?

When Kate's face filled his thoughts, he had his answer.

CHAPTER 28

Ewan video-chatted with his sister and her kids the next morning—a rare treat, since their internet was spottier than his. After doing a strong round of Chewbacca impersonations for his niece and nephew, he switched to voice-only and brought his sister up to speed.

It took his older sister all of four minutes to home in on his love life.

"You like her. Hang on: Enough you two! I'm trying to talk to your uncle!" Ailie interrupted his story about Kate and the Stone Garden to yell at the twins.

Ewan held the phone away from his ear while she hollered, amazed at her perception. "I haven't even told you her name yet."

"Sorry, Ewe. Go on."

He did his best to describe Kate, trying to sketch her with words and failing. The irony wasn't lost on him.

"Have you brought her flowers for no reason?" Ailie had asked. "I don't care how *unconventional* you say she is, she should get flowers for no reason. And I'm sure she'd love Bainbridge. Just saying."

He sighed. "I'll let you know when we get to the traveling together point."

"You *just* told me you took her to meet Michel."

His sister was still laughing at him when he ended the call.

Ailie's advice stayed with him, though, as he contemplated the tickets in his wallet for the string quartet.

Not long after, Ewan pulled the Scout into the garden center under a dark March sky that hinted at rain. He imagined Prospect Park would be starting to wake up, but here in the Champlain Valley, everything green still slept under the late-winter mud.

The hint of damp, verdant earth in the air suited his mission.

He stopped the idling engine and pulled the keys. There was a florist on the main drag, but he wanted something living. Nothing cut and pre-arranged for Kate.

The young woman he found in the greenhouse looked familiar. She was all of seventeen, sporting a Coulson's Lawn & Garden smock over ratty jeans and worn combat-style boots. She wore her dark, green-streaked hair in a long braid down her back. The name on her tag read *Danielle*.

When she looked up and greeted him, he asked, "Have I seen you at the Damselfly?"

"Yeah. I pick up some extra hours there on weekends if Ms. Grady needs me." She set down her shears and paused her pruning. "Can I help you find something?"

Ewan pressed his lips together. Faced with this scruffy but serious young woman, he suddenly felt this whole errand was a bit silly. Roses from Josephine's would have been fine. She continued to look at him; he caught a flicker of teenaged pity and steeled his resolve.

"I wanted to get a plant for my…for a friend's apartment. Something colorful." He pushed his hands deep into the pockets of his coat and studied a nearby flat of seedlings.

Danielle appraised him, doing her best to hide a patently teenaged smirk. "Does your friend garden, or is this just for decoration?"

"Just something pretty for her table. I thought it would be better than cut flowers…" He trailed off under the teen's scrutiny, but the girl arrived at a quick decision and came out from behind the counter she'd been working at.

"She'll like this." Danielle picked up a glazed ceramic bowl on a wide saucer, full of crimson, gold, and fiery orange cacti, their velvety pads filling the gaps between the blossoms. "They're grafted, but as long as they don't get over-watered, they'll do fine in warm, indirect light."

They were perfect.

"Did I say, 'she?'" He wondered aloud, feeling that flower buying shouldn't be this fraught.

"You said, 'her table.'" Danielle picked up the pot and headed toward the cashier's station near the door, throwing back a knowing glance at him. "And I know Ms. Pease a little from the Damselfly."

The arrangement hadn't set him back nearly what flowers cost in Manhattan, and that was about all that could be said for buying a woman flowers in a small town. Bad enough that Danielle had both known him, and known who the flowers were for without his saying, but teenaged girls weren't known for their discretion.

The dish of cacti sat on the dresser in his room, looking wildly out of place. A peal of laughter in a bland and soulless space.

They were perfect. In that, Danielle had been absolutely correct, and Ewan couldn't wait to give them to Kate. She might be too busy for dinner before the concert, but she'd probably make time for flowers, and to make up for the office incident, he'd managed a table somewhere special for afterward.

He contemplated a dress shirt, but went with a cashmere sweater and wool trousers. He understood that Kate wouldn't require him to dress up for her, but he also knew she'd appreciate the effort.

And he wanted to impress her. More than he was comfortable admitting, he wanted to impress her.

KATE HUNG UP THE PHONE AND SHOOK OUT HER CLENCHED HAND. A few long strands of hair clung to her fingers where she'd twisted a curl nearly into a knot talking to a vendor. She examined them, looking for early onset gray. On days like this she wanted to ditch the expansion and just go back to decorating wedding cakes in the back room of her parents' house.

"What was I thinking?" She spoke aloud to the empty room, and nearly dropped her phone when it answered her back.

"That you want more?" Her brother stood in the doorway between the kitchen and the dining room. "That you'd be amazing with more space to grow into, but you can't do that without the right stand mixer?"

"Jack!" Kate forgot the frustrating conversation with the restaurant supply warehouse and launched herself into her brother's embrace.

He hugged her hard. "You okay?"

"I will be." She stepped back, hands on her hips. "It's about time you showed up."

Jack had the grace to look ashamed. "I already said I was an ass."

"Do I get the real scoop now?"

Jack took a seat on one of her kitchen stools. "Nope. I figured I was overdue for a trip home, and Joss and I are taking Walt suit shopping tomorrow, so..."

"That's adorable." Kate perched opposite him, drawing her legs up and wrapping her arms around her knees.

"So," Jack went on, "I stopped by Mom and Dad's. They sent me over to invite you for dinner if you're free."

Her stomach flipped. "I'm not...free, I mean. I have to finish up here, then I'm going to a concert at the college with Ewan."

Jack missed very little. This was no exception. "Not so much maybe dating as actually dating?"

Kate paused; Jack pounced.

"Definitely dating." He leaned forward, hands on his knees. "Do Mom and Dad know?"

"No!" It came out more desperately than she intended. "I mean, yes. They probably know because everyone knows everything, but I haven't said anything, because I'm not sure where it...how long he'll..." She looked at her brother helplessly. "He's only here for a semester. There's no need to get their hopes up."

"Theirs? Or yours?"

Kate was grateful Jack questioned her gently. "I plead the Fifth."

"That right there is enough evidence for me." Jack stood, and jingled his car keys. "If you ditch your boyfriend later, we can grab some late night egg sammies at the Miss Morgantown. I'll even let you drive."

"I can drive, so you can interrogate me?" She did love that car. And late night breakfast food. "You're on. But brother dear, you have your own share of interrogation to face. You've got some explaining to do."

A flush rose up Jack's neck, and he pocketed the keys. "On second thought, maybe you should bring the writer."

KATE STOOD WHEN THE HOUSE LIGHTS CAME UP, WISHING IT WAS appropriate to whistle at a chamber concert. Around her was a full house, packed with students and faculty from the college, and more than a few familiar faces from town. They were sitting with some of Ewan's colleagues, including the Dancys, who were Sweet Pease regulars, and the English Department Chair, Murray Sporinger.

Kate loitered in the lobby with Meg Dancy while Ewan and Will brought the cars around. A gusting rain storm had blown in late afternoon, and the men were feeling chivalrous. Dr. Sporinger kept them company. He was already acquainted with Meg, and Meg was a big fan of Andy, Kate's favorite employee. Small talk came easy.

That ease was a blessing. She'd felt off balance since the night of Ewan's signing, though he showed no evidence of being upset at all. Somehow, she couldn't quite find her equilibrium again.

"Did you grow up here, Ms. Pease?" Dr. Sporinger asked.

"I did, and please, call me Kate. I spent some time away during college, and lived in France for a year, but other than that, this town's where I want to be."

The elder professor considered her for a moment; Kate thought about asking him what was on his mind, but Ewan and Will returned, shaking rain from their hair.

"Goodnight, Dr. Sporinger," Kate said after Ewan said his farewells.

Ewan's department chair kissed her hand. "It was a singular pleasure to make your acquaintance, Kate."

"What was that about?" Ewan ushered her outside to where the Scout idled, warm and inviting in the driving rain.

"I have no clue."

It was still raining when they returned to her apartment door. Ewan stepped inside to get out of the rain. She couldn't have said who reached for who, but a moan escaped her when he backed her against the entryway wall and threaded his fingers into the long tail she'd pulled her hair into. Kate sighed when a car passed his idling truck, honking at them on its way up Gristmill Alley.

"The door's still open," she said.

"So?" His smile invited another lingering, longing kiss.

"You're killing me." Her voice was hoarse.

He whispered in her ear, the brush of his stubble raising goosebumps. "Ask me in, then. I promise, we're on even footing in that department."

"I can't." She laughed, rubbing her cheek against his clean-shaven face. "My brother wants to talk, and I haven't seen him since…" Her voice trailed off as she considered the night of Nan and Joss's party. Her belly warmed at the memory of that first kiss.

"I know." Ewan kissed her one more time; this time a chaste good night. "Go, eat waffles and bacon with your brother." He touched her face with one fingertip. "I'll come by the bakery tomorrow between classes."

He climbed into the truck and shifted it into gear. He looked back to her, his expression full of naked wanting. Waffles and bacon with Jack seemed less important with every passing heartbeat.

"Ewan!"

He got out of the truck, but left it running. Seeing him standing there in the street-lit rain, Kate saw everything missing from every other man who'd been in that position before.

"If I texted you later, could I come by if you're still up?"

"I'll be up."

~

"WHAT CAN I GET YOU, HON?"

Paula had been serving the Pease siblings and their friends late-night breakfasts since high school. She was of an age with their parents, and had been working at the diner since forever.

Kate folded her menu. "Fried egg sammie with sausage and cheddar on a bagel, and a coffee frappe."

Her brother's menu was untouched. There were unfamiliar shadows deep in Jack's eyes; she wondered if something was bothering him, or if it was simply a matter of long hours at the office.

Paula turned to Jack, pen poised. Her smile was a touch mistier when she looked at Jack. He'd been close to both her kids; he'd dated her daughter Jenna, and Craig, the son she'd lost in Afghanistan, had been a regular around the Pease table growing up. "Two eggs, sunny side up, bacon, and cream cheese on an English muffin?"

The corners of her brother's mouth lifted at her remembering his favorite combo. "And coffee, please, Paula." When the waitress flipped her pad closed, Jack asked, "How's Jenna?"

Paula grinned. "Pregnant with her third. A boy this time. Poor little thing won't stand a chance, bossed around by all those girls."

Kate recalled that Jack's senior prom date was now married with two step-daughters, and two little girls of her own.

"Is Jenna still in DC?" Kate asked.

"As long as Geoff keeps his seat," Paula replied. "I hope it's long enough for me to get down there to visit."

Jack touched Paula's arm gently. "Give her my best, okay?"

Paula returned to the kitchen, and Jack took advantage of the lull in the conversation.

"So, Ewan Lovatt."

"Yep." Kate opted for keeping it simple.

"My assistant says she read one of his books for her book club." He paused as Paula returned to pour his coffee and deliver Kate's frappe. "You're dating a book club author?"

"I guess so." She dug a sundae spoon into the whipped cream. "I love this place."

But Jack wasn't having small talk. "Seriously, Katie, it's not like you to get into something like this without a plan. And an escape clause."

Kate thumped her glass down on the chipped Formica hard enough to startle the moon-eyed couple in the booth behind her brother. "What does that mean?"

"It means..." Jack kept his voice even while he added a couple of cream packets to his mug. "That I never catch you getting involved with someone temporary—with anyone, really—without establishing some boundaries, some structure."

He tore open three sugars and continued. "And you can't even give me a straight answer about whether you're dating the guy. 'I guess so,' isn't structure."

An angry comeback about Jack's flavors-of-the-month in recent years—not to mention his behavior at his best friend's engagement party—rose on her tongue, but she bit it back.

He was right about her.

She'd flown by the seat of her skinny jeans since she first confronted Ewan about the *Rose and Talon* quote. She'd ignored or dismissed his visiting status in favor of a couple of shared adventures and the delicious thrill she got just from being in his company. She'd flown off the handle at the idea of his inevitable departure, and let him twist in the wind when she couldn't get her shit together.

She'd forgotten, in the giddy rush of unpeeling his gruff public persona, to protect herself, and in those unguarded moments, she'd fallen into something much deeper than her failed Parisian love affair had even been.

Paula returned with their orders, and laid the handwritten check on the table between them. "If you two don't mind? Take your time eating, but my shift is over in ten minutes, and I need my beauty rest. Jenna is driving up with the little girls in the morning."

Jack eyed the bill and reached for his wallet. He handed over some bills with a smile. "No problem, Paula. It's late. You take care of yourself."

Paula pocketed the cash. "You're a sweetheart, Jack." She patted Kate on the shoulder. "You both are. Give my best to Cora and John."

When Paula headed for the register, Kate picked up her egg sandwich. "I can't be mad at you when you leave Paula a twenty-dollar tip on a fifteen-dollar meal."

"Craig was a buddy." Jack shrugged, and the love she felt for her brother swelled in her chest. Jack could be an ass, but he had a huge heart.

"Which reminds me," she said around a bite of warm egg and gooey cheese, "what's the deal with you and Anna?"

Jack choked slightly on his food. Clearing his throat, he looked at her with a touch of panic in his eyes. "I thought we were talking about your boyfriend?"

"He's not my boyfriend."

"There's no deal with me and Anna."

Kate wiped some errant ice cream from her lip. "Liar."

Jack finished chewing. "Pot. Kettle."

DESPITE HER TANGLED UP FEELINGS AND BEING GRILLED BY HER brother, she'd been thinking about Ewan since she left him. She couldn't get the image of his rain-kissed hair falling over eyes full of desire while he waited for her under the street lamps.

The rain had stopped, a cold wind off the lake replacing it. Jack's car purred away toward their parents' house, leaving Kate outside her apartment under a dark, quilted sky.

The sweet heat of their earlier kiss warmed her on the walk up the hill to Ewan's lodging. She pulled her phone out down the block from Lawrence House.

Still up?

His reply was instantaneous. *Very much so.*

She was no stranger to the odd booty call, but she really was a liar if she denied that this was so much more than a flirtation. So much more, even, than a short term affair. They were careening toward a cliff. The question was: would they stop in time, or tumble over, and did she care?

By the time she got to the porch, Ewan was opening the front door. He led her upstairs; the light touch of his hand around hers electric.

The click of his door in the jamb was like a starter gun. Kate wrapped her arms around him, stretching her body against his, feeling him shiver. When their mouths met, Kate released her hold on him to shrug off her jacket.

He touched her cheeks. "You are beguiling."

"I should have dated more writers."

She was playing, but his words nestled deep in her heart.

His writing desk was jammed under a window that faced County Road and a lonely green space. On the desk, his laptop slept. She thought of all the words in its memory, all the beautiful stories they would become. She let her eyes wander over the desk, covered in notebooks and sketchpads, index cards and reference pages.

Her own face looked up from the pages, at different angles, hastily penciled silhouettes, detailed blue ink drawings on college ruled notebook paper, her form in period dress, evolving from Victorian socialite to steampunk dream girl.

There were sketches of her, the Stone Garden, and the college. He had handwritten notes about moments they'd shared. His observations of her friends and neighbors spilled out over the desk: Nan's face, deep in concentration. George Cartwright's gallant carnation. Elisha McNair's tight physique.

He'd drawn an elaborate chart of Thornton, all points radiating out from a square in the center marked *Damselfly Inn/Bartram House.*

"Are we all just novel fodder? You didn't leave much out."

"You're the only woman I know who is offended at the idea of being someone's muse."

"I'm not offended, I just…" Tucked under his caption was a soft penciled outline of her sleeping face that he must have done from memory. Kate's breath left her all in a rush. "Muse?"

"Muse." The word took on the surreal quality of overused terms when he said it again. He turned back and leaned across her to close the laptop. "I don't use that word lightly. You're the only living woman who's inspired me like this. You've changed the trajectory of my writing."

Every time she thought she might be able to watch her step with him, he cracked open her defenses. It was too easy to just let him sweep her off her feet. She'd already thrown caution to the wind and let him into her life, why not embrace being his muse for as long as they had one another?

He called her beguiling; she would beguile.

"Is the bedroom over there?" She gave a little hip wiggle in the direction of one of the three doors off the main room.

"The other one." He gestured to a half-open door. "Do that again."

"What?" Kate shimmied. "This?"

Ewan took hold of her hips, tasting the sensitive skin from ear to shoulder. "Both."

Kate stepped away from him, improvising a series of moves from the bachelorette class that ended with her shirt trailing from her hand as she danced toward his bedroom. Ewan followed, but she pinned him in the doorway with a look, rolling her hips invitingly.

"You should take more of those classes."

Kate looked him up and down. "If I'm guaranteed to get this good a reaction, I may just."

She stripped down to bare flesh for him, reveling in the uneven pulse at his throat.

"Kate."

She laid herself back on his bed. "Come here, Ewan. I want you."

He was out of his clothes in a beat. She rolled him over and slid down his body, taking the silky hardness of him in her mouth. She drew out her teasing until he rocked his hips and moaned. It wasn't mercy when she slithered up his body, pressing her hips against him, giving him a taste of the wet warmth that waited.

She laughed out loud, delighted when he sat up. He brushed her nipples with his fingertips, bent to kiss one, then nuzzled the soft underside of her breast. She ground against him, ready for all of him, then gasped when he pushed her back and disappeared down her body.

Her first climax hit her fast and hard. She'd hardly had time to catch her breath before his clever mouth drove her up again. When she called his name, he chuckled. She felt the rumble of his laughter against her thighs.

"You taste like heaven."

"Come here, Ewan."

He did. He paused briefly to search the drawer next to his bed. When he joined her, they were both past reason. She took the length of him, matching his thrusts until they were both spent.

Kate slept by his side, waking at first light. She dressed in the half light, then smoothed the hair away from his face.

"I'll see you later."

He kissed her goodbye without fully waking, and Kate walked back to her apartment as the first fuchsia streaks of sunrise bled over the Green Mountains.

CHAPTER 29

Ewan woke to an email he had been waiting for. Will's historian connection had come through. A descendant of the Bartram family living in Lake Placid not only had some artifacts and papers belonging to Faye's father, but was also willing to tell him family stories pertaining to their mysterious ancestress.

He needed a breakthrough. While Alasdair and Cordelia were muddling along at a good pace, he couldn't find the rhythm of the Faye story. He wasn't sure if it was the film format, the story itself, or his own issues getting in the way, but it wasn't coming nearly as fast as Mallory expected.

He'd told Kate he would stop by Sweet Pease, but the visit, however tempting, would have to wait. He taught his morning class with one foot already out the door.

With his students on their way, Ewan shot a quick text to Kate, letting her know he had an errand that would take him out of town overnight. He considered adding a little something sexy at the end, but he couldn't shake the feeling that it was more ridiculous than sexy. He gassed up the truck just south of downtown Thornton, then looped back around campus and headed toward Chimney Point and the bridge to New York.

As he wound his way northwest into the Adirondacks, Ewan's voice recorder worked overtime. The prospect of meeting a living Bartram mingled with the memory of Kate's skin under his fingertips, and his imagination overflowed with story ideas. He jumped between the two books, dictating whole sections of both while he drove.

The Olympic ski jump took him by surprise. The snow was mostly melted in Thornton—only dirty plow piles remained in the college parking lots, and the mud was rising—but the silent, snow-covered alpine structure rose up above the tree line like a frosted sentinel.

Ewan pulled the truck over and got out, then reached back into the passenger seat for his notebook. The ski jump had no place in his current project, but to not sketch it would be wasting a tremendous opportunity. It was too interesting not to come back to; a moment's observation wouldn't set him too far behind.

A twig snapped, revealing a fully grown buck a stone's throw from where he stood by the side of the road.

Twelve points. Silent and unconcerned. Ewan froze, unable to look away. For a long while, they merely regarded one another. A truck passed, tossing salty slush onto the shoulder, and the deer leapt into the shadows.

The ski jump hulked over him, reminding him why he'd stopped, but he wanted to be on his way. Ewan snapped a photo with his phone. Not the same as putting pencil to paper, but good enough for the moment.

KATE HEARD HER PHONE CHIRPING, BUT THERE WAS NOTHING TO BE done about it. She was in the walk-in, pulling trays of pastries to proof overnight for Margot's shift. Without a free hand, whoever was looking for her would have to wait.

Once the pastries were secured in the proof boxes, Kate dug through the pile of papers on her desk to find her phone. The chirping had been Joss calling.

His voicemail was tense and clipped. A frozen pipe at the job site.

Water damage, material damage, timeline setbacks. Something about an inspection.

Kate looked at the wall clock in dismay. She had at least another hour of work to do at the bakery, but the light was fading, and she somehow thought any damage would look worse under the harsh work lights at the winery's barn.

The wedding cake she'd planned to start could wait until after closing. The library copy of *The Orchard Gate* waiting on her nightstand would have to wait.

That thought surprised her. She couldn't ever recall wanting to get back to a book, but Ewan's prose was so intimate, such an extension of the man he was, that she couldn't wait to read every word he'd published.

After asking Kim to lock up the back when they closed the bakery at six, Kate headed off to the parking lot at the bottom of Gristmill Alley.

It wasn't until she checked her phone again in the parking lot that she noticed a missed text notification from Ewan, and remembered he'd been planning to stop by earlier that day.

The warmth that kindled in her chest at the thought of him was especially welcome in the damp March chill. She could smell the green and brown of mud season in the air, and she knew that the steam from the sugar house at West's Farm would be rising over the Stone Garden.

See you tomorrow, maybe? Call me. She sent the message off with a little flutter, the heady mix of nerves and anticipation reminiscent of an adolescent crush.

She thought, as she drove, that the disappointment of Ewan's absence didn't sting too much, because she had so many plans and ideas for the remaining time they would spend together. She'd almost fooled herself into thinking she had come to terms with his impermanence.

Still, his absence wasn't made any easier by daydreams of his body tangled with hers in her double bed.

Once the van was in gear, her thoughts shifted to Sweet Pease North and her anxiety stretched with every mile she drove.

She passed the sign directing syrup tourists and Christmas tree cutters west into the valley. It was not lost on her that thoughts of Ewan had infiltrated many of her favorite haunts: the Stone Garden, Temple, the Thornton College campus, and now she wanted nothing more than to bundle up and take him to West's for sugar-on-snow before the sap stopped running.

The alchemy of hot maple syrup and snow, the collision of sticky heat and ice, taunted her. It was an imperfect comparison to Ewan and her, but there was a lesson in there about tackling the sweetness before it transformed from something soft into rock candy.

She would take him for sugar-on-snow and a real conversation about what exactly they were doing together.

Her brother was right; she didn't usually do undefined relationships. Casual, with clear parameters, was more her style. It was easier to live life on her terms without heartache and messy entanglements.

They could decide together. Put on the breaks, or rush into the abyss, but either way, they would know where they stood.

If Mathieu had been honest with her, maybe she wouldn't be in this position now.

The sight of her banner below the winery's sign brought her out of her head. She turned down the driveway hoping the "Opening August" part of the announcement wasn't off the table.

Joss's truck, as well as a few others, was parked near the lower entrance to the building, and in the quickly diminishing daylight, she could see that he wasn't alone. There was a crew busy inside.

An older man sat in the driver's seat of a running car, writing furiously.

She opened the door with her heart in her throat, but what greeted her was less a disaster scene than she'd expected. One of Joss's guys was running the Shop-Vac in the future service counter area, and she could see where the water had pooled before they'd started cleanup.

Joss heard the door and looked up.

"Hey, handsome." Kate fell back on levity until she had the truth of it. "What happened?"

"Bad luck," he said, shrugging in the direction of the cleanup effort. "We had windows open yesterday to ventilate and it looks like one didn't get closed all the way. It snapped cold overnight and a pipe froze. Stupid mistake, Kate. I'm sorry."

Kate tried not to let her frustration turn into anger. Joss was her friend; her best friend's fiancé. He was also excellent at what he did. And didn't she know that even the best had tough days? "So, what happens now?"

Joss shoved his hands in his sweatshirt and looked her in the eye. "The good news: the guy who left the window open owned up to it and is leading the cleanup. I'll eat the cost of that and we'll re-plumb the section that was damaged. We still have open stud bays, so there's no real impediments to the repairs."

Kate looked again at the young man vacuuming. "You scared the shit out of me."

Joss looked away.

Rarely had Kate seen him so ruffled. "And the bad news?"

"The guy you passed on the way in is the building inspector. He was supposed to be here today to do the rough inspection on the framing for your tasting room, but we weren't quite ready for him because I had the guys cleaning up. Looks like we caught him on a bad day. He says he can't come back for another week, and that's going to hold us up."

Kate crossed her arms over her chest. "Well, shit."

Joss's mouth tightened. "I'm sorry about all this. More sorry, maybe, because you're a friend, too. I'll suck up to the guy when I call his office, see if I can get a better reschedule. If I can't, I'll make the time up later. We've still got a long window before the summer soft open."

"Otherwise known as your wedding reception?"

"Yeah." One corner of his mouth betrayed his happiness, and any irritation she might have felt melted away.

"Can I help?" She looked around. Every hand was on deck, but maybe she could pitch in and speed things up. "I have a wedding cake to finish back in Thornton, but I can stay for a while."

Joss's gaze followed her around the room while his crew worked. "They've got it, but it means a lot that you offered. Go home and get the cake done so you can torture that poor novelist."

"He's out of town tonight. You guys have plans?"

"Nan wants to start the seating chart." He shook his head. "I told her I thought a buffet and some picnic tables would do."

Kate pursed her lips. "She gets points for not wringing your neck."

"Every day."

One of the guys waved him over, and Kate felt his attention shift.

"I'll call Nan later, see if I can get you out of seating chart hell."

"You're the best, Katie."

In the end, she worked late into the night on a hand-painted water lilies-style cake for a couple who'd fallen in love in Giverny.

She checked her phone for a reply from Ewan, but there was nothing to indicate he was going to be back, or where he'd gone and why.

So much of him was still a mystery. What was his second project? Was this part of his novel research? He'd called her his muse, which was flattering in the extreme, but she found that she didn't want to just inspire him, she wanted to be part of his work.

She wanted to be part of his life, but inspiration or not, he had no plans to stay beyond May, and it did her no good to linger on it now. She'd decided to keep it casual and let him go, and that was that.

She'd survived what she thought was heartbreak once.

Knowing better, she hoped she could survive the real thing now.

CHAPTER 30

Call me, Kate's message had said, so Ewan decided to make the hour and a half drive back to Thornton after dinner with Jeannie Starr.

The whip-thin, silver-streaked woman in her eighties—looking easily ten years younger in fleece and flannel-lined jeans—had met him at the door of her Craftsman cottage a half mile from the Olympic skating facility, and welcomed him in a deep, melodic voice.

"This house got here on the train, straight out of the Sears & Roebuck catalog. My uncle was the station manager." She pointed to a family photo on a nearby shelf. "Family connections to the railway, but you've figured that out."

Jeannie showed him books of photos and documents, let him take pictures of names and dates, told him a little about her uncle, who'd been a cousin, once-removed to Faye, though the generation had a huge age gap. Faye's adventurous, spinster life was nearly over when Jeannie's uncle was born.

The uncle had collected family memorabilia all his life, and Jeannie took over when he'd grown older. She knew more about the Bartram family than Ewan had hoped, and her enthusiasm was intoxicating.

"Your great-grandmother was her maid? Faye's?" Jeannie had read through his great-grandmother's diary with rapt attention. They'd talked all through dinner, with Ewan's recorder lying forgotten but running on the table between them. Now, with the hours of conversation safely downloaded to his laptop, he couldn't wait to flesh out his story.

He'd thought he'd get a room in Lake Placid for the night, give himself some time to decompress and write down his thoughts, but Thornton—and Kate—compelled him home.

Well, not home exactly…but back.

The word *home* stuck in his head as he drove.

The hint of invitation in her text tugged at him. There was definitely something witchy about her; he felt a lightness, a wonderful helplessness around her. She was a current he was swept up in, and he was beginning to question ever finding someone like her again.

Wondrous thinking, that.

He passed the ski jumps again around ten-thirty. If they'd loomed earlier, they lurked now, black shadows rising against the night sky. Thornton was no more than an hour and a half away. Kate, maybe five minutes more. Thoughts of her warm bed, of her sleek warmth pressed against him while the earth thawed outside clouded his tired eyes for one heartbeat too long.

He was wondering if a midnight text would be completely out of line, when the Scout clipped the deer in the hindquarters.

Ewan stomped on the brakes, swerving hard and screeching to a halt. He rushed out of the truck, only to find that the deer was nowhere to be seen. A bloody trail smeared away into the shrub by the side of the road.

He followed the trail, clambering over the icy rocks beyond the shoulder of the road. The muddy snow mingled with blood where the buck had churned through. Ewan couldn't have said why he needed to follow, but guilt propelled him deeper into the dark woods.

A horn blast from the direction of the road brought him back to rationality. The buck had a significant lead, and Ewan had no idea what he could do even if he caught up. He'd only seen a handful of trucks and the odd passing car on the roads. It wasn't as though he would be able to save the animal.

Or himself, if it came to that.

He got as far as the rocky outcropping near the road without incident. The Scout waited for him, haphazardly pulled to the side of the road, door ajar and headlights blazing into the woods opposite him. No wonder the truck had honked.

His foot slipped on frozen leaves. He overcorrected and pitched head first into the rocks. Though he put his hands up to block the fall, they slid over the ice and stone. His forehead struck a snow-crusted boulder and everything went black.

CHAPTER 31

"When this thing is a huge hit, and I'm rolling in money, the first thing I do," Kate muttered to herself as she let herself into the kitchen at Sweet Pease the next morning, "will be to hire a full-time assistant."

She caught sight of herself in the door's glass and amended that thought. First, a facial. Then an assistant. She looked haggard.

She was not the type to miss her sleep because a man didn't call. Even for two nights.

Ewan hadn't called. She hadn't slept.

Andy pushed through the doors from the service counter, holding the cordless phone and an order slip. "I thought I heard you. Some woman's been calling for you all morning, but she wouldn't leave a message, and you said not to give out your cell..."

Kate sighed. "Who?"

"Ally something..." Andy checked the slip for reference. "It's not a Vermont number."

Kate took the order slip and pinned it above her workstation. "If she calls again, come get me. If not, I'll call her back after lunch service."

She put on her apron and opened her production book. Margot

had checked off four huge items on the daily to-do list, which left her free to keep working on the two cakes that needed her attention. The phone rang just as Andy was returning to the front room.

He doubled back and handed it to her; she pinned it between her cheek and shoulder. "Sweet Pease Thornton, this is Kate Pease."

She was rummaging through a utensil drawer for her offset icing spatula as the woman introduced herself.

"Kate, my name is Ailie Dobrosky." The voice had a gruff kind of lilt, a touch of New York tang. "I'm Ewan's sister."

Something in Ailie's tone made Kate drop the spatula. The resulting clatter was far too loud.

"What happened? Where is he?"

Ailie sounded like she was speaking from inside a crowded tin can. "There was an accident the night before last. Somewhere in Upstate New York? He's in a hospital. I don't remember. He hasn't woken up." Her voice cracked a little, and Kate's heart lurched. "The truck is registered to my parents' address in Brooklyn. They're with him now. I'm on my way from Sea-Tac in a half hour."

Ailie broke off as what sounded like a boarding announcement filled in the space beyond her. Kate felt the oncoming rush of panic and squashed it.

"I'll be in Burlington later this afternoon," she continued, "and I know this is a huge imposition..."

Ewan's sister's voice hitched again, and Kate found hers.

"Is this your cell?"

"Yes..."

Kate dug out her cell phone and entered the number on the caller ID. "I'll text you my number. You send me your flight information, of course I'll come pick you up. It will save your parents a trip, and you a rental car from the airport."

"I..." Ailie's relief came clearly through the phone. "Thank you. I should go. That's my flight they're calling."

"No worries. You're welcome." Kate was already mentally shifting her workload. "Two things, though. Where is he? And how did you find me?"

"Let me check the message from my mom."

There was a heavy pause during which Ewan's life flickered in and out before her eyes.

"He's at Elizabethtown Community Hospital, and I Googled 'Kate bakery Thornton.'" There was a hint of wry levity in Ailie's voice. "You're the only game in town. I'll look for your text."

KATE WONDERED WHAT KIND OF WOMAN EWAN'S SISTER WOULD TURN out to be as Ailie Dobrosky's remarkable stride carried her toward the baggage claim. She moved like an athlete. Mathieu had loved that athleticism. He'd dragged her to enough games, talked stats, rankings, grace, precision. She'd been too infatuated to tell him she really couldn't care less about basketball.

The thought of Mathieu throbbed like a sore tooth, so she tucked the recollection away for the moment, and focused on Ewan's compelling sister.

Ailie was easily six feet tall, with a lean body and softer variations on her brother's stern features. Her cinnamon stick-colored hair capped her head in a stylishly shagged cut.

Kate knew a woman who was used to attention when she saw one. She was one, after all.

Kate had been on autopilot since Ailie called. She'd rearranged coverage at Sweet Pease, texted Joss that she'd be busy but to leave her messages if he needed her. Called Nan to let her know where Ewan was, then ignored Nan's frantic worry.

Crisis mode was easy.

Facing Ewan's sister was terrifying. Facing what might have happened to him was terrifying. Her feelings for him were likely to bring her whole facade down crumbling. Best to keep it all tucked away until she knew more.

"Ailie?" She called out from her vantage point near the carousels.

The tall woman's face relaxed slightly. The gravity of their shared situation stole Kate's breath for a moment.

She reached Ewan's sister as the baggage carousels clanked to life, spewing suitcases and duffels out from the belly of an unseen plane. Ailie kept one eye on the belt as she spoke.

"I appreciate you coming to get me. I really didn't want to handle this on my own." She leaned down and snatched a rolling bag off the carousel. "I more or less abandoned the kids with my husband and bailed."

Kate spoke without thinking. "Just how bad is it?"

Ailie's eyes widened. "Oh, Kate. I'm sorry. I just... I haven't seen him in half a year, and I just spoke to him the other night. I told him to buy you flowers..."

Kate couldn't help but smile. "He listened. They're beautiful. Potted cacti for my apartment."

"My parents dropped everything and drove up there; I panicked. I guess some trucker saw his car abandoned by the side of the road and stopped. Found him off the shoulder. The guy thought he was dead at first, but it was shock. He was cold and unresponsive. He radioed for help." Ailie shrugged helplessly and blinked back tears. "Ewan's the cool head in the family."

Kate took the handle of Ailie's bag. "Come on. Let's get my van and go find him."

In the van, Kate fidgeted, adjusting the heat. "Tell me if you're too warm to too cold..."

Ailie watched the darkness as they drove back toward Thornton. Kate rattled off local trivia to fill the quiet.

"That's where the winery is where I'm opening my café..."

Ailie turned and blinked at her, much the way Ewan had when Kate'd brought up exploring the secret haunts of her childhood.

"Hmm?"

"Nothing." Kate lapsed into nervous silence.

They were almost a half hour south of the airport when Ailie turned away from her vigil at the window and reached over to turn down the heat.

Kate noticed her long fingers and broad palms, and remember her observations in the airport, attempted small talk again. "Did you ever play basketball?"

Ailie grinned and, with that, the ice broke. "I played for two years in the WNBA after UConn. Did Ewe tell you?"

"No. I mean, we haven't talked about..." Kate squeezed the steering wheel hard. "I watched a lot of basketball with—when I lived in Paris."

Ailie seemed to sense her distress; Kate privately cursed Mathieu for the power he still held over her.

"Don't sweat it. Sisters demand girlfriend dish; boyfriends don't yammer on about sisters."

Kate relaxed her grip on the wheel.

"So, do you live in Seattle? All Ewan said was that you lived about as far from Brooklyn as you could get."

Ailie's laugh was so like Ewan's.

"Bainbridge Island. I got an offer to play in France, but I hurt my knee." Ailie smiled, and Kate felt a little more of her tension melt away. "I met Mike on a photoshoot for a piece on UConn alumna. He's a sports photographer. I told him he was it for me. He told me he lived in Puget Sound when he wasn't chasing a gig."

Sometimes, Kate thought, it worked out like that. Sometimes someone just gave everything up to be with the person they loved, and it ended like Ailie and her Mike. Could she give up Sweet Pease for a life in New York or some college campus? Could Ewan give up his wandering lifestyle and put down roots somewhere like Thornton?

Who said anything about love?

"What does an ex-pro basketball player do on an island in Puget Sound?" Kate asked.

"I coach and write a column for the local sports page." Ailie tapped her phone to bring up a picture of two jam-smeared, ginger-haired faces. "And I chase the twins around."

"They're adorable."

"When they're not horrible, yes." Ailie turned to watch the lake out the window. "How long 'til we get there?"

"Not sure, exactly. A while. The ferry would have been more

direct, but the last boat was at five." Kate glanced across at Ailie. "You're stuck with me."

"'Are we there yet?' I sound like my kids."

Kate's chest tightened. "No, don't feel bad." She flipped on her high beams to cut through the thickening fog. "I rely on snark to cope."

Ailie reached over and briefly squeezed her hand.

~

KATE DROPPED AILIE OFF AT THE MAIN ENTRANCE, THEN WENT TO FIND a parking space. She frantically checked her phone on the walk from the lot to the entrance, but there were no messages from Ailie, only a check in from Nan

Inside, she approached the reception desk. A young woman looked up from a computer monitor with a harried expression. "Yes?"

Kate set her keys and phone down on the counter. "I'm here to see someone."

"Visiting hours ended at seven."

"I just dropped his sister off, he was admitted early this morning. I think he's in intensive care."

"Last name?"

"Lovatt. Ewan Lovatt."

"And you are?"

"Kate… Katherine Pease."

The young woman peered up at Kate from between drawn brows. "Relationship?"

Kate's mouth opened, and she tripped over the answer. "Friend… of the family."

"Family only. If you're waiting, there's coffee in the cafeteria, and a vending machine across the lobby." The receptionist returned to her screen.

Kate grabbed her keys, clenching them. The metal cut into her palm, and she reminded herself the receptionist was only doing her job. She spun around and stalked across the lobby to an empty chair.

A home improvement show marathon flickered in silence, the

closed captioning flashing in it's black box at the bottom of the screen. Her phone stayed traitorously quiet.

As the wait stretched her nerves thin, Kate had time to examine her feelings. There was little to be done about any of it, the worry, the fear, and the gnawing uncertainty of her position in Ewan's life—something she would not yet have considered if she hadn't been thrust into meeting his family in the midst of a crisis.

Her overtired, hyper-aware thoughts kept circling around to the text he'd left her two days before. An errand in Lake Placid, an overnight stay. What had he raced off to do? Why had he not stayed the night there in the end?

By the time Ailie appeared in the doorway that led back to the patient corridors, Kate knew she was giving off sparks, but she was helpless to rein it in.

"I'm sorry, Kate." Ailie's apologetic half-smile resembled her brother's. "My mom was waiting for me, and they took me back to see him… I forgot."

"How is he? Can I see him?"

Ailie frowned. "It's family only until they move him."

Kate squeezed her lids against tears. She'd hoped wildly that the Lovatts had made an exception for her. "Of course."

"I'm sorry." Ailie took her hand. "He hasn't woken up, but he's breathing on his own. His core body temp was really low, and he's pretty banged up, but the doctors think he'll come around soon. Dad says they're going to move him once he does."

"I can wait."

Ailie fidgeted with her wedding band. "I have to go back. I'll tell him you're here when he wakes up."

Kate swallowed a sigh. "I'll go get some coffee or something."

Hospital time moved slowly. A tepid, weak coffee and two issues of *People* magazine later, Kate dared to look at her phone. Nothing from Ewan's sister. Seven texts from Nan.

She ignored Nan's messages for the moment. There was nothing to say, save that she was not family.

Her head snapped up every time anyone pushed through the heavy doors that led back to the patient corridors, but none of them was Ailie.

Finally, fatigue won out. She balled up her jacket for a pillow and let her eyes drift closed.

"Kate?" A hoarse voice pulled her from a fretful half-sleep.

Her first thought was that the older woman standing over her had given her son her smile. She pushed a stray lock of hair out of her mouth and sat up. "Mrs. Lovatt?"

"Call me Gail." Gail Lovatt squeezed her hand. "Thank you for bringing Ailie. We're very grateful."

"Is he okay?" Kate's mouth tasted like paste.

"He woke briefly, but not long enough to even realize we were there. I don't think."

Ailie pushed through the double doors, with a man who—from his dark eyes and the fall of his hair—could only have been Ewan's father.

Ailie hugged her, then introduced her. "Dad, this is Ewan's girlfriend, Kate. Kate, my dad, David."

Kate looked into two pairs of worried eyes. "I'm sorry we're meeting like this."

"It a surprise to meet you at all," Gail said. "If Ailie hadn't found you, we'd never have known."

Her breath clogged her throat.

"Mom," Ailie said, flashing a look at her mother.

"Oh, dear," Gail said. "I didn't mean for it to sound like that."

"No, don't worry. I get it." Kate hadn't told her parents she was seeing Ewan. Why would he share that with his parents? She glanced around for some evidence or direction of a cafeteria. "Can I get coffee or tea for anyone? Food?"

The offer diffused the weird tension between them.

"That's kind of you," Gail Lovatt said. "Tea, please, with a raw sugar if they have it, and a black decaf for David?"

Kate caught a slight head shake from Ailie, which she took for refusal. She left to seek out the hospital commissary feeling like an errand girl—and having no one to blame for it but herself.

Ten minutes later, she slid her way through an auto-closing door, narrowly avoiding sloshing Gail's Lipton all over her shirt, only to discover the Lovatts were missing.

She set the cardboard cup holder down on the reception counter. "Excuse me, but can you tell me where to find a patient?"

A new receptionist looked Ewan up, but her expression was disappointing. "Are you family?"

"No, I—"

"Family only. I'm sorry, ma'am."

"I'm here with the family. They said he was being moved..."

"I'm sorry, but right now I can't let you through."

There was no more information to be had, so Kate resumed her vigil on a scratchy chair. She drank another lukewarm coffee while Gail and David's drinks turned cold.

She waited through a shift change, and asked again, but the answer was still the same. She considered lying, but how to explain that to Ewan's family?

Since Ailie's call, she'd worn her crisis management hat, directing both her staff and herself through a to-do list that kept the worst of fear and worry at bay. Without a purpose or a place, she was left to her own thoughts.

Worry and fear for Ewan, but also for the chasm that opened in her heart at the thought of real harm coming to him.

That she might have lost him frightened her.

That she would lose him frightened her. To his continued career, to his next adventure, to his next book. Ewan had never meant to stay, and she had let herself fall for him anyway.

Finally, feeling like an interloper of the worst kind, she abandoned the now-cold drinks and left the hospital lobby.

Her phone pinged once on the way to the van, but it was Nan, wondering what was going on.

With only the moon for company, Kate put the van in gear and started out for home.

Ewan could hear the hospital sounds long before he could summon the energy to open his eyes. His whole body hurt. He'd dreamed of being small, pushing Matchbox cars off the dining room table, just to hear them crash, his mother singing in Gaelic to him.

He pushed his eyes open. There had been a crash. A deer. The woods. As the drifting, swerving tilt of the universe came rushing through his mind in high definition, he took in the unfamiliar room around him.

Double occupancy. He watched his fingers and toes wiggle in turn and sighed in relief. His roommate was a pale man in his fifties or sixties, propped up, watching muted local news with subtitles.

Ewan watched too, blinking his vision into focus until he knew the date. A day and a half had passed, judging by the date and timestamp on the Plattsburgh news scroll.

A day and a half.

He turned his face slightly—finding that it hurt to turn his neck—but couldn't see any personal effects nearby.

Did they know who he was? Had he come in as a John Doe?

Something must have alerted the staff he was awake. A nurse came in, greeted his roommate cheerfully, then progressed toward him through the sea of medical monitoring equipment around him.

"Hi there, Mr. Lovatt." She made notes on a chart with a huge, pink daisy-topped pen. "I'm Sue. How are you feeling?"

They at least knew who he was.

"Hi, Sue." His voice was sore, croaky. "I feel like hell, but from what I can recall, I think that might be a fine alternative to dead."

Sue smiled, but even through his discomfort and exhaustion, he could see she was already working through a checklist, and he fell silent. When she finished, she tucked his blankets in around him. Her gentleness was soothing.

"Your parents are getting some food, but I think they'll be back before too long. They're very sweet."

His parents? He wanted to wonder why they were there—and how long they'd been in...*where was he exactly?*—but the sunlight from the window was bright and his eyelids were heavy. Ewan slipped back into sleep with his questions unanswered.

He woke to his mother fussing with the blinds, as though she'd been able to read his last, disjointed thought.

His father was perched in a scratchy, utilitarian armchair, paging through a local tourism guide. His roommate appeared to be sleeping through an afternoon talk show.

"Hey, Mom. Dad."

"Ewan!"

His own craggy smile had its origins in his mother's face. A tall woman, a handsome woman, but not a beauty. His eyes told him as much, but the joyful pressure in his chest reminded him exactly how gorgeous she was to him.

His mom sat on the edge of the bed, attempting to arrange the blankets around his feet, which threatened to escape.

"They should find you a longer bed. And longer blankets." She clucked disapprovingly at the exposed skin above his sock-clad ankles.

"Gail," chuckled his father, "he's got plenty of room. The blanket's just caught up under his leg there."

She shot his dad a withering look Ewan knew well. She tugged the blankets out from under his hip, tucked them around his feet, then turned on him with a stern expression.

"And just what were you doing driving through the mountains in the middle of the night?"

Anxiety flared up, tingling in his extremities. "Does Kate know what happened?"

Kate would be in a marvelous temper if she didn't know, thinking he'd swanned off for days without word.

He wondered, though, what she thought if she did know.

His mother was inspecting his face, squinting slightly. "Yes. The basics anyway. Your sister thought to find her and tell her, and your Kate offered to drive her from the airport in Burlington."

His dad looked up from his guide pamphlet. "Ailie says she's sweet."

Ewan's attempt at laughter ended in a grimace. "Ailie hasn't gotten to know her yet."

The idea of Kate on her way, of Kate in her hot-pink van with his sister, was both comforting and disturbing.

His eyes drifted closed. He felt his mother's hand on his forehead, and her voice lulled him back to sleep.

CHAPTER 32

Kate's crew met her in the kitchen at dawn, concern in their expressions.

Andy handed her a revised schedule sheet. "We re-worked everything so you can go back to the hospital. Margot is going to cover production."

Two hours of sleep left her eyes gritty and her head pounding. She took the schedule from Andy and glanced at the coverage. "I'm going to have to promote you. This looks great."

"Is he okay, Kate?" Moira's hands were wound tight in her apron.

"I don't know." Kate's lip trembled; she bit it and breathed in through her nose. *I don't know, and I'm too damn stubborn to just text his sister and ask.* "I'm on my way there find out."

She thanked them and they dispersed, leaving her alone in the kitchen. She leaned against the counter and scrubbed her tired eyes. Ewan was everywhere, in the stool opposite, teasing her about sugar sculpting, kissing her senseless behind the swinging door, doing a passable job of cleaning up her mess.

She ran the tap on the handwashing sink and splashed her face, then pushed through the door to the front.

"Andy?"

"Yeah?" He set down the window spray he'd been holding. "What do you need?"

"Is the espresso machine ready to go? I think I'm going to need some high octane coffee to get me to Elizabethtown."

"I'm on it."

Kate sat in the booth by the window where she'd told Ewan George Cartwright's story. She'd never asked him what he and Mr. Cartwright had talked about that day, walking the slushy sidewalks of Main Street together.

Now she found she wanted to know.

"Double strength," Andy said, setting a to-go cup in front of her. "And a date-coconut bar. You need breakfast."

"Thanks, Andy. You're the best." She slid out of the booth and left her staff to finish readying the bakery for the day.

By the time she reached the hospital again, a new face sat behind the reception desk. This time, she was given a room number, and directions to find the nearest nurses' station to check in.

The double espresso had settled into her bloodstream; she felt almost human approaching the young man behind the computer. "Hi. I'm looking for room 562."

"Left at the T, fourth door on the right, but I think there are already two in with him. Have a seat over there, and I'll check."

David Lovatt appeared from the same direction she'd come, bearing a trio of steaming cups. He blinked owlishly at her before recognition brought a smile.

"Good morning."

Kate stood. "Hi. Can I help you carry something?"

"Oh, haven't you been in?"

"No," she said. "Someone just went to check who was there."

Ailie strode around the corner, the nurse trailing her by a few steps. "Kate, I'm so sorry. We just left you, didn't we?"

"Is he awake?" She didn't care that they'd forgotten her, not when Ewan was so close.

"He is. Come on."

Kate followed Ailie, drawing David in her wake, but the Lovatts sent her into the room alone. She shot a grateful glance back at them as she moved past his roommate's bed.

Ewan was too pale, and the faded cotton johnny was definitely not his best look.

"Hey..." Kate's greeting fell flat. Even the lighting discouraged levity.

Ewan smiled to see her and patted the mattress near his hip. "Thanks for bringing Ailie over."

Just for bringing Ailie?

She perched more than sat, searching Ewan's face for injuries, and hating herself for her sour thoughts. He had a broad bruise blooming on one shoulder, from what she could see peeking out from under the neckline of his hospital gown. The purpling matched the bruising near his hairline where a deep gash was stitched together.

Kate wrapped her fingers around his, blinking back tears stinging in her eyes.

Ewan squeezed back. "I'm glad you're here."

Humor won out. "There are easier ways to get me to pay attention to you."

He started to laugh, but winced; the laugh ended in a wheeze. "Shit," he muttered. "Can't even laugh at your completely inappropriate flirting."

The failed mirth left Ewan's face even paler and beaded with sweat.

"Are you okay?" Kate couldn't help the edge in her voice. She had no idea how to behave, how to worry without tipping her hand and revealing the depth of her feelings.

A different nurse popped her head in. "Everything all right?"

Though Ewan nodded, this nurse checked his monitors and looked him over. She gave Kate a stern look; Kate released Ewan's fingers with a guilty twitch.

He reached for her hand again, but Kate edged off the bed, hugging her upper arms and studying the view between the blinds while the nurse finished her notes and exited the room. "Your nurse doesn't like me."

"She doesn't like me, either." His voice was weak. "Or she's been on all night."

"Do you need anything? Water?" Kate saw that a paper cup was half full on the table adjacent to his bed. "A blanket?"

Ewan patted the mattress and winced.

"What is it?" Kate asked.

"Shoulder hurts." He retracted his outstretched hand. "Damn."

He was fading with the exertion of talking to her.

"You're tired. I'm not helping." Kate shoved her hands into her jacket pockets to confirm the presence of her keys, wallet, and phone. "Should I send your mom and dad back in?"

"Sure." He sounded like a tired little boy. "Kate?"

"Mmm?" She turned back, wondering suddenly if she should have kissed him goodbye, wanting for all the world to curl up beside him and fall asleep to the beeps and pings around them. A fleeting hope that he'd ask her to stay crossed her mind, but Ewan's eyes were already closing.

Out in the hall, Ailie and her parents were nowhere to be found. Kate made her way back to the small waiting area near the nurses' station, but stopped when she heard her name.

"… do about Kate?" Gail's voice rose at the end of an unheard question.

"Mom, I honestly don't think she's that interested." Ailie's response sounded weary. "Ewan didn't think so when I mentioned it earlier."

"She's here, though." Ewan's mother sounded unsure.

"She's a busy woman with her own life to get back to."

"You're probably right," Gail said. "I won't say anything."

The coffee soured in her belly. Kate gambled on the corridor having an exit stairwell somewhere and fled in the opposite direction.

THE RETURN TRIP TOOK HER PAST THE DAMSELFLY INN. SHE TURNED into the driveway, thinking the timing was perfect for some tea and sympathy.

"So, when's he being released?" Nan fussed with the teapot and sugar bowl on the tea tray destined for the parlor.

Kate was making a show of folding dish towels, half-sitting, half-standing at the kitchen island of the Damselfly Inn. "I don't know. The Lovatts had everything under control." She looked up at Nan's shocked expression and added, "He's not in any serious danger."

"You. Don't. Know." Nan carried the tea- and pastry-laden tray toward the swinging door to the foyer, her gaze lingering as she hip-checked it open.

"I'm hardly the Florence Nightingale type." Kate grumbled at the basket of towels.

"You'd look great in one of those Civil War nurse's aprons, though." Anneliese had slipped in through the well-oiled screen door, bringing a breath of the mild weather in with her. "How's Ewan? I take it that's who gets to see your Florence Nightingale get-up?"

"He's bruised. Tired." Kate sighed.

"But alive." Anneliese set down a stack of notebooks, a planner, and some flyers. "We've all been worried. Seems we've gotten used to having him around."

Kate could only nod. *Alive.* And she had been worried. Worried, frightened, but not family. Not interested enough to be part of the conversation.

Her head hurt. She needed sleep.

Nan came back from delivering afternoon tea to the parlor. She spoke over the rush of water from the faucet as she soaped her hands. "Have you told him yet?" She reached for a freshly folded towel to dry her hands and waved at Anneliese. "Hi, Anna."

Anneliese glanced between Nan and Kate. "Told who what?"

Nan hung the used towel on the oven door handle. "Kate. Told Ewan she's in love with him."

"Oh, that." Anna smiled in Kate's direction, but one look at Kate halted the curve of her lips. "I'm guessing not."

"I'm right here," Kate snapped. "And I'm not in love with him."

Even to her own ears, her denial sounded the lie it was, but it really didn't matter if she was in love with him or not.

He wasn't staying.

She wouldn't fall for another man who couldn't give her forever.

Anneliese pressed on. "Do you remember what you told me about what was missing with Seth? Fluttery, sinking, champagne-lust, I think you said?"

Damn her. "Yeah."

"Look us in the eye and tell us you don't feel like that about Ewan." Anneliese's voice took on the firm, soothing tone she used when Chloe was being unreasonable, and Kate's temper flared.

"I have somewhere to be." She did her best to sweep out the door, patting her pockets for her keys and phone as she did. The gesture brought Ewan's lost expression when she'd left him.

She hadn't figured on an interrogation.

Or accusations of love.

Her friends could see it, but Ewan hadn't. His family hadn't seen it. They only wondered what was to be done with the stranger who'd blundered into their son's life. Ailie had said it; Kate just hadn't heard it.

You're the only game in town.

She put the van in gear and backed out of her space, her gaze lingering on the sun sinking over the Adirondacks—over the hospital in Elizabethtown—as she checked the east-bound side of the road.

With a small head shake, she dismissed thoughts of Ewan, and turned herself and her van toward town. There were cakes to finish, supplies and marketing materials to order, and emotions to bury.

CHAPTER 33

Joss Fuller was the last person Ewan expected to be the first to turn up at his door. His parents and sister had overseen his hospital discharge, lingering in Thornton for a couple of days until he insisted they all go home.

Their concern only reminded him of the person missing from his recovery.

Once he'd replaced his damaged phone, he'd called, left voicemails, and texted, but Kate wasn't replying.

"Joss."

"Hey." Nan's fiancé had a fine layer of sawdust on his shoulders. "Saw the rental outside. How's the Scout?"

"Banged up." He opened the door wide enough to admit the other man. "I had it towed back to the guy in New Jersey who restored it for me. Cost me a fortune, but I love that truck."

"It's a beauty," Joss said. "How're you feeling?"

"Like crap," Ewan admitted. "But it could have been worse."

"Listen, Elisha told me you were out of the hospital," Joss said. "I ran into her downtown. She said you weren't going to be back in the classroom for a few more days. Nan and I thought maybe you'd like to use my cabin. It's quiet."

"That's a great offer. Thank you."

Joss hadn't mentioned Kate at all, an omission Ewan had to assume was intentional.

Kate, as far as he could tell, was finished with him.

Neither the prospect of holing up in the apartment, nor the awkward possibility of bumping into her while trying to write or research appealed to him.

"It's pretty well-stocked with the basics, so you only need fresh groceries. Just let me know."

"I'd love to."

Joss's sympathy was silent, but evident. "You want to come by the Damselfly later and pick up the key?"

Gym. Work. Plan. Read. Sleep. Repeat.

She'd bored herself silly, but the idea of eating more than the samples her livelihood required or conversing with people turned her stomach.

She'd turned to Ewan's first novel for solace. His words, his warm voice, the way he touched her, she lived it all in his prose. He was that good, and she was that much of a masochist. *The Orchard Gate* made every sad movie she'd ever seen look like a comedy, and yet she couldn't put it down. She knew it would end badly, but when it did, her tears shocked her.

She'd downloaded the three novellas in his lighter steampunk series, and was making her way through them in the evenings, after working herself to the point of exhaustion.

At first, Ewan had called. He texted. He did all the right things after she escaped his hospital room.

And when she didn't reply, he stopped. Which was the plan. Ignore him until he stopped calling. Let him leave town; let her get back to the business of baked goods and casual flirtations.

She'd broken her own damn heart, and more thoroughly than her once-upon-a-time lover ever had.

Mathieu had been a girl's first love. An infatuation flavored with young lust and the magic of Paris. In the quiet, bone-deep honesty of midnight, she could admit what Nan and Anneliese already knew to be true.

She did love Ewan. Fiercely.

THE WORLD OUTSIDE JOSS FULLER'S FOREST RETREAT WAS ALL DIAMOND frost and tender green, like nothing Ewan had ever seen. Inside, it was both snug and simple. Ewan had lit a fire and the Goldberg Variations played from his laptop over Joss's impressive sound system. The pantry and bar were well-stocked. The innkeeper's fiancé knew the exact balance of solitude and comfort required to ease a man's shoulders.

He reached for his mug of coffee and was momentarily distracted by a thin beam of morning sunlight breaking beyond the deck. He rose, pushed open the doors, and whistled in appreciation. He hadn't realized the full drama of the cantilevered balcony when he'd arrived the night before; in the cool of dawn it soared out over the hillside.

He wanted Kate beside him.

Her silence, and with it the distance she imposed upon them both, cut deeper than he'd been prepared for.

He wrote long into the night, against his doctor's orders. He was supposed to be avoiding fatigue and eye strain, but both Faye and Cordelia sang siren songs. In the dark hours, he'd placed Cordelia in peril, allowed Alasdair to engineer her rescue and then fail to secure her affections. Like her real life counterpart, Cordelia would be a challenge. Because he got to play god with his characters, Alasdair would eventually have what his author could not.

In the light of day, however, there were pages of notes, copies of Bartram family photographs, and hours of interview recordings to wade through. He pushed thoughts of Kate Pease aside and got to work.

The words had never come faster. By the end of a few days of feverish drafting, he had the first act of Faye's story down, and a full three novella arc for Cordelia and Alasdair plotted out.

He returned to teaching under strict orders to call his physician if he had any headaches. Ewan had to laugh, the attending doctor at the hospital in Elizabethtown had clearly never been a teacher. Will had held down the fort in their shared course lectures and enlisted some help from his senior thesis students to lead Ewan's discussion groups. Between email and the shared server, he'd even managed to catch up on grading essays between long stretches spent writing at Joss's cabin.

That he had to take more frequent breaks to rest his eyes was something he resented. Unfortunately, he had no one to blame for the situation but himself.

His students were all incredibly kind. He'd returned to emails and social media posts wishing him a speedy recovery, and the first lecture had been delayed nearly fifteen minutes while all the rumors of his near-death were clarified. He found himself having to disabuse more than a few of them of the notion that it was all a little romantic.

Their attention, however, did nothing to fill the hole left by Kate's absence.

As far as he could tell, she had driven south from Elizabethtown and seamlessly reentered her existence without him. Alone in the quiet of his apartment, his imagination spent from furiously drafting the novel in his free hours, he had to admit his fantasy—a tender Kate bearing sympathy, and maybe sweets, to surprise him—was a stretch.

Especially since she never returned to the hospital, never reached out to his sister, never returned his voicemails or texts.

He couldn't understand it, and it hurt.

Murray Sporinger arranged meetings about his replacing Caroline Waterford at Thornton, but Ewan delayed them. A future here was less rosy without Kate. Instead, he called Mallory.

"Ewan," she said. "I was beginning to think you were going to bail on me."

He could hear squawks on the other end of the line that sounded suspiciously like an infant. "Did I catch you at a bad time?"

"What? Oh. The baby." Mallory laughed. "I've got my niece here.

My brother and sister-in-law are down from New Hampshire. So, do you have the script ready?"

"Almost. I've been busy." *My personal life is a train wreck, but I've been writing.*

"Great. I'll let Mitch and Yvonne know. They're dying to read it."

Ewan wrote the two names on an empty corner of a page of notes. "They don't even know what it's about."

"They've got you and a mysterious, romantic, period piece. What else do they need?"

"Okay, Mal," he said. "Go play with your niece."

"Start looking at flights in June," she said. "We're going to Hollywood."

Instead of looking at flights, he worried at his pain like a sore tooth. Hours of thinking about Kate when he ought to have been reading essays and prepping exams led him to wonder if it wasn't just him she was running from.

The idea that Kate, in all her strength and fire, might have been hurt, took root in his imagination. California didn't have to be their end.

What might she do if he barged into Sweet Pease demanding answers?

CHAPTER 34

As interventions went, Kate supposed, starting with a round of slices at Fantastic Pizza was pretty tame. Her friends, led by her brother—whom Kate hadn't even heard was in town—had shown up at her apartment and dragged her away from Ewan's first novella. They frog-marched her out the door in her sweats and messy bun.

Nan voiced their collective opinion that she was turning into a boring recluse, and needed airing out. It was probably true. She'd read more in the last couple of weeks than she had in all the years since high school.

She convinced herself she was only immersed in *Alasdair Sledge* because it was an excellent read, not because she missed the author to the point of agony.

Jack had been called home from Boston to help with Operation Kate, but with the band back together, talk turned inevitably to Nan and Joss's wedding. The men planned their stag night, Anneliese and Nan fell into place cards and flower girl attire, leaving Kate to stew.

"Kate?" Anneliese was looking at her with questions in her eyes.

"Hmm?"

Nan answered. "Sorry, Kate. We were a little caught up in when to do photographs. Before or after the ceremony."

"Before." Kate said. She heard the dullness in her own voice and winced. "I mean, of you, and us. The rest after."

Anneliese reached out to lay a hand on Kate's arm. "We're not doing a good job of cheering you up, are we?"

"Not really." She pushed herself out of the booth, intent on escape. "You know, I think I prefer whiskey to pizza and beer."

~

EWAN WAS NEARLY JOGGING WHEN HE ARRIVED DOWNTOWN IN SEARCH of Kate, but Sweet Pease and the apartment above were dark. He stood outside her building, catching the wet, green scent of the spring runoff in the river, thinking back to the last time he'd found her windows dark.

He hoped she had the comfort she needed tonight.

He hadn't ventured much farther than the co-op for food since the accident, preferring to let teaching and writing occupy the places where pleasures had previously lived, including his stomach, but he passed the steamed over windows at Fantastic Pizza and caught a whiff of marinara in the air.

A man could only be so strong.

Ewan missed New York pizza; the town's pizza place was a decent one, but nothing compared to his favorite slice.

For one thing, you couldn't fold this stuff in half and eat while walking. He set his pizza on its paper plate on the small table near the door, and did his best to tune out the noise around him.

"Ewan?"

He turned to find Anneliese at his side. He swiped some stray sauce from his lip with his thumb. "Hi, Anna."

Looking past her, he noticed Kate's brother and Joss in a back corner booth.

"You can join us, if you like."

He looked at what remained of his dinner. "I don't know."

She sat lightly on the chair opposite him. "How are you feeling? We were all worried about you."

Ewan glanced past her again to where Kate's brother was watching them. "I'm pretty sure Jack wasn't worried about me."

"Jack is worried about his sister. You should talk to her."

He pushed the paper plate away. "I tried. I called her twice a day for a week, left messages, texted. She's done with me."

"I don't think she is."

Anneliese held his gaze with her steady blue eyes. She hadn't raised her voice, hadn't accused him of anything, but he felt as though he'd let her down.

"A smart man knows when a woman isn't interested anymore."

"A smart man would go for a drink at Temple and reconsider that position." She smiled, rising from the chair. "Now."

Only Nan followed her out of Fantastic Pizza and down the street to Temple, pulling up a stool with her as if she hadn't had a grown-up tantrum in front of her best friends and probably half of the high school softball team.

Nan nursed a beer while Kate worked her way through a second Manhattan. The first had gone down too quickly, and the whiskey wasn't doing anything to improve her mood; sadly, neither was Nan.

"You ghosted."

"I didn't." Kate twirled the skewered cherry in her drink. The bar was noisy, but it was a genial buzz. The weeknight crowd was there for drinks and company. She was as close to anonymity here, at a bar with her best friend in the heart of her hometown, as she would be anywhere in town. "I just haven't had time to really talk to him. Sweet Pease needs my attention now more than–"

"Save it," Nan snapped. "You cut ties and are hoping he'll be a gentleman and vanish quietly so you don't have to feel like a bitch. You're being pigheaded."

An astonished giggle, fueled by drink and the shock of Nan calling her on her crap, rose up along with her dander. "Are you calling me a bitch?"

"No..." Nan sipped delicately, giving Kate the side-eye. "I suggested you prefer to be the one who leaves, but you're in too deep, so you ghosted."

"They said I wasn't interested."

Nan set her glass down. "Who said that?"

"Ailie. Or Gail. Both. They were talking about me, and they said Ewan said I wasn't interested."

"In him?" Nan snorted. "He had a head injury. He was obviously not in his right mind."

"I don't know what. I was sick of being Kate the Forgotten, so I bailed."

Nan fixed her with an incredulous gaze. "You. Bailed."

"Shit." It was no use. Nan knew her too well. "You're right."

"I do not, for one moment, believe he thinks you're not interested in him. Why don't you just talk to him? Maybe he's as conflicted as you. Maybe he wants to stay in town, woo you, and raise a dozen gorgeous kids here."

"A dozen?" Kate eyed Nan's pint glass. "How many of those have you had?"

"One. I'm driving. And trying not to end up too wide in the hips for that dress you made me order."

"The corset will sort you out." Kate pushed her empty highball glass away. "And I didn't make you order anything."

"Mhmm." Nan drained the remaining beer from her glass. "I'm not drunk; he just strikes me as a candidate for the secretly-wants-twelve-kids type."

Kate felt the blood drain out of her face even as she imagined a couple of kids and a farmhouse out in the woods near the Stone Garden. Somewhere spacious so Ewan could write and she could have a test kitchen...

And that was exactly why she'd avoided Ewan since his accident. She didn't want to want that cozy, settled future. Not with a man who was living in rented space and likely already negotiating his next move.

There it was, though, as clearly as if she'd read it in one of Ewan's stories. A wedding, babies, a home. All the things she'd never let herself think of, never wanted with anyone since Mathieu, because wanting meant risking your heart.

Nan leaned her head on Kate's shoulder. "I know you're hurting. I can see it on your face. Does he know any of how you're feeling?"

The tenderness in Nan's voice was Kate's undoing. Two fat tears welled up and dipped down her cheeks before she could stop them. Like the best friend she was, Nan flagged Dee for the check and handed Kate a dry cocktail napkin.

"Joss isn't expecting me home at any particular time. Why don't I walk you home and we can figure this out?"

Kate sniffed and dried away the evidence of her tears. "With ice cream? And something on cable with a Hemsworth?"

"Solving the world's problems, one Australian at a time, I see."

Ewan's voice startled her. A shiver rolled along her skin.

The bruising was gone. Only a small scar near his hairline gave away his accident. Alive, Anneliese had reminded her.

All her wit deserted her. "Hi."

"Hi." A small smile played around his eyes, and even though his lips didn't follow, relief followed the thrill of his voice along her nerves. He might be upset, but he didn't hate her. "You're a hard woman to find."

Kate tilted her head. "Not if you know where to look."

The attempt at flirting fell flat; the smile around Ewan's eyes faded. Nan set some cash down on the bar with the bill and slid off the stool.

Ewan looked back at Nan's retreating form. "She ghosted."

Laughter was preferable to tears, and Kate cackled away at the unlikely coincidence of his words. "I prefer to call it a French exit."

"Kate." A gruff plea laced her name, and her laughter dried up. "Please talk to me."

Kate could feel a bubble of quiet forming around them. People were paying attention, and people loved to talk. "Not here. Let's walk."

She left another bill on the bar and went out, confident Ewan would follow.

The night outside was cool and clear, but soft, as if summer were pressing up against the early spring chill. Kate wrapped her oversized boyfriend sweater tightly and belted it, shoving her hands into the deep pockets as Ewan's footsteps fell in sync with hers.

"Kate." Ewan's voice was barely audible over the high-water tumble of the Thorn River.

She kept her stride even, resisting the urge to bolt. For one thing, she was an adult. For another, she knew if she ran, she'd end up on her parents' porch. And again, she was an adult. "I already said that."

Ewan looked at her. "What?"

Kate opted not to admit he'd caught her thinking out loud. "Over there."

He followed her across the street and onto the town common, where benches lined the ash- and maple-ringed green. Choosing one across from the Historical Society's dark windows, she sat. Ewan sat next to her, his body tall and solid. He leaned forward, elbows on his knees.

Kate waited as the night settled around them, punctuated by the occasional car on Route Seven and the laughter and chatter of Temple's patrons coming and going from the bar. There was music playing somewhere nearby, something bluesy on the breeze.

"How did you know I was there?"

Her face was cast into deep shadow, dappled silhouettes of leaves and streetlight rippling over her features. Ewan caught the glint of her eyes in the darkness and held her gaze.

"I ran into Anneliese. She suggested I go to the bar."

Kate hunched a bit and hugged herself. "So much for *sisters before misters*."

"I did try to talk to you. I didn't abandon you, Kate."

"But I abandoned you?"

She was infuriating. "Yes." he said. "Where have you been? I thought we were starting something together. I missed you, and you've been going about your business here without so much as a word."

"You didn't need me. You had your parents and your sister."

"What are you talking about?"

A long beat passed before Kate spoke. "I heard them talking about how you didn't think I was interested, how I was a busy woman with my own life."

He wracked his brain for any kind conversation she might have misconstrued. When he realized what she'd heard, he sighed.

"They asked me if they should invite you to go to dinner with them. My head hurt, and my mom was being nudgy. Ailie was snappish; she missed Mike and her kids. I told them you probably had things to get back to in Thornton."

He wrapped his hand around hers.

"I was trying to do you a favor," he said. "I did need you. Badly. Who else flirts me out of a mood and bosses me around and makes the sun shine through endless weeks of grey, muddy misery? Who else makes me laugh and feeds me things I don't know I love yet? How could I not need that, stuck in a hospital bed on the wrong side of the damn lake? I needed you, and I needed my laptop." His breath heaved. "That's all I want to need for a good long while."

"What good will needing me do, when you're wherever you're off to when you leave?"

Her voice was so small; diminished Kate broke his heart far more than absent Kate.

"More good than you know. I wasn't looking for you two months ago, but for the life of me, I can't see why. I should have been."

She said nothing, only watched the empty street in front of them. Her silence was unsettling.

"Who was he? The guy who left you?"

"Matthieu." The name, whispered in a lilting accent, was a blade to his throat—swift, sharp, lethal. "I…We…were together when I lived in Paris. I loved him. He walked away from me a month before I was due to finish my internship."

There was a tearful wobble in her voice now. The urge to find—

and hit—the bastard who'd made her cry was as violent as a rangy, bookish kid from Brooklyn could muster.

"I was ready to tell him I would stay. In Paris. That I'd give up my family and my dream of this place for him. For us."

"Kate." Three times; the writer in him heard it. Three times he'd spoken her name. If he was weaving a spell, he hoped he was casting it correctly. Gone was any lust for vengeance. He gathered her into his arms and held her while her grief spilled over.

"I loved him, and he left me like I was a tourist he hooked up with in a club."

The fight drained out of her body along with her tears. He touched his lips to her temple and whispered comfort.

"I'm sorry he hurt you." He stroked her hair, cradled her against his chest. "I'm not racing away from here. From you. Not if I have a reason to consider staying."

Somewhere in the distance, the music slowed. Kate tilted her head and the light caught damp tracks on her cheeks. She peered into his face, and he wondered what she saw there. He felt raw and naked, his soul exposed to the fire in her gaze.

There was a new seriousness in her voice when she spoke. "Does the reason have to have a lot of strings?"

His heart leapt into his throat, choking his response. "None at all if you don't want them."

"You have one, then. A reason. To consider staying."

"And if I have to go to California?"

"You can come back when you're done."

Her caution warred with the wild happiness in his chest. "I'd like that."

She leaned forward, slowly, deliberately, and touched her lips to his. He held back, waiting to see what this change in her would bring. She traced his jawline and ran her fingertips through his hair. When her palm smoothed down his neck to slip beneath the collar of his shirt, she tugged him closer. Her mouth opened, drew him into the kiss.

She braced her weight on the bench; he brought them closer still. Her kisses were leisurely, exploratory, but still he held back.

She arched against him and tasted his lips with tongue and nipping teeth. There was whiskey and sweetness on her breath. Her lips were seasoned with tears.

Holding back was no longer an option. She drowned out the melody, the waterfall's babble, the stars above them. He gave in to the magic, realizing as he did that it was never him who cast the spell. How long they made out like high school kids on a park bench he neither knew nor cared until Kate shivered hard, drawing away. The wooden slats around them were damp with dew and the moon had reached its tipping point, falling into the western sky.

She tucked her head under his chin so that he felt her speak as much as heard her.

"I'm cold. Come home with me."

"Of course." What else was there to say? He would go where she asked, as long as she wanted him there. He didn't remember crossing the road or walking past Temple again to reach the arched brick doorway on Gristmill Alley that was her apartment door. There was only the buoyancy of their fingers entwined, the scratchy softness of her sweater's cuff rubbing his wrist, the night sounds of the campus up the hill and the sleepy village through which they walked.

Once inside, Kate tossed her sweater over the back of her sofa and turned to face him. Under the bulky cardigan, she wore a Thornton Union High T-shirt and the sweats her traitorous friends hadn't let her change. She was already pushing off her left shoe with her right foot. The casual removal of her canvas sneakers sent a fresh jolt of lust through him. He unbuttoned his jacket, laying it next to her sweater on the sofa back.

She reached back and pulled out her ponytail holder. Her curls and waves fell down over her shoulders; she gave a little head shake as they settled, then finger-combed the loose strands around her face.

Barefoot and tumble-haired, arms akimbo, she said, "Can you stay tonight?"

"Of course." He knew he was repeating himself. "I —"

"I'm glad." In two long strides she was in his arms.

~

Without question, Kate had missed this. Ewan held her as though she were a precious and capable machine; she felt both elegant and strong in his embrace.

She slipped her hands into the waistband of his khakis and pulled the tail of his button-down shirt free. Under that, the soft cotton undershirt, and then the warm valley at the small of his back. He shivered when she offered him her mouth, exploring the ropy muscles of his back, the angles of his shoulder blades. She deepened the kiss, then stepped back, giving him a sly look as she ran her hands around his ribcage and pushed his shirt up.

Taking her cue, Ewan shrugged off his button-down and helped her along, tugging the undershirt over his head. She laughed when his shaggy hair tumbled back down over his forehead, and reached to smooth it back. He caught her hand in his and pressed his mouth to her palm.

With her free hand, Kate lifted the hem of her shirt, slowly revealing champagne lace as she did. Ewan caught the shirt and pulled it over her head.

She shimmied out of her sweats, leaving only her lacy things.

"I could get used to that look."

"You like?" Kate twirled in the discarded pile of clothes.

"I like."

They laughed together when she stumbled slightly, but the laughter gave way to the music of breath and sighs when skin touched skin. Kate pressed against him, fumbling with his belt buckle and fly while he twined his fingers through her hair.

Somehow, the awkward tango across the room, from sofa to bed, was sexy as hell, and the moment when he knelt between her thighs to slide down her panties was tender and thrilling. When his long, rangy body stretched out next to hers, he paused to look at her. For the first time that evening, shyness stole over her; she held his gaze and fought a blush he wouldn't see in the dim light of her tiny bedroom.

When he spoke, his voice was raspy. "I'm glad you invited me in tonight."

"I'm glad you found me." *Tonight, and when you came to Thornton.* This time when she kissed him, there was no awkwardness, no laughter, no teasing. There was only the magic of desire and the heat between them. Where he touched her, she felt it all along her limbs. Where her hands explored him, shudders ran along his skin. Without speaking, they each drew out the pleasure, feather-light kisses and teasing caresses.

She arched against him when he followed fingertips with kisses. He tensed when she scraped her nails through the hair on his chest. When their breathing was labored with wanting, when she could no longer wait to have him inside her, she rolled him onto his back, pausing only to reach in her nightstand drawer. Even that final step was charged, hot. He moaned when she readied him, gasped when she took him inside.

His fingers dug into her thighs as he rose to meet her. She rocked against him, slow and steady, building to a thrumming crescendo. She felt the delicious pressure flare deep in her belly and arched back, feeling her body tighten around him. She cried out when he touched her, and then he was driving them up again.

This time they hit the peak together.

It was a long time before she was willing to stir from his side. He was quiet, his palm skimming idly from her knee to her hip. She could almost hear his contentment, and her own sang counterpoint. The shade of her earlier misgivings crept into the room, but she pushed it back. The lightness she felt when they were together was too precious for doubt.

When they woke, it was to Kate's phone gonging.

"What is that?" Ewan rubbed his eyes.

"A reminder." She reached for the phone. "I have to check in with Anneliese about Nan and Joss's wedding. It's only two months away."

She rolled over, propping herself up on one elbow. The doubts she'd struggled with in the night faded in the warmth of Ewan's body heat. "Would you consider staying for the wedding?"

"Is that an invitation?" He grinned. "Or do I need to ask Anneliese? Or Elisha?"

She slid her leg invitingly along his. "It's an invitation."

CHAPTER 35

Mallory called a few days later. Ewan was dressing for a cocktail party at the Sporingers' home.

"Mitch and Yvonne have the last weekend in June free. They're on location in Malaysia before that, and on a scouting trip the week after."

"Mal," Ewan began.

"If this thing goes well, they'll be headed east to scout for sites in New York, maybe even in that little town you're in. You could fly back and show them around."

"Mallory." It came out sharper than Ewan intended.

"What?"

He could hear her mental gears grinding to a halt through the phone, so he gave her a beat. "I can't fly out to L.A. in June. Maybe later, but not June. I'll send you everything I have and you can talk to them, but I have to be somewhere."

"They really want to meet you."

"And they will." He straightened his cuffs with the phone crooked between his chin and shoulder. "But the script should speak for itself."

"Ewan…"

"I'm staying here. As long as I can. I'm in love, Mal, and it matters.

Mitch and Yvonne can have Faye if they want her. You figure the financials out, and we'll all celebrate in the fall."

Mallory was silent for a moment.

"Well, then," she said. "Who am I to put a man's career before his heart? I'll meet with them, and I'll sell the hell out of you, but you have to tell me one thing."

"Sure."

"Will I like her?"

Ewan laughed out loud. He felt as carefree as the man in the reflection looked. "You will love her."

He whistled—badly—as he walked the half mile across the campus to the Sporingers' house.

Diane Sporinger had whipped up a feast of cheese, olives, bread, wine, fruit, and an impromptu performance of Sondheim songs had begun over an argument about Broadway classics. A *salon*, she called it, like a French patron of the arts. Two music students, a math professor, and an art history professor who sang in the community choir were taking turns at half-forgotten lyrics punctuated with laughter and shouted corrections.

Murray Sporinger's granddaughter Livy, a recent alumna who was preparing for a summer research internship in New Zealand, was trash-talking Reed Sharpe when the sing-off began.

Suddenly, Livy looked up and smiled. "Professor McNair? Over here."

Ewan turned to find none other than Elisha shrugging off a jacket and unwrapping a mile of Hermès from her stylish throat. She smiled her dazzling smile and made her way across the room.

"Livy." The two women exchanged warm hugs.

"Professor—"

"Elisha; you're not my student anymore."

Livy rolled her eyes, but the gesture was more affectionate than anything. "Elisha, this is Grampa's new project, Professor Lovatt."

It was Ewan's turn to roll his eyes, but Elisha took pity on him.

"We've met. How are you, Ewan?"

Livy excused herself. Ewan saw her seek out her grandmother amongst the crowd.

"I'm enjoying myself. It's unexpected."

Her bell-like laugh rang out. "You're funny when you don't mean to be."

"Intimate parties where I am expected to appear knowledgeable and charming? Total nightmare."

"I love them." She took in the room. "Frank Marshall sings?"

Ewan watched the lauded statistician belt out something that definitely wasn't Sondheim. "Apparently. Is that Lloyd Webber he's doing?"

Elisa cocked her head fetchingly to one side, listening. "I think it is. *Jesus Christ Superstar,* if I'm not mistaken. I had no idea."

"It's a crazy world." Ewan shifted on the sofa to make room for her. "You want a seat?"

"I'm going to grab a drink and some food. I skipped dinner. Do you want anything?"

His own glass was still half-full. When she returned from the sideboard, she sat; the Broadway concert was only getting more raucous. "Do you like theatre?"

"Not this stuff. I mean, it's fine, but I like plays better than musicals. Except opera." He glanced at her over his glass. "I have a secret weakness for opera."

"We should see something at the Met this summer. Are you going to be in New York in June?"

When he didn't reply immediately, she forged on. "Do you have something else planned? I'm going to be in Newport with my family for a month in July, but it's not that far to Manhattan."

"I'll be here in June. Not sure about July."

He had an invitation to the wedding of the year.

Elisha was watching him with a knowing twinkle in her eyes. "You and Kate, hmm?"

Somehow, he wanted to tell her. He wanted to say out loud the crazy idea that had bloomed in his heart after making up with Kate.

She was another outsider, another crazy transplant to this place, and he felt—with the strain of flirtation removed—a kinship with her.

"I'm going to ask her to marry me. Hopefully she'll say yes, and I'll be here in July and August and the next fifty years."

"There's something in the air here." Elisha touched his arm. "I hope she does. Say yes."

"You hope who says yes, Ms. McNair?"

Murray Sporinger had materialized from another room.

Elisha stood and smoothed her already perfect hair. "Dr. Sporinger. Thank you for the invitation."

"Murray." Ewan also stood. "Diane throws a great party."

"Is Ms. McNair convincing you to stay? Or has that lovely pastry chef I met at the string concert already done that?"

Ewan felt the heat rise up his neck. *Was he so transparent?*

Elisha laughed again. "Didn't I tell you at the engagement party, Ewan? She's a force."

"I see." Sporinger's expression was knowing, but also happy. "You'll finish applying for the position, then?"

"I suspect he will," Elisha said. Her lips curved over her glass.

Ewan suspected he ought to feel trapped by the conversation, but the merry band at the piano had switched to jazz standards, and he knew what he had to do.

The hardest part would be waiting for the right moment, and to shorten the wait, he pulled out his phone and texted his mother. There was something in Brooklyn he needed.

CHAPTER 36

No potted plant this time, Kate noted. Ewan turned up at the bakery just before closing with a beautiful bouquet of roses from Josephine's.

She hadn't seen him in two days due to a wedding cake and a faculty party on top of their mutually harried spring schedules, and the urge to tuck herself in under his chin and breathe him in was nearly overpowering. She settled for stretching up on her toes to kiss him.

"Let's get pizza and go to bed early," she whispered in his ear.

"I have a better idea," he said, hugging her. "Let's go for a drive."

Ewan surprised her by taking the road southwest past the athletic complex and the performing arts center. Kate expected that he would head in the direction of the Damselfly. The truck's headlights lit the road ahead; the pastures and woods rolling out beyond the campus borders melted into the darkness around them.

Kate watched the sky overhead as a layer of quilted clouds drifted in to obscure the starlight. There would be April showers before dawn.

It was late enough that only scattered lights from the farmsteads and lonely developments reminded her they weren't alone in the world. As her eyes adjusted to the dark, the shadowy, nighttime beauty of her home washed over her.

Ewan didn't speak; he was mulling something over. She could feel the intensity of his thoughts from across the truck. They passed through the sleeping village of Shoreham; Ewan wordlessly and purposefully steered them south and parallel to the shore of Lake Champlain.

Ewan's silence unnerved her. There was no anger in it, no temper. If he was upset, it didn't show.

"Is everything okay?"

"Yeah, fine." His fingers drummed the steering wheel, and he scanned the turns as if looking for signs that never appeared.

She opened the window to let the air from the lake fill the car. The verdant scent on the breeze calmed her. The black of the water winked in and out of sight as they traveled, vanishing and reappearing between orchards and freshly turned fields.

When he pulled the car over in the gravelly turnoff just before the Ticonderoga Ferry, Kate's curiosity got the better of her.

"It's a long wait for the first boat."

He turned the key, cutting the engine but leaving the music playing. Without the low rumble of the engine and the static of the open window, Kate recognized Otis Redding. The radio dial was tuned to WTCR. Some student DJ was indulging in late-night soul.

"I missed the turn." Ewan spoke softly, and Kate leaned in a little. "Here's as good as anywhere."

"Where did you mean to go?" She couldn't help herself; he'd seemed so sure of himself.

"Part of it was I wanted to see where Marian lived," he admitted. "That sounds really weird when I say it out loud."

Kate didn't mean to laugh, but he was right. "Yep. It does."

He chuckled softly, but he didn't volunteer anything more.

"You said, 'part of it.' What was the other reason?"

He started to say something, then backtracked. "Do I need another reason? Isn't your company enough?"

"I'd like to think so."

She hadn't meant to sound so sharp, but he was being secretive, and it worried her.

He took her hand in response, smoothing her palm with his thumb.

"It's more than enough." His voice had gone husky. "I wanted to explain California. I never did. My agent, Mallory, ran into a friend from college who has a small production company. They got to talking, and I came up."

"As you do," Kate teased.

"Yeah." Ewan drummed the steering wheel. "Well, Mal mentioned the idea I'd pitched her for a Faye Bartram novel, and they asked her if I'd consider a script instead."

"Holy shit. Really?"

"I've never done one before, but Mal was certain this was it. This was the break in my career that would make Alasdair a household name like, Hawk goddamn Johnson."

Kate was missing something. "Huh?"

"Reed Sharpe."

"Oh." Kate still wasn't sure where this was going. "Have I seen a trailer for that?"

"Probably." Ewan turned to her. "I've been writing this script all semester, on the assumption that I'd meet with her friend Mitch and his partner this summer. Mallory was trying to warm me to relocating out west."

"I see."

"No. You don't. June was on the table, but I don't want it. I sent the pages to Mallory and told her to pass it along. If they want the script, we can negotiate, but I don't need to be there right now. I can take a trip in the fall, or whenever, but none of that means more to me than being here with you."

His confession shocked her even as the last of her reservations crumbled. Doubt lifted off on the breeze, dissipating over the water, leaving her feeling both drained and brimming with affection.

With love.

"You could have told me," she said.

"I should have."

"I should have told you about Mathieu."

"You could have."

Kate laughed. "We're idiots."

"We blundered into one another, I think." He turned to her suddenly. "If I could rewrite us, I'd have stumbled into Sweet Pease on a beautiful morning, seen you come through that swinging door in your hot pink jacket with flour on your nose, and been able to say just the right thing to charm you. You'd have wrapped me around your finger, and that would have been that."

He laughed lightly, his expression painfully earnest in the dashboard light.

"I write better meet-cutes than I live, apparently."

Kate felt it in her chest, the sweet ache of what she felt for this man. Even so, she could see his version of events, could see how she would have flirted circles around him until she had him exactly where she wanted him.

"You should write that one into a story, but I'll keep us as we are." Kate touched his cheek. "You saw my worst the moment you met me. There were never any illusions for you, and I didn't know until now how important that is."

The yielding when he leaned into her touch thrilled her, but it was the glint of his smile and the lifting of her cheek against her palm that sent a current of warmth through her blood.

"You've changed everything, and I love you for it."

"You love me?" The floor of the truck seemed to sink away from her, like an elevator that lifts too quickly.

"Every intractable, shimmering cell of you, Kate."

His hands were shaking. She could see the quiver in his fingers where they wrapped around hers.

"My elusive heroine has your face because I am thoroughly bewitched by you, but it's a pale tribute. Words don't do you justice."

He traced her cheek, and she felt the anxious energy in his touch.

"I love you, Katherine Pease. You have my heart, and I have no idea what to do."

"Stay." The wish became a word before her fear could rein in her heart. "Not just for the wedding. Stay all summer."

Hope kindled in his eyes, and the rest of her precious, fragile plea came free from its tethered place inside her. "Don't leave. Stay here with me. Write your books, teach, eat too many of my experimental sandwiches."

She squeezed his hand and smiled through the tears that filled her eyes.

"Stay, and marry me."

"Yes." He didn't hesitate. Not at all.

"'Yes?' Just like that?"

"Yes." His smile lit his eyes, and he pulled her across the bench seat. "We'll get a little house of our own, maybe rent out your apartment. You can run your pastry empire, and I'll write in the garret."

"A writing garret?" Kate leaned into him. "Very Brontë."

"Well, I can't have Rochester's attic. I'm fresh out of madwomen. If it doesn't have a garret we'll hire Joss to build one."

"You really don't want to go to California?" She scrutinized his face, looking for regrets and finding none.

"No." He considered a moment. "Well, yes. But I never really wanted to live there. That was Mallory's dream for me. Turns out, I want to live and write here, take the occasional meeting if this Faye Bartram movie thing works out, write a feisty, clever, accomplished woman into Alasdair Sledge's bachelor world, seriously pursue the position Murray Sporinger spoke to me about." He ran a hand up her denim-clad calf. "Very contentedly."

"Flatterer." Her voice hitched. "Wait. Murray Sporinger offered you a job?"

"Not formally offered, but there's potential there."

"Why didn't you tell me?"

"I didn't want to scare you off with talk of the future."

"Fair enough. I'm not scared now." She caught her reflection in the rearview mirror. Her cheeks were pink with pleasure. They were getting married. "When?"

Once again, he didn't hesitate. "Sometime over the winter?"

Kate had a vision of crackling fireplaces, hot chocolate, and winter-white silk.

"But far enough out," Ewan said, "that we wouldn't be stealing Nan and Joss's thunder."

Kate curled her body against his. "That's the perfect answer."

When he kissed her, she tasted promises and magic, sweeter than anything she'd ever known.

He laced their fingers together, and Kate relaxed into him, his tall frame supporting her, cradling her. He kissed the spot where her hair tucked behind her ear.

"Do you remember that day when I walked with George Cartwright?"

"You were so kind to him. It took my breath away."

"He asked me if I had a girl."

Kate smiled. "What did you say?"

"I told him the truth." Ewan spoke against her temple. "I didn't have one then. He told me I should find a girl who was a good cook. I wondered how you'd react if I asked you to go steady."

She giggled, turning her face to his. "I might have said yes, if you brought me a corsage when you asked me to the VFW dance."

"When I'm old and I forget things, I'm going to remember you telling me about the Cartwrights, and I'm going to tell everyone how I fell in love with Kate Pease in her bakery on Main Street."

Kate snuggled in closer. "And I'll tell them that you took too long, so I asked you to marry me."

"I took too long?" He nipped playfully at her ear, then kissed the spot.

"You'll be old and forgetful; everyone will believe me."

"What have I gotten myself into?"

Kate sat up a little, and turned to him. "A lot of trouble, that's what."

"Will you come with me to New York to tell my parents?" He hugged her in close again. "And my sister will probably want us to come out to Washington."

"They won't assume I'm a horrid eavesdropper?"

"How could they?" Ewan asked.

"You know," Kate recalled her first meeting with Gail Lovatt, "you get your talent for sticking your foot in your mouth from your mom."

Ewan belly-laughed. "You're going to get along just fine."

She considered the prospect of immediate travel, hoping it wouldn't be a deal breaker. "Can we go after the opening? I'm flat out until then."

"Of course." He kissed her again. "But don't be surprised if they come to us in the meantime."

"It would be nice to see them somewhere besides a hospital corridor."

"Speaking of my family..." He produced a ring box from his jacket pocket. "Can I give you my grandmother's diamond? Even though you asked me?"

It was beautiful. Perfect in that old diamond way, and the intricate, antique setting took her breath away. He took her hand, sliding the ring over her knuckle. It was too big, but she kept it on.

"You were planning to ask me? After everything I put you through?" She flexed her fingers, catching the ring's sparkle in the light from the parking lot. "You might be the bravest man I know."

He chuckled. "I just might be. But also the luckiest."

He kissed her lightly, but she held him close, her lips a breath from his. "I'll show you lucky."

This time his laugh was deep and true.

"You have a filthy mind, Kate Pease. But I'm happy to oblige."

Kate was still giggling when he made the turn back up toward Shoreham.

EPILOGUE

Kate checked her mascara in the mirror over the fireplace in the Damselfly's parlor. She hiked up her fuchsia silk bodice, and twisted to check her hair.

Jack batted her hand away from her hair. "Okay, Maid of Honor; you're perfect. Let's do this."

Her brother offered his arm and they stepped out into the foyer. The four-part string arrangement of *Ode to Joy* poured in through the open doors and windows, and Kate blinked back tears.

It wasn't every day your best friend got married.

She met Nan's eyes as they passed the staircase. Like a living portrait, Nan paused on the landing, backlit by June sunlight in her veil. The bride was nothing short of luminous, her gown trailing up the stairs, blush parade roses and ferns spilling from her hands. Molly Fuller was tucking a delicate scrap of blue-embroidered cloth into the bouquet's wrapping, and a flood of feeling caught in Kate's throat.

"She's a vision, isn't she?" Walt Fuller whispered from where he stood at the bottom of the stairs, waiting for Molly and Nan.

Kate was quite sure he was referring to his own bride as much as Nan, and a stray tear ran down her cheek.

"No tears, sister. We've got to get these kids hitched." Jack blew a kiss up the stairs to Nan. "See you out there, kiddo."

Kate peered over her shoulder, looking for the photographer, who was already taking rapid shots of the moment on the landing from her unobtrusive position near the front door.

Jack steered her toward the door to the terrace. "Madison is on it. Stop managing everyone. Anneliese has got everything under control."

It was true and, what was more, Anna herself was beckoning from the end of the aisle. Kate grinned; half the town was assembled on the Damselfly's lawn, waiting for Nan to meet Joss under the wisteria-wound pergola.

Chloe Thompson waved at them. She stood beside her mother in a cloud of pale pink tulle, clutching a silver-metallic paint bucket full of petals and waiting for her Auntie Molly and Uncle Walt to escort her down the aisle ahead of the bride.

Kate followed the aisle down to the groom. Joss stood there, looking dapper and anticipatory in his dove gray suit, while Reverend Marcotte smiled serenely at his side. Kate knew weddings were his favorite perk of the job.

And then her gaze—and her heart—found its home. Ewan stood in the second row on the bride's side, tall and elegantly turned out, eyes only for her.

She felt her lips curve into their secret shared smile; one wedding down, one more to plan.

And then the string melody shifted to a dreamy version of *Fever*, and Kate straightened. It was time, as Jack so eloquently put it, to get those kids hitched.

When, some hours and a few glasses of champagne later, she pulled Ewan onto the dance floor at her nearly-finished Sweet Pease North space, Kate decided it was sweet to be the better dancer. She tucked herself in close to his body, the better to convince him he was the one leading. With her three-tiered masterpiece of ivory buttercream and edible seed pearls safely in Margot's capable hands, she was ready to dance until dawn.

Ewan let her spin out and reeled her back into his arms, catching her lips for a quick kiss. "See? I'm not entirely a mess."

"You are a disaster on two left feet, but you're mine."

The crowd lowed around them, and Kate basked in their energy.

When Stevie Wonder gave way to Anne Murray, her heart flipped over as her parents and Molly and Walt drifted into the center of the dance floor. Nan and Joss watched the older couples from where they swayed in a bubble of newlywed bliss. Ewan gathered her close and sang along in a barely passable baritone.

Could I have this dance for the rest of my life...

"If it turned out you wrote *and* sang brilliantly, I might have hated you a little bit." She was teasing, but the feeling of his rumbly voice serenading her filled her with joy. She laid her cheek against his lapel. When people spoke of cherishing one another, this was what they meant.

Ewan chuckled. "Don't hate me. Pity me. My mother sent me to cotillion. With both my left feet. In the nineties."

She blinked, gracing him with an astonished side-eye. "The eighteen nineties?"

His only response was to croon along with Anne Murray.

She watched her parents dance, watched the Fullers—old and new—hold each other close, and dreamed of the future with a full heart.

Turn the page for a sneak peak at Family Practice, book three in the Thornton Vermont Series...

FAMILY PRACTICE

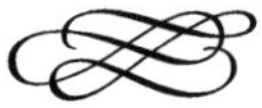

CHAPTER ONE

CHAPTER 1

Anneliese Thompson's back ached from painting, but come hell or high water, tomorrow her five-yer-old daughter would have her first big-girl bedroom. The cottage next door to the Fletcher Hotel—with its wild garden and faded picket fence that faced the town common—only needed some love and a little girl's laugh to come back to life.

In that way, she and the cottage were a lot alike.

Her phone buzzed from the drop-cloth covered bed behind her. She kept rolling pale turquoise swaths, hoping to finish the last wall before the real world interrupted.

Her voicemail alert pinged, then her email. Someone wanted her attention.

She navigated the maze of her childhood furniture, crammed into the room at odd angles, holding her paint-smeared hands up for her own inspection.

The phone rang again, and Anneliese jogged down the stairs. Twice in a row usually meant her mother. A brief maternal worry for Chloe fluttered in her chest, but she quashed it and nudged the kitchen tap open with one wrist. No paint on the phone screen.

The missed call from California set her heart racing afresh. The only person who would call her from California was the last person she wanted to hear from.

She tapped through to the messages with trembling fingers.

"Anneliese, hi. My name is Amy Letourneau. I'm in charge of putting together a wedding bash in your area, and you come highly recommended. Would love to talk to you about it. Give me a call as soon as possible. Thanks."

The name didn't ring a bell, but it wasn't her ex. She set the phone down on the drainboard and braced her hands on the sink. Three thousand miles and the better part of five years and just the spectre of Chad could send her whole world tipping off its axis.

Tears threatened, and she smeared her eyes with the back of one hand. When she blinked away the wetness, she saw her neighbor and landlord wave through the kitchen window. Jeremy, in his straw hat and Bermuda shorts, was tending the butterfly garden he maintained in the sunny side yard of the Fletcher House Hotel. She smiled and waved.

Time to finish Chloe's room, and call Amy Letourneau back, whoever she was.

By the time she'd rolled the walls and cleaned the brushes, the morning was gone, and part of the afternoon with it.

She pulled out her client notebook and opened a fresh page. Amy Letourneau picked up on the third ring.

"Hello. Amy here."

"Hi, Amy. Anneliese Thompson. I'm returning your call."

"Awesome. Hi. I hope I didn't call too early. I'm in New York for work, but I still haven't adjusted to the time zones."

"Not at all. So, what's the wedding?"

"About that. I'm a P.A. My client is getting married. Her fiancé wants a New England wedding. She wants an Event-with-a-capital-E, and it's my job to make that happen. I need someone to partner with, and your name came up."

"Who's the client?"

"That's confidential for now. They're not social media official, if you take my meaning. There would be an NDA if you decide to work with us. For now, though, I'd love to come up there… Thornton, it's called? See some potential locations, that kind of thing."

What could it hurt? "Sure. When do you plan to be in the area?"

"I can take a train up tomorrow. Or rent a car. How far is it?"

Anneliese laughed. "You'll want to rent a car. The train's a ways from here. Is this a mobile number? I'll text you the name of a cafe where I meet clients. It also happens to be the home of the best wedding cakes in the state."

"Now we're talking. I'm going to say late afternoon, since I literally have no idea how far from Manhattan Vermont is."

"Sounds about right." Anneliese laughed again. Despite the mystery—or maybe because of it—she liked this effervescent voice on the phone. "Text me when you get to town. My day is pretty flexible."

"Great. I totally have a feeling about this."

Amy Letourneau was gone before Anneliese thought to ask who'd referred her. She didn't know anyone who rated a non-disclosure agreement.

Time enough to worry about that tomorrow. For tonight, she was on her own in her newly rented house. No mother to question her parenting choices or remind her she was single and on the other side of thirty. No daughter with bottomless curiosity and rapid-fire questions.

Time for tea and a book on the screened in porch, and supper when she felt like it.

She plugged in her new electric tea kettle and filled the reservoir, humming to herself. She fussed over the tea leaves while the kettle boiled, then took her mug out to the porch.

Beyond the shabby screening, the garden was in unruly, riotous bloom. It had gone too long without a caretaker. Leggy phlox leaned against the pickets. A climbing rose had fallen over and was creeping along the flagstones. Crab grass sprouted anywhere there wasn't something hardy to hold it back, and the daylilies were crowded up against the patchy remains of spring daffodils and tulips.

She had her work cut out for her.

Jeremy and his husband Glenn were inspecting the wisteria vining the hotel's front porch. Glenn caught her eye and ran down the front steps and over to the low picket fence that surrounded the carriage house.

"We've got a late robin's nest, come on over."

Anneliese put her tea down on the porch floor and made her way out of the front garden and around to the Fletcher Hotel's grand front entry. They'd pulled up a four foot ladder and Jeremy was angling his phone to get pictures of the nest without getting too close to the babies.

"Hey, Anneliese." He peered back over his shoulder. "We didn't see the nest before because of the flowers, but Mama's nesting late, so we didn't miss the action!"

Anneliese laughed, but she was touched by their enthusiasm. "I can see living next door to you two is going to be an adventure."

Jeremy stepped down. "Go on up and take a look. Glenn will spot you. I've got to get back to the front desk."

Anneliese gave his departing back a wry look. "I think I can handle a glorified step-ladder."

"You're no fun," Glenn teased. "Holding the ladder is my duty as the man of the house."

Three tiny blue eggs and one wet, skinny fledgling were snugged in the carefully constructed nest. She felt a kinship with the absent mother. She was nesting too, and hoping her fledgling would thrive, though she was grateful she had more than a few weeks to launch her baby into the world.

"Nests are happy things, Anneliese." Glenn was watching her with open concern when she stepped off the ladder.

"Oh, I know." She smiled at him. "I was just thinking about children and nesting and…"

"You're entirely too sweet." Glenn gathered her into a fraternal hug, tucking her head under his chin. His t-shirt was impossibly soft and smelled like Old Spice. "And you have company."

Anneliese stepped out of Glenn's arms and looked back at her garden gate with a smile.

"Nan! Kate!" She waved, then turned to Glenn. "See you later."

She met her friends and led them through the gate and onto the porch. Kate was carrying a huge basket wrapped in cellophane and a yellow bow.

"We brought you a present."

Nan hugged her. "Congratulations. I couldn't leave without coming to see it."

Anneliese took the basket from Kate. "Sit. No, wait. Come see Chloe's room. I just finished it. Then we'll sit. I can make more tea."

Kate took in the shabby-but-not-yet-chic walls and floors on the first floor with a hopeful eye. "You're allowed to paint?"

"I started upstairs."

They followed her up the narrow stairs to the small landing between her room and Chloe's.

"Oh, it's perfect. What's the color called?" Nan asked.

"Pearl Reef. And that's all my old white iron furniture from my parents' place under the sheets."

"Chloe's going to love it." Kate turned her attention to Anneliese's nearly empty room with a delicate lift of one brow. "Your space needs a little something."

"I know the mattress on the floor isn't much, but..."

Kate pursed her lips. "It'll do, but you are going to have to upgrade for proper booty calls."

Anneliese sighed dramatically. "Yeah, because I have so many of those lined up."

"Nan, we need to get our girl laid."

Nan laughed. "Give her five minutes to get settled."

Kate shrugged. "I'm going to think about it. In the meantime, you need curtains..."

"I have ideas. Let's go enjoy the porch. Nan can tell me what she and Joss have planned for their babymoon[Don't forget the babymoon!], and I can show you my ideas for the rest of the house."

It took a few minutes to find her idea scrapbook. When she stepped outside the kitchen door, she knew something was very wrong. Nan perched on the porch swing, watching Kate listen to someone her phone. Kate's face was bone white, her eyes frantic.

"I'll be there in five minutes. Hang on, Daddy." Kate's voice broke over her father's name. Kate looked at her friends, but Anneliese didn't think she was seeing them.

"What happened?"

"My mom... something happened. She was non-responsive when they put her in the ambulance. I have to go." She started to leave, then patted the pockets of her skirt. "You drove."

Nan pulled her keys from her bag. "I'll take you over there now. You need to call Ewan."

"Right." Kate was trembling; her voice wobbled and cracked. Tears spilled over her lashes. "I can't."

Anneliese touched her shoulder. "I'll call him. Tell him to meet you there. It's going to be okay."

Nan was already bundling Kate out the door and down the garden walkway.

Anneliese watched them go with a heavy heart. The Peases were a tight-knit clan, and Kate's mom Cora was the heart of it.

Jack.

Kate's brother would know by now, too. Was he already on his way north? For all his expensive habits and flashy city living, Jack was fiercely devoted to his family. She pictured him, white-knuckling the wheel of his sleek car, pushing the engine to get him home to his mother before—

It didn't bear thinking about, and she'd made promises to her friend. Time to call Kate's husband.

Anything to take her mind off of worrying about Jack Pease.

To read the full first three chapters of *Family Practice*, subscribe to my newsletter at http://bit.ly/CDGNewsletter

Need more Thornton? Pick up your copy of *Sugaring Season: Stories from Thornton & Beyond*, today!

ALSO BY CAMERON D. GARRIEPY

The Thornton Vermont Series

Damselfly Inn

Sweet Pease

Family Practice

Sugaring Season: Stories from Thornton & Beyond

Standalone Romance

Buck's Landing

Short Fiction in Anthologies

Valentine (Metaphysical Gravity)

Requiring of Care (Echoes in Darkness)

Christmas Mini-Romances

Bread & Promises (Yuletide)

Cinnamon Girl (Wish)

The Soloist (Joy)

Star of Wonder (Merry Little Christmas)

Santa's Photographer (Secret Santas)

Merry's Christmas (Atlantic to Pacific)

Twelve Days 'til Christmas

~

Children of the Parallels

Speculative Middle Grade Short Fiction

Parallel Jump

Parallel Hunt

ABOUT THE AUTHOR

Cameron D. Garriepy attended a small Vermont college in a town very like Thornton. She's missed it since the day she packed up her Subaru and drove off into the real world. Some might say she created the fictional village as wish fulfillment, and they would be correct.

She is the author of the Thornton Vermont series and the founder of Bannerwing Books, a co-op of independent authors. Prior to Bannerwing, Cameron was an editor at Write on Edge, where she edited three volumes of the online writing group's literary anthology, *Precipice*. Cameron appeared in the inaugural cast of *Listen to Your Mother - Boston,* and irregularly contributes flash fiction to the Word Count Podcast.

Since her time at Middlebury College, Cameron has worked as a nanny, a pastry cook, and an event ticket resale specialist. In her spare time, she cooks, gardens, knits, reads avidly, and researches hobby farming--chickens and goats are just waiting for her ship to come in. She writes from the greater Boston area, where she lives with her husband, son, and a geriatric pug.

Connect with Cameron online at www.camerondgarriepy.com
Hear first about sales and new releases via Cameron's newsletter—subscribe at
www.bit.ly/cdgnewsletter
Join the conversation in Cameron's Facebook group at www.bit.ly/thorntonfbgroup

amazon.com/author/camerondgarriepy
facebook.com/camerondgarriepy
twitter.com/camerongarriepy
goodreads.com/camerondgarriepy
bookbub.com/authors/cameron-d-garriepy
instagram.com/camerongarriepy
pinterest.com/camerongarriepy

ABOUT THE PUBLISHER

Bannerwing Books is a writers' co-op founded in 2012 by Cameron D. Garriepy, and completed by Angela Amman and Mandy Dawson. Currently residing on Slack, somewhere in the ether between Boston, Detroit, and Paso Robles, Bannerwing presents works by Stephanie Ayers, Ericka Clay, and Liz Zimmers, as well as collections featuring Andra Watkins, Kate Shrewsday, and Kameko Murakami.

www.bannerwingbooks.com

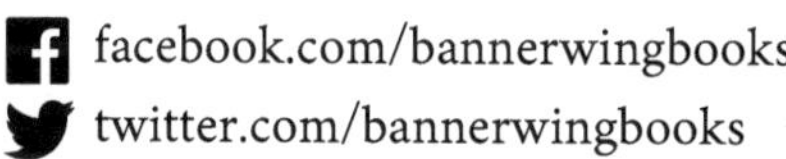

Made in the USA
Middletown, DE
17 November 2021